MORE ACCLAIM FOR THE ROMANCES OF
BARBARA DAWSON SMITH:

FIRE AT MIDNIGHT
"An unsurpassed historical romance that will keep you riveted with its intense suspense and intrigue . . . I couldn't put it down!"

—Affaire de Coeur

FIRE ON THE WIND
"Superlative . . . A fabulous treasure."

—Rendezvous

"Again and again, Barbara Dawson Smith stretches the boundaries of the genre."

—Romantic Times

DREAMSPINNER
"A page-turner filled with love and intrigue . . . Make room on your bookshelf."

—Romantic Times

"Barbara Dawson Smith is wonderful!"

—Affaire de Coeur

St. Martin's Paperbacks Titles
by Barbara Dawson Smith

A GLIMPSE OF HEAVEN
NEVER A LADY

Never A Lady

BARBARA DAWSON SMITH

St. Martin's Paperbacks

NEVER A LADY

Copyright © 1996 by Barbara Dawson Smith.
Excerpt from *Once Upon a Scandal* copyright © 1996 by Barbara Dawson Smith.

ISBN: 0-312-95936-2

Printed in the United States of America

St. Martin's Paperbacks edition/November 1996

10 9 8 7 6 5 4 3 2 1

Dedicated to
my own two little ladies,
Jessica and Stephanie.
May you always
be young at heart.

Acknowledgments

My heartfelt thanks to my editor, Jennifer Enderlin, and to my critique group, Joyce Bell, Christina Dodd, Betty Gyenes, and Susan Wiggs, for their many helpful and inspiring comments. Your work is appreciated!

≈ Chapter 1 ≈

M ary Elizabeth Sheppard waited in the gloom beside the caravan. Here, beyond the pool of torchlight where the villagers were gathering, she felt safe, cocooned by the shadows of evening and hidden by the swaybacked nag. Here, she stood close enough to go forth and do her Christian duty when the time came.

Striving for calm, she reached into her apron pocket and extracted the carrot she had saved from dinner. George the Third accepted the morsel, his huge teeth tickling her palm. The sound of his crunching drifted through the warm night air like a counterpoint to the hum of conversation.

The rising moon cast a silvery sheen over the people sitting on the village green. They were a typical lot, yeomen farmers slumped from a day in the fields, ruddy-cheeked women dressed in homespun, barefoot children dashing to and fro. They looked weary but content, conversing with the ease of long acquaintance. Mary knew a familiar wistful desire to join such a circle of family and friends whose roots were sunk deeply into the soil of their ancestors. What was it like to live in the same cozy cottage year after year, to watch the same garden flourish and grow, to greet the same genial neighbors each day?

The question was fleeting, fanciful. Over the past eighteen years, she had traveled every hill and vale in England. This snug wooden caravan was her home on wheels, the only home she had ever known.

The vehicle shifted and creaked as a man emerged into the starry night. Clad in sober black, the Reverend Thomas Sheppard lowered his head to avoid striking the painted sign that pronounced "The Wages of Sin is Death."

Usually, Deacon Victor Gabriel walked out first, his divinely handsome profile and charismatic smile eliciting sighs from the women in the congregation. But today, Mary's fiancé had left for Dover to fetch a bundle of new tracts from an American ship, and he would not return until the morrow. She felt an uneasy gladness, for his absence brought respite from the secret shame he roused in her.

From her stance beside the caravan, Mary could see her father's back and the iron-gray tonsure that circled his bald pate like a crown of thorns. Thomas Sheppard stood on the top step and extended his arms to the ragtag crowd as if to embrace each and every one of them.

Talk ceased. Someone coughed, a hacking sound that died away into the night. A baby wailed and its mother shushed it.

"Welcome, brethren." His voice rang out like the peal of a church bell. "We have come together tonight to rejoice in the word of the Lord, to renounce worldly wealth and the temptation it brings. 'Him that cometh unto me, I will in no wise cast out.' Let us begin now by lifting our voices in song."

That was her cue.

Mary pressed herself to the warm neck of the old horse. Her heart thundered against her whalebone stays. Her throat choked up until she could scarcely breathe. She longed to run into the darkness and hide herself in the deep black shadows of the hedgerows that bordered the fields of wheat and mustard.

"Come forth, my daughter," Thomas Sheppard commanded. "God has given you the voice of an angel. You must use it to His glory."

So he said every night. And every night Mary obeyed him.

Her fingers trembling, she reached up to make certain that none of the reddish strands had slipped the mooring of her braids. Would she never lose the innate shyness that made her dread facing an audience? Only her father's watchful eyes gave her the strength to forge on. Clutching the hymnal to her high-necked gown, she forced herself to walk into the torchlight and take her place at the base of the steps.

Thomas Sheppard sent her an encouraging smile. She managed a shaky smile back before opening the hymnal and pretending to consult the verses that were engraved on her memory.

She peeked at the multitude of expectant faces. In the front row sat a weaselly man with gold-capped teeth, a weather-beaten housewife with hopeful eyes, a group of boys elbowing each other. Moistening her lips, she wished desperately for Jo. These ordeals had been more bearable when she and her twin sister had clasped hands, their clear soprano voices rising to the heavens in harmony.

Those times were gone forever. Mary's reluctance dissolved into an immeasurable sadness tinged by remorse. This was her penance, her punishment. She drew a deep breath and began to sing: "He who would Valiant be. . . ."

The crystalline notes seemed to float over the people, over the thatched roofs of the night-shrouded hamlet. She focused her attention on a nearby oak tree and pretended she was alone. The branches swayed in the breeze, and the leaves rustled an accompaniment.

Then Mary saw her.

A woman clad in a diaphanous white gown ran out of the darkness beyond the tree. A banner of red-gold hair streamed behind her. In the torchlight, her eyes glinted green in a face so lovely, so achingly familiar it made the song die in Mary's throat.

"Jo," she whispered, then louder, through a sob of exultation, "Jo! You've come *home!*"

Mary barely heard her father's exclamation. Dropping the hymnal, she dashed through the crowd on a zigzag path. A muttering of surprise arose from the villagers. She paid them no heed in her haste to greet her sister.

Jo halted at the rear of the multitude, her eyes wide and curiously frightened. The nightdress swirled around her, and dark splotches marred the white front. Blood?

"Mary! Oh, please, Mary, save me!"

Fierce emotion beat inside Mary's breast. Whatever had put the stark fear on Jo's face, Mary would banish it. They were two halves of one whole—at least they had been until that fateful night three months ago when Jo had fled to London and embraced a life of sin.

But Mary could not think of that now. Her sister was back. Nothing else mattered.

She opened her arms to hug Jo. Instead of warm flesh, she clasped a rush of cool air. The image of her twin shimmered and vanished into the black velvet night.

"No!"

For an instant, Mary stood in frozen denial. The shadow of her sister's panic haunted her heart. Then she sank to the ground, weeping, her gray skirt pooling on the grass. She felt hot and cold and shivery. God have mercy. Jo wasn't here.

It had happened again. Mary had been cursed by a vision.

For many months she had resisted the inhuman link with her twin. She had prayed and fasted to cleanse herself of the powers of darkness. But now she knew with mingled fear and alarm that she had failed to sever the bond between their minds.

Her father came striding forward. "Mary Elizabeth! What is the meaning of this disruption?"

"I saw her, Papa. Jo was standing here. Right here." The agony of loss inundated Mary again.

His stern face bore lines that hadn't been there half a year ago. He sucked in a ragged breath. " 'Tis the devil's work again. I warned you against it."

"But she was calling me," Mary whispered. "Oh, Papa, something's amiss with her. Something terrible."

An excited buzzing came from the villagers. Several people made a superstitious sign against evil.

Thomas Sheppard released her and stood with his head bowed. When he looked at Mary again, his gray-green eyes held a bleak verdict. "Heed me well," he said. "Josephine is no longer my daughter—or your sister. She chose the path of damnation, and if God so wills it, she must suffer the consequences."

"How can we turn our backs on her? She needs us!"

"The devil is tempting you into a life of sin. Be strong, daughter. Resist the call of his darkness."

Turning, he walked with measured steps back to the caravan, where he resumed his stance on the stairs. He lifted his hands to the heavens. "My good daughter, Mary, has seen a sign this night. It is a sign that warns us to renounce the vanities of the wicked world. Let us pray, brethren, for all those weak souls who have been seduced by the fleshly excesses of the aristocracy. Their transgressions must not be allowed to taint righteous folk like yourselves."

Mary sat on her heels and hugged her knees. She struggled against the wayward thoughts that pushed past her conscience. She should honor her father's judgment. She should kneel in quiet prayer and ask God for strength. She should act the dutiful daughter as she had always striven to do.

Yet she could not forget the image of Jo, bloodied and begging for help.

Since childhood, she and her sister had shared a strange connection. They could feel each other's emotions, hear each other's thoughts, even see images of each other. She had known the time her sister had fallen into a well. She had rescued Jo. Likewise, Jo had known when her twin was set upon by bullies. Jo had raced to her aid. When their father denounced the unnatural skill, Jo had talked Mary into fostering it in secret. She had convinced Mary it was not evil, but the whispering of their hearts.

Now Mary knew with appalling certainty that her sister was in grave danger. She had to answer the call even if it meant incurring the wrath of God.

And her father.

London
14 May 1817

Adam Brentwell, the fifth duke of St. Chaldon, wanted a bride.

Yet he stood in a quiet alcove at Almack's and deliberately avoided catching the eye of the patronesses enthroned against the far wall of the assembly room. He was bored with introductions to doll-faced debutantes. He had no wish to join the gentlemen who were leading ladies in high-waisted gowns onto the dance floor. He had already fulfilled his duty by dancing with an array of dull-witted beauties. It was a relief to steal a moment alone with his dark thoughts, to brood on his afternoon visit with Josephine Sheppard, and to plan his next move.

"Hiding from the title hunters, St. Chaldon?"

Out of the assembly room strolled a dandy with Byronic curls and a lush lower lip. A longtime family friend, Lord Harry Dashwood struck a languid pose in skintight salmon trousers, a high starched cravat, and a lilac coat so slim-fitting it undoubtedly required the aid of a corset. He went on, "What say you we fly this dreary nest and catch us a pair of ladybirds?"

A discreet liaison appealed to Adam. But he had Sophy to consider. "It would be uncivil to leave so early."

"Civility be damned," Harry grumbled. "You should take a leaf from your brother's book."

Adam tensed. "Meaning?"

"Meaning Cyril had the good sense to save himself from this tedium of lemonade and stale cake. No doubt he's tasting the delights of his own white dove as we speak." Harry cast a sly look at Adam. "By the by, two days ago the woman was seen marching up the front steps of Brentwell House. What could be the reason for *that* indiscretion?"

Bloody busybody. Adam subjected him to a cool stare. "I would never permit a whore to enter my home."

"The hard-hearted duke. Miss Austen should pen a novel about you. She could title it *Pride and Priggishness.*"

Adam was not amused. He had to distract the man before the entire ton learned the disgraceful truth. "Speaking of gossip, word has it you're low in the pocket these days. Rather than stealing away from here, you would do well to shop at the marriage mart yourself."

With a shrug, Harry lifted his quizzing glass in a lazy survey of the ladies on the dance floor. Music drifted from the orchestral balcony, and the chandeliers blazed with golden light. "So both of us are in the running for a wife. You out of dreary duty, and I out of sheer desperation."

"There comes a time for all men to settle down."

"Yes, Father," Harry mocked, still scanning the crowd. "Ah, there's one who's rumored to have caught your eye. Lady Camilla Crockford is quite the heiress. Have you settled on her yet?"

The dark-haired girl was dancing the cotillion in perfect, mincing steps. Adam assessed her neat figure, so slender and graceful. She would make a lovely ornament for any gentleman's arm. Yes, he would ask her. But he felt no urge to hurry.

"I'll announce my choice in due time."

"Don't tell me. You attempted to kiss her and found out she's the Goddess of Winter." Grinning, Lord Harry bent closer in confidence. "I confess to have sampled those porcelain lips myself. Nary a trace of warmth in that heavenly body."

Adam fixed him with a freezing scowl. "Take care how you speak of the lady."

"Ah, you must learn to smile, old chap." Lord Harry returned to his idle survey. Then he stopped and stared through the round quizzing glass. "By gad, who is that golden nymph near the orchestra? I thought I'd met every lady here."

Bored by the farcical game, Adam stepped forward to have a better view into the assembly room. At first he missed the girl. Several women chatted in the shadow of the balcony, all of them dark of hair. Except for one bright-eyed miss laughing with a lanky gentleman. A virginal white gown clung to her full figure.

Adam compressed his lips. "She's hardly out of the schoolroom. Not your type."

"Au contraire. Look at those plump curves. Only think of what a happy handful those breasts would make."

"Don't think," Adam said in his iciest voice. "She is not for you."

Harry lowered the quizzing glass. "Do you know her?"

They would meet sooner or later. Adam supposed it was better done now, under his watchful eye. "Come. I'll introduce you."

He led the way through the throng of people. Ladies dipped curtsies and smiled fawningly at him. He nodded in imperious acknowledgment, not stopping to speak. They were enamored of his title, his wealth, his eligibility. Did any of them consider him as a man, not a commodity? Did they wonder if he might wish to marry, not to secure the succession, but to find a woman with whom he could share his innermost thoughts and feelings?

He banished the nonsensical questions. Sentiment only clouded a man's judgment. He would choose his duchess based on her beauty, her biddable nature, and most importantly, her breeding. That was the way to achieve harmony in a marriage.

The blonde girl spied his approach and wrinkled her nose like an ill-bred child. For one furious instant, he expected her to stick her tongue out at him. Then her gaze slid to his companion, and a flirtatious smile brightened her face. She sallied forth to greet them.

He told Harry in a harsh undertone, "To save you the trouble of ferreting out the information, she has thirty thousand settled on her."

"Thirty—?" Gulping, Lord Harry dropped his quizzing glass so that it dangled on its gold ribbon. "Gadzooks! Why have I not heard—?"

The girl glided within earshot. Adam took her by the elbow and brought her forward the final two steps. "Lady Sophy, may I present Lord Harry Dashwood. Harry, my sister."

As if his starched cravat had shrunk several sizes, Harry turned an interesting shade of red. He bowed over her gloved hand. "My dear lady. I confess, I quite nearly didn't recognize you. You've grown up to be the fairest of all the angels—"

She thumped her closed fan onto his padded shoulder. "Do stop your ridiculous banter. Don't think I've ever forgiven you for making me kiss that slimy toad."

"You were all of twelve and begging to be teased."

"I was merely nine and you were cruel to trick me. But you did teach me a valuable lesson." She looked him up and down. "That a croaking frog can never be transformed into a prince."

His ruddiness deepened. "Kind lady, you must give me

the chance to redeem myself. May I beg the honor of this dance?"

She eyed him, her face as glowingly ripe as a peach. Adam saw the interest in her expression—and the naïveté, too. "I'm afraid she's promised this one to me."

"Hah," Sophy said. "Mama isn't here, so I shan't hold you to your silly duty. Not while Lord Toad is in desperate want of my company."

With that, she sailed toward the dance floor. Adam snatched hold of Harry's arm. "No samples."

He smirked. "Word of honor."

As the rake sauntered after his quarry, Adam grimly watched them. This particular fortune hunter had a knack for digging out gossip. Could Sophy manage to guard her tongue about the problem with Cyril? Or would she spill the scandalous secret before Adam had the chance to settle the matter discreetly?

Lady Camilla Crockford glided out of the crowd. She sank into a curtsy at his feet, her dark curls complementing the pale blue gauze of her gown. "My lord duke. Forgive my forwardness, but you promised me a second dance."

She rose before him in regal splendor. Her lips formed a perfect porcelain smile. The Goddess of Winter.

He offered her his arm. "Shall we?"

On the dance floor, he placed one hand at her slim waist, the other on her dainty shoulder. Camilla waltzed with lightness and grace. She had a diplomatic way of imparting gossip so that it seemed amusing rather than offensive. No doubt she could pour tea for a chosen few or greet hundreds of guests at a ball. She would make the perfect duchess.

Beauty. Biddability. Breeding.

Yet he found himself wondering if she were capable of deep emotion. Unable to answer the question and unsure of why it should matter, Adam let his attention stray to his sister. Sophy and Harry made a handsome couple, whirling around the dance floor. But Lord Harry Dashwood was a sixth son with no prospect of an inheritance. And Sophy was easy prey for his outrageous charm.

As soon as the waltz ended, Adam excused himself from Lady Camilla. He drew Sophy firmly away, and despite her protests, he made certain she chose more suitable partners for the remainder of the evening. Lord Harry disappeared, no doubt on the prowl for the inviting white thighs of a Fashionable Impure.

Adam, too, felt the urge for physical release. He had a sinking feeling this would be one of those nights when he would pace the bedroom, unable to sleep. Slumber had eluded him of late, and he couldn't fathom why. He had always scorned people who could not govern their own actions. The insomnia left him frustrated and somehow ashamed at his inability to control what should be a natural function.

Of course, there was the vexing business with Cyril's mistress. Her cleverness infuriated Adam. The temerity of the female, to toss him out of her house as if he were a pedlar. He resolved to return on the morrow. Once and for all, he would put an end to her scheming.

As the ball neared its close, he escorted his sister to their coach. The street lamps cast brave little pools of light into the gloom of the city. Sophy sat yawning on the plush blue seat opposite him. Despite their disagreement over Lord Harry, she chattered like any girl caught up in the thrill of her first Season.

Eleven years separated them in age, and Adam felt ancient by comparison. Had he ever been so passionate about life? Surely before the responsibilities of the dukedom had been thrust upon him at the tender age of fourteen, he had played games like other children. He had grown up too fast, that was all.

It seemed a lifetime ago that he had been summoned home from school in haste when his father had been stricken by a heart seizure. Adam remembered vividly the sickroom smell of the ducal bedchamber, the wail of the winter wind outside the mullioned windows, the shuffle of his shoes on the carpet as he approached the massive four-poster hung with gold brocaded silk. It was the first time he had ever seen his father lying in bed. Even more shocking was the paleness of the duke's skin and the blue tinge of his lips. His eyes were closed. Had not the counterpane moved with his faint, whistling breaths, he might have been a corpse.

Stopping near the foot of the bed, Adam was aware of each dull thud of his heartbeat. He had learned from an early age to speak only when spoken to. Yet today he could not bear to wait for the duke to notice him.

"Father?"

The duke lifted his sparse gray lashes. His blue eyes were sunken in folds of flesh. "I am dying, my son," he said without preamble. "The time has come . . . for you to be . . . St. Chaldon."

Pausing only to take gasping breaths, he went on in his dispassionate manner to describe various improvements underway on the estate, to delineate his extensive financial investments, to expound upon the duties of his exalted rank. Adam listened as if through an icy fog. Over the past few years, he had become aware that his father was much older than the fathers of his classmates, that the duke had been well on in years when he had married and sired three children. Now he lay dying. Soon his lifeless body would be interred in the cold ground.

Denial hammered at Adam. He fought the unmanly sting of tears. He had grown up in awe of the duke, always striving for a word of praise and never quite succeeding. The very thought of wearing the ducal coronet panicked him. Would he never have the chance to win his father's love?

Desperate for reassurance, Adam fell to his knees beside the bed. "You must live, Papa." A sob escaped him, and he groped for his father's hand. It was cold, so cold. "You *must.*"

"Don't snivel, boy. 'Tis vulgar." Wheezing, the duke withdrew his hand and stared with his critical gaze. "Stand up. Show me . . . the St. Chaldon pride."

Adam scrambled to his feet and snapped to attention. His cheeks burned as if he'd been slapped. "Yes, Your Grace."

"A duke is born to command. Never forget . . . that you are superior to other men." Then his father had dismissed him and turned his head away.

Even now, fifteen years later, Adam could recall the utter loneliness and misery he had felt. His father had died the next day, and Adam had been plunged into the myriad duties of his new rank. He had left behind the carefree amusements of childhood, the youthful hunger for affection. In time, he had come to see that he had been blessed with a sacred trust. He had learned to rule wisely. His adolescent need for approval had vanished with maturity.

"I don't believe you've been listening to me at all," Sophy complained. Across the dim carriage, his sister sat pouting.

"I beg your pardon," Adam said automatically. "What scintillating tidbit of gossip did I miss hearing?"

She wrinkled her nose. "I merely wondered if you knew who's come to call on us so late. Look."

Adam peered out as the coach rolled to a stop in front of Brentwell House. Unlike the terraced town homes surrounding the rest of Grosvenor Square, this porticoed mansion stood in regal solitude behind iron gates, as fine a dwelling as any country house. Strangely, despite the lateness of the hour, the windows were ablaze with candlelight.

His gaze sharpened on a carriage waiting on the drive. He thought he recognized the insignia on the door. The doctor's carriage?

Mother. Had she taken ill again?

He forgot his intention to leave Sophy off and then depart on his private search for comfort. He leaped from the

coach and took off at a run, striding up the wide marble
steps.

Sophy ran behind him, her slippers pattering like a
child's. "You let the door slam in my face," she accused. "I
knew it. You're only polite in public."

He ignored her. He thrust open the door just as a
sleepy-eyed footman in azure and silver livery sprang to
attention in the domed entrance hall.

Adam barked, "Where is the duchess?"

"Upstairs, Your Grace. If I may say, there's been a terrible doing tonight—"

"Adam!" his mother called. "Thank heavens, you're
home."

She descended the grand staircase, clinging to the
wrought-iron railing as if she could not hold herself upright. Rusty splotches marred her dressing gown, and her
silver hair straggled down her back. Her dishabille startled
Adam; she always took great pride in her appearance.

"Mama!" Sophy cried. "Whatever has happened?"

Adam mounted the steps and met his mother halfway.
Though she was a regal woman who seldom invited closeness, he took her into his arms. Tremors rippled through
her. He saw to his shock that the stains on her gown were
blood.

"Someone's been hurt," he said. "Who?"

"It's all the fault of his mistress," she cried. "Didn't I say
that ill-bred hussy would be the ruin of your brother?
Didn't I?"

Her voice rose to the high pitch of hysteria. Disciplining
his fear, Adam rubbed his hands soothingly over her back.
"Calm yourself. Tell me what she did now."

The duchess lifted her chin and took a shuddery breath.
Wetness shone on her patrician cheekbones. "Oh, Adam.
That horrid female has shot my Cyril."

๑๑ Chapter 2 ๑๑

London
15 May 1817

"Have ye gone mad? Why've ye come back here?"

Standing in the doorway, the hulking old servant stared at Mary with his mouth agape. Fine red lines marbled his bulldog face, and a fleece of tight gray curls capped his head. The light from the peg lamp held by his grizzled paw glinted off the brass buttons on his green livery. Beside him, a mangy dog wagged its stub of a tail.

Before Mary could answer, the man peered up and down the dusk-shrouded street, where the smell of soot permeated the rain-soaked air. Then he yanked her inside the town house so fast she nearly tripped on the threshold. "Make haste, Miss Josephine. Them bloody Bow Street Runners are watchin' fer ye."

The front door with its lion's head knocker banged shut. Mary found herself standing in an elegant foyer. She tilted her head back and the stairwell seemed to go on forever, vanishing into darkness. Her hem dripped rainwater onto the marble floor, and her arm was weighed down by the valise that contained all of her worldly belongings.

Her teeth chattering from the damp chill, she pushed back the hood of her sodden mantle. "I'm not Josephine. I—I'm her twin sister, Mary."

His breath whistled out in amazement. " 'Tis uncanny."
He squinted at her up and down. "I knew she had a sister,
but ye're the very spit o' her. Skin like snow and hair like
fire. But Miss Josephine never wore braids trussed up tight
as a spinster's—ah—purse."

"Please, sir. I—I've come a long way. Where is my sister? And who are the Bow Street Runners?"

"Miss Josephine would want ye to have a cup o' tea
first," he said in a gruff voice. "Then I'll tell ye the foul tale
from start to finish."

Turning, he limped down the passageway, one of his legs
dragging unnaturally. The mongrel stayed by Mary, nudg-
ing her hand until she scratched its head. Foul tale? What
could the servant mean by that?

Filled with foreboding, she hesitated in the foyer, wondering if he meant for her to wait here. She knew little of
accepted behavior in a fancy London house. Compared to
the caravan, the place was breathtakingly huge. Gilt-
framed paintings adorned the walls. The curtains of the
parlor were drawn against the dreary gray dusk, and shadows cloaked the furniture like dust covers. She felt lost and
bewildered, stretched taut by the need to *know*.

Her gaze followed the one man who could answer the
questions that had plagued her for the past twenty-four
hours, ever since Jo had begged her for help.

Mary dropped the valise with a thump and scuttled after
the manservant. The smoky trail of his lamp tickled her
nose. The door at the end of the corridor had already
flapped shut in his wake. She pushed it open, descended a
steep flight of stone stairs, and found herself in a large
cellar kitchen. A crackling fire lit the room with cozy
warmth, shining over rows of copper pots and silver plates
on the shelves. A one-eared tabby stared down from the
top of a cabinet, its green eyes glinting.

The grizzled retainer scowled at the cat and muttered to
himself. He took up a ring of keys and unlocked a small,
multi-drawered chest set against the wall. He scooped a

spoonful of tea leaves into a pot, then limped over to the hearth to pour steaming water from the kettle there.

Mary hung back, unsure of her welcome. She had plumbed the reserves of her courage to make the journey from Sussex in the crowded confines of the mail coach. A tradesman flaunting ginger-colored whiskers had gawked at her most of the way and, with a wink, offered to escort her around the city. She had managed to elude him at the depot by slipping into the swarms of people. She had walked for hours before finding the address she'd known from the only letter Jo had ever posted.

Sinking down on the lowest step, Mary petted the dog again and smoothed her hand over the patchy fur. The animal whined in pleasure, and its warm body comforted her.

Never before had she been on her own. Always she'd traveled with her father and Jo; then later Victor Gabriel had joined their mission in the role of deacon.

The thought of her fiancé filled Mary with mingled awe and guilt. She felt a strange sort of relief at not having to face him yet. He was so pure, so utterly *good*. Until now, she had shown him no sign of the dark side she battled in herself. Now she had proven herself unworthy of him by defying her father.

Was Victor even back from Dover yet? Had he and Papa mounted a search for her?

No. Papa had not come after Jo, either. He would never follow Mary into the den of iniquity that was London. She was alone in her desperate quest.

She imagined for the hundredth time Thomas Sheppard finding the letter she'd written before creeping out of the caravan long before dawn. How angry he must have been! And worse, how disappointed in her. For all his sternness, he loved her . . . and Jo. She treasured the memories of him reading to them at bedtime, applauding the biblical plays they put on, teaching them the skill of skipping stones across a lake. She cringed to think of hurting her father when he had already suffered from Mama's death and Jo's descent into corruption.

For the past three months, Mary had striven to make up for her sister's desertion by acting the obedient, virtuous daughter. She had cooked his meals and copied his sermons and raised her voice in song at every prayer meeting.

Until the vision last night had changed everything.

"I see ye've met Prinny," the servant said, a teapot of brown crockery in his hand. "Ye must have a way wi' creatures like yer sister does."

Mary's eyes welled with tears. Jo had fed starving strays and bandaged birds with broken wings in defiance of Papa's edict to let nature take its course. The sharp knife of memory stabbed Mary. If only she hadn't shut Jo out of her heart. If only she hadn't succumbed to wicked temptation. . . .

The man stood at the table and poured a mug of tea for her. "Come and have a drink," he said, not unkindly. As Mary rose from the step and approached the table, he tilted his woolly head at her. "Ye're a bashful one. Yer sister would'a been chatterin' like a magpie, askin' questions and demandin' answers."

Mary removed her wet mantle, perched herself on the edge of a rush-bottomed chair, and took a sip of tea. "Please, sir, I've been traveling all day. Will you tell me now where she is?"

"After ye take a few good swallows. Ye look pale as a ghost."

Impatient for news, she obliged. The heat of the liquid spread through her body. At his gesturing motion, she drank until the mug was nearly drained. "Thank you, sir."

"Just call me Obediah. I be the footman here, even though them curst Frenchies shot off my foot." He grinned at his own jest and unabashedly lifted his trouser leg to display his wooden peg. "I came beggin' one day at Miss Josephine's door. She took me in when nobody else would hire an old war horse."

How like Jo. "For mercy's sake, where *is* my sister?" Mary asked, unable to contain herself any longer. "What's happened to her?"

"She disappeared." Obediah remained standing, his face set in grim sadness and his forearms resting on the table. "She run off last night. Right after she shot Lord Cyril."

The mug slipped from Mary's fingers and thunked onto the table. "Shot? Who is Lord Cyril?"

"Her protector, Lord Cyril Brentwell. He's younger brother t' the duke o' St. Chaldon."

Jo had withheld the name of the man who had lived with her in sin. To hear it now knotted Mary's throat.

Obediah went on, "Last night his lordship come by for dinner with Miss Josephine. I served 'em meself, cauliflower soup and joint o' lamb just the way his lordship liked. But the lovebirds weren't cooin', if ye know what I mean."

In a haze of disbelief, Mary shook her head. "They quarreled?"

"Aye. Seems his brother—Adam Brentwell, the almighty duke—ordered Lord Cyril t' renounce yer sister. Miss Josephine left the dinin' room in tears, poor dear. Lord Cyril dashed upstairs after her. Whilst I cleared away the dishes and come down here t' the kitchen."

Obediah paused, his gaze clouded as if he were lost in memory. The coal fire crackled in the silence. Tense with dread, Mary prompted, "And then?"

" 'Twere after midnight, I was lockin' up like I do every night. I found the front door standin' wide open. Thought a robber might'a come in, so I hastened upstairs to tell Miss Josephine. But she was gone. Lord Cyril was lyin' in a pool o' blood. Shot in the head."

Mary pressed her hands to her icy cheeks. "Merciful God," she moaned. "He's dead?"

"Nay. Out cold, an' still is, I hear. The doctors say 'twill be a miracle if he lives."

She sat in numb denial. Blithe, kind-hearted Jo attempting murder? Impossible.

Impossible.

"Did anyone see Jo? Were there any other servants about?"

"Housemaid and cook and tweeny was all asleep in their beds down here in the cellar." He gestured toward a dark passageway off the kitchen.

"Then how can you blame my sister?"

" 'Twas the Runners that said so." Obediah rubbed the network of broken veins across his nose. "They was sent by the magistrate at Bow Street. If ye'd come earlier, ye'd a seen 'em. They swarmed the place all day, trampin' up and down the stairs like the King's own regiment. Them and His Grace."

"His Grace?"

"The duke," Obediah said blackly. "Ye don't want t' cross that one. 'Twas he who sent the Runners away to check every hellhole in London. He swore he'll see Miss Josephine hang."

Obediah was right about the blood.

Hesitating in the doorway of the bedroom, Mary held a heavy branch of candles. The servant had cautioned her not to go into her sister's bedroom. Now she understood why.

From here, she could see the irregular rust-brown stain on the patterned carpet and could smell its faint coppery odor. Her stomach lurched. Lord Cyril Brentwell had been shot here in this room. Near the foot of the canopied bed. By Jo.

Mary squeezed her eyes shut. She wished the dog had come upstairs with her so she could hug it tightly. Surely Jo could never harm any living creature. Yet who would have thought her capable of becoming a man's doxy, either? Perhaps she had fallen deeper into a pit of sin than Mary had imagined.

Mary! Oh, please, Mary, save me!

The memory of her sister's desperation gripped Mary's heart. Jo had been the victim, not the perpetrator. Obviously, a robber had crept into the house, believing the occupants gone for the evening. London teemed with ruffians and thieves and ne'er-do-wells. Jo must have witnessed the horrid crime and fled for her life. Even now she might be hiding somewhere, afraid to return.

The thought galvanized Mary, and she ventured a few steps inside. The candles cast long shadows over the walls and ceiling. She was supposed to retire to one of the guest chambers, but curiosity waged a winning battle with common sense. She wanted to see her sister's domain, the place where Jo had lived for the past three months.

The grandeur of the room awed Mary. Other than the occasional visit to a croft or cottage, she had never been in a real house before. This one chamber was many times the size of the caravan. Gold curtains draped a bank of windows. The white and gilt furniture included a dressing table with a mirror, a huge wardrobe, a chaise and chairs, and a washstand with a china pitcher.

The bedsheets were rumpled as if Jo had just arisen. Drawers hung open and articles of clothing were strewn on the carpet. Papa had always scolded Jo for her carelessness. Only Mary understood her twin's absorption in the fanciful dreams that overshadowed the mundane details of daily life. The knot drew taut in her throat. The least she could do for Jo was to set things to rights.

She tiptoed to the bedside table, making a wide berth around the bloodstain, and put down the branch of candles. It was then that she noticed the mirror over the bed.

It was tucked inside the canopy and framed by festoons of golden fabric. How perplexing. Had her sister grown so vain that she needed to admire her beauty while lying abed?

Odd that, for Mary herself had developed an aversion to mirrors. After Jo's impetuous departure, Mary had given away her lone handmirror. She could no longer bear to look into it. To do so meant seeing not only herself, but the face of her twin, her lost half.

Plucking a delicate painted fan from the floor, she felt the comfort of Jo's presence envelop her. Her dear sister had touched this fan. Here, in this room, Jo had gone about her daily ablutions. Here, she had dressed and laughed and slept. Here, she had lain in bed with her lover. Did she still like to whisper secrets in the dark after the candle was blown out?

Mary struggled against the resentment that poisoned her mind. How she despised Lord Cyril Brentwell for seducing her vulnerable sister. Papa was right to condemn the aristocracy for its evil excesses. Jo might have returned home had not a nobleman tempted her with the glamour of riches.

And had not Mary herself barred the door to her heart.

Stung by regrets, she went to the open wardrobe and picked up a silk stocking. Its cool smoothness evoked in her a comparison to her own plain worsted stockings. Decadent attractions abounded inside: gowns of satin and brocade and India muslin, tippets of fur and feather, fine kidskin gloves, an array of plumed and beribboned bonnets. Mary regarded it all with a sort of fascinated aversion. She and her sister had grown up wearing castoff clothing from charity bags. But now Jo arrayed herself like a lady in these rich and sensual garments.

Mary glided her fingertips over a silk chemise, then snatched back her hand. How smooth it felt, how tempting to know the feel of it draped over her body. It was like a hunger in her, a hunger born of the desire to know if Jo had found her heart's desire. Had giving up her family been worth the price?

Clasping her clenched fist to her breast, Mary stepped to the dressing table. She kept her eyes downcast to avoid looking into the mirror. Flagons of perfume and pots of cosmetics littered the table. Out of habit, she lined up the containers in neat precision. Then she lifted one to her nose and drew in the heavenly aroma. Roses.

Her throat ached. As girls, she and Jo had often crept away from the caravan to weave crowns of wild roses and pretend to be princesses. Her face shining, Jo described the palace where she would live someday. Instead of a tiny cubicle, she would sleep upon a huge gilt bed. Instead of her worldly possessions fitting into one small trunk, she would own a different gown for each day of the year. Instead of railing against the aristocracy, as their father did, Jo declared that she would marry a nobleman.

But how wrong she had been. Her lord had offered only a shameful liaison.

A jewel box lay open, its contents winking in the candlelight. Had the intruder been frightened off before plundering it? Mary picked up a necklace of emeralds set in gold, and the gems weighed as heavy as sin. Had Jo regretted her choice? Were jewels and gowns an adequate replacement for the loss of her decency? Her very soul?

Where *was* Jo?

Determined to find the answers, Mary found herself fastening the piece around her neck. She risked a quick peek at the mirror before lowering her gaze. Yet the pull of curiosity overcame her reluctance, and she slowly lifted her chin.

Her reflection was solemn and mirthless, her green eyes too grave to invite any comparison to the gemstones. The extravagance of emeralds glowed against the high-necked bodice of her gray gown. She looked like a schoolgirl playing dress-up.

A queer sense of unreality enveloped Mary. She looked like . . .

Her drab costume melted into an expanse of white bosom and an indecent décolletage. Her severe coronet of braids unfurled into a cascade of red-gold curls. Her unsmiling features transformed into an animated face of haunting beauty.

Jo.

*She wore a gown of rich green that matched the emerald
necklace at her throat. As she ascended the steps to a porticoed mansion, her escort turned his blond head to smile at
her, and the sharp-sweet thrust of longing in her mixed with
dread.*

*Mary, is your heart listening? I'm so excited, so afraid. I
wish you were here with me. . . .*

The scene misted over in Mary's mind as if viewed
through a window rimed with frost. No matter how hard
she tried, she couldn't recall the image. Only a lingering
tension remained.

With shaking fingers, she reached up and unfastened the
necklace. The gemstones slithered downward and coiled
like a snake in her cupped palms.

Sweet heaven. She had seen her sister wearing this very
necklace. And who was the man with Jo? Lord Cyril
Brentwell?

It must have been a scene from the past. Yet how was
that possible? Always before she had sensed events as they
had actually happened. Never had she witnessed an occur-
rence after a passage of time.

Mary's heart beat faster. Their father had declared the
mind bond a tool of the devil, and he had forbidden his
daughters to use it. Yet they had continued to do so in
secret until the day when Mary had shut her sister out.
Had she become so adept at suppressing the skill that her
ability to control it had died?

A guilty yearning tempted Mary. She could resurrect the
unnatural power, use it to contact her sister. Perhaps she
could coax Jo back into the family fold. And then Mary
could beg her forgiveness.

"What the devil—?"

The guttural voice jabbed into her thoughts. Holding the
emeralds, Mary spun around.

A stranger loomed in the doorway of the bedroom. A
greatcoat framed the breadth of his shoulders, though she

could see the elegance of the attire beneath, the white
cravat against a burgundy coat, the fawn breeches, the
black knee-high boots. His hair was as dark as the shadows
behind him, and his face was harshly handsome, thin-
lipped and threatening.

They stood staring at each other for what seemed an
eternity. His hostile presence unnerved Mary. Where was
Obediah? She parted her lips to scream for him but only a
dry croak emerged.

Abruptly the stranger lunged at her.

Gasping, she ran. He blocked her escape to the door.
When she tried to dash around him, he caught her by the
arm and flung her onto the bed.

In a haze of terror, she struggled to sit up. The doorway.
She could see the gloom of the passage beyond. Safety.

His body came down on hers, and this time she cried
out.

His gloved hand clamped over her mouth and stifled the
sound. His black eyes glowed in a face so sinister it looked
like Satan himself. With his free hand, he wrested the
necklace from her fingers and hurled it away. The piece
fell to the floor with a metallic clatter.

"Greedy wench," he growled. "I was right to think you
would come back for the jewels."

His words mystified her. His hand smelled of soap and
leather. Despite the barrier of her gown and petticoat, she
felt the power of his muscles, the heat of his body. The
mirror over the bed reflected the back of him like a great
winged beast that had trapped its quarry.

Horror-stricken, Mary bit down on his fingers. Her teeth
sank into the soft leather and met the hardness of flesh.

Cursing, he loosened his grip. She flipped onto her
stomach and scrambled toward the foot of the bed. But the
rain-dampened skirts hampered her legs. He slammed
onto her in an instant, pinning her facedown to the mattress.

She couldn't move, couldn't breathe. The goose-feathered counterpane muffled her cries. Her bottom was snuggled into his groin. They were pressed together as closely as lovers.

"Murderess!" he snarled. "I'll see you swing for shooting my brother."

Merciful God. *Merciful God.*

He was Adam Brentwell. The almighty duke of St. Chaldon.

She managed to turn her head to the side. "I'm Mary. N-not Jo." Her voice sounded weak and unsteady, and she was filled with shame at her helplessness. "Jo is m-my sister."

For a moment he lay immobile. She felt the furious beating of his heart against her spine. Gooseflesh prickled over her skin, and the hotness of him stifled her. Obediah's warning whispered through her mind: *Ye don't want to cross that one.*

"I underestimated your cleverness," the duke said, his breath heavy and moist against her ear. "You must have found yourself a very rich, very gullible new lover."

He shifted his weight slightly and yanked up her skirt. The pressure of his gloved hand met her stockinged ankle and slowly moved up her leg. "This is what you like, isn't it? This, from any man willing to pay your exorbitant price."

Shock bolted through her. She squirmed, desperate to evade his relentless assault. With inexorable firmness, his fingers slid over her knee and onto her thigh. A nightmare of panic pulsed inside her, and she heard herself whimpering, panting, driven to the verge of a swoon.

"The truth, Josephine," he said in a harsh whisper. "Admit that you shot Cyril."

He was a madman. A demon. She resisted the writhing darkness that threatened to suck her down . . . down . . . down.

"No. *No.*" Out of the depths of her soul rose a frantic prayer. " 'The souls of the righteous are in the hands of

God, and there shall be no torment touch them. . . . they shall be greatly rewarded: for God proved them, and found them worthy—' "

"For Christ's sake."

Just as he neared her most private place, the duke removed his hand and his weight lifted from her. A blessed rush of cool air set her teeth chattering. He grasped her arm, hauled her to her feet, and brought her closer to the branch of candles on the bedside table.

There, he took hold of her chin and turned her face to and fro. He assessed her features from the prim, braided hair down to the quivering lips. In the light, she saw that his eyes were not black at all, but a very dark blue, and the glow from the candles was reflected there like tiny stars flung against the dusk sky.

When he released her chin, the imprint of his warm fingers lingered. As did the ghostly sensation of his hand on her leg.

"I should have known," he said. "You aren't nearly as handsome as Josephine."

"You aren't so handsome yourself. And how dare you treat me so shabbily." Mary fell silent, shocked at her boldness. That tussle on the bed must have rattled her senses. Her body trembled like a spoonful of jelly, and she rubbed her chilled arms.

The duke cocked one black eyebrow. The expression gave him an imperious aspect, as if he were gazing down his aristocratic nose at a beggar. Quite unexpectedly, he unfastened his greatcoat and settled the heavy garment around her shoulders. The remnants of his body heat made her distinctly uneasy. Yet she was grateful to hide herself, to burrow into the voluminous folds.

"Josephine was never wont to quote the Scripture," he said, his brusque voice belying any kindness. "But the physical resemblance is considerable. You're twins?"

"Yes."

"Yet Josephine has a mole to the left of her mouth, and you've one to the right."

Warily she nodded, shaken by his perception of a detail that few people noticed. She and Jo were mirror images—a fact their father had viewed with disquiet. Thomas Sheppard had forced Jo to use her right hand when her left was more adept; he had disapproved of her exuberant spirit and ordered her to behave like quiet Mary.

The duke peeled off his glove and examined the fingers she'd bitten. She felt a twist of spitefulness. "Are you hurt?"

"A minor soreness." He looked her up and down. "And you?"

He brought to mind the scandalizing intimacy of his touch. Resisting a shudder, she shook her head.

He watched her closely while he paced the shadowed bedroom. It was as if he expected her to bolt out the door at any moment. And she would if her legs didn't feel as weak as water.

"What are you doing here tonight?" he asked.

"I came to call on my sister."

"Do you live in London?"

"No."

"Where are you from?"

"Nowhere in particular."

"Don't be evasive. Everyone comes from somewhere."

His arrogant attitude fostered a rare rise of temper in her. This was the sort of man her father preached against—one of the decadent minority, the privileged few who believed themselves born to rule. Yet this duke was no better than she was.

She met his chilly gaze. "Not everyone. An appalling number of homeless people wander the streets. I was shocked to see so many pitiful souls roaming the city, while the rich ride about in fancy carriages—"

"Spare me the social commentary and answer my question."

Mary swallowed painfully. So much for her brief show of pluck. That dictatorial tone had her quaking in her wet shoes again. "My father is a traveling minister," she said, willing her voice not to crack. "We were making our way through Sussex."

His blue gaze bored into her. "Then how did you know Josephine was in trouble? There wasn't enough time for a message to be sent and for you to respond."

Mary's tongue felt tied in knots. How could she admit that she had seen Jo in a vision? The duke would laugh at her, scorn her as a liar.

She kept silent.

"Well, Miss Sheppard? It is Miss, isn't it?"

"Yes," she whispered.

"Tell me the truth. Did Josephine send you here to fetch her jewels?"

"No! I don't know where she is."

"Then how did you know to come here, today of all days? Unless she ran straight to you." He took a step closer, a menacing step. "Admit it, you know where she's hiding."

"That isn't true!" Mary cast about frantically for an answer. There was no getting around it; she would have to lie. Begging the Lord's forgiveness, she stammered, "It w-was mere coincidence that I came to visit at this time. Ask Obediah. He'll assure you that I know nothing of Jo's whereabouts."

Adam Brentwell stalked nearer. Mary backed up to the bedside table and huddled within the folds of his greatcoat. Her stomach churned. He looked so bitter, so furious, so *male*. Unwillingly, she recalled the hardness of his body pressed to hers.

"Stop right there, or I shall scream for Obediah."

The duke halted. His black eyebrows were lowered so that he appeared annoyed to the limits of his patience. "Rest assured, Miss Sheppard. I have no intention of ravishing you—so long as you cooperate. And you will cooperate. I shan't relent until I see justice done for the sake of my brother."

Her gaze flitted to the bloodstain on the rug. She forced herself to ask the question: "Has . . . has he died?"

"There's been no change in his condition."

Mary folded her hands in fervent prayer. "Praise God for that."

"Praise God that Cyril lies insensible? Better you should implore the Almighty for the swiftness of His vengeance upon your sister."

The duke's words were cold, heartless. His belief in Jo's guilt roused the fire of denial in Mary. "You've made a terrible mistake. You should be seeking a ruffian, not an innocent girl."

"Then we have differing views on your sister's character. She was anything but *innocent.*"

Mary bristled. It was as if he had attacked her own honor, her own integrity. And little did he know of the guilty secret that prodded her. "Jo would shoot a man only in defense of her life. Your brother must have abused her."

"I beg your pardon. Your sister was a spider, snaring him in her web of greed and seduction."

With rare stubbornness, Mary shook her head. "That isn't the Jo I know."

The duke reached inside his coat and drew out a square of paper, which he unfolded and handed to Mary. "Perhaps this will convince you."

Mary blinked down at the note.

> *Cyril—*
> *With great sorrow, I must tell you that I've met a new love, the man of my heart. Forgive me, darling. Know that I shall always treasure the fond memories of our months together.*
> *I am away to the Continent tonight. Do not follow me.*
> *Adieu, Josephine*

"That letter," said the duke, "was found lying on the floor beside the bed. She must have been preparing to depart when my brother walked in on her. No doubt he tried to stop her. He was rewarded by a bullet to his skull."

Sickened, Mary stared at the squiggly words. The handwriting was Jo's. And yet it was not. Where were the blots, the words crossed out, the ill-formed letters? Often Mary had copied over Jo's work to spare her a lecture from their father. In fact, the letter looked more like Mary's neat writing.

She lifted her gaze to the duke. The light from the candelabrum etched hollows beneath his cheekbones. Judging by the smudges under his eyes, his lordship hadn't slept any better than she had the previous night. Against her will, Mary felt a twinge of compassion. He was as worried about his brother as she was about her sister.

"This isn't Jo's penmanship," she said. "It's far too tidy. And Jo favored curlicues. If you don't believe me, only compare it to something else written in her hand."

The duke snatched the letter back and glanced over it again. "If you're saying this is a forgery, that's nonsense. Who would go to such lengths?"

"Perhaps someone who wanted us to believe she shot your brother." Mary voiced the horrid thought that seized her. "Someone who hated your brother enough to shoot him and then kidnap Jo."

৩ **Chapter 3** ৩

Adam curbed his rising temper. Considering her vulgar parentage, what else could he expect from this country bumpkin but unfounded accusations?

Mary Sheppard was the offspring of an itinerant minister who preached sedition to the uneducated masses. She didn't know it, but only days before the shooting, Adam had sent his steward to make discreet inquiries about Thomas Sheppard.

The preliminary report had described a firebrand cleric who wrapped himself in a cloak of godliness even as he advocated the overthrow of the nobility. The dispatch had failed to mention the existence of a twin sister. Adam would have to chastise his man about *that* little oversight.

Mary Sheppard looked startlingly like Josephine in drab disguise. Only eighteen, she already had the prim aspect of a spinster on the shelf. The braided, scraped-back hair made her face appear too thin. Her thick-lashed eyes were a fine shade of green, yet the color was dulled by her pallor and nondescript clothing. His greatcoat swallowed her slender figure—or as much as he could see of it from the shapeless dress that she wore.

Guilt pricked him. Never in his life had he treated a woman so callously. He had behaved like a beast, pinning her to the bed and shoving his hand beneath her skirt. He had wanted to punish Josephine.

Instead he had assaulted the Virgin Mary.

Unwillingly he recalled the warmth of her skin through her rough stocking, the shapely curve of her leg, the softness of her thigh and the tantalizing heat beyond. He was appalled to think of how tempted he'd been to take her against her will.

Even now, he burned to discover what other secrets lay beneath her ugly gown. He wondered if Mary Sheppard could be persuaded into bed, if she could be coaxed to wild abandon. As swiftly as the thought came, he banished it. In a mistress, he preferred a worldly woman, not a pinch-lipped maiden.

"I can prove I'm right," she announced. His coat swirled around her as she turned and marched to the bedside table. Pulling out the top drawer, she began to search through the contents.

He stalked to her side, watching as she drew out a spare candle, a quill pen, a silver inkpot, then a pamphlet, a stack of blank vellum, and a cheap gothic novel.

Unaccountably annoyed, he asked, "What are you doing?"

"Looking for a sample. . . ." From the book, she plucked out a scrap of paper that must have been used as a marker. She glanced at it, then waved it in triumph. "Ahah! There you go, sir. This will prove the letter to be a sham."

He took the paper from her. It appeared to be shopping list. *3 pr. stockings (silk), pink ribband (1 yd), sheet music (5?), leather collar (Prinny). . . .*

As Adam scanned the rest of the items, uneasiness stirred within him. He didn't want to think of Josephine Sheppard as an ordinary person who purchased musical scores for her pianoforte and collars for her dog. Nor did he wish to place any significance on the childish penmanship or the ink blots.

"See?" Mary Sheppard said. "You cannot deny the difference between that neat letter and this sloppy list."

"I concede to a disparity in the styles. Yet it only proves that she took more care with the farewell note."

"It proves there was no random intruder." Her gaze intent on him, Mary took a step closer. "Please, sir, trust me to know my own sister's writing. She had to have been abducted by someone who despised your brother. And you must help me find her."

The appeal in those green eyes tugged at him. Tucking the list in his pocket, he strove for dispassion. "You're mistaken about Cyril. He is much loved by all who know him. He has no enemies."

A dubious frown puckered her brow. She flashed him a wary look from the coppery veil of her lashes. "Perhaps he did something *you* don't think of as wicked."

"Explain yourself."

"Lord Cyril might have dallied with the wife of a jealous man. Aristocrats think little of lustful indiscretions."

"My brother has been inordinately faithful to your sister."

"Then perhaps he incurred a gaming debt so large he couldn't repay it. The person he owed shot him."

"He would have come to me or to my mother for the money."

"Might he have won a wager, then, and beggared another lord? There *must* be a reason. It only makes sense that one of his own kind shot him."

"And what, pray, is his kind?"

"A wicked rake. A heartless noble who thinks nothing of luring a poor commoner into sin."

"For God's sake," Adam exploded, prowling back and forth. "You do not even know Cyril."

"Then tell me about him. *Is* he a gamester?"

How irritatingly direct she was! Adam resented this wisp of a girl for putting his stricken brother on trial. "If someone had had a quarrel with Cyril, he would have challenged my brother to pistols at dawn. An ambush in the dead of night is the act of a jealous lover, not an honorable man."

"Nor of an honorable woman," Mary Sheppard said. "Yet you do not hesitate to accuse Jo of the hideous deed."

"Pardon my bluntness, but your sister was hardly engaged in a respectable profession."

Mary's eyes widened, and he saw the pain there. She stepped away from the bedside table and glared at him. "Do not sully my sister's character. Your brother was an equal partner in their liaison. If you consider Jo to be dishonorable, then Lord Cyril is guilty of the same sin."

Underlying her angry tone was a sorrow that Adam did not care to contemplate. He wanted to dismiss Mary Sheppard as a tart-tongued termagant. To denounce her as a judgmental shrew who dared to fling fire and brimstone at a duke.

Yet he felt curiously ashamed. She showed pluck in defending her twin. And she forced him to look at the situation in a new light. Cyril had a knack for trouble and a winning charm for talking his way out of it. Only last week he had bid an extravagant amount on a matched pair of grays at Tattersall's and then persuaded the duchess to foot the bill. With all the careless flair of a gentleman, he often lived beyond his considerable means.

Mary stood with her arms folded as if to protect herself. *Was* there another explanation for Josephine's disappearance?

No. She was a fugitive from justice. She had written that farewell note. This kidnapping theory was too outlandish.

Adam paced the bedroom. His eyes felt gritty from lack of sleep, and his temples throbbed. The bloodstain on the carpet served as a constant reminder of his mission: he must apprehend his brother's assailant.

Until the Runners uncovered a clue to Josephine's whereabouts, Mary Sheppard was his only hope. She might know something that could be of help to him, but he would have to tread carefully.

"Let us assume—only for the sake of argument—that your sister was abducted," he said. "It follows that my brother got in the way of a man who wanted her for himself. Thusly, the villain could be one of the suitors she rejected."

"Suitors? But I thought . . . your brother was . . ."

"Her only bedmate? Not at first, Miss Sheppard."

He had the pleasure of seeing Mary blush again. The pinkish tint across her cheekbones lent a sweetness to her thin features. It had been a long time since he had met a woman so lacking in artifice.

He disliked being the one to disillusion her. But it was bound to happen sooner or later.

"Your sister collected quite a stable of admirers," Adam continued. "You see, Cyril met Josephine on her first night in London. Apparently she was wandering the streets in search of a place to stay. He was captivated by her rustic charms and made her an offer, but she coyly refused to become his mistress."

"There was nothing coy about it." Mary Sheppard lifted her chin and stared him in the face. "Of course, Jo refused him. She often spoke of marrying a man who loved her. A man who would treat her with all the respect she deserves."

"Permit me to finish. Never one to refuse a challenge, Cyril set her up in this house and gave the other gentlemen a sporting chance to win her favor. For a month, they courted her in droves. Ultimately, after toying with countless male hearts, she chose my brother to share her bed."

As he spoke, Mary had lowered herself to the edge of the four-poster. Now she sprang back up and glanced askance at the rumpled sheets. "H-how many suitors did she have?"

"A fair number. You can be certain I will investigate the matter immediately." The spark of an idea flared in Adam's mind. An idea so outrageous, so risky, it just might work. Slowly he added, "With your help."

"My help?"

"Yes."

Caught up in analyzing the possibilities, Adam strode toward her. He lifted the greatcoat from her shoulders and dropped it on the bed. "Sir!" she squeaked. "Whatever are you doing?"

"Wondering if I might turn the ugly duckling into a swan."

He plucked out the cheap pins that secured her braids and then unraveled the tight twists of hair. Glorious, red-gold waves unfurled into his hands and glinted in the candlelight. He rubbed a silken strand between his fingers.

She flinched away, her arms clasped over her bosom as if she expected him to strip her naked. "Get away from me, you . . . you lecher."

He wanted to smile at her virginal outrage, but the breathy catch to her voice stopped him, as did the dramatic change in her appearance. With her hair spilling down, the ends curling around her breasts, she looked like a woman who had a secret yearning to be ravished.

Perhaps his scheme wasn't so farfetched, after all.

In a fever of inspiration, Adam strode to the wardrobe and chose a gown at random. The scent of roses wafted over him. Closing his mind to the woman who owned it, he gathered up the confection of silk and ribbons, took it to Mary Sheppard, and held it against her shoulders. The rich bronze fabric brought the glow of color to her pale cheeks.

The indecent décolletage would complete her metamorphosis. From their encounter on the bed, he suspected that Mary Sheppard possessed the same magnificent bosom as her scheming twin.

"Perfect," he muttered. "A little polishing, and you could tempt a saint."

She stood stiffly, backed against the bedpost. "Remove your hands from me at once. Or I will be forced to scream for help."

"Then I shall be forced to stop your mouth with my own."

Her lips parted. But she didn't make a sound.

Again he felt a fleeting tenderness and resisted it. "I have a plan, Miss Sheppard. Together, we shall find your sister."

"Then you truly believe she was abducted?"

He looked straight into her green eyes and lied. "Truly."

As cautious hope dawned on her face, he reasoned that his falsehood might enable him to avenge the wrong done to his brother. Josephine had shot Cyril in cold blood and run off with another man. To snare the bitch, Adam had no choice but to play on Mary's belief in her sister's innocence.

He quieted his clamoring conscience with the memory of Cyril lying white-faced and motionless in bed, his head wrapped in bandages, his eyes closed. Perhaps forever.

A tempest of dread and love raged in Adam. He might have been born to command, but he could not order God to spare his brother's life. With effort he controlled his emotions and gazed down into her eyes. "If you believe Josephine to be blameless, you will help me flush out the villain who captured her."

"Yes! I'll do anything." Unexpectedly, Mary Sheppard pressed her hand to his, and her warmth penetrated to a deep, cold place inside him. "But how will we manage it?"

"It's quite simple. You shall pose as your sister."

She should never have agreed to the outrageous plan, Mary told herself for the hundredth time.

Lifting the blue silk curtain of the coach, she risked a peek out at the hazy morning. At this early hour, only tradesmen and servants hastened about their tasks, for the rich could not be expected to arise before noon, or so Obediah had told her. It was a wonder the duke could manage to bestir himself.

I'll see you swing for shooting my brother.

A shudder gripped Mary. The duke had said as much when he'd believed she was her twin. No doubt a man of his stature could make good his threat. Praise God he now accepted that letter as a forgery, and they were united in the effort to find Jo. The scheme required swift action and strict secrecy. It was vital that Mary make a success of her transformation.

The curtain slipped from her gloved fingers. Sweet heaven. She was in the wicked city of London, on her way to meet the duke of St. Chaldon at his private residence. So that he could teach her to behave like a fallen woman.

A jittery sensation danced in Mary, the same nervousness that had wreaked havoc with her stomach since the previous evening. Was it a sin to participate in this brazen charade? A part of her longed to be perched between Papa and Victor while the old horse, George the Third, drew the caravan along some rural road. The constant traveling was wearisome, yet achingly familiar. She could almost hear the creaking of the wheels, the twittering of larks and sparrows in the hedgerows, the deep voice of her father explaining a passage of the Scripture. . . .

"Hot cross buns," shouted a man just outside the coach.

The streetseller's hoarse voice cast her squarely back into the present. At the appointed time, she must convince the spurned suitors that she was Jo. Accordingly, she had followed the duke's orders and garbed herself in Jo's wicked clothing. Because her own coarse cotton shift would make lumps in the silk gown, she had been forced to don fine undergarments, too. She had gulped upon stealing one peek in the mirror, and swiftly covered the gown with her old, green mantle.

She had been ready when, promptly after breakfast, his carriage arrived to fetch her to his house. She would overcome her reticence and act as vivacious as her twin. Odious as the task might be, she would pretend she had escaped her captor and sought sanctuary with the duke.

Mary took a deep breath redolent of expensive uphol-

stery and the soot of the city. If it meant finding her sister,
she would mimic even the corrupt ways of the nobility.

"Jo," she whispered to the dim interior of the coach.
"Jo, where are you?"

The muffled clopping of the horse's hooves and the rattle of the wheels over the cobblestones filled the silence.
Mary swayed between hope and fear. Perhaps she would
never be able to renew the severed bond with her twin.

Perhaps it was too late.

No. She wouldn't torture herself with horrid conjectures.
Jo had to be alive, or else Mary would know somehow. She
would *know*.

The coach drew to a halt. A footman opened the door
and set down the steps. Mary descended to the pavement
and teetered on the unfamiliar high heels. She walked
slowly toward a modest brick town house, not the lavish
mansion she had expected. The street was quiet with few
passersby. An iron fence embraced the minuscule front
yard with its perfectly clipped shrubbery. The overall effect
was rather formal, and irrelevantly she found herself longing for a blaze of hollyhocks and a tangle of roses.

No sooner had she knocked than the door swung open.
An expressionless butler stepped aside to allow her entrance.

"Miss Sheppard, I presume." His eyes were focused on a
point just above her shoulder. "May I take your cloak?"

She started to obey. Just in time, she clutched the worn
folds around herself. "No, thank you."

Without further ado, he ushered her into a drawing
room decorated in blue and silver. She found herself tip-
toeing as if she were an interloper rather than an invited
guest. The doors closed behind her with a subtle click.

Then she saw him.

Seated at a secretaire in the corner, Adam Brentwell put
down his quill pen and frowned at her. His weariness
struck her first: the smudge of shadows beneath his eyes
and the tension bracketing his mouth. How coldly superior

he looked in his dark blue frock coat, the white neckcloth, the fawn breeches and black knee boots. He was a fancy version of his namesake, a sinner expelled from the Garden of Eden.

Rising, he came toward her, the carpet muffling the sound of his boots. She had the ridiculous urge to retreat before his advance, to run back to the safety of Jo's town house. Only with effort did she hold herself still.

Offering no greeting, he studied her critically. "I see you've anchored your hair into those dreadful braids again."

"I know nothing of fancy styles."

"And you should have had the sense to veil your face. Someone might mistake you for your sister."

"I thought that was the point."

He raised one eyebrow in that disdainful way of his. "Not yet. Didn't Rayburn offer to take your wrap?"

"The butler? He did, but . . . I'm chilled."

"Nonsense. We've a morning of hard work ahead of us. I won't have you looking as though you're about to dash out the door."

His long fingers were already freeing the buttons at her throat. A mortifying shiver danced over her skin, but he didn't appear to notice. Without so much as a "by your leave," he removed the mantle and tossed it over a chair. His frown deepened to a scowl as he cocked his head and stared at her dress.

Heat rushed up her half-bare bosom and into her cheeks. She lowered her gaze to his snowy cravat and forced herself not to fidget. His scrutiny made her insides feel as fluttery as a captive butterfly.

The gaudy topaz silk clung to her breasts and cascaded to the floor. Even this, the most modest gown in her sister's wardrobe, exposed an alarming amount of flesh. Fortunately, Mary had found a swatch of lace buried in a drawer. She had soothed her sensibilities by tucking the semi-sheer fabric into the décolletage.

Though she would die before admitting it aloud, she took guilty delight in wearing the fine garb, right down to the cambric petticoat and frilly drawers, the silk stockings that felt like a cool caress against her skin. She tempered her vanity with a single poignant thought. Jo had worn these things; for a brief time, Mary could experience her sister's new life.

Adam Brentwell stepped closer. "You shan't be needing this."

Before she realized his purpose, he pulled out the makeshift modesty piece. His fingers brushed her bosom and her heartbeat surged.

Gasping, Mary pressed her hands to the mounds of her breasts. If she'd felt indecent before, now she felt utterly shameless. "Give that back to me."

"No." Turning, Adam Brentwell tossed the lace onto the coal fire.

She raced to the hearth. Tongues of flame licked the airy cloth so that it glowed orange before darkening to black. Without thinking, she snatched at it with her gloved fingers. The lace fell onto the fender and dangled in a smoking, ruined pile.

She swung back toward the duke, intending to vent her rage at his high-handed act. The scathing setdown died on her tongue.

Oh, God have mercy. He was gazing at her heaving bosom in a way that could only be compared to the smoldering lace.

She clapped her hands back over her breasts in a futile effort to hide herself. "You shouldn't have done that."

To her alarm, he drew nearer. One corner of his mouth lifted, though she could not call it a smile. "Little Virgin Mary."

An undertone of laughter roughened his voice. He found her modesty amusing. Amusing!

Her blush deepened, stinging her face. "Don't be blasphemous."

"Then don't play the prude." He caught her wrists and drew her hands down. "The good Lord gave you a beautiful form. If you're to play your role convincingly, you must grow accustomed to men staring. You'll even come to enjoy it."

In his midnight blue eyes glowed a mixture of appreciation and something darker, something Mary couldn't identify. His gaze seemed to penetrate her skin, as warm as the fingers that held her wrists. For no discernible reason, she recalled the solidness of his body pressing her to the bed, the shocking sensation of his hand on her leg. Would his clean-shaven face feel hard to her fingertips? She had the strangest urge to find out. A sensation like heated honey drizzled through her limbs and melted her knees. If she were bolder, she would lift herself on tiptoe and brush her mouth against his.

Awareness drenched her in an icy wave, and she stepped away from the duke. No respectable female would consider kissing a near-stranger, especially when she was already promised to another. Even Victor only permitted himself an occasional chaste peck on her cheek.

It must be the ruse. Her mind was adjusting itself to the role of wanton. "I'm not performing at the moment. I'll wear my mantle."

"You'll do nothing of the sort. We can afford only a day or two of preparation." Adam snatched up the green garment and carried it out of the room, reappearing in a moment to shut the doors again. When he turned, resolution tightened his jaw. "Henceforth, you shall dress and act exactly as Josephine. Unless you wish your sister to remain at the mercy of a gun-wielding villain."

The reminder abashed Mary. "No, of course not." She took a step toward him. "How is Lord Cyril?"

"The same," he said, his voice heavy. "The doctors don't know when or if he will recover."

"May I . . . go upstairs and see him? Perhaps I could say a prayer at his bedside."

Frowning, the duke tilted his head to one side. "He isn't here. He's at Brentwell House."

"But I thought this was your home." In confusion, she gestured at the magnificent room.

"Hardly. I needed a convenient place for assignations."

"Assignations?" She blinked in puzzlement. "Do you not have meeting rooms in your house?"

A subtle gleam entered his eyes. "I am referring to discreet affairs, Miss Sheppard. This is where I entertain females who are not received in society."

"Oh." Mary feared she was blushing again. Not so much at her own ignorance, but at the thought of him bringing women here for the purpose of carnal acts. Unwillingly she pictured him kissing a woman in a scarlet frock, pressing her down on the bed, putting his hand beneath her skirt. . . .

Beyond that, her imagination went blank.

The duke walked away to the secretaire in the corner of the room. He returned, bearing a sheet of paper. "I've compiled a list of suspects. These five men were the most avid in regard to winning Josephine, and none can account for his whereabouts on the night of the shooting. I'll send them each a message to come here in two nights' time. One by one. But instead of me, they shall find you. Or shall we say, Josephine."

Panic swept over Mary in a giddy wave. It was ludicrous. She couldn't carry through with the ruse. Those jaded gentlemen would see straight through her disguise.

She busied herself with peeling off her soot-stained gloves. "What if the kidnapper has fled London with Jo?"

"It's the height of the season. It would look suspicious if any of these men were to leave town abruptly."

"May I see?" She extended her hand for the list, and he gave it to her. None of the names were familiar, and she feared to think of the consequences if they overlooked Jo's kidnapper. "Are you certain there are no others?"

A curious blankness came over his face. He took back

the list, carefully folded it, and tucked it in an inner pocket of his coat. "I know of only these men. So unless my brother regains consciousness and gives us additional names, we have no choice but to proceed. Now curtsy as you should before a man of rank."

His command caught her by surprise. "To you?"

"Yes. These men will expect obeisance from a commoner."

An ingrained resistance stiffened Mary. "My father taught me that I am the equal of any aristocrat. The Scripture says, 'Whosoever exalteth himself shall be abased; and he that humbleth himself shall be exalted.' "

"Then rest assured, Miss Sheppard, you are destined for sainthood."

She wouldn't let his sarcasm deter her. It suddenly became imperative to her to make him *understand.* "Must all people bow and scrape before you? Are you truly more worthy in the eyes of God than the man who polishes your boots or the one who drives your carriage?"

He clasped his hands behind his back. "God made me heir to the dukedom. It is my duty to act accordingly. Every society needs its rulers, else chaos would reign."

"Yet why must one class be more deserving of respect than another? We are all people. Even servants have hopes and fears, joys and sorrows."

His lips thinned as if he found her words undeserving of a rebuttal. "That is neither here nor there. Lest you forget, we dare not do anything to alert these men that you are not who you claim to be." The duke gestured at her. "Now, curtsy."

He crossed his arms and waited imperiously. It was galling to genuflect to a nobleman as if he were the Almighty. Yet Mary could see his point. She must set aside her objections. For Jo's sake.

Gritting her teeth, Mary bobbed up and down.

The duke shook his head. "Try again, and this time sink

almost to the carpet. And don't flail your arms. Hold the
sides of your skirt if you must."

She obliged, wobbling on the high heels. For one appalling moment, Mary feared she would tumble into a heap at
his tastefully shod feet. Just in time she managed to steady
her balance. "Was that acceptable, my lord?"

Something glinted in his fathomless blue eyes, though
his mouth was unsmiling. "Your Grace," he corrected. "It
seems you have forms of address to learn as well as a
proper curtsy. Then there's wielding a fan, flirting, and of
course"—he cocked one dark eyebrow—"conversing without preaching."

She longed to get the ordeal over with and done. "Why
is all this preparation necessary? Each man need only take
a look at me. If he's the kidnapper, I'll know straightaway
by his reaction. He'll think I've escaped him. And that's
that."

Adam Brentwell strolled to a window and peered out.
She couldn't help but notice how the sunlight dramatized
his noble profile, how tall and fit and elegant he was, how
perfectly at ease in these sumptuous surroundings. "We
must also discover where the villain is holding Josephine,"
he said. "With charm and cunning, you must persuade him
to lead you there. I shall be right behind you."

A chill prickled Mary's skin. For all his refinement, he
exuded an aura of menace, and she wondered suddenly if
he was lying. Perhaps he had some secret, diabolical plan
in mind. As quickly as the suspicion arose, she buried it.
No, he merely wished to apprehend the man who had shot
his brother.

With the duke's aid, she would soon see Jo's sparkling
eyes and sunny smile. She would embrace her sister and
make amends for shutting her out. Painful hope swelled in
Mary's breast. She owed so much to the duke.

She crossed the room to him. Gazing at his proud features, she felt a surge of shyness and braced her hand on
the back of a gilt chair. "Your Grace, forgive me for ever

doubting you," she said in a breathless rush. "Please know the depths of my gratitude. It's ever so kind of you to help me rescue Jo."

He narrowed his eyes. Again, she was struck by the impact of dark and sinister emotions churning inside him.

"I am not a kind man, Miss Sheppard. Make no mistake about that." He clapped his hands. "Now curtsy again to me. And do it right this time."

After endless hours studying protocol and memorizing rules of etiquette, she returned to Jo's house with a long list of tasks to practice. Half wilting, Mary climbed the stairs. The door to her sister's chamber was closed, hiding the brownish bloodstain from her sight.

In the guest bedroom, she couldn't resist a glance into the pier glass. Except for the severe hairstyle, the resemblance to her sister was uncanny. She looked slim and refined, very much the fashionable lady, her face and bosom glowing in the dusky light. Was she truly so pretty? Or did these lewd trappings merely disguise her plainness?

Had the ugly duckling become a swan?

Recalling the duke's words made Mary feel strangely warm. She mustn't succumb to vanity. She kicked off the high-heeled shoes, slipped out of the topaz silk, and donned her own gray gown. It was shabby and shapeless, but she welcomed its comforting familiarity.

A day in Adam Brentwell's tyrannical presence had taken its toll on her fortitude. She reminded herself that he, too, wanted Jo waiting at his brother's bedside when Lord Cyril awakened. That goal gave the duke a true nobility of character, not just an empty title bestowed by an accident of birth.

So why did she feel as if something was amiss?

Restless, Mary wandered back downstairs. She was on edge from being in a strange place, from being forced into a distasteful role, from learning to behave in a manner so contrary to her upbringing. Had Jo experienced the same difficulties upon coming to London? If only Mary could ask her.

She roamed through the downstairs, the spacious rooms dim and lonely without Jo to brighten them. There was the parlor with its fancy chairs and tables, the drapes drawn against the daylight. At the back of the house, she found a music room with a pianoforte.

She danced her fingers over the gleaming keys, and the tinkling of notes lifted her spirits. Jo had meant to buy sheet music. Was she taking lessons? That had been her desire, one of her grandiose plans for the future. It seemed a lifetime since they had spoken of their dreams on an idle afternoon, riding in the back of the jolting caravan, their bare feet swinging and the sunlight dappling their hair. Jo would spin fantasies about a dashing lord who would slay dragons for her, who would face unimaginable dangers to win her heart.

It had come as a surprise when Jo had allowed herself to be courted by the quietly zealous Victor Gabriel. Perhaps it was his mesmerizing voice and his heavenly handsomeness. Or perhaps his true attraction lay in his unwavering devotion to God. Any woman would long to draw such worship toward herself. . . .

"What mischief did the duke want wi' ye?"

The gravelly voice came from behind her. Mary spun around to see the stoop-shouldered servant limp out of the passageway, the dog at his heels. "Obediah! You startled me."

"Ye went off in His Grace's carriage afore nine an' ye been gone all day." The footman shook his clenched fingers. "Duke or not, if he took liberties wi' ye, he'll taste my fist an' spit out a few teeth."

"His Grace treated me like a lady. We spent the day planning how to find Jo." It wasn't a lie, she told herself. Just a simplification of the truth.

"Humph." Suspicious blue eyes peered from his rough,

red-veined face. "Well, next time warn me when ye're comin' back. Dinner ain't ready yet."

"I'll try, thank you. And please tell the cook not to prepare a big meal for me. I don't want to be a bother."

"She's gone, an' good riddance. I'll be fixin' yer victuals."

"Gone?" Mary blinked in surprise. "But where?"

"I sent her packin' the mornin' after the shootin'. The housemaid an' tweeny, too. 'Tweren't practical t' keep 'em on with the mistress run off."

"Don't you think you acted in haste? What will Jo do when she returns?"

He shrugged. "I'll hire new servants, ones that ain't lazy like that Missus Gilbert. Only lifted her hefty arse t' eat." The servant mournfully shook his grizzled head. "I told Miss Josephine, but she were too soft-hearted t' sack the slug." Muttering to himself, Obediah shuffled out of the music room, and a moment later, the kitchen door slammed.

Mary frowned. He seemed to assume that Jo wouldn't return soon. Why? Did he, like the Bow Street Runners, think she had fled from the scene of an attempted murder?

Worried, Mary escaped out a glass door and found herself in a derelict garden behind the town house. Prinny padded after her, circled a patch of late sunshine, then lay down to watch her. The small, rectangular area was bordered by a high brick fence. An X-shaped walkway made of flagstones divided the garden into four triangles. Overgrown vegetation choked every inch of earth, and dead leaves spilled over onto the pathways.

Out of habit, Mary crouched down and pulled a few weeds. One stubborn plant resisted her fiercest tugging. She walked to a potting shed in the corner of the garden and opened the door to a raucous creaking of the hinges. From a nail on the wooden wall hung a rusted trowel. Taking it and a pair of clippers, she sank to her knees before a flowerbed.

The tip of the trowel cut through the hard packed earth and the weed popped out, dirt clinging to the white roots. The scent of fresh-turned loam perfumed the warm evening air. Mary breathed deeply, filling her lungs with the rich aroma as she cleared away the layers of humus.

Yearning rose from a place hidden deep inside herself. During childhood, Jo had been the rescuer of stray and wounded animals. But Mary had found pleasure in things of the earth. She cultivated little gardens in the woodlands, transplanting poppies and primroses and creeping thistle from hedgerows, working for a scant few days at a time before she had to move on with her family in the caravan.

If she married Victor, she would resume the nomadic way of life. *If.* Her emotions seemed as hopelessly tangled as this garden. Would her fiancé still want to marry her? Would her father forgive her and allow her to return?

Did she *wish* to return?

The wayward thought disturbed her. Of course she would marry Victor. He was a fine, saintly man who set a high standard of morality. At times, he would go off into the countryside and pray in solitude like a prophet of old, spending hours in devoted reflection. She had tried to do likewise, but her mind had an exasperating habit of wandering from holy contemplation. Perhaps she would never be as good as her fiancé.

A sense of unworthiness crept over Mary. Thrusting it away, she shut her mind to past and future and then dared to dream. Someday . . . somehow she would have a plot of land to call her own. A cottage with a garden abounding with honeysuckle and lilacs and daffodils.

A sense of peace settled over her as she worked. She liked to think gardening was a form of worship, this tending of God's earth. The muted sounds of the city drifted from the distance: the rattle of carriage wheels, the cry of a streetseller, the clanging of pots from the kitchen. She hummed as she labored, determined to make a beautiful retreat for Jo.

Clipping away some dead branches, Mary found a cluster of pink blooms clung to a prickly bush. She plucked one and breathed deeply of its fragrance. A boundless awe filled her. Roses. Her sister's favorite flower.

Mary . . . please . . . are you listening?

The words appeared in her mind as clearly as if they had been spoken aloud by a companion. She sat back on her heels, her heart beating fast and furiously. No image came to her, only a rush of despair that enclosed her in a cold mist.

Yes, I'm here, Mary's heart whispered. *Jo, I'm here!*

She closed her eyes and a passage stretched out into darkness. A star of light glowed at the end. Through the tunnel tumbled a cataract of emotion, a deluge of sorrow and hopelessness that flooded Mary's chest.

Mary . . . you never answer . . . don't shut me out . . . I need you . . . please answer . . . please . . . please. . . .

Merciful God! Her sister didn't hear her. With every ounce of her energy, Mary concentrated her mind on the radiance of her sister.

Jo, tell me what's happened. Tell me where to find you.

Her answer came in a surge of raw desperation that poured through her in an icy wave. A fear so potent, so poisonous, that bile stung her throat.

He's coming back . . . Mary, save me . . . he's coming back. . . .

The voice fell abruptly silent as if a door had been slammed shut. The bright dot winked out, leaving a dense and lonely blackness.

Something cold nudged her arm. Mary slowly opened her eyes to the purple light of dusk and the mournful regard of the mangy dog. She sat in the garden beside a heap of fragrant humus.

And the rose lay shredded in her lap.

❧ Chapter 4 ❧

"Bring me another neckcloth, will you, Fenwick? This one bloody well won't tie properly."

Adam tossed the wrinkled strip of starched linen onto the dressing table. He extended his hand, and the valet obligingly delivered another pristine cravat.

"If I may, Your Grace, I would be happy to arrange the cloth for you."

"That might be wise. I seem to be ruining far too many this morning."

Fenwick stepped in front of the duke and deftly worked at the tie. He was a small, sober man with a receding hairline, and as meticulous as a Bond Street tailor. What did he think of as he went about his duties? Adam realized with a start how little he knew of the man's personal life, beyond that Fenwick was a bachelor.

Even servants have hopes and fears, joys and sorrows.

The observation had nagged at Adam ever since Mary Sheppard had spoken it the previous day, her green eyes bright with zeal in a face too thin and judgmental for his tastes. How dare she question his decency to his servants. Their well-being concerned him, not their personal idiosyncrasies. He needn't brood on her self-righteous accusations, especially not now, when the health of his brother weighed on his mind.

Yet he found himself saying, "You've been in my employ for over ten years, have you not, Fenwick?"

"Yes, Your Grace. Twelve years to be precise."

"Are you contented in my household?"

"Contented?" The valet glanced up, then lowered his lusterless brown eyes as he gave the neckcloth a finishing flourish. "Most certainly so."

"You have all your wants met here? You have a comfortable life?"

"Yes, my lord duke."

"Come now, you must have some complaint that I can rectify."

The valet kept his head respectfully bowed. "None, Your Grace. I could not wish for anything more than to serve you."

There. That proved it, Adam thought, as Fenwick brought over a navy blue coat with silver buttons and helped him into it. To inquire further into the man's private affairs would be a breach of etiquette between master and servant. One did not, after all, chat with one's employee as if he were a crony across the gaming table at White's. They had nothing in common.

Fenwick stood waiting, his expression deferential. "If I may, Your Grace, I should like to extend my sincere wishes for Lord Cyril's swift recovery."

"Thank you, Fenwick. That is deuced kind of you."

Adam had sat part of the night at his brother's bedside. The candle flickering on the table had cast Cyril's pale face into sharp relief. The animation was gone from his features. He had looked so frail lying there with his eyes closed and the white bandage wrapping his blond hair. And so utterly still.

A hot coal of pain burned in Adam's chest. Cyril was the happy-go-lucky charmer, eight years younger than Adam and more like a son to him than a brother. It was strange how birth order had made them so different. Cyril lived the life of a dashing gentleman, gambling and horse racing

and flirting with the ladies, while Adam shouldered the
duties of the dukedom.

*A duke is born to command. Never forget, you are superior
to other men.*

Now that he was older, Adam understood his father's
words. He appreciated the privilege of being master of five
vast estates, and he ruled his tenants and servants with a
firm but fair hand. He especially loved the family seat in
Derbyshire where he had lived as a child. He looked forward to the late summer when he could escape to the
country, ride over his lands, supervise the harvest, and visit
his tenants.

Of late, he had thought of raising his own sons there.
And so he had determined to settle on a wife. It was time
he married and secured the succession. He had only to
carry out the formality of asking Lady Camilla Crockford.
Yet he had dawdled, loath to endure the fuss made over
newly betrothed couples. He could wait the few weeks until
the end of the Season.

Now a grimmer reason stopped him. He would give
away his ducal coronet if only he could ensure his brother's
recovery. And if only he could spare his mother the grief of
losing her beloved second son. On the night Cyril had been
shot, she would have gone to Almack's with Adam and
Sophy had she not felt ill from a nervous ailment Adam
attributed to her one disastrous encounter with Cyril's mistress.

Josephine Sheppard. Damn her ambitious soul to hell.

The effects of a restless night had taken a toll on Adam.
His head felt thick, his eyes gritty, his muscles sore. In the
cheval mirror he looked fit, though shadows underscored
his eyes. He wondered if Mary Sheppard had rested well,
or if she had lain awake too, fretting about her sister, tossing and turning in bed. God. What a blow it must have
been for her to learn that Josephine had vanished in the
wake of a heinous crime. He almost regretted gulling
Mary. He had lied to her, told her he believed Josephine

innocent of shooting his brother. Mary thought him a hero for seeking her twin.

Instead, he intended to see Josephine hang.

He shouldn't feel guilty about misleading Mary. He could waste no sympathy on a naive girl who was tied to him by tragedy. Whenever he looked at her, he saw the face of his brother's assailant.

He strode from the ducal suite and into the passageway. At this early hour, the house was quiet and dim, and his footsteps echoed on the marble floor. He went downstairs to the dining chamber, where a footman served him from the steaming silver dishes on the sideboard.

He sat at the immense dining table, alone with his thoughts. Alone to ponder the suspects, to speculate on which man Josephine had cast her spell upon. She had to have bewitched him with her body, for no true gentleman would harbor a woman who had shot her noble lover. Was Josephine even now sleeping in the arms of her new protector? Did she plan to lie low until the Runners gave up on finding her? Would she flee to the Continent? Or to America? The very notion tightened the ball of fury inside him.

He had men watching every ship at the docks of London, Dover, Bristol, and elsewhere. He would snare her. This ladybird would not fly from the wrath of St. Chaldon.

"Good morning," chirped a cheery voice. "What a positively beastly hour to arise from bed."

Sophy breezed into the dining chamber. Gowned in pale green gauze that clung to her plump curves, she headed straight to the sideboard and fetched her breakfast.

"Why are *you* up so early?" Adam asked.

"I wanted to speak to you, of course." Sophy carried a plate heaped with eggs and kidneys and toast to the table. "Thank heavens I caught you in time."

"What is it now?" he said in exasperation. "Did you see a bonnet you fancied at the milliner's? Charge it to my account if you like, and do not bore me with all the tedious particulars."

While slathering orange marmalade on her toast, Sophy stuck her tongue out at him. "I'll have you know a woman's head is filled with more than fashion and gossip."

"Pardon me. We mustn't forget flirting, either."

"Beast. If you were not my brother, I would cheerfully expose you to the ton as a woman-hater."

"Your charity is admirable." Too preoccupied for further squabbling, Adam drained his teacup. "If you'll excuse me."

"Wait." Sophy swallowed a forkful of coddled eggs. "That's precisely why I came to speak to you. Where *are* you off to so early in the morning?"

"My business is private."

"You were gone all day yesterday. Has it to do with that woman who shot Cyril?"

Adam pushed back his chair and rose to his feet. He had enough headaches dealing with the prickly Mary Sheppard. The last thing he needed was for his meddlesome sister to get wind of his plans. "You are not to trouble yourself over *her.*"

"But I'm right, aren't I? You're working with the Bow Street Runners to find Josephine Sheppard."

"Don't be fanciful. The only contact I've had with them is the reports they've brought me."

"Then you're searching for her yourself?" Sophy dabbed her mouth with a napkin and sprang to her feet. "Wait for me, then. I insist upon helping."

"Sit," he said in a freezing tone.

She sat, albeit with a sullen cast to her mouth. "You needn't get all dukely with me. Ordering me about like a pet dog."

"I will order you as I see fit. And I'm warning you—"

"I have a perfect right to offer my assistance. Cyril is my brother, too."

"So nurse him back to health, then." Adam pointed his

finger at her. "And heed me well. You are to stay here and out of trouble. That is my final word on the matter."

Sophy watched Adam stride out of the dining room. She considered sticking out her tongue again, then decided the effect would be wasted.

Frustrated, she dove back into her breakfast, using a bit of toast to mop up the gooey remains of her eggs. So he expected her to molder in a sickroom while he chased down the murderess. Well, there were physicians aplenty to care for Cyril. And besides, she couldn't abide sitting all day like a brainless ninny. She wanted to *do* something.

Adam must be on the trail of Josephine Sheppard; Sophy was sure of it. Did he mean to search for clues at her town house? That was the logical starting place. Unfortunately, Sophy had no earthly idea where Cyril's mistress had lived. Ladies weren't even supposed to know that gentlemen kept women for pleasure. But Sophy secretly found the notion fascinating. And this was her chance to see a genuine love nest.

Could she bribe a groom or the coachman to take her there? Perhaps, but the staff was infuriatingly loyal to Adam.

Then a brilliant idea struck Sophy. Her fork clattered to the china plate. She knew just who to ask for help.

"Carry the fan in your left hand," said the duke of St. Chaldon. "That indicates you are interested in making the man's acquaintance. Like so." He transferred the fan to his other hand.

Perched at the opposite end of the chaise, Mary obediently mimicked his action with her own fan. She stifled an untimely urge to giggle. How ridiculous Adam Brentwell looked. His fingers were large and dark against the ivory sticks. The lace-edged fan contrasted with his tailored garb and stern face. She wondered if he ever smiled.

It was the middle of a long afternoon. They were closeted in the drawing room of his town house, the dwelling he used for his carnal assignations. He sat an arm's length away, his cravat perfectly tied, his shoulders squared beneath the navy blue coat, his long legs outlined by fawn breeches and tassled black Hessians. She could smell the subtle spice of his shaving soap. It brought back the memory of lying crushed beneath him on her sister's bed, his body hard and muscled and shockingly male. And the rush of heated agitation she had felt as he pressed his hand up the length of her leg.

"Very fetching," he said. "How did you manage to summon a blush at will?"

She realized the duke was staring at her. Her cheeks grew hotter. "By pondering the sinfulness of this charade."

"Come now, Miss Sheppard. I doubt you've committed a sin in your entire life."

If only he knew.

Flustered by the turn of her thoughts, she glanced down at the scene delicately wrought on her own fan of stretched chicken skin. That was another mistake. Painted on the folds was a bawdy picture of satyrs romping with half-naked maidens. She snapped the fan shut.

"Excellent," Adam Brentwell said. "Closing the fan means that you are ready to speak to the man."

"Oh."

"Now draw it across your face. Like this." Folding his own fan, he sketched it over his smooth-shaven cheek.

It was an incongruous move for so powerful a duke. Again she resisted an errant bubble of laughter. "What does that mean?"

" 'I love you.' "

He spoke in a toneless voice. The mirth died in Mary as the emptiness of his words depressed her somehow, and she let the fan fall to her lap. "You can't really expect me to tell such a bald-faced lie to these men."

"You will say whatever is necessary to win their confidence. Remember, your sister is in danger."

The duke's face was taut, resolute. He was right, of

course. She would do anything to save Jo. But she could not imagine herself whispering that phrase to any man but Victor Gabriel.

Not that she had ever done so to him. She had felt too guilty over betraying her sister, too ashamed of the wicked longings he roused in her. But somehow she would atone for her sins. She wanted to be his wife, to devote her life to Victor.

If he forgave her for tearing off to help her sister. She could not forget how furious he had been when Jo had abandoned him for the bright entertainments of London. He had disappeared into the forest for two days of fasting and prayer. When he returned, he was again the dedicated missionary. Jo's departure was a sign from God, Victor had announced, a sign that he had chosen the wrong daughter. To Mary's disgraceful delight, he had asked to betroth himself to her instead.

"Do not toy with your fan, Miss Sheppard. That will be taken as a sign that you are bored."

Mary blinked at the duke. His silver-flecked blue eyes regarded her with disdain. "Perhaps it wouldn't be far from the truth," she said.

"Do not be impertinent, either. Your purpose is to bewitch these men with the beauty of your voice and the allure of your looks. Use your body to entice them just as your sister did."

He made Jo seem cold and heartless and manipulative. Mary slapped the fan onto the chaise. "That isn't like her at all. Jo is warm and giving and loyal. Not a . . . a hussy."

Adam Brentwell sat silent a moment. She sensed a struggle behind the rigid expression that masked his thoughts. "Pardon my choice of words," he said mildly. "My only purpose is to find the villain before he flees the city with your sister his captive. I dare allow but one more day to train you in the art of seduction."

One more day. The impending deception plunged Mary

into a panic. She sprang up from the chaise and paced the length of the drawing room. "What am I thinking of?" she moaned in an undertone. "I'm no flirt."

"You're mumbling," the duke called out. "Come back here. I have no wish to shout."

At the bank of windows, she turned. He sat straight and unsmiling and imperious, like a monarch on his throne. He had been raised to believe himself better than the rest of humanity. To snap orders. To take charge. She must not let his arrogance deter her from finding Jo.

"And this time," he added, "don't run like a hoyden. Take slow, dainty steps and sway your hips."

"Sway my . . ." Scandalized, Mary couldn't bring herself to utter the word. "I can't behave so lewdly. I won't."

"Yes, you will. You must."

He's coming back . . . Mary, save me . . . he's coming back. . . .

Jo's desperate voice reached across the dark passage of memory. One of the lords Mary would deceive tomorrow evening might be her sister's abductor. And this was her one and only chance to catch him.

"Sway my . . . hips," Mary muttered through gritted teeth.

She undulated her body in an exaggerated imitation of the women she had seen on the streets of London. The motion was exceedingly awkward, especially while wearing high heels and performing under the critical scrutiny of the duke.

Resolutely, she shifted her gaze to a gilt-framed painting of the English countryside on the wall behind him. She imagined herself walking through the caravan as it jounced over a rutted road. To keep her balance, she would swing her hips back and forth, shifting her shoulders to and fro. For good measure, she poked out her head like a goose.

Her heel caught on the fine carpet. She grabbed at a rosewood side table to steady herself. A rectangular silver case went skidding across the polished surface. The lid flew open and playing cards rained over the floor.

"Oh, I'm sorry." She sank to her knees and gathered up the pieces of pasteboard decorated by red and black shapes. Suddenly she noticed the drawings on the backs. "Sweet heaven!" she gasped. "These women haven't a stitch of clothing."

Ominous silence emanated from the duke. Hastily tucking the last lewd playing card into its silver box, she slammed down the lid. Only then did she risk a look at him.

He sat with the fan half covering his face. What a bumpkin he must think her! An unsophisticated child. A failure at the feminine arts. She told herself not to fall victim to his dissolute standards, not to care a whit for his debauched opinion. Yet a part of her wanted him to view her as a woman equal to the ladies of his closed circle.

His broad shoulders quivered. He lowered the fan, and his mouth twitched. His eyes danced with a mirth so alien to the brusque-tempered nobleman that Mary sat back on her heels and stared in amazement. A warm attractiveness lit his face, banishing the harsh superiority. The transformation gave him the aspect of a man of many facets, a man who was worth knowing once she looked past the snooty exterior. A man who could laugh.

Mary realized she was gawking like a moonstruck maiden. She smoothed her skirt and straightened her spine. "Don't make fun. It was an accident."

"Forgive me," he said, though his twinkling eyes gave him a decidedly unrepentant look.

"You oughtn't have these bawdy cards lying about, anyway." Scrambling to her feet, she slapped the case onto the table. "They are Satan's tool. They encourage the vice of gambling."

His mouth took on a devilish tilt. "Mistress Mary, quite contrary. You've much to learn about the pleasures of corruption."

"No, thank you. I've had quite enough lessons for one day."

"You," he said, "have only just begun."

With languid grace, Adam Brentwell rose from the chaise and walked toward her. He carried the folded fan and slapped it rhythmically against the palm of his hand. His approach stirred an agitation within her that was part fear and part fascination.

She crossed her arms. "I shall not practice that silly walk anymore."

"Then we'll overlook the swaying hips for the moment and return to the fan. Hold the handle to your lips like so."

He touched the ivory sticks to his mouth. His firm, masculine mouth. Mary watched, mesmerized. She felt the shocking impulse to know the feel of his lips pressed to hers.

"Your turn," he said.

As he handed over the fan, their fingers brushed, and a peculiar melting sensation weakened her knees. Ever so slowly she lifted the fan to her lips. She couldn't stop herself from wondering if it was the very place his mouth had touched. He watched her action with far more interest than the simple lesson warranted.

She lowered the fan. "What does it mean?"

"Kiss me."

"Kiss . . . ?" For one outrageous moment she thought he meant himself, and longing broke over her in a powerful rush. Then realization struck. "You mean . . . those lecherous lords?"

"Perhaps."

Struck speechless, Mary could only stare at Adam, at the way his gaze deepened to a midnight glow. He stood so close she could smell his clean scent, so close he could draw her into his embrace.

"Have you ever been kissed by a man?" he asked.

She thought of Victor's chaste peck on her cheek, and

her face heated. She had long wanted more. Much more. But the dark pull of secret desires frightened her.

"So you haven't," the duke said, his narrowed eyes assessing her. "It occurs to me that you are sorely lacking in experience, Miss Sheppard. One kiss, and these men will know straightaway that you're not Josephine."

"It occurs to *me* you are being impertinent. I've no intention of letting them touch me in any way."

"Nevertheless, you must be prepared. And it seems the duty of educating you falls to me."

With that, he tilted up her chin and lowered his mouth to hers. Mary gasped, but her squeak of surprise was muffled by his lips. She stood stiffly, unyielding, her father's voice booming in the maelstrom of her mind: *Abstain from fleshly lusts which war against the soul.*

And then the warning slipped away as the full pleasure of the kiss assaulted her senses. Oh, sweet heaven. His mouth was soft, searching, seductive. His tongue traced the seam of her lips and then somehow, she felt his moist heat invade her. He tasted of dark sin and voluptuous desire. Awash in blissful shock, she was aware of the fan slipping from her grasp, aware of herself catching at his muscled shoulders for support, aware of him stroking her hair as if she were a woman who mattered to him.

An irresistible enjoyment ascended within her, the feeling so divine that she was powerless to stop herself from luxuriating in it. This was kissing? Her dreams in the darkness had been a pale shadow of glory, a maiden's tame imaginings.

The pressure of his body against hers felt good and right. His hand drifted downward, leaving her flesh tingling in its wake. And then he touched her bosom. The pads of his fingers brushed a light caress over the skin exposed above her bodice. Something buried deep inside her drew taut, and his warmth flowed downward, down to that aching tension. Shaken by the pleasure of it, she moaned and pressed herself closer to him.

The warmth of his mouth left her. Still caught in the net of enchantment, Mary blinked at the man holding her, the chiseled mouth, the noble cheekbones, the glittering eyes. Reality slapped her in the face.

The duke. She had kissed the almighty duke of St. Chaldon.

Worse, she had reveled in the experience. Her hair cascaded down her back; she hadn't even realized he had unbraided it. All her father's teachings had vanished at her first taste of temptation.

Adam Brentwell scowled down at her. "You show promise," he said. "Yet you kiss like an innocent. We shall have to work on that."

His cool assessment mortified her all the more. She was trembling when he didn't appear affected in the least. Of course. To him the kiss was merely another tedious lesson.

"Once was quite enough for me," she said, unwilling to show her guilt at the sudden thought of Victor. "Thank heavens, some men value innocence."

His hands tightened on her shoulders. A line appeared between his black eyebrows, giving him a look more brooding than haughty. Did her lack of sophistication trouble him so much?

Before she could ask, the muffled sound of voices came from the foyer. The double doors abruptly clicked open. Mary half turned in his arms to see a young woman march inside, a gown of pale green gauze adorning her lush curves. Golden curls framed the lovely features of a cherub. A dandified gentleman garbed in yellow pantaloons and a rose-red coat followed her, as did a grim-faced Rayburn.

The duke released Mary so swiftly she felt cast aside like unwanted rubbish. "What the deuce—?" he snapped at the newcomers.

"Forgive me, Your Grace," said the butler, wringing his gloved hands. "I informed the lady that you were otherwise engaged, but she was most insistent—"

The lady waved the servant to a stop. "I told you, Adam is never too busy for me."

"You may go," he told the butler. "I'll settle this matter."

Rayburn bowed and left, closing the doors.

"Now tell me, dear Sophy," Adam said in a grim tone, "what is the meaning of your coming here? I've a good mind to subject you to a sound thrashing."

Mary frowned. Sophy? Who was she? She looked too young to be one of his women.

Sophy walked closer to Mary and halted. Her hand lifted to her curvaceous bosom and her china-blue eyes widened. "Perish me! Adam, how could you? While Cyril is lying on his deathbed, you've been dallying with Josephine Sheppard!"

✤ Chapter 5 ✤

Adam rubbed his throbbing temples. He should have seen this coming. Sophy had been far too biddable at breakfast.

He strode past Mary and approached his sister. "Young lady, you've disobeyed my order to stay home and out of trouble. I suggest you get to your carriage immediately and hope I forget you ever came here."

Sophy had the effrontery to glower, tapping the toe of her slipper on the carpet. "I shan't go until you tell me exactly what you're doing with *her*." With the flourish of a Covent Garden actress, she pointed her finger at Mary.

Mary ducked her head as if she longed to shrink into the white-painted woodwork. A charming blush pinkened her cheeks. She tugged self-consciously at the bodice of her gown, though the gauzy jade fabric lifted only a fraction over the mounds of creamy bosom. Ah God, he remembered how lush and warm she had felt in his arms. The cloud of red-gold hair drifted around shoulders as white as alabaster. Only moments ago he had sampled the softness of her lips. There was so much more to Mary Sheppard than he had imagined.

"I say, old chap," drawled Lord Harry Dashwood. "Never thought you'd stoop to stealing your own brother's ladybird."

The dandy devoured Mary with his eyes, and Adam felt

a rush of unreasoning fury. "I would have thought *you* would have more sense than to convey my sister here."

Harry lifted his manfully padded shoulders in a shrug. "Who am I to deny the request of a lovely nymph? Can't say I'm sorry, either. Things look far more . . . entertaining than I had anticipated."

"You were supposed to be assisting the Runners," Sophy accused Adam. "Not trifling with the murderess yourself. Wait until Mama hears about this!"

At least Mary's disguise was a success; he could take small satisfaction in that. Much as it irked him, he had no choice but to set his sister straight. "Mother will hear nothing. Now, may I present Miss Sheppard? Miss *Mary* Sheppard."

Sophy's mouth dropped open: For once, she was speechless.

Lord Harry let out a hoot of astonished delight. Bowing to Mary, he clicked the heels of his Hessians—boots that were polished to so high a sheen his valet must have added champagne to the blacking. "Enchanted, my dear."

Mary peered doubtfully at him from beneath the fringe of her lashes. "May I ask your name, please?"

He swept up her hand and brought it to his lips. "Forgive St. Chaldon's lack of manners. I am—"

"Lord Harry Dashwood, society's most prolific gossip. Who, by the way, is about to learn the meaning of discretion." Adam scowled at Harry until he released her hand and stepped back. "His accomplice is Lady Sophronia. My sister."

"You never let on that you had a sister. Of course, we've barely known each other two days." Mary dipped a credible curtsy, then took a hesitant step toward Sophy. "I'm pleased to meet you, your ladyship."

"Oh, do call me Sophy." As if studying a French fashion doll, she strolled around Mary. "The likeness is amazing. You and Josephine must be identical twins. You even sound like her. Why, how positively famous!"

Mary brightened. "You've met Jo?"

"I have, indeed."

"Where? When? Please, you must tell me. It's been months since last I saw her, and I've missed her so."

Sophy leaned forward confidingly. "Well, it happened just last Sunday. Jo was wearing the most cunning green silk dress—"

"That is quite enough gossip," Adam broke in. "We agreed not to speak of that incident."

Mary whipped her head around and glared. "I'll thank you not to interrupt. She might have valuable information."

She wore a fierce expression, the delicate coppery brows lowered over eyes as green as a woodland bower. He found himself fascinated by the glimpse of wildness in her, the passion of a mother vixen protecting her pup. His rush of attraction annoyed him.

"Sophy can tell you nothing of importance." He turned a pointed stare at Sophy. "Come, I'll escort you out."

Lord Harry ambled forth to block their path, his thumbs hooked in the waistband of his yellow pantaloons. "Try not to be a prig, St. Chaldon, though I know you can't help it. If Lady Sophy has met Cyril's mistress, I for one would relish hearing all the delicious particulars."

"As would I," Mary said. "It might shed light on where my sister has gone."

"See?" Sophy cocked her head in pouty triumph. "What harm would come out of telling? Lord Toad is your trusted friend."

"My amphibian lips are sealed." Harry pressed a finger over his smirk.

Adam gritted his teeth. The last thing his mother needed to upset her fragile health was for that deplorable event to besmirch the family name. "There was a brief, chance encounter that is of no significance. Now, the subject is closed. Forever. I will have your word on that."

Sophy wrinkled her pert nose. "As you wish, O Great Duke."

"Mind your manners, O Impudent Lady. Especially in light of your blatant lapse of propriety today."

"No one of consequence saw me enter here, if that's what you mean," Sophy said with a sniff. "I was clever enough to disguise myself in a hooded cloak. The only person who noticed me today was that dreadful manservant."

"Manservant?" Adam asked, frowning. "Did Rayburn insult you?"

"Not him, Josephine Sheppard's footman." Sophy walked to a side table and picked up the silver card case, turning it to and fro in her gloved hands. "I vow, he was a curmudgeon. Refused to divulge any information about you or Cyril's mistress."

"You must mean Obediah," Mary said. "He's truly kind once you come to know him."

Adam snatched the card case out of his sister's hand before she could examine the erotic contents. The pounding in his head had intensified. He glared at Lord Harry, who made a strangled sound in his throat.

"So you went to Cyril's house, too," Adam said. "What if a journalist from one of the news rags had been hanging about?"

"Let her be." Mary stepped forward, her skirts whispering. "My staying there doesn't make me a fallen woman. Nor should a mere visit ruin your sister's reputation."

"Hear, hear." Sophy craned her neck to peer at the carved chimneypiece, the muted silk-papered walls, the blue and silver upholstered chaises and chairs. "A pity this is so dull and proper, though. Not at all as I imagined a love nest would be."

Lord Harry examined his fingernails. Adam felt heat rise from his stiff cravat. God help him, in a moment he was going to enroll his sister in a school for wayward girls.

"You're so terribly discreet," she went on blithely. "I never guessed you kept mistresses. Does Mama know?"

Adam marched Sophy to the double doors. "You are going straight home. You'll spend the remainder of the day in seclusion. No, make that the rest of the month."

She jerked ineffectively at his grip. "But you haven't even told me what you're doing with Josephine Sheppard's sister."

"I don't intend to."

"Wait!" Just as they reached the doorway, Mary came hurrying up, the wealth of her hair shining in the dull afternoon light. "I would welcome Lady Sophy's help. She can prepare me for the masquerade tomorrow night."

"Masquerade?" Sophy repeated.

"Masquerade?" Lord Harry echoed. "I've a salver stacked with invitations, but none for a masked ball."

Both of them looked at Adam.

"Never mind," he said. "It is a small, unimportant affair—"

"On the contrary, it is matter of life and death." Mary turned to his sister. "You see, I am to pose as Josephine in the hopes of catching her abductor."

"Her abductor?" Sophy said on a rising note of surprise.

"Yes, your brother and I have determined that she is innocent. He's so very kind to help me clear her name. Didn't you know?"

Sophy and Lord Harry exchanged astonished glances.

The dandy cocked an eyebrow at Adam. "What is this harum-scarum tale?"

"It is quite simple," Adam stated, feeling himself sink into a mire of guilt and lies. "A villain who wanted Josephine for himself used a pistol on Cyril and then took her hostage."

"We hope to catch the man before he flees the city with Jo," Mary added. "If he hasn't already."

Harry leveled a stare at Adam. "Indeed."

Adam stared back, daring him to dispute the story.

"What a curious twist," Sophy said. "Josephine did seem too amiable a woman to be a murderess."

"She's blameless," Mary averred. "My fondest wish is for your brother to wake up and tell you so, all of you." Lifting her gaze to Adam, she bit her lip. "If only I could pray at his bedside, perhaps I could implore the Almighty for his recovery."

Sophy clapped her hands. "What a smashing idea. Cyril would hear your voice and think you're Josephine."

And then he'd suffer a relapse. "No," Adam said. "He's in the care of the best doctors already. I will not alter my plan."

"The duke intends for me to trick the kidnapper into believing Jo has escaped," Mary added. "He has been good enough to teach me how to behave accordingly."

She curved her lips into a smile directed at Adam. A smile so pure and trusting that he felt another throat-choking rush of guilt. When she learned of his deception, she would no longer look on him with blind faith; she would despise him.

"Ah," Harry said. "And clearly you conduct your lessons quite thoroughly, St. Chaldon."

Recognizing the deviltry in Harry's eyes, Adam kept his expression bland. Damn that kiss. And damn himself for being seduced by Mary Sheppard's winsome naïveté. Unwillingly, he remembered his dizzying sense of her awakening sensuality. His need for her had transcended mere lust. In spite of himself, he had felt the urge to protect her, to forbid her from playing her worldly-wise sister, to keep her sweetness and fire all to himself.

Some men value innocence.

He resisted the lash of shame. Certainly he was attracted to Mary, but he hardly planned to seduce her. Though for a prim little preacher, she had the makings of a fine sinner.

"I've no experience in hair dressing or other feminine arts," Mary said shyly. "You might help me, Lady Sophy. If it isn't too much trouble."

"Why, certainly—"

"No," Adam said in alarm. "My sister is hardly a servant."

"Then who shall help her to bathe and dress?" Sophy asked with a cunning smile. "You?"

A fantasy flashed into his mind, of stripping Mary naked, lowering her into a copper tub, washing every inch of creamy feminine flesh. . . .

"Not that it's any concern of yours," he stated, "but I've engaged a suitable abigail."

From London's most exclusive bordello, he added grimly to himself as he guided his sister into the foyer. He glanced back into the drawing room to see Mary again fussing with her décolletage. If that jade-green creation put her to the blush, then tomorrow night she would feel as naked as the Venus de Milo.

She had no inkling of how perfectly he meant for her to resemble a whore.

"Are you certain this is wise?" Mary asked again. "Won't the duke be furious?"

She and Lady Sophy rode side by side in the hired coach. The gentle rocking of the springs should have been soothing, but Mary felt a fluttery foreboding in her belly. In the middle of the afternoon, Sophy had put in a surprise appearance at Jo's town house. She had insisted upon taking Mary to Brentwell House to visit Cyril.

Now, she patted Mary's gloved hand. "Don't fret. I know how to handle my brother. Besides, no one of consequence shall see us. Mama always naps in the afternoon. And Adam has gone to consult with the magistrate at Bow Street. I'll have you back, safe and sound, before he can discover you've gone."

Mary fervently hoped so. Tonight was the masquerade, and she had awakened in the predawn darkness, too tense to sleep. It was worse than waiting to sing at one of Papa's prayer meetings. This outing provided a diversion, at least, as did Lady Sophy's chatter about fashion and gossip and the people who entertained in a social circle far beyond Mary's world of farmers and shepherds and housewives with large broods of children.

Garbed in yellow sprigged muslin and an enormous bonnet trimmed with feathers and ribbons, Lady Sophy embodied the excesses of the idle nobility. Mary's father had taught her that only by renouncing wealth and status could any aristocrat hope to win salvation.

Yet Lady Sophy was warm and friendly and kind. Did her generous nature reflect a pure soul? Or was this bright-eyed girl doomed to burn in hell for all eternity simply because she had been born to privilege? That did not seem right.

It confused Mary even more to realize that she was drawn to Sophy. Like Jo, Sophy regarded life as a grand adventure. Rules and restrictions could not contain her exuberance. What a trial she must be to her brother, who lived by rigid laws of propriety.

Hypocritical laws, Mary amended. St. Chaldon was concerned only with appearances. No lady of the ton was supposed to know that he kept a private house for indulging his vices. A house where he brought his lovers, kissed them, touched their bared breasts. . . .

Sweet heaven, how thoroughly he had kissed her. His tongue had penetrated her mouth. His arms had held her against his hard body. Just the thought made her hot and restless.

You kiss like an innocent. We shall have to work on that.

To her shame, she wanted him to instruct her. Craved it with a mortifying hunger. Was this the allure of Satan, this desire to let the duke have his way with her?

Releasing a shuddery breath, Mary willed away the temptations of the flesh. Better she should satisfy her curiosity about the Brentwell family. She wanted to know what it was like to grow up in luxury, to have roots sunk deeply into the soil of heritage. And she wondered what sort of

boy Adam had been, whether he had acted mischievous or
as mirthless as he was now. Had arrogance come with his
ascension to the dukedom? Surely at one time he had been
a lad with tousled black hair and impish blue eyes. . . .

"Look," Sophy said. "We're here."

Mary peeked past the leather curtain as a vast marble
building loomed into view. Her lips parted in awe. Six towering pillars supported the huge portico. Figures from
Greek mythology were carved into the stone around the
doorway. Scores of gleaming windows marched across the
endless front of the structure.

A peculiar sense of unreality descended over her. Gazing at the mammoth house gave her the curious feeling
that she had seen it before . . . somewhere. . . .

She blinked, and the uncanny sensation slipped out of
her grasp. "Merciful God," she breathed. "It's a palace."

Sophy laughed. "What, this old pile? You should see the
ducal seat in Derbyshire. Why, you could get lost for days
in that house. Once when Cyril took me exploring, he ran
away and left me. It was hours before Adam found me,
wandering through the upstairs." She snapped her gloved
fingers. "Quick now, your veil. No one must know who you
are."

Mary drew the fine veil over her face just as a footman
in powdered wig and livery opened the door and let down
the step. She accepted his proffered hand and emerged
into the sunny afternoon. Her shoes met a thick bed of
straw strewn over the curved front drive.

Sophy grimaced as the straw clung to her hem. "An un-
tidy mess, isn't it? But it muffles the sound of horses'
hooves and carriage wheels so that visitors don't disturb
Cyril."

"I thought he was insensible," Mary said. "Wouldn't it
be better if he *was* awakened?"

"Tell that to Adam. No one dares to disobey his edicts."

Except his sister, Mary thought, following Sophy past the
gigantic entrance and down a flagstone path lined by per-

fectly clipped boxwoods. Though she wore her nondescript green mantle buttoned tightly over one of Jo's gowns, it was hard to be inconspicuous while accompanying Sophy in her yellow spencer with the red epaulettes and the bonnet with its tall, bobbing feathers. As she and Sophy circled around to the side of the house, she fancied someone could be peering down at them from the windows, a servant or relative. She prayed no one would report to the duke about seeing a veiled lady. Why did his approval matter so much to her?

Sophy went up onto a loggia and opened a door made of glass panes. Her eyes sparkled with high spirits. "We can sneak inside here," she said in a stage whisper.

Misgivings nagged at Mary. "Perhaps we should go back."

"Don't be a ninnyhammer. What can it hurt for you to visit Cyril?"

Sophy took hold of Mary's elbow and propelled her over the threshold. Mary found herself in a cavernous library. She craned her neck to gape at the rows of tidy volumes that filled the walls, the veil fluttering with her every breath. She had never seen so many books in her entire life. Above the shelves, gilt-framed portraits of ducal ancestors glared down at her. She inhaled the pleasant reek of leather bindings and beeswax polish.

"Have you read all of these books?" she asked.

Sophy drew her across the checkered carpet. "Perish me, no. Why read when one can have real adventures?" Reaching an arrangement of salmon-colored chaises, she tugged off her bonnet and unfastened her spencer.

Mary did likewise, though she left on her veiled hat. She felt exposed in the low-cut gown of pale gold cambric, and, not for the first time, mourned the loss of her modesty piece.

Sophy stuffed their wraps into a space behind the couch. "There. Now no one will ask me where I've been. And if

anyone stops us, you're Lady Freestone's timid niece from
the country."

She went to the doorway and poked her head out into
the corridor. Abruptly she ducked back inside. "Oops."

"What is it?" Mary whispered.

Sophy looked pale as if she'd seen a ghost. She panto-
mimed to Mary to keep quiet. The sound of approaching
footsteps came from the passageway.

Mary's heart thundered against her ribcage. She flattened herself against a wall of books, clasped her shaking
hands together, and prayed for deliverance. The heavy
footfalls grew louder, then faded away into silence.

Sophy released a loud breath. "That was close."

"Who was it?"

"Oh, no one important. Let's hurry while the way is
clear."

As she went out, Mary was struck by a poignant reminder of Jo. When they were growing up, Jo had been the
instigator of mischief, sneaking out of the caravan at night
or playing a trick on a bully. Once, when a village girl had
snickered at Mary's patched dress, Jo had snitched the
girl's Sunday frock off a clothesline and tied the garment
onto a pig. She'd slapped the animal on its rump and sent
it squealing down the road. Even Mary had laughed at the
resemblance to a fat matron. And she had felt a sinful
surge of gladness when the animal dove into a ditch and
wallowed in the mud.

She felt a similar thrill now, the thrill of the forbidden.
Chastising herself, she focused her mind on her secret
goal. God forgive her, she had come to Brentwell House
for more than to pray for Cyril's recovery.

She hoped to open herself to another message from her
twin.

With renewed resolve, she hastened after Sophy, who
was mounting the stairs at the end of the passage. Situated
in a corner, this could not be the main staircase. Yet Mary
was awed by the delicate plaster designs on the walls, the

glittering crystal chandelier, the intricately wrought balustrade. Perhaps it seemed all the more romantic when viewed through gauzy lace.

How could this place be called a mere house? It was a mausoleum, a monument to wealth and privilege. The residence of the duke of St. Chaldon.

Adam Brentwell was master here. He need not creep like a thief through the maze of wide corridors. This was his home. This was where he ate and entertained and slept. How strange to picture him in his familiar surroundings.

He had grown up amid this opulence with servants to do his bidding. Her own upbringing had been full of simple pleasures, riding at the back of the caravan with the sun warm on her face, planting tiny gardens along the roadside, snuggling with her sister on winter nights. Her pastimes had been ordinary things such as reading a book or skipping stones with their father. Could she have been happy in a place so grand?

Uncertain, she followed Lady Sophy past statues on pedestals, past framed paintings and gilt chairs. Once, they had to duck into a deserted bedroom while a pair of chambermaids went by, toting armloads of folded linens. At last Sophy stopped at a door decorated by gilded moldings. A silver vase of flowers sat on a table nearby. She turned the scrolled handle and peeked inside, then motioned for Mary to follow.

It was like entering an immense tomb. A few candles were lit here and there, creating small oases in the dimness. The only other light came from a fire crackling on the hearth, for the draperies on the bank of windows were shut against the afternoon sun. Mary wrinkled her nose at the smell of the sickroom, a sharp, medicinal odor.

As Sophy approached a colossal four-poster bed, Mary tiptoed behind her. The ivory silk hangings were partially drawn, and Mary felt a tingling anticipation. At last she would see the man for whom her beloved sister had forsaken her family.

Out of the shadows in the corner stepped a dark figure.

Startled, Mary turned from the shrouded bed and blinked behind her veil at a cadaverous man in a gray periwig, his collar so high and stiff that it met the underside of his sharp chin.

He bowed to Sophy. "My lady."

"Has there been any change, Doctor?" she murmured.

"None, I regret. I employed the leeches again, but to no avail."

Mary shuddered. "Might not the ill humors in his blood be improved by opening the windows?" she ventured. "My father has never been ill for more than a day or two at a time, and he says his good health comes from living out in God's fresh air."

The physician raised his thin brows. "I beg your pardon, Miss? Noxious, chilly air would be certain to send his lordship to his grave."

Mary flushed and fell silent. She had not meant to draw attention to herself. The last thing she wanted was for Adam Brentwell to learn she had been here.

"You may be excused, Doctor," Sophy said. "My companion and I will sit with Lord Cyril for a while."

"But His Grace insists that a physician be present at all times—"

"It's only for half an hour or so." Sophy widened her eyes, a charming smile on her rounded features. "I'll ring if I need help. Go on now, you'll be wanting to have a bite to eat in the kitchen. Cook is baking prune tarts today. Your favorite."

The pointed tip of his tongue flicked out like a lizard's. "If you insist, my lady."

"Oh, and if you should happen to see the duke or the duchess, don't tell them I'm here." She winked. "I'm supposed to be resting in my room."

The moment he stepped out and the door closed quietly behind him, Sophy drew back the bed hangings. The impishness slid from her face, and melancholy tugged down the corners of her mouth.

Mary lifted the veil up onto her hat as she approached slowly, her gaze riveted to the still form lying beneath the embroidered counterpane. A bleached muslin bandage wrapped his head, and wisps of fair hair poked out the top and sides. Someone must have shaved him, for his finely chiseled features were as smooth and pale as a marble statue. She concentrated on him, studying every minute detail, willing her mind to connect itself to Jo.

A sense of unreality whispered through her, and the man in the bed no longer seemed a stranger. Drawn to him, she sank onto the edge of the mattress and leaned closer, drinking in the sight of his honey-brown lashes, the narrow nose, the elegant mouth that could laugh and kiss and bring such bittersweet joy.

She felt dizzy, as if she had tumbled into her sister's life. Abruptly his features wavered and dissolved into horror. . . .

The gunshot jolted her awake. She jerked upright, her heart drumming. Only a faint light from the corridor outside penetrated the gloom of the bedchamber. A shadow moved near the foot of the bed. But she felt only a fleeting fear, for another sight riveted her.

Cyril lay sprawled on the floor. Blood matted his pale hair and puddled beneath his head, staining the carpet. His eyes were shut as if in death.

A primal scream burst from her. "No!"

She scrambled from the bed and sank to her knees, taking his head into her lap. His blood dyed her hands and seeped into her nightdress and she screamed again and again.

The shadow sprang at her. Arms locked around her like the jaws of a trap. A smelly gag muffled her voice. Yet the sound of her cry went on and on, echoing inside her brain, and she wanted to run and run and run into whirling blackness. . . .

Mary! Oh please, Mary, save me!

"Mary, stop! Please, oh, please stop."

The nightmare receded like a dark tide. Dizzily, she blinked at the rosebud mouth pursed tight and the blue eyes screwed up in worry. Lady Sophy. Her soft, scented hand was pressed against Mary's mouth.

"Are you all right?" Sophy asked. "You're not going to cry out again, are you?"

Mary managed to shake her head.

Sophy slowly lowered her hand. "Perish me! You yelled loud enough to wake the dead. I nearly leapt out of my skin! I hope to heavens no one heard you."

"I . . . I . . . it was the shock." Half-expecting to see blood, Mary looked down at her shaking hands. The fine kid gloves were as pristine as they had looked in her sister's drawer. "It was the shock of seeing your brother lying there as if he were dead."

It was a lame excuse, but Mary dared not reveal the truth. A shudder coursed through her as the frightful scene released its talon-like grip on her mind. Sweet heaven, she had achieved her goal. She had witnessed the night of the shooting.

But this time, she hadn't merely seen Jo. She had *become* her sister.

Just as her father proclaimed, she had been cursed by an unnatural power, a power born of the dark forces of evil. She had resisted the affliction through prayer and self-restraint. But now she had achieved an eerie success. She had descended into terror, felt all that her sister had felt.

If only she could have seen more. If only she had discerned a face on that shadowy figure. A thought buoyed her flagging spirits. Perhaps Lord Cyril had seen the gunman.

She bowed her head. "Please, God. Let him awaken soon. Please."

"Cyril is too stubborn to die," Sophy said, tenderly touching her brother's arm. "He'll soon be plaguing me with his teasing again." She sounded as if she were trying to convince herself.

Mary could see the faint movement of the coverlet as his chest rose and fell. A rush of emotion had preceded the vision. She had felt bliss and longing and vibrant passion in her sister.

"She loves him," Mary whispered. "She truly loves him. That's why she never came home to me."

"Do you mean your sister?"

"Yes." Then bitterness seared Mary's heart as she studied the boyishly handsome features of the man on the bed. "Jo deserved to have her love returned. If only Lord Cyril had wed my sister, no man would have dared to abduct her. She would be safe now."

Sophy twisted her hands together. She drew in a breath, then heaved a gusty sigh. "You must know the truth no matter what Adam says. You *deserve* to know."

"What truth?"

"It's what Adam didn't want anyone outside the family to find out. Only two days before Cyril was shot, he brought your sister here to this house. You see, he wanted all of us to meet her."

Mary sat up straight on the bed. She remembered looking into Jo's mirror and seeing a vision of her twin dressed up in emeralds and a fine gown. Lord Cyril had been walking at her side, up the steps to a porticoed mansion . . . Brentwell House. "Surely the duke would never have invited Jo to set foot here."

Sophy leaned forward and grasped Mary's hands. "He didn't. In fact, Adam tried to toss her out on her ear. He and Cyril almost engaged in fisticuffs right in the grand saloon, in front of me and Mama."

Mary's heart bled for Jo, who had been dismissed as unfit to enter the home of the man she loved. "Why would Lord Cyril bring my sister here? It was cruel of him to subject her to insults."

"But he *did* love Josephine. Or rather, he *does*. Enough to defy convention—and Adam." Sophy's face lit up with unholy delight. "You see, Cyril intends to marry her."

⚓ **Chapter 6** ⚓

Pacing the library, Adam frowned at the man he had sent to investigate Josephine Sheppard. Oswald Dewey was a weaselly man with eyes like black beads and skin the color of sallow leather. As steward, he had served Adam for many years and his father before him. Although a bit rough-edged, Dewey was the soul of discretion. Yet he, too, had failed to find the fugitive.

Adam had spent the afternoon at the Bow Street station, where the magistrate had paraded forth a line of red-haired females purported to match the description of Josephine Sheppard. They ranged from gin-sotted sluts to weeping shop girls, but none had the face of a goddess and the eyes of a she-cat. Adam had been grilling a team of Runners when a message had been delivered that Dewey waited at Brentwell House. Hoping the steward had located Josephine's hiding hole, Adam had mounted up and ridden hell-bent through the teeming streets of London.

Now, he settled himself on the edge of the library desk. His haste had been in vain. The news Dewey had come to report was a bitter disappointment.

Dewey leaned forward on his gilt chair and picked up a quill, twirling the feather in his skinny fingers. "Didn't you hear me aright, Your Grace? There's a twin sister who's the spit of Miss Josephine Sheppard."

"I know about Mary Sheppard."

"You do?"

"I do."

The servant used the quill to scratch his sparse brown hair. A tiny shower of dandruff sprinkled his dark coat. "Then did you know she's vanished, too? Just three days ago, it was. She must've gone to her sister, I'd hazard. They could be hiding out in the rookeries somewhere here in London Town."

Adam retrieved the quill and set it back in its silver holder. "Mary Sheppard is safely in my custody. Now, have you anything useful to disclose?"

Dewey tugged at his knotted cravat as if it choked him. "I been keeping a watch out for Miss Josephine, day and night, like you ordered. But she didn't run off to her father. Ever since Miss Mary left, the Reverend Thomas Sheppard's locked himself in that caravan."

Suspicion gnawed at Adam. What manner of man could sire twins who were so different, one a demoness and the other an angel? "And you're certain he stayed in the caravan?"

Dewey nodded. "Sneaked a look through a window, I did. His nose was stuck in his Bible."

"No visitors? No one suspicious hanging about?"

"Only person who's been in and out is that holy deacon, Victor Gabriel." Dewey shook his head, and a few more white flakes drifted to his shoulders, "The luckless rotter. Left at the altar for the second time."

That caught Adam's interest. "Explain yourself."

Apparently pleased to have surprised the duke at last, Dewey grinned, displaying several gold-capped teeth. "Gabriel was planning to wed Miss Josephine first, but three months ago she jilted him and came to London. Now his intended bride is Miss Mary."

If a thunderbolt had struck Adam, he couldn't have been more astonished. Mousy little Mary, betrothed? No, not mousy. She was gorgeous when she unbraided her hair, when she donned a gown that flattered her figure, when she was pink and flustered from a man's kiss.

Adam sprang up and resumed pacing. He felt unaccountably annoyed that she had never breathed a word about a fiancé. Or had she?

Some men value innocence.

Her chastisement still irked him. He was not accustomed to having his honor as a gentleman challenged. And why the devil should she speak to him of her private life, anyway? It wasn't as if they were members of the same social circle. She was nothing to him. Nothing but his means to entrap Josephine.

"Tell me everything you know of this Victor Gabriel," Adam said.

"Lemme think." Dewey reached out to set a small globe spinning in its wooden stand on the desk. "Gabriel assists Thomas Sheppard, sometimes preaching to the flock, sometimes passing out tracts and leading the prayers. He went off searching for Miss Mary a day or two, like his godly heart was broken. The man's a right proper saint, he is. And as handsome as his namesake, the archangel. All the females fall into a swoon over him."

With one fingertip, Adam stopped the motion of the globe. "He must have a fault or two. A weakness for drink or the cards."

"Not Deacon Gabriel. He's pure as a maiden's cunny. The womenfolk hang on his every word, they do. Ain't fair to the rest of the gennlemen, especially when he harangues 'em about fleshly lust. Why, after one of them sermons, a man can't buy himself a decent tumble in the hay."

Victor Gabriel sounded like a paragon of virtue. A cold fish who had taught his fiancée nothing of her sensual nature. He was a fitting husband for the little Virgin Mary.

Somehow that notion didn't improve Adam's disposition. "Go back to Sussex and keep a watch out for Josephine. I expect you to report any suspicious moves by

Thomas Sheppard, too. Here's something for your traveling expenses."

Opening a drawer, he extracted a gold sovereign and flipped it to Dewey. The little man caught the flashing coin in a nimble paw; then he bobbed a bow amid another flurry of dandruff. "You're a right generous man, Your Grace."

He slipped out the garden door, leaving Adam alone in the library. Alone with his black thoughts.

So Mary Sheppard was to wed her sister's spurned suitor. No doubt Thomas Sheppard had arranged the match so that one of his daughters would marry his successor. Adam wondered if it hurt her pride to be second choice, to accept her sister's castoff.

He acknowledged a twinge of discomfort. He too had been more drawn to the vivacious Josephine. But Mary's drab clothing and bashful manner were merely a disguise for a spirited, opinionated, and utterly exasperating young woman. Did Victor Gabriel see that? Would he admire those qualities? Or would he crush them?

Soon Mary would return to the uncertainties of a vagabond's life. Of course, that was all she knew, wandering over the hills and vales of England with her firebrand father and holy husband-to-be. What did they talk about while traveling all day? Scripture readings? The next evening's sermon? Or did they laugh and tease each other like a warmhearted family?

Adam paced the length of the library and paused to stare unseeing out one of the tall windows. How strange, not to want a plot of earth to call one's own. He himself prized his many holdings, most notably his country estate, where he was free from the tedious round of parties, free to ride over his land. Did Mary ever yearn for a real home? Or was she content to live in cramped quarters and never to stay in one place? She was a mystery to him, all starch and vinegar one moment, and the next, melting in his arms as if he was the man of her heart.

Restlessly, he prowled toward the door. The devil take

his curiosity. Better he should concentrate on the masquerade. In a short while, Mary would dress for her role. He
would fetch her from her sister's town house and make
certain the abigail had accomplished the task of transforming the angel into a whore.

After tonight, he would have no further use for Mary.
She would return to her caravan and her fiancé. And
Adam would have his revenge. He would see her sister
swing from the gibbet at the Old Bailey.

As he walked past a chaise, he spied a patch of yellow
fabric sticking out from behind the salmon velvet uphol-
stery. Frowning, he reached behind the sofa and pulled out
a bundle.

A single bonnet tumbled to the carpet. The rest of the
parcel consisted of two wadded garments. Both were familiar to him. The yellow spencer trimmed in red belonged to
Sophy. And the other, a mantle in a putrid shade of olive
green, belonged to Mary Sheppard.

Realization blazed through him. They were here. In his
house.

He could think of only one reason why. Cyril. *If only I
could pray at his bedside.* . . .

Adam stalked out of the library and made for the nearest staircase, taking the steps two at a time. The carpet
runner muffled the thud of his riding boots. Blast that pious minx. He didn't want her anywhere near his brother. If
Cyril awakened, he might mistake her for his fickle lover.
He would name her as his assailant and Adam's plan to
catch Josephine would lie in ruins.

As he rounded the corner, the situation went from bad
to worse. A woman hastened toward Cyril's bedchamber.

He caught up to her a scant few feet from the door.
Gently grasping her arm, he brought her to a halt.
"Mother. Why aren't you resting?"

"It's Cyril." In a rich bronze gown, her silvery hair piled
atop her head, Eleanor St. Chaldon looked every inch the

duchess. Yet her manner was agitated, her hands twisting the lace at her throat. "I must go to him. I must!"

And find Josephine's identical twin in there? "That isn't a wise idea just now. You mustn't exert yourself. Let the physicians tend to Cyril." Adam spoke calmly, guiding her away. "I'll fetch you if there's any change."

"You don't understand," she said with a moan. "One of the maids passed by here a few minutes ago. She heard someone scream in there. Oh, my darling boy must have died!"

She wrenched herself out of his grasp. Before he could react, she darted away, running with an utter lapse of dignity. She reached the door and flung it open. Then she reared back and stiffened, her fist clutched to her bosom.

Adam came up behind her. Out of the shadowy bedroom floated the haunting sound of a woman singing. The clear soprano notes were sweet and soothing as a lullaby. No, it was a hymn. Something about God and hope and chariots to heaven.

Mary.

His pulse surged with anger and attraction. She knelt beside the bed, a dainty angel framed by the ivory hangings. Her hands were clasped in prayer and her face was lifted to the candlelight. A simple bonnet adorned her red-gold hair. The beauty of her voice enveloped him like the softest silk. Against his will, he felt his soul lifting, soaring, yearning for something he could not name.

In that moment of high exultation, he wanted her. Wanted more than the fleeting pleasure of her body. He wanted her smiles, her confidences, her joys, and her sorrows. He wanted to own her heart.

He was brought jarringly back to earth when his mother burst forth into the bedchamber. "Strumpet! Murderess! Have you come to finish off my son?"

Mary gasped in mid-note. She swung around on her knees and looked up at the duchess. "Please, I've done nothing but pray—"

"Move away from him. Now!"

Mary hastened to stand, nearly tripping on her hem. She scuttled to the foot of the bed and seized hold of the post. Her bosom was heaving, her breasts like ripe peaches nestled in the golden cup of her bodice.

The duchess leaned over Cyril. With a visibly trembling hand, she touched his brow, his cheek, his neck. "Praise God, he's still alive." Her voice shook. "Praise God."

Adam fixed his arm around her frail shoulders. "Mother, come away. Let me handle this."

"No! I will not be coddled like an invalid." She seemed to gain strength, drawing herself up as she wheeled toward Mary. "How dare you creep into my house. Adam, send for the Runners. We must not let this trollop escape the noose of justice."

Mary stood watching, wide-eyed, like a cornered doe. The look on her face was part fright and strangely, part compassion. "I'm sorry," she murmured. "I never meant to cause you more pain."

Judging by the tight-lipped fury on his mother's face, Adam saw no recourse but the truth. "She is not Josephine Sheppard. This is her twin sister, Mary."

The duchess twisted around to stare at him. "That is absurd. Two women could not look so much alike."

"They are not perfectly identical. Observe the mole near the right side of her mouth. Josephine has one to the left."

His mother glowered at Mary. The sputtering fire on the hearth bathed the bedroom in a heat that bordered on the uncomfortable. Sweat prickled down Adam's neck, a reminder that the physician had ordered Cyril be kept warm for fear of his taking a chill.

"Adam is right, Mama." Sophy stepped out of the gloom on the other side of the bed. "Her name truly is Mary. She's sweet and shy and well-mannered."

Adam groaned inwardly. He had been so concentrated on Mary that he had completely forgotten to look for his sister.

"Sophronia?" the duchess said in a chastising voice. "Whatever could you know of this . . . this common creature?"

Sophy held her chin at a defiant tilt. "I only met Mary yesterday. Quite by accident. And she is a perfectly respectable person. Adam can tell you all about her."

His mother directed her most imperious frown at him. "I await your explanation."

He would sooner lie to God Almighty than deceive Her Grace of St. Chaldon. But lie he must. "Mary Sheppard came looking for her sister. I told her that if the Bow Street Runners could not find Josephine Sheppard, then how could I?" He paused to compress his lips. "Miss Sheppard begged to pray for Cyril at his bedside. I could see no harm in granting her request. Sophy was kind enough to chaperon."

Sophy flashed him a thankful smile, then resumed her sober mien.

"Have you gone mad?" his mother said in a deceptively quiet tone. "My daughter cannot chaperon rabble. Associating with this lowly being will ruin Sophronia's reputation."

Adam had never thought of the duchess as a mean-spirited person, and her contempt disturbed him. As did the sight of Mary with her gaze downcast. "Mother, I must ask you to refrain from insulting a visitor to my home."

The duchess's eyes widened. "Do you care so little for your family, then?"

"I care to maintain civility. I care to see my guests treated with all due respect."

"No harm has been done, Mama," Sophy pointed out. "Only you and Adam are here. And we did so hope that Mary's singing would reach poor Cyril."

"He stirred once," Mary offered hesitantly. "While I was singing, I saw his eyelashes flutter."

Adam's chest constricted. Drawn by reckless hope, he stepped to the bed and leaned down, scrutinizing his brother's face. There was no movement, just the faint rise and fall of his chest. His skin was pale, so unreflective of the boisterous spirit that struggled for life. Aware of the sting of moisture in his eyes, Adam kept a firm grip on his emotions. Gently he touched his brother's cheek, and its warmth gave a measure of reassurance.

He turned on his heel and walked to Mary, grasping her shoulders. The delicacy of her bone structure belied her inner strength. "Are you quite certain?"

"Yes, Your Grace—"

"She's deceiving you," the duchess said. "No doubt, she wishes to raise false hopes in us. Before long, she will be asking you to reward her with money and jewels."

Releasing Mary, Adam turned to Sophy. "Did you see Cyril move?"

She lifted her hands in a helpless gesture. "Well . . . I . . ."

"The truth now."

"I'm sorry, Adam. I must not have been looking."

"It happened," Mary insisted. "Please, Lord Cyril might have mistaken me for Josephine. Lady Sophy herself told me that our voices sound alike."

"Then let us hasten you away from him," the duchess said in a low tone. Lifting her hand in a majestic wave, she motioned the group over to the door. "God forbid my son should hear the voice of the woman who tried to kill him. It might be enough to send him to his grave."

Mary lifted her chin. "My sister didn't shoot Lord Cyril. Jo would never harm a living soul. Ask the duke. He'll tell you."

Adam's muscles tightened. All three women gazed at him, his mother incredulous, Sophy worried, Mary so very trusting.

How the devil was he to get out of this tangle?

"The case is still under investigation," he said. "We shan't know the whole story until Josephine is found . . . or until Cyril comes to his senses. Until such time, I suggest you ladies refrain from distressing yourselves unnecessarily."

Before his mother could object, Adam seized hold of Mary's arm. "Allow me to show you out, Miss Sheppard. Sophy, if you would be so kind as to escort Mother back to her chambers."

He swiftly steered Mary out the door and into the passageway. She directed a cryptic glance at him but said nothing. At his side, she marched like a soldier of the Lord, lips pinched and eyebrows winged together in a frown.

No doubt she would take him to task for sidestepping the issue of her sister's guilt. Little did she know, he had a few things to say to her, too.

Their footsteps echoed down the grand staircase and through the entrance hall with its high vaulted ceiling painted by a Venetian artist who had been commissioned by his great-grandfather, the second duke. As a child, Adam had liked to lie on the cold marble floor and gaze up at the adventurous scenes from the life of Julius Caesar. As an adult, he permitted himself a quiet pride in being master of this magnificent domain.

But he felt no pleasure now.

"Have my carriage brought 'round," he told the footman standing guard at the double doors. "The landau."

As soon as the servant departed, Mary said, "Lord Cyril did move, I'm sure of it."

"Perhaps what you saw was a trick of the candlelight."

"It was no trick! If I try again, he might respond to my voice. He could awaken."

"He is under the care of the best physicians in London," Adam said in a low tone. "When I agreed to work together with you, it was with the understanding that you would abide by *my* rules. You violated my trust by sneaking into my house."

The fervor lighting her face faded away, leaving her cheeks pale. "I nearly forgot your lofty proprieties, m'lord duke. What an outrage if anyone in Society should learn that you had allowed a commoner into this hallowed place." She shook her head, wisps of red-gold hair dancing at her brow. "How can you value such artificial nonsense above your brother's health? His very life?"

Adam tamped down the rising fear for Cyril. Upon awakening, his brother would indict his mistress. It was too soon for Mary to find that out. "There is the health of my mother to consider, too. I will not have her unduly distressed."

Mary bowed her head a moment. When she raised it, she looked him full in the eyes. "Lord Cyril must regain his senses. If the masquerade fails, only he can clear Josephine's name."

He clasped his hands behind his back. "It's highly unlikely that Cyril saw the gunman. Her bedroom was surely dark. It's best we go ahead with our plan for tonight."

"Why are you being so obstinate? We should explore every possibility." Mary balled her hands into fists at her sides. Those green eyes were clear and cold and accusing. "Unless you disapprove of your brother's choice of a wife. So much that you're plotting to keep them apart."

Wife. Adam's blood ran cold. Damn Sophy and her loose tongue. And damn the masquerade that required him to pretend approval of Josephine Sheppard.

He walked back and forth, his footsteps sharp on the marble floor. "I wish to find Josephine's captor as much as you do. I want to see my brother's assailant behind bars. Beyond that, I have no plans."

She stepped into his path. "Then why did you not tell me about their betrothal? I shouldn't have had to learn the truth from your sister."

"It was an oversight. I've a considerable amount on my mind at present."

"But—"

"Enough. Now is neither the time nor the place for a private discussion."

He flicked the veil over Mary's face, then grasped her arm. Without waiting for the footman to return, he opened the great door and hauled her out onto the portico. The breeze had picked up, carrying the scent of cinders and horse dung, the familiar taint of the city. He burned to get Mary back to the town house and have the masquerade over with and done.

His timing was perfect. A team of matched bays was drawing the closed black landau from the stables. Adam steered Mary down the wide front steps and over the layer of straw that served as a reminder of his brother's critical injury. A footman opened the plain door, which bore no ducal coat of arms as did the town coach. Today, Adam required anonymity.

The moment he had settled himself on the leather cushions and the vehicle set off on its gently rocking ride, Mary leaned forward from her seat opposite him. "Will you grant your blessing on their marriage?"

Curse her persistence. "Miss Sheppard, I believe we should locate your sister first before we begin planning weddings."

"You don't approve, then." She sat back, the veil hiding her features, though he fancied he could see a scowl lowering the fine lines of her eyebrows. "Do you think if you sweep their love under the rug, you can pretend it doesn't exist?"

"Love has nothing to do with the crime under investigation."

"It most certainly does. It proves that Jo would never shoot Lord Cyril. Which, by the way, you ought to have told your mother. Why didn't you?"

"At the risk of repeating myself, her health is precarious."

"And she wants my sister to be found guilty. That would put an end to the wedding quite handily." The veil billowed with her huff of displeasure. He imagined Mary pursing her lips in the annoyingly pretty manner that made him want to kiss them into softness. "One would think," she went on, "that the duchess would set aside her prejudices. She should congratulate her son on finding the happiness of true love."

"Love," Adam stated grimly, "is of little consequence in choosing a wife. To a man of noble birth, marriage is a dynastic alliance, the union of two eminent families."

"What twaddle. A man and a woman should be allowed to determine their own happiness, rather than letting others dictate the course of their private lives."

"And have you followed your own preaching? Or have you let your father select the sainted paragon you intend to marry?" The moment the words were out, Adam knew his temper had goaded him into a blunder.

In the dimness of the carriage, she sat very still. "You know of Victor? How?"

Adam supposed she would find out sometime. "I sent a man to Sussex to learn what he could of Josephine, perhaps to gain a clue as to her whereabouts."

"You've been spying on my father?"

"I merely wished to leave no stone unturned."

"Why would you think Papa would know who abducted Jo?" Her fingers bunched the golden fabric of her gown. "Unless . . ." she said slowly, "unless you've been lying to me. Perhaps you don't believe that she was abducted at all. Perhaps you think she shot Cyril. And that she might have run to hide with my father."

Each word sounded forced as if Mary struggled against disbelief. She pressed herself backward against the cushions, her body rigid, her breasts rising and falling.

God. She was too quick, too insightful.

Affecting a casual laugh, Adam leaned forward and closed his hand over her tensed fingers. "My dear contrary Mary. I've spent the past two days teaching you how to fool your sister's kidnapper. I wouldn't have bothered to do so if I were insincere. You can trust me."

"Can I? What else haven't you told me?"

Her hand nested warily inside his. The interior of the carriage closed them in an intimate bower. She looked mysterious and unattainable, a bride-to-be meeting her intended husband for the first time. A lady who wanted wooing.

How foolish. She was no lady. Nor could she ever be his duchess.

Yet Adam felt strangely like a bridegroom as he lifted the veil from her face. And he found himself coveting Mary Sheppard with a fierceness that caught him unawares. His gaze lingered on the oval shape of her face, the pert nose and the stubborn chin, the mutinous mouth. Their clasped hands rested in her lap, and he was keenly aware of the slim, silken thighs beneath her gown and petticoats.

"There *is* something I haven't told you," he said.

She bent nearer. "Yes?"

Her eyes were deep green pools of curiosity, and he wanted to see them soften with desire. Lifting his hand, he caressed the velvety bow of her lips. "I haven't told you," he murmured, "how much I've thought about our kiss. Or how I ache to continue our lesson."

Her eyes widened. Her lips parted to his touch, and her breath warmed his fingers. Lured by her innocence, he leaned forward and brushed his mouth over hers once, then again. He tasted her with his tongue, savoring the small sigh that gusted from her. A curious tenderness warred with the heat in his loins. He found himself wishing he had met her at another time, in another place, under happier circumstances. A time when he would have the leisure to seduce her by degrees. A time when he could court her and win her heart. A time when he could tempt her into becoming his mistress—

Abruptly she pulled back. She launched to her feet and banged her fist on the roof. "Stop this carriage at once," she called to the coachman. "I wish to get out."

"What the deuce—" Adam began.

Mary grabbed the door handle. He caught her slender wrist. She jerked against him so hard that he feared to break her fine bones, and he loosened his grip.

As the landau slowed, she threw open the door and jumped down to the busy street.

෨ **Chapter 7** ෨

M ary landed with a jarring thump on the hard cobblestones. Her skirts twisted around her ankles, and she fell to her hands and knees. Pain bolted up her legs and arms, but she didn't care. She had to escape. Just down the street, the coachman was drawing the horses to a stop; the duke poked his dark head out and grabbed the swinging door.

She hauled herself to a sitting position. Passersby stared, though none stopped to help her. A vendor pushed his pie cart and hawked his wares in a loud singsong voice. A plump matron waddled along with three young children following like ducklings.

The fashionable Mayfair district had given way to the quaint, gabled buildings of the Strand. The brisk breeze carried the odor of the river. Mary looked wildly about the shabby, genteel street. Surely she couldn't be more than half a mile from Jo's town house.

The rumble of wheels caught her attention. Coming down the road was a horse-drawn dray piled high with wooden casks. The vehicle was headed straight toward her.

She pushed to her feet and her knees wobbled precariously. Stars floated before her eyes. She blinked against the sudden dizziness, and the harsh shout of the driver assaulted her addled senses.

A pair of masculine hands clamped around her waist, lifted her over the curbstone, and planted her on the foot pavement. The dray rattled past, leaving a fog of beer fumes.

The duke of St. Chaldon loomed over her. "Good God! Are you hurt?"

"N-no." It was only half a lie, Mary rationalized as she brushed the dirt from her gold skirt and gathered the shreds of her composure. Her legs felt decidedly stronger, though her knees still stung from the impact.

"That," Adam Brentwell said, taking hold of her hands and examining the stains on her gloves, "was an act of utter witlessness. You might have broken a bone or bruised yourself. You might not have been able to go on with the masquerade."

Somehow it hurt to be reminded that she was only a pawn to him. "Then I'd be completely useless to you, wouldn't I?"

"You're damned lucky you didn't kill yourself."

"Don't curse at me. Perhaps none of your proper ladies have ever leaped from a coach, but Jo and I often jumped down from my father's caravan while it was still moving."

"Then your sister is as cockle-brained as you are."

"So much for civility. You're as ready with the insults as your mother." Mary wrested her hands away. "If you hadn't tried to force your attentions on me, I would not have had to resort to escape."

He smiled, a rare and sinfully attractive quirk of his mouth. "Forced, Miss Sheppard?"

A blush bloomed on her cheeks. She felt weak at the knees again. Before he could spy her telltale reaction, Mary spun around and limped down the street. She *had* wanted to kiss him. To feel those firm male lips pressed to hers again. To breathe in his scent and let his vitality surround her. To taste, just once more, the forbidden fruit of passion.

Merciful Lord. She must have cobwebs in her brain. Or a hex upon her heart.

It was shocking and shameful, this secret stirring inside

her. The truth of her wanton nature mortified Mary. She had promised herself to a man of the cloth. She *wanted* to marry Victor. She intended to spend her life striving to be worthy of him. And even if she were free, Adam Brentwell was a heartless aristocrat, an arrogant devil who expected her to curtsy before him and to fall adoringly at his feet as if he were the Almighty Himself.

She slanted a glance sideways to see him walking straight and tall beside her. He cut a fine figure in a frock coat of military blue over buff-colored breeches and tassled black boots. How did he keep so fit when he led such an indolent life? Like all noble bloods, he rode in plush carriages, attended lavish parties, and thrived on worthless amusements. Her father had said as much, preaching that men like the duke drank and whored and gambled the night away, sometimes losing a fortune at a toss of the dice. The dark circles beneath his eyes gave testament to his nocturnal hours.

So did his private town house. He openly admitted to engaging in lewd activities there.

She felt herself blushing again and kept her chin tucked to her chest. She must never forget that the duke of St. Chaldon had but one use for a woman of her station.

Lord Cyril must be different, for he had agreed to make a respectable woman of Jo. The news roused both joy and fear in Mary. How wonderful for her sister to find love; how horrid that her fiancé's family disdained her. Somehow, Mary vowed, no matter what her father or Victor said, she would stand by Jo in the face of the tyrannical duke and his imperious mother.

If only she could find her sister.

Ahead, the coachman drove the landau slowly down the street. The stench of manure drifted from a livery stable. As someone in the throng jostled Mary, Adam Brentwell caught her around the shoulders and drew her closer. For a moment she was clasped against his solid body, her bosom pressed to his chest. Surely he could feel the maddened beating of her heart.

"Come back into the coach," he said.

"I would rather walk." Twisting free, she increased her pace. "You needn't attend me. I can find my own way to Jo's house."

"I am not questioning your sense of direction. Rather, the advisability of a young lady strolling unescorted."

Mary didn't know whether to laugh or to sneer at his pompous speech. She settled for gesturing at the street which teemed with housewives and tradesmen, urchins and merchants. "You forget, Your Grace. I am one of the masses. Not a delicate lady of—what do you call it?—the *haut* ton."

"Ton will suffice. And may I point out, you are my charge. I shan't allow any harm to befall you." His eyes narrowed to an intense blue that glinted with mystery. He tugged the veil over her face again. "Tonight is too vital to my plan."

Mary felt a shudder of nerves. Half of her thrilled to his protectiveness; the other half whispered that he might be using her for his own nefarious purpose. Did he truly wish to help her catch the kidnapper? Or had he been lying to her all along?

As they crossed the busy thoroughfare and headed north, suspicion gnawed at Mary. She was still shaken by the revelation that the duke had investigated her father and Victor. Leave no stone unturned, Adam had claimed. Could she believe him?

His strong fingers held her elbow, conducting her over a stretch of uneven pavement. She had the sudden giddy feeling of being swept away by the tide, not knowing where she was going. Never had she been more conscious of her lack of sophistication, her isolation in this vast city. Like it or not, she had to trust an aristocrat. Jo's life depended upon it.

They neared a corner where a barrel-chested man held

out his cap. One of his sleeves was empty and pinned to his patched shirt. The grimy uniform marked him as a former soldier in His Majesty's army. Over the past few days, Mary had noticed other veterans aimlessly wandering the streets. According to Obediah, when the war against Napoleon had come to a victorious conclusion at Waterloo, thousands of enlisted men had been discharged. They had inundated the capital, and jobs had grown scarce.

The duke slipped a coin into the soldier's cap. The man touched the duke's arm in gratitude. "Thank ye, yer worship, sir. Yer generous to them less fortunate."

Inclining his head in acknowledgment, his lordship continued with Mary down the street.

Her sense of righteousness won a battle with her innate shyness. "He needs more than alms. He needs a livelihood."

"At least he'll eat for a few days. If he doesn't squander the money on cheap gin."

"For shame, Your Grace. That man lost an arm in service to his country, and you assume the worst of him. How arrogant of you to believe that the poor are more subject to vice than are the rich."

"And how presumptuous of you to know my opinions."

His mockery roused her to greater indignation. "You might have offered him a job. It would be no hardship to add another servant to your staff. Unless you're prejudiced against the disabled of the world."

Adam sent her a black look. "Climb down from the pulpit, Reverend Sheppard. That soldier also relieved me of three silver buttons."

He showed her his sleeve. Threads dangled where the buttons had been sliced from his cuff.

Shocked, Mary glanced back over her shoulder, but the bustling throng blocked the street corner from her view. She lifted the veil a moment so that she could see more clearly. "Are you certain he did that? I never even saw a knife."

"It was there. He'll sell the buttons at Petticoat Lane for a few shillings apiece."

Mary felt the need to go after the soldier and convince him to repent. On the other hand, she feared the duke might take it into his mind to cart off the man to Newgate Prison.

Adam resolved the issue by taking her arm and directing her around a pothole in the pavement. "Have a care, Miss Sheppard. Things are not always as they seem to be. 'Judge not, and ye shall not be judged.' "

The hint of a smile on his face annoyed her. Before meeting him, she had never traded insults with a man; her father expected her to behave modestly as befitting a woman's role. "The Scripture also says, 'Go and sell that thou hast, and give to the poor, and thou shalt have treasure in heaven.' Decent folk are starving for want of wages, while the rich wallow in splendor."

"Then you will be pleased to know that I employ well over a hundred servants and support several thousand tenants on my estates. A beggar has never been turned away from my kitchen doorstep without a parcel of food."

"Truly?" Surprised, Mary glanced admiringly at his noble profile before remembering his decadent nature. "Still, you should hire the needy, give them the pride of working for their daily bread rather than soliciting handouts. As Jo did."

His steps slowed. "Explain yourself."

"She made Obediah her footman when he came begging a meal at her door."

"He never mentioned the circumstances of his employment," Adam said musingly. "Though admittedly, I asked more questions about the other servants. The ones who ran away before they could be interrogated about the shooting."

"Ran away?" Mary asked in puzzlement. "Obediah told me he'd sacked the cook for her laziness. And the housemaid and tweeny as well."

Adam gave her a sharp, considering scrutiny. Yet she doubted he could see past her veil. "You must be mistaken."

"I don't think so." Mary blinked at him; then another idea distracted her and she touched his sleeve. "As soon as we find my sister, I shall encourage her to hire several new servants in addition to the ones who left. It's only fair that we do our part."

"Part?"

"Hiring the disadvantaged. Just think, if every aristocratic household were to create a few extra jobs, the number of poor would be greatly reduced."

He arched one black eyebrow. "A fanciful notion. But families of quality keep sufficient staff already. They would not take kindly to the additional expense."

When the traffic cleared, Mary started across the side street. "Yet the gentry fritter away many times more than a meager salary in a single hand of cards. They see no wrong in squandering hundreds on gems and gowns. It is far better that the money go to a good cause."

"Would you put the jewelers and dressmakers out of work? And the card manufacturers and club employees as well? That seems contrary to your crusade."

Sparks of silver flashed against the blue of his eyes. Was he teasing her? The very possibility irked Mary.

She stopped in the middle of the street and set her hands on her hips. "You, sir, are appallingly blind to the plight of the homeless, the humble, the wretched of God's earth. You, who keep a second house solely for the purpose of your own carnal lust."

His gaze was deep, devilish. "And you, Miss, are determined to tar me with the blackest of motives. All because I desire discretion in my romantic affairs."

"No. Yes! Your behavior is wicked and sinful."

"On the contrary, as an unmarried man, I am not bound by any vow of fidelity." He guided her to the side of the road just as a phaeton driven by a smartly dressed young blade rattled past. "It is my belief that the good Lord created in us a capacity for passion, for a man and a woman to take joy in each other's body." The duke looked her up and down. "He created that need in you, too. If you would but allow yourself to explore it."

An involuntary shiver coursed through Mary. He aroused the memory of lying beneath him on the bed as he lifted her skirts. He had shaped his warm hand to her leg, subjecting her to his unwanted caress. What would the experience have been like if he had touched her in pleasure rather than in anger? If she had been his willing partner, rather than his terrified captive? And why, now, did she feel the dark heat of desire for him?

She cudgeled her wayward thoughts into obedience. "Do you know what's wrong with your character?"

"I've a suspicion you are about to enlighten me."

"You don't regard the lower class as real people, people who weep and bleed and suffer. You toss them a coin or a crust of bread and consider your duty done."

His lips tightened. For a long moment he gazed at her, a muscle working in his jaw. Then he sketched a bow. "Your point is well taken, Miss Sheppard. If it so pleases you, you may choose some poor soul for me to employ."

If he had announced he was offering her his honored name in marriage, she could not have been more surprised. "Now?"

He lifted his gloved fingers in a negligent gesture. "Now. Here. Whomever strikes your fancy."

He must be jesting. Yet a sober expression graced his noble features. He looked the perfect gentleman, and as darkly handsome as Satan himself.

Mary lost no time in her search. By peering down the side street, she could see the genteel district where Jo's house was located in a row of charming Georgian dwellings with columned stone facades. Here on the main thoroughfare, people walked to and fro, some hurrying on errands and some strolling from shop to shop. A servant lad toted an armload of parcels and trotted after a stout housewife. A coster with a hacking cough trudged behind his barrow of pickled whelks. A ruddy-faced girl hawked muffins from a tray.

Then Mary spied the woman lounging against the pole of a gas lamp. A basket of apples perched on her hip, she looked strong yet careworn. An apron that had once been white cinched her stout waist. A ragged black shawl draped her sturdy shoulders. Judging by her straggly salt-and-pepper hair, she looked to be in her middle years.

What wrenched Mary's compassion was the appleseller's face. A bruise darkened her puffy cheek and one eye was swollen half shut. Here was a woman who had suffered, likely at the brutal hand of a man.

Mary hesitated, tongue-tied at the notion of speaking to a stranger. But she had a point to prove to the duke.

She approached the matron. "Ma'am? My name is Mary Sheppard. Are you by chance in need of steady work?"

The woman exuded the musty odor of sweat and suspicion. "I got me apples ta sell. I ain't no cadger." She narrowed her good eye, peering at Mary's veiled features, then assessing her revealing gold gown.

Mary stealthily tugged up the bodice. "I'm not suggesting charity. I'm only asking if you're interested in a better position."

"Well, now, that depends. I'm a 'onest woman, I am. Don't think ta cozen me into a bawdy 'ouse. The ones wot cater ta bloods like 'im." She jerked her thumb at the duke, who stood at Mary's elbow.

His lip curled ever so slightly. "I assure you, madam, my household is quite respectable."

"He's the duke of St. Chaldon," Mary confided.

"Is 'e, now?" Interest gleamed on the woman's plain features. She lurched away from the post long enough to bob a curtsy. "Mrs. Primrose, I am. Wot d'ye be offerin' me?"

"A position on my staff at Brentwell House," the duke said. "Perhaps in the kitchen—"

"An upstairs maid," Mary put in. She would not let him hide the woman in the scullery.

Mrs. Primrose clutched her basket of apples. "Fer a decent wage?"

His expression remained bland. "Naturally, provided you do your tasks to my housekeeper's satisfaction. And you must reside in the servants' quarters. Would that arrangement be permissible with your husband?"

"Ain't got no 'usband, no family, neither." She tapped her bruised cheek with a dirty fingernail. "If yer wonderin' about this 'ere, it come from bumpin' into a door."

"I'm sorry."

Adam Brentwell managed to imbue the words with disdain. It only made Mary more determined to puncture his lordly hauteur. She wanted him to see Mrs. Primrose and others like her as flesh and blood human beings.

A lightning bolt of inspiration struck her. With his connections and her ideas, they could do so much good for the unfortunate. They could start a movement to create more jobs for the poor. Yes! As soon as she found her sister, Mary resolved, she would concentrate on converting the almighty duke of St. Chaldon to her father's cause of equality.

Adam's day went from bad to worse when he arrived at Josephine Sheppard's town house and walked into a fracas.

It was annoying enough that he had allowed himself to be maneuvered into hiring the redoubtable Mrs. Primrose. She had no sooner entered Brentwell House than she had refused Fenwick's request to follow him downstairs, carrying a sack of laundry for him. Adam had been obliged to reprimand her and then soothe the valet's sensibilities.

So much for Mary's noble experiment.

Yet she had managed to stir in him an uneasiness about his attitude toward the common class. Though he gave alms to the poor, and his mother and sister performed charitable works, Adam seldom thought of the masses as individuals. Until today.

Today he had been struck by curiosity about street women like Mrs. Primrose. Did she live in a filthy tenement infested with rats? Were the few pence she made selling apples adequate to buy food and clothing? *Was* it his responsibility to look after people who couldn't care for themselves?

Adam had pondered the questions all the way to Josephine's house, where Mary was preparing herself for the masquerade. He stepped down from his plain black carriage into the gray drizzle. The dreary weather had driven most people indoors. He saw only a humpbacked watchman at the end of the block, starting his nightly patrol of the neighborhood.

When no one responded to Adam's knocking, he tried the door and found it unlocked. The dim light of dusk lit the small entrance hall with its gilt-framed paintings and crystal chandelier.

Claws clicked on the marble floor. The mangy gray dog loped forth from the direction of the cellar. Adam absently rubbed the animal's matted head; then the dog paced to the stairway and whined.

The sound of raised voices floated downward. One male, one female.

Adam grasped the newel post and cocked his head to listen. He couldn't discern the words, only the harsh undertone of anger. Who, besides the abigail, was with Mary?

"Stay," he commanded the dog.

The cur settled down to wait at the base of the stairs.

Adam mounted the narrow flight of steps and followed the cacophony to the opened doorway of Josephine's bedroom. Since his last visit on the day of Mary's arrival, the chamber had been tidied. The lingerie had been put away, the accessories stored, the four-poster bed made up with clean linens. In the middle of the counterpane slept a tabby cat that was missing an ear.

One change struck Adam like a blow. The stained rug had been removed. A bleached spot showed where his brother's blood had been scrubbed from the bare planks.

In the middle of the room, Obediah bent nose to nose with a tiny woman clad entirely in black.

"Cochon!" Madame Fournet snapped, gripping a silver hairbrush and drawing herself up to her full four feet, ten inches. "English swine. You would dare to meddle with my *pièce de résistance*—"

"Talk the King's English, ye curst Frenchie. I ain't gonna let ye turn this flower o' virtue into a half-naked whore."

He pointed at Mary. Like an alabaster statue, she stood in front of the dressing table, her fingers twined together and the light from a branch of candles limning her slender form.

Adam's mouth went dry. He was looking at the mirror image of Josephine Sheppard.

Except for the tiny mole to the right of her mouth, Mary could have been her scheming twin. And just like her sister, Mary exuded the sensuality of innocence ripe for the tasting.

The airy gauze gown molded to the fullness of her breasts and hinted at the curve of her waist and hips. The fabric was the warm ivory shade of her skin, lending her the illusion of nudity. Her hair was caught up in a mass of red-gold curls. Several strands tumbled onto her bare shoulders in the sweetly tousled effect of a woman just arisen from bed. Touches of carmine gave her cheeks the illusion of a blush and her lips the pouty invitation to a kiss.

In vivid detail, Adam recalled the flavor of her mouth. He thought of the softness of her body beneath his, and a surge of unholy heat seared him. God. He wanted to call off the masquerade and make long, slow love to her.

Instead, he must throw her to the wolves.

He approached the servants. "What is the meaning of this? Obediah, why are you not tending to your duties?"

"I come t' check on the lass, and 'tis good I did. She ain't goin' nowhere dressed only in them underclothes." Obediah set his bulldog face into a scowl. "An' that's me final word."

Madame Fournet brandished the hairbrush like a dueling pistol. "Ignorant peasant," she said with a Gallic sniff. "Miss Sheppard is wearing the finest gown ever to adorn a woman. Beside her, all others would look like faded flowers."

"Please, stop quarreling." Mary stepped to Obediah and touched his arm. "I only wish to find my sister. If my garb helps me to achieve that purpose, then so be it."

Madame Fournet's sharp features softened. "This sister, she is beloved of you, *non?*"

"Yes," Mary said. "I would do anything for her. Anything at all."

Her quiet voice trembled with emotion, and she lifted her gaze to Adam. The proud determination there made him feel tainted by deceit. Yet he forced himself to return her stare with cool directness. It would not do for her to guess again at his own hidden purpose. By the time she realized the truth, and her trust died beneath the shock of understanding, it would be too late for her to save Josephine Sheppard from the gallows.

"Time grows short," he said. "Veil yourself for the carriage ride."

Mary looked appealingly at Madame Fournet. "Surely there is nothing more that you can do for me."

"Un moment, s'il vous plaît." The abigail dipped a curtsy to the duke. "Only permit me another moment with the curling wand. My artistry was interrupted by this . . . this *diable.*"

Obediah shook his fist. "Stop yer gabblin'. We Brits won the war and we're still cursed by ya bloody frog-eaters."

As madame puffed out her flat chest, Adam gestured to

Obediah. "Go on downstairs. I should like a word with you."

Grumbling, the old retainer stomped away, his peg leg thumping on the wood floor.

"Five minutes and we shall depart," Adam told Mary, then followed Obediah down the stairs.

In the entrance hall, the dog wagged its stubby tail hopefully. But Adam had too much on his mind to bother with one of Josephine Sheppard's strays.

Except for the human variety.

He motioned the footman into the drawing room and closed the doors. Gloom shrouded the furniture, and the lonely ticking of a table clock marked the passing seconds. It reminded Adam of how little time he might have to catch his quarry.

Obediah drew back the draperies to let in the meager light. "There ye go, Yer Grace. Though if yer plannin' t' give me a scold about that slut-maker upstairs—"

"I have a question to pose to you. About the other servants employed by Josephine Sheppard."

"Ye mean that fat slug of a cook? I told the Runners she an' the tweeny an' housemaid ran off like scared rabbits. They was afraid the law might pin the blame on one of 'em."

"According to Mary Sheppard, they were sacked. By you. Right after my brother was shot."

Obediah's hand froze on the curtain. The weak light glimmered over his red-veined face, the bulbous nose. Silence stretched out in the dusty air.

"Well?" Adam prompted. "Did you say as much to her?"

The servant gave a rusty laugh. "Ye caught me flat out, Yer Grace. I was only meanin' to spare the tender-hearted lass from knowin' the truth. What would she think, the staff bein' so disloyal to her sister, not standin' fast and waitin' fer her return?" He shook his grizzled head. " 'Twas best fer Miss Mary to think they was lazy good-fer-nothin's who deserved the boot."

"And you have no further knowledge of where the women went?"

"Scuttled off to the rookeries, mark my words," Obediah said darkly. "The Runners'll be lucky t' find 'em in all those broken down tenements."

Adam watched him keenly. "Quite so."

The footman glowered back. "Long as we're askin' questions, Yer Grace, I got one fer ye, too. Miss Mary won't tell me yer plan, only that she's t' pose as her sister. What are yer intentions with her?"

I'd like to ravish her.

"It is no concern of yours."

" 'Tis every concern. Not havin' family meself, Miss Josephine and Miss Mary are like me own daughters. I won't abide any harm comin' t' either of 'em."

Interesting, Adam thought. Would the man lie to protect Josephine?

He paced toward Obediah. "Do you think Josephine shot my brother?"

Obediah shifted his gaze, but only for the barest moment. "I was downstairs in the kitchen, dozin' by the fire. I never heard a sound that night."

"I'm not asking for facts. Only for your opinion."

"She couldn't've hurt a fly, then. Not a durned fly."

He sounded vehement. Too vehement.

Adam noted how the servant averted his face and stumped to the desk to light a candle with flint and steel. He had the distinct impression the old man knew more than he would admit.

Hearing the patter of footsteps on the stairs, Adam set aside his questions for the moment. Cold resolution flowed through his veins. It was time to escort Mary Sheppard to his town house.

❧ Chapter 8 ❧

An aura of cozy intimacy glowed in the drawing room at Adam Brentwell's town house. A fire hissed on the hearth. Here and there, golden pools of candlelight nestled in the veiling of charcoal shadows. On a side table near the blue-striped chaise, decanters of wine glowed like fat rubies.

It was a scene set for seduction. Not, Mary thought, that she wanted to be seduced.

Pressing her damp palms together, she paced from the tall secretaire at one end of the room to the windows at the other. She parted the velvet draperies to peek outside. The flickering sconces on either side of the front door barely illuminated the small yard with its clipped boxwoods marching in military precision along the wrought-iron fence. The row of discreetly elegant houses loomed against the night sky. The street was deserted.

But not for long. In a few minutes the first of Jo's spurned suitors would arrive.

Mary's stomach felt even more jittery than it did on singing nights. *Sweet Jesus, save her.*

She couldn't act the coquette. She knew nothing of beguiling a man. Especially not a parade of sophisticated lords.

"Nervous, Miss Sheppard?"

Sweet Jesus, please save her.

Her heart dancing, she whirled around. His Grace of St.

Chaldon stood in the doorway. His chiseled features held that look. His customary remote expression had been replaced by one of keen interest. His eyes were the deep, dissolute blue she had noticed when he had first beheld her disguise in her sister's bedroom. It was as if he found her . . . beautiful.

Pleasure burned like a flame inside her, igniting an uneasy mix of guilt and shame. She should loathe him instead of hoarding the crumbs of his admiration. A libertine nobleman was far less worthy of her notice than Victor, whose purity of soul kept him from regarding her in so bold a manner.

But she was no longer certain that the duke was entirely corrupt. He did, after all, donate money to charity. He had given Mrs. Primrose a post in his own household. And he had touched his brother's cheek with unmistakable affection. Besides, without Adam's help, she might never rescue Jo. That alone softened Mary's heart to him.

Feeling shy under his scrutiny, she resisted the urge to fold her arms over her half-exposed bosom. "Of course I'm nervous. Any woman would be at the prospect of facing all those strange men."

His mouth twisted into a grimace as if the notion displeased him, too. He closed the double doors behind him, then walked to her and settled his big, warm hands on her cold shoulders. Awareness of his touch tingled down to her breasts. And lower.

"You need pretend to be Josephine in front of only one man at a time," he said. "I've sent a message to each of the five suspects, requesting an audience. They're scheduled to arrive at thirty-minute intervals. That should give us ample time to interview each one."

"And I'm to identify her abductor from his reaction."

"Precisely. If we're lucky, he will demand to know how you escaped him."

"What if he's cunning? What if he senses a trick and pretends ignorance?"

"Then say what we rehearsed."

"What if I can't tell if he's lying?"

"I'll know. Remember, I'll be listening from behind the screen in the corner of the room."

"And if he sees through my disguise?"

"Then let me deal with him."

Mary shuddered at his grim tone. She hadn't let herself think about the threat of danger, that she might be facing a desperate man. The villain who had left Lord Cyril for dead. The knave who now held her sister hostage.

The duke cupped her jaw in the palm of his hand. "Chin up, now," he murmured. "No harm shall befall you. Just behave as I've taught you, and you've nothing to fear." He looked her up and down. "You're lovely and nubile enough to charm any man."

Blessed heaven, that smile. It transformed his features from intimidating and haughty to handsome and roguish. Somehow, he was no longer the domineering duke. He was a man. A man who viewed her as a beautiful woman.

His hands tightened infinitesimally on her. His smile faded into that Look again. The look of concentrated awareness that crept past her defenses and roused a wanton yearning in her.

For all that she knew it was wrong, secretly she was proud that she attracted him. Mary had never thought of herself as possessing a nubile form; she had never even seen herself naked. She had bathed by running a wet cloth beneath her shift. She had bound her hair in a tightly braided coronet. She had swathed herself in shapeless gowns buttoned to the throat.

Until now.

These past few days in London had been replete with sinful luxury, a luxury in which Mary reveled: the caress of fine fabrics against her skin, the taste of rich desserts, the softness of a feather bed, the delight of living in a real house with rooms so large she could twirl with her arms outstretched and never once send a book or a plate crashing to the floor.

Even more wicked and wonderful was the duke himself. Except for his white cravat and shirt, he wore stark black, and the dark beauty of him dazzled her senses. She found herself longing for his kiss again, a ridiculous fancy considering the unbreachable wall between them.

His thumb caressed the sensitive corner of her mouth. "Mary, I'm sorry."

Caught in the swirl of strange new feelings, she blinked at him. "Pardon?"

"I'm sorry you've been forced into this deception. If things don't turn out as you hope . . ." He looked as if he wanted to tell her more. But his lips compressed into a thin line.

She felt another treacherous melting in the region of her heart. Touching his arm, she found his muscles taut. "You mustn't blame yourself. Without your help, I wouldn't have known who had courted Jo. I couldn't have executed this clever plan to identify the culprit." Mary took a deep breath to ward off her misgivings. "Your Grace, even if we don't find the kidnapper tonight, I owe you so very much."

His scowl deepened, as if she had displeased him again. Before she could ask why, a faint clopping sounded in the distance.

They sprang apart. Feeling warm and flustered, Mary retreated to the draperies and peered outside. At the corner, a single gaslight shone on the cobblestones, and a carriage headed down the darkened street. A pair of prancing horses drew the black boxy vehicle to a halt in front of Adam's house.

Releasing the curtain, she was seized by a shiver of panic. The time was nigh. In a moment, she would have to play her role. She folded her hands and breathed a prayer, beseeching the Almighty for courage. And for the good fortune to find her beloved sister.

The duke cleared his throat. When she opened her eyes,

he was again the glacial nobleman, his face an impenetrable mask.

"Our first visitor is Viscount Bellford. His given name is James. Stand by the fireplace so he sees you immediately. Be quick now. There's no time to waste."

Mary hurried into position and snatched up her fan. Her legs felt wooden; her lungs strained for air. The snapping of the fire faded before the roaring in her ears. All of her strength seemed to trickle away.

The duke disappeared behind a filigreed ivory screen in a shadowed corner of the drawing room. Exotic carvings of foreign gods and writhing serpents decorated the tall panels. Mary longed to be the one in hiding. But there was no backing out now.

A discreet rapping made her jump. Just in time, she spread her fan to conceal her scandalous bodice. The door to the drawing room opened and Rayburn stepped inside.

The dour-faced butler bowed to her. "His Grace's guest has arrived."

"Send him in."

The words squeaked out of her. Immediately she chastised herself. She mustn't behave like a timid mouse. She must assume her sister's persona. She must act animated and merry and brave. She must charm his lordship into revealing what he knew of Jo's disappearance.

The servant vanished. A moment later, a man ambled into the room. Viscount Bellford had a florid face and a ridiculously elaborate cravat that ill suited his portly physique. His head shone as pink and bald as a pig's. Gold buttons marched down the front of his bright green frock coat. His legs were squashed into pea green pantaloons, white tights, and gold-buckled shoes.

He squinted at Mary. "I say, it cannot be . . . Why, is that you, Miss Josephine?"

Astonishment creased his ruddy features and he stopped dead in his tracks. Mary tensed, scrutinizing him for any sign of anger or alarm. There was none that she could see, only the blankness of bewilderment.

Disappointment stabbed her. Identifying Jo's abductor would not be simple.

Mary curtsied. "What a pleasure to see you, m'lord."

Leaning on his gold-topped cane, the viscount stepped closer. "What, pray, are *you* doing here? Where is the duke? He sent an urgent message begging me to wait on him at this very hour."

She moistened her lips. If Bellford were playacting, could she lead him on and draw out the truth?

"His Grace had to step out for a few moments," she said, hoping her voice sounded sultry. Lowering the fan, she teased him with a view of her breasts. When his eyes goggled, she sat on the chaise and patted the cushion beside her. "Come, sit with me. We have much to say to each other."

His gaze roved hungrily over her dress. He had that look in his dark, piggy eyes. But coming from Bellford, it repulsed her.

He remained standing, his face wary. "You, my fine game hen, are wanted for attempted murder. The Runners have been searching the length and breadth of London for you."

"As you can see, they have not been clever enough to find me."

"Damme! You are hiding out here? On St. Chaldon's approval? You shot his brother, by Jove."

"That was a terrible misunderstanding—"

"It was a scandal, an outrage!" The viscount paced back and forth, the gold tip of his cane tapping on the rug. "How shocking, a female wielding a pistol on a man of Lord Cyril's rank. To what depths has this great nation sunk?"

Was his demeanor a pretense? Because he scented a trap? Mary had the dismal suspicion that his bafflement was genuine. Yet she had to be certain.

118   **Barbara Dawson Smith**

She rose from the chaise and glided toward him, swaying her hips as Adam had taught her. "I am an unusual woman, you must allow."

He licked his lips and stared greedily at her. "More so than I ever thought."

"We both know that you want me." She winked at him as if to share a private jest. "Enough to abduct me and have me all to yourself."

Bellford recoiled. The lust vanished from his expression. "Abduct? Good God, woman! Do you think to cozen me into becoming your accomplice in crime?" He backed toward the door. "I am a gentleman!"

Mary matched him, step for step. "Come now, you needn't hide the truth. You captured me, and I pretended to fight you. It's such a delicious game."

"I don't know what you are babbling about."

"I think you do."

"P-please, Miss Josephine." He pulled out a handkerchief and mopped his brow. "Why are you interested in me of a sudden? You spurned my honorable offer to take care of you. You allowed me only one dance at the Cyprian's Ball. You even sent all my expensive posies to some ragtag hospital for the poor. You surely cannot have changed your mind."

She tapped him on the arm with her fan. "Enough of this sport. I wish for you to take me back to our love nest."

"Our . . . what?"

With a thump, the viscount backed into the wall beside the door. He stood there with his arms splayed, looking like a plump green butterfly pinned to a corkboard. He was staring at her as if she were a madwoman.

She terrified him. She could see it in his eyes. At any moment he feared she might whip out a pistol and shoot him stone-cold dead.

Viscount Bellford was telling the truth. He knew nothing of Jo's abduction.

She forced a smile. "I confess, I was teasing you, m'lord.

It was a lark, nothing more. You had best be off now. Else the duke might think you were trifling with me."

"Quite so, Miss Josephine. Whatever you say." Cane in hand, Bellford edged toward the doorway.

"One more thing, m'lord."

"Yes?"

She almost laughed at how quickly he froze. "I must ask that you not breathe a word of my presence here, not to anyone." Pointing her finger at him, she imitated her father at his most thundering magnificence. "Remember, I have no patience with treachery."

"M-my lips are sealed. Locked tight as a bank vault." Raising his plump hand to his mouth, he mimicked the turning of a key. "If you don't mind, I'll just slip on home now. Give my regards to the duke."

With that, he dashed out into the entrance hall, his shoes rat-a-tatting on the marble floor. Then the door slammed. In the ensuing silence, the clapping of hands startled her. She swung around to see the intimidating figure of the duke emerge from behind the screen. She had been so caught up in her role that she had forgotten he was watching.

"Excellent," he said. "A performance worthy of a Covent Garden actress."

Mary looked at him uncertainly. "But it was to no avail."

"Certainly it was. We can cross poor Bellford's name off our list."

Shivering from the aftermath of tension, she rubbed her bare arms. "Thank heavens Jo had the sense to refuse that lout. Imagine, he actually fancied his offer to her an honorable one."

"You cannot have expected him to propose marriage."

"Your brother did."

The duke gave her a long, narrowed inspection. "Cyril often acts without thinking. However, that is neither here nor there. We have other, more important concerns tonight."

Still feeling edgy, Mary took umbrage at his sidestepping the issue. She walked toward him and poked him in the chest with her folded fan. "As head of the Brentwell family, *you* should be the one to whom the obligations fall. Why haven't *you* married?"

He stood straight and tall, his hands clasped behind his back and his eyes chilly. "If you must know, I intend to remedy the situation very soon."

Was he betrothed, then? Deep inside, Mary felt a stirring oddly akin to loneliness, as if a light had winked out in her soul. What should his plans matter to her? They were not friends, only allies in the campaign to rescue Jo.

"Your Grace, I'm certain you've chosen a lady who is perfectly suited to your exacting standards. I wish joy to you and your noble bride."

Adam stared at her with something rather like regret. "And shall I wish the same to you?"

The affirmation stuck in her throat. He didn't know about the appalling wrong she'd done her sister. He couldn't fathom the guilt she'd felt at accepting Victor's proposal of marriage.

"I hear another carriage," the duke said, his head cocked to the side. He consulted his silver pocketwatch. "It seems our next quarry is six minutes early."

He snapped the timepiece shut. Mary caught her breath, anxiety returning with full force. Dear God. What if this second man were the one?

But the Honorable Simon Wiggins took only cursory notice of her when he strutted into the drawing room a few moments later. His curling blond tresses had been artfully arranged around a face of classic perfection. As he minced past a wall mirror he struck a pose, his manly chest thrust out, his square jaw raised, a shapely leg in skintight pantaloons turned to its best advantage.

He was so enraptured by his own handsomeness that Mary knew straightaway he was incapable of sullying his white kid gloves with an act of violence. After a few probing questions, she extracted his vow to keep silent about her and dismissed him.

The third would-be suitor was Sir Barney Guinness, a rich coal merchant who had purchased a baronetcy and thought he could buy whatsoever he wished, Josephine Sheppard included. A flicker of his heavy eyelids showed his surprise; then a crafty look came over his broad face and he proposed to bribe the Bow Street Runners. He would spirit her to his manor in Northumberland, where she would enjoy every manner of luxury, provided she agree to be locked up with no access to weaponry. She was, after all, a notorious murderess.

When he attempted to slip a gold guinea into her bodice, Mary slapped away his hand and sent him packing.

The fourth suspect arrived on foot. Clad in a shabby suit with frayed cuffs, Lord Jeremy Enderlyn gave a dramatic start upon seeing Mary. Snatching up her hand and clutching it to his sunken chest, he fell to his knees and launched into a flowery ode to Josephine's beauty.

When Mary suggested he might have come to court her on the night of the shooting, he turned into a watering pot. He cried that he had suffered her rejection many weeks ago. Didn't she know he had spent every moment since then pining in his garret, composing reams of poetry to her? Would she now be content to await his inheritance from his pinchpenny grandmother, and to accept his courtship?

He was so pathetically eager for her affection that Mary couldn't help but concede his innocence. She doubted even a kidnapper could have faked those tears.

She held out a desperate hope for the last man on the list. After making her wait for a quarter hour, the earl of Peterbourne strolled in, fashionably late and unfashionably dressed.

Rigged out in green satin, he wore a powdered periwig some four decades out of style. The wrinkles on his face marked him as old enough to be her grandfather. But his strong, craggy features hinted that he had once been extraordinarily handsome.

He stopped a few feet from Mary and fumbled for his quizzing glass. He tilted his head to scrutinize her, and strangely, it looked like a listening pose. None of the other men had noticed the positioning of the tiny mole near her mouth, the one difference between the twins. Would he?

Dear God, don't let the earl see through my disguise. Let him believe that I am Jo.

Laughter burst from Peterbourne. "Eh, what's this? Josephine Sheppard? Have you come to murder St. Chaldon, too?"

Relief eddied through Mary. "Were that the case, I hardly think Rayburn would have let me in here."

"You're chasing St. Chaldon, then. Couldn't wait for his brother to be buried." The earl sauntered closer, one pale greenish eye magnified by the glass. "Or maybe you've been the duke's lover all along, eh? A wench after my own heart."

"The duke is not my lover." Mary fought to keep her anger under control. How dare he assume her sister behaved in so shameless a manner. It made Mary all the more determined to find out if he was the one. "You of all men should know where I've been these past few days."

A smile touched his sensual mouth. "The devil you say. I don't care what you've done or where you've been. So long as you give me a bite, my juicy little tart."

Dodging his outstretched hands, she went to the side table. "May I offer you a drink, m'lord?"

"Port, and don't stint. Bring it here and bide awhile with me. Quite a lot's happened since last we met, eh?"

He seated himself on the chaise, and Mary fancied she could hear his bones creaking. She took her time pouring the wine into a crystal glass, and wished she dared to take a drink herself. Something about this earl stirred uneasiness in her, something more than his crude manner. He looked vaguely familiar to her.

But that was impossible. Surely she would have remembered encountering such a lewd man.

She delivered the goblet to Peterbourne. His papery skin brushed against her fingers, and she jerked back from a jolt of energy. Revulsion burst like a rotten fruit inside her. With it came the half-formed impression of darkness.

Dear God. Jo?

Mary closed her eyes in an effort to probe the feeling before it slipped away. But she was too late. The sentiment vanished in a twinkling, leaving her with a queasy sensation in her belly. She concentrated her mind in a desperate search for the passage to light that led to her sister.

Jo. Jo! Are you listening? Help me know the truth. Did Peterbourne kidnap you? Is he the one? Please, please, you must answer me. . . .

Peering through the network of tiny holes carved in the ivory screen, Adam bit back a curse. Mary had been playing her role with a finesse beyond his highest expectations. She had changed herself so skillfully that had he not known better, he would have sworn she was a seasoned ladybird.

He had saved his prime suspect for last. Peterbourne was an indifferent huntsman who might well botch a shot at close range. Lacking any scruples, he was addicted to bedsport. He had a taste for whores, the younger the better. Most of all, he possessed a title and wealth far beyond Cyril's means. Yes, Peterbourne would be a ripe plum for a schemer like Josephine Sheppard.

But now Mary was about to ruin all Adam's plans. Limned by golden candlelight, she was standing as if in a trance, her eyes shut, her hands clasped together, her perfect body swaying sinuously as if to an inner chant. Christ. Now was no time for her to stop and pray. Acting the saint was sure to make the rascally earl suspicious.

But Peterbourne was scowling down at his trousers. Wine dripped from his fingers and made a dark splotch on his green breeches. "Clumsy chit! You spilled port all over me."

Mary blinked, awareness dawning on her face. "Merciful heavens." She snatched up a lace doily from the silver tray and dabbed at the stain.

"A mite higher there, my Lady Minx." Peterbourne closed his skeletal fingers around her wrist and jerked her down beside him on the chaise. With an agility that belied his advanced age, he drew her hand toward his crotch. "Now there's the way to win my good graces—a nice massage for Tall Dick."

A pulse hammered at Adam's temple. His muscles tensed with the effort of holding himself back. In all his planning for tonight, he had not foreseen this powerful urge to grind his fist into that libertine's belly.

Her cheeks flaming, Mary snatched her hand back and scooted away. "M'lord! Behave yourself."

Peterbourne gave a croak of mirth. "You always were a playful one, leading me on a merry chase. We make good partners, you and me."

Partners. Adam narrowed his gaze at the earl. Had Josephine run off with him? Had the aging rake been jealous of the younger Cyril, and aided her in hatching the murder plot?

Mary spread her fan so that Adam could see only those come-hither eyes and the glimpse of shadowy cleavage. The sight put him in the same predicament as Peterbourne. It was his own fault for transforming her from a psalm-singing spinster to a skilled seductress.

"So," she purred. "You abduct me and then I escape you. Have I done my part well thus far?"

Peterbourne sidled closer, so that their knees touched. "No more games, my sweet nymph. Allow me a taste of your succulent flesh."

She used the fan to swat his grasping hands away. "Have a care, the duke could walk in. When he's angered, he can be quite the ogre."

"Bah, there's enough of you to share. Besides, St. Chaldon invited me here. Perchance he means to join our game."

At first she blinked in innocent puzzlement; then shocked understanding brought a blush to her face. "How clever of you to include His Grace. Shall I summon him? Then you can escort the both of us to our secret love nest."

Bravo, Adam thought. If they could gain entrée to the earl's private quarters, Adam might have Josephine Sheppard in his custody at last. He resisted considering the terrible look of betrayal that would wipe the innocence from Mary's face.

"You've made me too randy to walk," Peterbourne said with a leer. "I'll have a go at you first. Right here and now."

He lunged and she recoiled. "I don't think—"

"Won't do for a pretty piece like you to think. Just lie back and spread your legs. There's a good girl."

"Please, m'lord! Let me up!"

Peterbourne pressed his squirmy captive against the back of the chaise. Every muscle in Adam's body went rigid. How dare that old goat lay a hand on Mary. He would pay for this.

"I've a new game," Peterbourne said. "You play the wild mare, and I'll be the stallion. Lift your tail for me now."

As he tossed up his head and loosed an excited whinny, she wrested her arm free. Her open palm connected with his cheek. The smack resounded through the drawing room.

Peterbourne reared back, his hand to his square-jawed face and his wig askew. "Bitch!" Then his voice lowered to a raspy growl. "Have a care how you treat me, girl. We're not who we seem to be, are we?"

Adam absorbed the puzzling remark through a red haze of fury. The lecher pinned Mary to the cushions, his hands stroking over the mounds of her breasts. Adam could tell she was trying to ease away without rousing the earl's suspicions. Her struggle filled him with intolerable tension. Bloody hell. Bloody *hell.* How could he have pitted a vulnerable girl against that walking phallus?

Exerting tremendous restraint, he forced himself to stay behind the screen. He must not ruin the charade, not when he was so close to victory. He must not squander this chance to avenge his brother. He must not. . . .

The sound of ripping fabric rent the air. Mary gave a keening cry of distress that pierced the armor of Adam's control.

He exploded out from behind the screen. Four long strides took him to the chaise. He snatched the earl by the back of his green satin coat and dumped him onto the floor.

Uttering a howl of pain, Peterbourne landed on his bony bum. His wig flew off, revealing a shining bald pate. His legs were splayed like the skinny limbs of a rooster. His watery green eyes squinted up at Adam.

"St. Chaldon," he acknowledged with a terse nod as if he were enthroned at court instead of lying in an inglorious heap. He groped for his wig and jammed it onto his head. "Didn't mean to exclude you. Be delighted to share in a *ménage à trois.*"

He was a tough old bird, Adam had to concede that. "I don't engage in forced ravishment."

"She wants it, my little hobbyhorse." The earl jerked his head toward the chaise. "Take a look. Isn't she a prize filly?"

Mary sat huddled on the cushions, her eyes wide with shock, her tousled red-gold curls tumbling to lily-pure shoulders. Her arms were crossed over her gaping bodice, and the sheer silk shift had been torn so that Adam could see the fullness of her uncorseted breasts. Yet she embodied the innocence of an angel.

"See?" Peterbourne said with a laugh. "She ain't protesting. Just playing another of her teasing games—"

Adam grasped the earl by his padded shoulders and

hauled him to his feet. Through gritted teeth he said, "You'll speak of Miss Sheppard with respect."

"Poppycock. She's only a chippy— Oww!"

Adam's fingers fisted in the satin lapels of the earl's coat, so that he dangled in the air. An odor of decay emanated from him. "Obviously you need a lesson in manners. You may begin by apologizing."

"Didn't mean to poach. Forgive me."

"Not to me, you dolt. To her."

"Don't be absurd. Let me down."

"Beg the lady's pardon first."

"That one's no lady—"

Adam tightened his hold until a purplish hue colored the earl's once-handsome face. "Do it."

Peterbourne gasped for air. His crabby hands clawed at his throat. His eyes bulged with fear. Then abruptly he went limp. "S-sorry . . . Miss," he choked out. "St. . . . Chaldon . . . turn . . . me . . . loose."

"With pleasure."

His anger unsatisfied, Adam carried his prey across the drawing room. He shouldered open the double doors, marched past an astonished Rayburn who recovered himself in time to swing open the front portal, and deposited the earl in the wet loam of the garden.

"A pity there isn't a sewer handy," Adam said. "I suggest you depart while I'm still feeling merciful."

Peterbourne released a raspy groan. He stood up, stooped as if in pain, clods of mud decorating his breeches. With one darkly furious glance at Adam, he scuttled down the front walk and a footman helped him into the waiting carriage. It was only as the vehicle was disappearing around the corner that Adam uttered a low, savage curse.

Caught up in his intent to punish Mary's assailant, he had completely forgotten about Josephine Sheppard.

❦ Chapter 9 ❧

W hen Adam returned to the drawing room, he stopped just inside the doorway.

Mary no longer cowered on the chaise. A wealth of bright curls drifted down her slender back as she stood before the row of crystal decanters. The candle glow gilded her exquisite profile, and the sheer gown revealed far too much of her delectable figure. But that was not what caught him off guard.

With one hand, she clutched together the torn edges of her bodice. With the other, she held to her lips a goblet brimming with wine.

Her slim white throat worked as she gulped the wine. Adam stared in fascination. He had never seen a woman drink as swiftly as she did. Then again, no lady of his acquaintance had had to endure what Mary had endured. If she needed to drown her sorrows, he could only blame himself.

She grimaced suddenly, and a fit of coughing seized her.

He strode forward and touched her warm shoulder. "Such a choice vintage is meant to be savored."

Gasping, she jerked herself away from him. Holding the goblet to her bosom, she retreated to the marble mantelpiece. Her deep green eyes glinted with wary bravado. "Must you creep up on me?"

A quaver took the edge off her sharp tone. Despite the

ruined gown, she looked less like a lightskirt than a virginal girl.

No, not a girl. She was a woman. All woman.

He disciplined his baser instincts. He had already hurt Mary in his lust for vengeance. The last thing she needed was another man ogling her body.

"I'm sorry," he murmured. "More than you can imagine."

Taking care not to frighten her, Adam removed his coat and draped it around her shoulders. She flinched again, though she did not refuse his offering and drew the coat together. With her skin pale against the dark fabric and the overlarge garment hanging halfway to her knees, she looked like a little lost waif.

She lifted the glass and drained the last few drops. "I need more wine." Making a wide berth around him, she returned to the side table with its array of bottles.

As she reached for a decanter, he wrapped his fingers around its crystal neck. "I've a suspicion you've never imbibed spirits before."

"My father says drink is the tool of Satan. But what can one more sin matter?"

Adam frowned. "Sin?"

"I played the temptress tonight. 'All wickedness is but little to the wickedness of a woman.' " Hiccoughing, she put her hand to her mouth and lowered her gaze. "Papa made me memorize that passage."

"Bloody h—" Adam bit off the curse. "You're the most virtuous woman I know."

"Not always," she whispered.

Her slim fingers rested beside her parted lips. She looked up at him from beneath the fringe of her lashes. In any other female, the pose would have been coy. But Mary exuded a genuine shyness, as if she feared he would think ill of her.

If only she knew. He yearned to hold her in his arms, to

let his tenderness atone for Peterbourne's rough treatment of her.

Adam set her goblet on the table and motioned her to the chaise. "Sit down, please."

She sat, huddling in his coat, her teeth worrying her lower lip. "I'd really like more wine—"

"Not yet. We need to talk." He deliberately seated himself at the other end of the chaise. "First of all, women are no more inherently wicked than men."

"Hah. Dressed this way, I'm like Eve holding out the forbidden fruit."

"For pity's sake, don't don your hair shirt. Peterbourne is a worthless, foul-mouthed lecher. You didn't invite him to assault you." Resting his arm on the back of the chaise, Adam leaned toward her. "What happened was in no way your fault."

Mary ached to believe him. Papa always said that a woman who behaved like a wanton brought destruction upon herself. And with the earl's smelly breath on her face and his nimble fingers groping her bosom, she had remembered those prophetic words.

Shuddering, she drew the coat more securely around herself. It carried a hint of spice, the comforting scent of Adam. "You don't . . . despise me?"

"On the contrary, I admire you. You were wonderful tonight, brave and brilliant. And beautiful."

His husky tone raised the fine hairs on the back of her neck. His gaze flitted to her lips. Or perhaps it was only her imagination, the effect of the wine. Already she felt a pleasant giddiness inside her head. The rigidity within her mellowed, the guilt and shame sloughing off like shed skin.

"I'm not brave," she murmured. "I was quaking inside the entire evening."

"Any woman in her right mind would have felt the same," the duke said. "If you wish to cast stones, then do so at me. It's my fault for sanctioning the masquerade. It was my plan, my folly."

His vehemence somehow delighted her. "Now who's wearing the hair shirt?"

His stern look endured a moment. Then he laughed. It brought a brightness to his face, a lightening of the dark mystery that too often masked his true feelings from her.

Mary knew she was staring, but couldn't help herself. He looked so magnificently ordinary, sitting there in his shirt and waistcoat, his arm stretched across the back of the chaise, and his booted legs crossed.

Not ordinary. Her befuddled brain searched for the right description. Friendly? Agreeable? Undukely?

"Human," she muttered.

"I beg your pardon?"

She had not known it was possible to blush so hotly. But this one set fire to her face. "Nothing. I was thinking aloud, that's all."

"Well, then." He cocked a black eyebrow. "I don't suppose we should sit here all night trading the blame back and forth."

"You're right," she said, seizing on the distraction. "We should plan our next move."

He gave her a long, assessing look. "I've already taken care of that. I've dispatched Rayburn to watch Peterbourne's house."

"The butler?"

"Yes. If Peterbourne tries to spirit Josephine away, my man will stop him." The duke stood up and prowled the drawing room. "Though to be honest, I rather doubt that Peterbourne has her in his custody. He acted too blasé about your presence here."

Mary thought so, too. Yet what of that keen impression of darkness? Had she sensed his corruption?

His cryptic words dripped like cold raindrops in her memory.

Have a care how you treat me, girl. We're not who we seem to be, are we?

"You're not who you seem to be," Adam said. "Could he know that Josephine has a twin?"

How peculiar, Mary thought. No one but Jo had ever been able to read her thoughts. She sensed a warm connection between her and Adam, not the link she had with her sister's mind, but a bond nonetheless.

And when had she started thinking of the duke by his Christian name?

He watched her quizzically, and she realized she must be staring. "Perhaps Jo mentioned me to him. Perhaps she told him about this." Mary touched the tiny bump of her mole. "Though I can't imagine why she would."

"Hmm. It bears further investigation. And not by you. I should never have let Peterbourne within a mile of you."

The duke wore that scowl again, as if he could not bear the thought of another man touching her. But of course, he was a gentleman. His code of honor required him to protect all women.

Nonetheless, pleasure glowed within her. The wine muddled her thinking, but it was an agreeable state in which her worries floated like a distant dark cloud. The awful stain of violation had vanished, too. She could feel herself smiling, and she didn't know why she should when the charade had failed.

"No wonder people drink spirits to escape their troubles," she mused.

Adam looked up from his contemplation of the hearth. "The answer is no."

"No?"

"No more wine or you'll have the very devil of a headache come morning."

"It's *my* head." On that childish protest, she lowered her chin to the fine fabric of her coat.

Not hers. His. Just moments ago, the garment had clasped his upper body. Wearing it now felt deliciously sinful, like a stolen embrace.

"Mary?" He went down on one knee before her as if he

were about to make a declaration of the heart. The thought enraptured her for a moment . . . the almighty duke of St. Chaldon falling madly, passionately, irresistibly in love with a commoner.

"Are you all right?" he asked. "You look lost in a dream."

She was. But he mustn't know the dream was of him.

He knelt so close she could feel the heat of him. Warmth nestled deep in her bosom. Unlike Victor, Adam had an aggressive quality to his handsomeness. His black hair and swarthy skin gave him a pagan aura. He exuded an earthy vitality, the strength of an oak in its prime.

Struck by an unusual boldness, she touched a pale line on his jaw. "Where did you get this scar?"

Adam went very still. "I was chasing after Cyril, and tripped on a tree root. It happened long ago." He cocked his head and peered intently at her. "You're smiling. May I ask why?"

"Mmmm."

She mustn't admit that the feel of his stubbled jaw enthralled her. Or that she could be content to gaze at him for an eternity. He had that Look in his eyes again. Oh, those eyes. The diamond-starred blue pulled her like a tunnel of light, calling to her, drawing her away into another world. . . .

She could feel him staring at her from across the crowded theater, though he sat in the shadows of his private box. The glitter of those blue eyes raised a chill on her skin. Why did he always watch her so? He must surely know by now that she would never forsake Cyril.

If only Mary were here to advise her. Solemn, levelheaded, sensible Mary. . . .

Mary came back to herself with a gasp. Her hands felt for the leather arms of the theater chair and met the silk of the chaise instead. Her heart pounded and goosebumps prickled on her cold skin. She blinked to stop the room from revolving.

The candlelight created a golden island in the gloom of the drawing room. Adam's drawing room. She took his hand into a tight grip. She needed him. He was her lifeline in a storm-tossed sea. "Dear God. It happened again. I was *Jo.*"

He frowned. "Of course you pretended to be your sister tonight. But that's over, and it's high time I took you home."

"No! Please. You must listen." The concern on his face suddenly inspired Mary to share her remarkable secret. "Let me explain. I can see into Jo's mind. I can see things that happen to her. I can hear her call to me. And ever since I came to London, I've even sensed some of her memories."

The duke raised an eyebrow. "The wine has affected you more than I'd thought."

"Wait," she said, holding onto his hands to stop him from rising. "It's *true.* It has something to do with our being twins. As far back as I can remember, I could sense when Jo was in trouble. She knew the same about me. Once, a pack of dogs cornered me in the woods. She came running half a mile and beat them off with a stick. Then another time—"

"Allow me to clarify," Adam broke in. "You believe that you can see what your sister is doing even when she is in another place."

"Yes. But Jo is more skilled at it than I." The reason why weighed on Mary's conscience like a millstone. Not even her father knew the whole of it. She lowered her eyes and prayed to be forgiven the half truth. "I closed my mind to her . . . when she ran off to London. Papa said I must cut her out of my life, lest I be tainted by her wickedness."

The devil is tempting you into a life of sin. Be strong, daughter. Resist the call of his darkness.

A lump clogged Mary's throat. More than her father's edict had provoked her rejection of her own sister. Every time she had sensed a communication from Jo, she would block it out by concentrating her mind on passages from the Scripture. The method soon had become second nature to her. But the guilt had never ceased to plague her.

Mary bowed her head, remembering the long nights she had lain awake in her tiny cubicle, her father snoring gently nearby. The black shadows on the ceiling of the caravan had reminded her of the stain on her soul. She had prayed as much to erase that blot as she had prayed for Jo's safety.

Adam extracted his hands. "If you can truly see your sister, then you should have led me straight to her. You could have spared yourself the trouble of the masquerade. And I would have been treated to a clever parlor trick."

His voice rang with mockery. Alert and aloof, he crouched on the rug and watched her as a warden might watch a madwoman.

Why had she thought he would believe her? Very few would. Yet even though it was farfetched, she'd hoped that he would be different.

She gathered his coat against her aching heart. "It isn't so simple. I can't control when the images come to me, or what they show me. I know only that Jo is terribly afraid."

Adam stood up, towering over her. "No one can see into someone else's mind. You mistake me for a lackwit." He pivoted on his heel. "I'll ring for my carriage."

"No!" Mary surged to her feet and lurched between him and the bell rope. To steady herself, she grasped at the marble mantelpiece. "How do you think I knew to come to London when I did? On the night your brother was shot, I *saw* Jo."

"In Sussex?"

"I don't mean she was actually there. It was like . . . like a waking dream. I was singing a hymn at a prayer meeting when Jo appeared at the back of the crowd. She ran toward me with her arms outstretched." Heedless of the rent in her bodice, Mary threw out her own arms. "She called out to me, begging me to save her."

Hands clasped behind his back, the duke paced in and

out of the shadows. "Are you quite certain you hadn't been sipping the communion wine?"

"Oh, you . . . you *lout.*" Mary yanked the edges of his coat together. "You're blind to anything that doesn't fit your narrow-minded view of the world."

"And I suppose your father approves of your delusions."

With effort, she swallowed her ire. "No, he doesn't. He calls it an evil curse. But at least he believes me."

Adam said nothing for a moment. She felt the searing force of his stare. "All right," he said, "convince me. Find Josephine."

"I can't," Mary whispered. "I've tried and tried, but I've received only one faint message. Yet I've glimpsed a few of her memories. Incidents in London when she called to me." *And I didn't answer,* Mary thought in anguish.

Adam resumed pacing. "Explain yourself."

"Once, I saw Jo wearing a green dress and her emerald necklace and walking up the steps to your mansion. I think . . . it must have been when Lord Cyril brought her to meet your family."

"Obediah could have told you what she was wearing that day."

"Another time I saw your brother lying on the floor. His head . . . was bleeding. And then . . ."

"Then?"

"A man sprang out at her from the darkness. She screamed, but he slapped a gag over her mouth."

Adam turned sharply toward Mary. "Describe him."

"I didn't—or rather—*she* didn't see him. But it proves she was kidnapped."

"It proves you were dreaming."

He was making her dizzy with the way he walked back and forth, back and forth. Mary drew a shaky breath. "Just a few minutes ago, I saw my sister at the theater. A man was watching her."

"What man?"

She lifted her shoulders in frustration. "I don't know.

Someone who wanted her to end her relationship with Lord Cyril. Perhaps because he wanted to court her himself." Mary curled her fingers into fists. "She was frightened of him, I think."

The duke's gaze burned into her. A tingling heat crept over her skin and burrowed deep inside her breast. With just one look, he could melt her like a snowflake on warm skin.

Warm skin. She wondered what it would be like to run her fingertips over his bare chest, to see if his flesh were hard or soft, rough or smooth. She wanted to let her hands explore him . . . lower. Even with her head spinning, Mary was shocked at herself. The wine must have put that unnatural thought in her mind.

"You saw nothing more of him?" Adam asked.

"Who?"

"The man at the theater," he said impatiently.

She focused her whirling senses. "The place was dark. He was seated in a private box. But he had blue eyes. I'm certain of it." Mary snapped her fingers. "None of the men who came here tonight had blue eyes. That means we missed the true kidnapper!"

"We had already determined as much."

His cool tone irked her. "Don't you understand? This is an important clue."

"Then I shall alert the Runners to arrest every blue-eyed gentleman in the realm. Myself included."

"You're jesting."

"Of course I'm jesting." He prowled toward her. "Surely you see the absurdity of the situation. I can hardly tell the magistrate that you divined this clue from a dream."

There was no convincing him. The realization struck Mary silent, and disappointment lodged like a stone in her belly. She had bared her soul to Adam, and still he scoffed at her.

He drew on the velvet bell rope. A footman materialized in the doorway to receive the duke's instructions. Then

Adam came toward Mary. "I'm taking you back to your sister's house. A good night's rest should put these fantasies out of your mind."

She crossed her arms. "I'm not sleepy."

He raised one black eyebrow in that infuriating way. "Mistress Mary, quite contrary. How does your mettle grow?"

He thought he was so clever, so superior. She fired back, "With noble swells and aging rakehells, and doubtful dukes all in a row."

That caused his other eyebrow to lift, too. With unholy satisfaction, she savored his surprise. Then he threw back his head and laughed for the second time that evening.

"I do believe I underestimated you at our first meeting. I thought you were merely a self-righteous radical."

"Well, I thought you an arrogant devil. And I still do."

"Touché." Taking her arm, he guided her out the door and into the gloomy foyer. "However, a quick wit is of little protection against men like Peterbourne. I was wrong to involve you in dangerous matters."

She was aware of his closeness, the yearning she felt in spite of herself. "It isn't your fault. I involved myself."

"So you did." Opening the door to a small cloakroom cleverly disguised in the paneling, he lifted her lilac satin spencer from a hook. "Nevertheless, things are about to change."

Mary watched in bemusement as he brought the garment to her. She slipped off his coat and saw his gaze linger on her bosom. A blush stung her cheeks. She clutched the coat to her ruined bodice. "Change . . . how?"

Without answering, he helped her into the spencer. The form-fitting garment ended just below her waist, but at least she could fasten the ivory buttons. She was halfway done when Adam made a startling move. He closed his big hands around her shoulders and began to massage them.

The sudden intimacy of his touch stunned Mary, and she went as stiff as a curling wand.

Until the divine pressure of his fingers soothed the tension from her muscles. A slow heat flared in the region of her stomach. She must remember that she was betrothed to another man. That it was wrong to feel this craving for the duke. It was wrong because . . . The reason evaporated from her mind. Somehow she found herself drifting backward against his chest. His broad, solid chest. She gave herself up to his scent, his warmth, the security of his body.

His breath stirred her hair. His coat slipped from her arm and landed in a crumpled heap on the marble floor. A secret hunger grew inside her. She wanted him to do things to her that she knew not how to name. If this awe-inspiring state was desire, no wonder so many women were lured into sin.

It seemed the most natural thing in the world to turn in his arms and lift her face to him. She sensed hesitation in him; then his lips came down on hers with a tenderness that made her feel like swooning. He kissed her long and deeply, holding her so close she touched every part of his body as if they were one. Yet she felt no fear, only a boundless need to stay in his arms forever.

Slipping his hand into the unbuttoned top of her spencer, he cradled her neck, and his thumb brushed the sensitive hollow of her throat. Her head swam as he slid his palm lower until it lay warm and heavy on her upper chest. She wanted him to touch her bosom. With astonishing intensity, she wanted him to replace the awful memory of defilement with a new and wondrous celebration of sensuality.

Abruptly he withdrew his hand and placed it at her waist. His lips brushed her temple, his breath heating her. "I didn't mean to do that."

She pressed her cheek to his lapel. "Yes, you did. I wanted you to. Oh, Adam, I've never felt this way before."

There was a prolonged silence in which she absorbed the

deep thudding of his heart. Again she sensed an inexplicable bond with him, as if she could see into the dark turmoil in his mind. He too must realize that their association could never go beyond a kiss. Yet she clung to him, unwilling to end the moment.

He lifted her chin. Through the shadows, his commanding features held a hint of mystery. "Do you trust me, Mary?"

She could gaze for hours into his intensely blue eyes. Odd, that she felt safe with a licentious nobleman in his house of sin. "Yes."

"Then I should like for you to do something for me. Something very important."

God have mercy. Did he want her to disrobe? Perhaps he was no different from the other wicked lords. And perhaps she was not so virtuous, either, for she felt the outrageous urge to do just that.

"I need your cooperation," he went on. "I shall arrange to have a coach fetch you come morning. Be packed and ready at dawn."

She blinked, sure she had misheard him. "But . . . where will I go?"

"Home. You shall return to your father in Sussex."

The announcement struck her like a sobering splash of ice water. "Return . . . ?"

"You'll be safe in the country. Your grievous experience tonight shan't be repeated. And meanwhile, I shall do everything in my power to track down the criminal."

Like velvet manacles, his fingers held her waist. She stood frozen, her hands braced on his forearms, his muscles hard and thick beneath the fine linen shirt. Even now, she felt a mortifying attraction to him. Even when he used his persuasive appeal to manipulate her. How naive she was in the ways of men.

"I'm staying in London," she said.

"Perhaps I have not made myself clear. Your leaving is

not a matter of choice. If it pleases you, I shall send you daily reports."

Mary wrenched herself from his embrace. "Pleases me? Since when have you cared to do what pleases me?"

He took a step toward her, his hands stretched out like a sculptor wanting to mold a piece of clay to his will. "Try to understand. I am only acting to benefit your welfare—"

"No, you're acting on your own behalf. For your own convenience." Her throat knotted with the urge to weep. "Since the masquerade failed, you have no further use for me."

"Mary," he said, his voice low and vibrating, "you showed a great deal of pluck tonight. More than any lady of my acquaintance would have done. But I cannot imperil you any longer."

That gently chiding tone almost undid her. Almost. "I won't cower in the country while my sister is at the mercy of a vicious scoundrel. Especially as I am the only person who can communicate with her."

"Ah, yes. The mystical mind link."

"Scoff if you like. Your opinion means nothing to me. And in case you've forgotten, I am a free woman. I am not bound to obey you or any other puffed-up lord."

Silence cloaked the shadowed foyer. Somewhere down the darkened passage a clock bonged the hour of midnight. Mary teetered between surprise at her own vehemence and pride at her backbone. A few days ago, she would never have dared to speak to a man in so bold a manner. Her newfound defiance felt good, sinfully good.

She held her head high, determined not to shrink and spoil the effect. The duke's face might have been carved from granite. There was no hint of the compassionate man who had refused to let her blame herself, no hint of the benevolent lord who had helped her in her quest to find Jo.

The hollow clopping of hooves sounded outside. "My carriage," the duke said tonelessly.

He picked up his coat and eased into it. Then he opened

the door and stood waiting, the perfect gentleman. She stepped past him into the chilly May night. Dark clouds blotted out the stars. The rain had given way to a fine mist. The candles in the outside sconces guttered within their paned glass, and the feeble light shone on the black bog of the garden.

Wrapped in gloom, a long dark vehicle stood at the curbstone, drawn by a single sway-backed horse. It was not the duke's carriage, after all. It looked like . . .

Mary skidded to a stop on the slick flagstone path. Adam's arm came around her to keep her from falling. But his warmth could not penetrate her frozen body.

Two murky shapes clambered down from the driver's seat. The taller one stepped back in a deferential manner. The other man wrenched open the wrought-iron gate and stormed up the path.

She pressed backward against the duke. Her mouth was so dry she could not whisper more than a single word. "Papa."

❧ **Chapter 10** ❧

"Get away from my daughter, you noble infidel. Lest you taint her with your perversion."

Not since he had worn short pants in the nursery had Adam obeyed the command of an underling. Yet he released Mary and stepped slightly ahead of her. Given the circumstances, he deemed it prudent to make an exception of the Reverend Thomas Sheppard.

So this was the man who had taught Mary to hate the aristocracy. Somehow Adam had expected a more impressive personage. The watery light from the sconces glinted off Sheppard's balding head. Of average height, he wore black from neck to toe. Stern lines cut into his craggy face as if he seldom smiled.

The man who remained in the shadows was more physically imposing, though the darkness obscured his features. Victor Gabriel, no doubt. He neither greeted his fiancée nor inquired of her well-being, a fact that grated on Adam.

"No one has tainted me, Papa. Pray, don't be angry with the duke—"

"Silence. Do not add a falsehood to your list of sins."

"I'm sorry."

At her meek whisper, Adam turned so that he could see Mary. She stood with her head bowed, and her neck gleamed pale and vulnerable through the gloom.

He glared at her father. "She's done no wrong. If anything, you should praise her. Only a true Christian woman would have the fortitude to travel alone to London to search for her missing sister."

"Josephine is no longer kin to us," Sheppard said in a guttural tone. "Mary knew that. Yet she defied me and here is the result. I find her dressed and painted like a whore."

Mary hunched her shoulders. Her fingers trembled visibly as she fastened the top buttons of her spencer. Only moments ago, she had stood straight and proud. Until her father had shamed her back into the role of timid mouse.

Adam controlled his temper. "Perhaps we should go inside and discuss the situation in more congenial surroundings."

" 'The Lord's curse is on the house of the wicked.' " Sheppard walked to Mary and placed a proprietary hand on her sleeve. Beads of mist clung to his coat. In the uncertain light, his eyes glittered a shade paler than hers. "I have come to save my prodigal daughter from your den of iniquity, Mr. Brentwell. Not to see her bask in the company of a fornicator."

"It is customary to address me as *Your Grace.*"

"I pay homage to the Almighty, not to a heathen who sets himself above the honest folk of England." Sheppard brandished his fist. "Your reign is doomed to fall, you and all your kind. One day the true Lord will rise up and smite you with His mighty sword."

"Bide your threats, preacher. You venture close to sedition."

The older man stared a challenge, though he pinched his lips together. Adam knew that in the years since the revolution in France, the discontent of the English lower class had caused unease among the aristocracy. That fear had peaked in January, he recalled, when a shot had been fired at the Regent himself. The government had promptly enacted laws prohibiting the assembly of more than fifty citizens near Westminster. Magistrates were given the power to imprison any person who so much as spoke of revolution.

Adam had supported the laws. Conceivably, fanatics like Sheppard could stir the masses to violence, and Adam had no wish to see a guillotine erected in Pall Mall. Yet he also found himself remembering what Mary had said.

You don't regard the lower class as real people, people who weep and bleed and suffer. You toss them a coin or a crust of bread and consider your duty done.

That vehement crusader had vanished, for Mary stood with her chin tucked to her chest. She was likely blaming herself again. Damn her overdeveloped sense of guilt. And damn the father who condemned her without letting her speak in her own defense.

A gust of wind rustled the bushes. Sheppard tightened his grip on her arm. "Come, Mary Elizabeth. I am taking you away."

Thomas Sheppard would crush her fledgling spirit. Adam knew he should not care, yet he did. He stepped into her path. Very quietly, he said, "Would you prefer to stay?"

She lifted her chin and looked at him. Her eyes reflected a blank acceptance of her fate. She shook her head in reply, then lowered her gaze again. It was as if the sharp-tongued reformer who traded insults with him had ceased to exist.

Adam moved back and let her pass. He should be relieved. Thomas Sheppard had saved him the trouble of convincing Mary to quit London. Before she poked further into her sister's disappearance and discovered a certain damning truth.

Yet he felt an ache in his chest as he watched her walk to the caravan with her father. He had felt this hollowness once before, when he was eight and his favorite pony had been sold. His father had declared Adam man enough to own a hunting mare. He had forced Adam to watch as the new owner rode away on the pony down the long, oak-shaded drive at the ducal estate.

Adam remembered the heat on his cheeks. And the thrashing he had received for his tears.

It was ridiculous to think of that now. The long-forgotten memory had nothing whatever to do with Mary Sheppard.

As she reached the caravan, she paused a moment beside the horse. She stroked the animal's side, and the nag turned its head and nuzzled her palm.

Just moments ago, those small hands had touched him, first tentatively, then with passion. And what of that kiss? He had not meant for it to happen. He had never meant to do more than rub her shoulders to relax her before breaking the news that he was sending her away. Yet when she had turned in his arms, he had been unable to resist that soft, wanting mouth. Ah, the taste of her had been worth the indulgence. It had been a fitting way of saying goodbye to her.

Victor Gabriel emerged from the shadows of the garden. Instead of retreating to the caravan, he approached Adam.

Mary's fiancé wore a black cassock over his muscular frame. With his finely molded features and pale golden hair, he might have been a painted angel come to life. Adam recalled his steward reporting that Gabriel's startling perfection had been said to make the women in the congregation swoon.

He seemed unaware of his magnetism. As he stopped a short distance from Adam, he kept his head slightly bowed and his hands pressed together like a supplicant.

Some men value innocence.

Mary had been speaking of her betrothed. Soon she would lie with this paragon. To him, she would give the pleasure of caressing her body. To him, she would submit in the most intimate way possible. *If* such a godly man permitted himself to feel physical passion and to share that joy with his wife.

Adam realized the deacon stood motionless, waiting. "Well, man? Have you something to say?"

"Your Grace, I beg your pardon for intruding." Gabriel's voice was smooth, mellifluous, riveting. And deferential for a member of a radical sect. "If I could but broach a delicate topic."

"Go on."

"I should like to inquire as to the health of your brother."

Adam pulled his attention away from Mary, who was clambering up to the front of the caravan. "What do you know of Cyril?"

"Only what little news I gleaned while determining Miss Mary's whereabouts. He is said to be insensible yet."

"That is true."

"Have the doctors given you any hope for improvement?"

"They hope for the best, of course." Pricked by suspicion, Adam added, "Why do you wish to know?"

"If it pleases my lord duke, I would like to pray at Lord Cyril's bedside for his swift recovery."

Mary had made a similar request. The memory burned in the void of Adam's chest. Prayers were all these religious folk could offer. Prayers, when Cyril's assailant roamed free.

"Save your entreaties for Josephine Sheppard." He peered closely at the deacon. "Perhaps you know how to contact her."

Gabriel flicked a glance at him. Adam had the impression of pale, earnest eyes before the deacon lowered his square-jawed face. "I, Your Grace?"

"You were once betrothed to her. Is it so odd to surmise that she might have come running to you in her hour of need?"

"Miss Josephine had no use for a man of God. Months have passed since wealth and status lured her away from the fold of her family. We have not seen her since."

"Surely she sent letters. Something that might give you a clue to her whereabouts."

The deacon shook his head sadly. "There is nothing. I pray for her nightly, though I fear her soul is lost forever." He bowed. "I hope my request did not offend you, Your Grace. I will add your brother's name to my prayers." Slowly he walked back to the caravan.

Dislike festered in Adam. So there went the man who had accepted Mary as second best. He was a holy fool for not seizing her in his arms and kissing her.

On the front seat perched the scarecrow figure of Thomas Sheppard. Beside him, a dark, dainty shape was silhouetted against the moonlit sky. Mary.

Adam fancied she was watching him, and the notion made him strangely light-headed. Why should he care if she looked his way? She had served her purpose. And now he knew she was as mad as her father, to believe she could peer into her sister's mind. He should be glad to see the last of her.

And yet he could not take his gaze from her.

Suddenly she did something that Adam would have missed had he not been straining to see her through the shadows. She lifted her pale hand in a furtive wave.

Thickness expanded his throat. He felt the undignified impulse to wave back. He caught himself in time, curling his fingers into a fist at his side. After a moment, she ducked into the caravan, and the fleeting bond between them was severed.

Victor Gabriel climbed aboard and took up the reins. The single horse began plodding down the cobbled street, drawing the curious vehicle that creaked and squawked like a grumpy old aunt.

Adam stood there long after the caravan disappeared around the corner, long after his own carriage appeared and he sent it away. From the distance came the growl of traffic. Somewhere, fashionable people traveled home from an evening at the theater. Somewhere, gentlemen drank and gambled. Somewhere, ladies laughed and danced.

While the darkness settled around him.

"Here's yer tea," Obediah said, plunking a silver tray on the rough-hewn table. "An' a plate o' meat pasties to fill yer bellies."

A branch of candles cast light and shadow on the pots and dishes stacked on the wall shelves. A fire crackled on the hearth, doing little to dispel the damp chill in the air. To save the expense of an inn, Mary's father had decided to pass the night in the caravan, which was parked in the mews behind Jo's town house. He had descended to the cellar kitchen, Mary knew, only because he wanted to have words with her.

As Obediah puttered by the hearth, adding more coals to the flames, she poured the steaming tea into mugs, sugared one for Victor and set a plain one before her father. To her own she added a dollop of cream, then wrapped her cold palms around the blessedly hot mug.

It was a relief to have a moment to gather her thoughts while the men ate a late supper. Her head ached from the aftereffects of the wine, and her stomach churned. During the short journey here, as she braided her loose hair into its familiar coronet, she had been riddled by self-doubt. How swiftly she had slipped back into her role of obedient daughter. The woman who had stood up to the duke of St. Chaldon had lost all confidence at a sharp word from her father.

She had swallowed the urge to speak her mind when he had ordered her to ride inside the dark interior of the caravan. Always before, she had welcomed the chance to hide herself away from the rest of the world. Yet this time the caravan felt like a prison. The closeness of the walls, the scents of book bindings and ink and stale food, even the familiar rocking and jolting had only made her long for escape.

She wanted to run back to the duke's house. She wanted
to throw herself on his mercy and beg him to take her in.
Standing there against the backdrop of the shadowed
house, his hands on his hips, he had looked so solid and
dependable, so competent.

Unlike her.

She made a face at her mug of muddy tea. Odd that she
and Adam had been quarreling over her departure at the
very moment her father and Victor had come to fetch her.

A throaty growl drew her attention. Prinny stood alert,
watching Victor, no doubt wanting a scrap to eat. The deacon ignored the dog as he had all of Jo's creatures. He was
never cruel to them, of course, only oblivious, as if his
mind were focused on more spiritual matters than a hungry animal.

Mary crumbled a bit of meat pie and slipped it under the
table. The dog loped forward and wolfed down the piece,
then sat on the flagstone floor, one paw raised, his stubby
tail working furiously. He looked at her with dark, heart-
melting eyes until she fed him the rest of the pie.

Her father made a small motion to Obediah, and the
two men glowered at each other in a wordless exchange.

Mary had but a moment to puzzle over it when the footman rose from his stool by the hearth.

"Quit yer beggin', ye scurvy cur," he told the dog. " 'Tis
time fer the both o' us t' check the locks." Obediah went
up the stairs, his wooden leg thumping. The dog hung back
a moment, whining as if he feared to leave Mary alone with
two strange men.

Mary made a shooing motion. "Go on, Prinny. I'll be
fine."

After one last longing look at her, the dog padded up
the steps. Mary wished she could follow. Her muscles were
tensed as she braced herself for the axe to drop.

And then it did.

"Now," her father said, "I will have a full confession

from you, Mary. What were you doing with that noble-man?"

His forbidding countenance had always made her feel small and insignificant. Yet he could smile, too, and had done so often in happier times. With effort she managed to keep her chin raised. "The duke was helping me find Jo's kidnapper. We had . . . interviewed several men who knew her."

"You were alone with him. In the middle of the night. And you expect me to believe he didn't try to ravish you?"

"He didn't."

I wanted to ravish him.

What would her father think if he learned of that kiss? What would Victor think?

Too miserable to look at her fiancé, she watched her father's thick fingers clench his mug. She told herself he was only concerned for her. "You didn't ask if I met with any success."

"Did you?"

She shook her head. "Oh, Papa. I'm so dreadfully afraid for Jo."

He lowered his head to his hand and rubbed his brow. When he gazed at her again, weariness hollowed his eyes. "I'm more troubled by what's happened to you in just a few days. Look at yourself, dressed in the garb of a whore. Has this wicked place stripped you of all decency?"

She shifted uncomfortably, thankful at least that the but-toned spencer hid the damage done by Peterbourne. "Per-haps by coming to London I did my first decent act in months."

"What nonsense. You were always the good child, tracta-ble and dutiful." Thomas Sheppard's moody gaze flicked down to his empty mug. "Unlike your willful sister."

"Jo has a generous heart. Have you forgotten how she can nurse any creature back to health? Or how she could make you laugh? She made everyone around her smile." Mary stole a glance at Victor, who sat contemplating the fire as if oblivious to the conversation. "I've always wished I could . . ." She bit her lip and fell silent.

"Could what? Be more like her?" Her father slammed his fist onto the table so hard the dishes rattled. "God forbid that you, too, should have inherited the bad seed."

This was not the first time he had made reference to her ancestry. Always before he had deflected her questions. But after all she'd been through for her sister's sake, Mary would not be put off again. "I want to know about this bad seed. I have the right to know."

"There is no purpose in the telling. 'Tis better you pray for guidance toward the path of righteousness."

"Was it my mother?" she persisted.

"No!" His face softened as if he gazed into the far reaches of happier times. "Ruth was as saintly a woman as ever walked this earth. 'Tis a mercy she's no longer here to witness the fall of her daughters."

Mary subdued a stab of pain. She had only a hazy memory of a dark-haired woman who sang sweet lullabies. "Who was this bad seed, then? Your mother? Your father? A grandparent?"

His features hardened again. "Don't press me, Mary Elizabeth."

When he spoke in that tone, she had always obeyed him. But not now. Once already tonight she had proven to herself that she had backbone. She flattened her palms on the scarred surface of the table. "Papa, I have to know. Else I'll never understand why you've always resented my sister even when we were children."

He passed his hand over his face. The age lines seemed to cut deeper than ever, and the heavy rasp of his breathing filled the silence. "Perhaps 'tis time you learned the truth. I've borne this black burden all my life." He paused, and she sat very still, waiting. " 'Twas my father," he said, "your grandfather. May the wicked earl burn in hell."

"An earl?" she said in astonishment. "You have noble blood?"

"As do you. All because a worthless libertine forced himself on a God-fearing serving maid. When he learned she was with child, he cast her out. Had not a kindly family seen fit to take her in, she would have starved to death." The merry crackling of the fire underscored his grave tone. "And I in her womb."

Mary could scarcely credit the news. Yet it explained so much. No wonder her father denounced the aristocracy. No wonder he condemned the waywardness in Jo. "Who was this earl?"

He turned the mug round and round in his big hands. "His identity matters not. He ceased to exist for me long ago. I was only a lad of six when my mother succumbed to a lung ailment. I found work in a vicarage, where I learned to worship the Lord. As a young man I took the name of Sheppard and vowed to devote my life to the flocks of worthy poor, to vanquish the evil seed with good works. Until your sister undid all my toil."

"You've misjudged her." Mary thought of Adam's words. "No woman is inherently evil. Jo is only misguided."

"She is lost forever." Thomas Sheppard closed his eyes, his hands steepled beneath his chin. " 'From the lips of a loose woman drip honey, and her speech is smoother than oil; but in the end she is bitter as wormwood, sharp as a two-edged sword.' "

" 'And a virtuous woman is a crown to her husband,' " Mary countered. "Oh, Papa. Wait until you hear. Jo and Lord Cyril are betrothed."

His eyes opened. "Betrothed?"

"Yes. They are to be married. Cyril's sister told me so, and the duke confirmed it."

"Only if Lord Cyril recovers." Victor spoke suddenly from his stool at the end of the table. "And if the Almighty takes pity on Miss Josephine."

A fathomless compassion shone in his gray eyes. There was no sign of the jilted fiancé who had cursed Jo in fury

the morning after she had run away to London. But for
that one lapse, he dwelt on a spiritual plane above frail
human emotions.

Returning her gaze to her father, Mary leaned forward,
her elbows propped on the table. "We'll find Jo. She isn't
like your father. Surely now that she's betrothed, you can
find room in your heart to forgive her."

Mary waited for his mouth to curve into a rare smile,
waited for him to reassure her. He could be jovial and
kind, a loving father. But now he lowered his head and ran
his hand over the fringe of his hair. "She was living in sin in
this very house. Marrying will not absolve her of that."

"Don't you trust in a forgiving God? Did not Jesus save
the soul of Mary Magdalene?" When her father's face remained stony, she slipped off her chair and touched the
gnarled back of his hand. "You cannot forsake your own
daughter. Jo has been kidnapped. By the same villain who
shot Lord Cyril."

Victor said, "Talk about town says that *she* shot him. She
broke one of God's commandments, and so we must leave
it to Him to punish her."

The two men exchanged a glance. Her father was the
first to look away. He stared down into his mug.

So that was the way of it. They were banding together to
vilify Jo. Mary blew out a huff of frustration. "You've
wronged her, both of you. Just as I did by not coming after
her sooner. To you, Papa, women are either whores or
saints, and there is no room for human mistakes."

Thomas Sheppard sat with his shoulders slumped. "I can
see that the city has changed you already, Mary Elizabeth.
You never before spoke to me with such disrespect."

Tears burned her eyes. "I'm sorry, Papa. But perhaps I
was too obedient until now. Too eager to please instead of
thinking for myself." She took a deep breath to relieve the
pressure in her chest. "I won't go with you in the morning.
I must remain in London until I know my sister is safe."

He gazed at her, haggard creases on his face. "Stay

here," he said heavily, "and you will be no daughter of mine."

His words struck like a stake into her heart. How could he ask her to choose between him and her beloved sister?

Jo, who had sent that message of terror.

"I cannot leave," she whispered.

"So be it, then." He rose from his stool, brushed past her, and started for the doorway.

Without thinking, she ran to embrace him. For a brief moment he leaned into her, and she felt the warm clasp of his arms, breathed in his familiar scent of horses and sweat. She hoped with piercing fervency that he might yet change his mind. Then he pushed her away. Without a backward glance, he trudged up the stairs to the ground floor.

Her father looked so old, so fatigued. His departure had the stamp of finality. Mary could feel it in every painful beat of her heart. Dear God. Would he ever accept her back? Or was she truly on her own now?

"He prayed for you, day and night."

Victor's deep voice reached out to her. She turned to see him regarding her with tender sympathy, the firelight haloing his golden hair. The dark swirl of guilt enveloped her. He was a simple man guided by his faith, a man whose goodness lifted him above mere mortals. So how was it that she had felt a sense of rightness with Adam—an aristocrat—when Victor had a purity of the soul?

He had entranced her from the moment of their meeting less than half a year ago. Appearing out of a throng of worshippers, he had come forward like King David striding into battle. He had fallen to his knees before her father and begged to serve the Lord.

And so Victor had joined the vagabond mission. The new deacon often rode ahead to post broadsheets advertising the next prayer meeting. He slept beneath the caravan at night, seemingly impervious to cold or rain. All the while, Mary was enraptured by the spell of her own unchaste desires. When he spent hours in solitary prayer, she prayed for him to notice her. She imagined him kissing her, touching her. She drifted dreamily through the weeks, buoyed by fantasies she kept secret even from her sister. Until the day when he asked Jo to be his wife.

Beautiful, vivacious, sparkling Jo.

For the first time, Mary had resented her twin. She managed to hide the demon jealousy, to study and cook and clean as if her heart weren't rent in two. And she closed her thoughts to her sister. Each time she sensed Jo speaking to her, she blocked her out by reciting a passage from the Scripture. That had been the start of the estrangement between them.

A vast regret flooded her now. She remembered Jo's distress, her attempts to identify the source of her twin's aloofness. And Mary had added another black mark to her soul. She had told her sister that she agreed with their father; the special bond between them was the curse of Satan. They had exchanged heated, hurtful words. And that night, Jo had run away to London.

In the darkest region of her soul, Mary knew she was responsible. She had driven her own sister away. Because she had coveted her sister's betrothed.

And now . . . now she desired Adam. Was she a wanton who valued a godly man less than a dissolute lord?

Victor cleared his throat. "Did you not hear me? Do you not wish to reconcile with your own father?" He went on in that gentle, reproachful tone. "Set aside your waywardness, Miss Mary. The Reverend Sheppard left his mission for your sake. Do not hurt him again after all he has suffered in his lifetime."

She lacked the strength to argue. "Is my grandfather still alive? Has my father ever told you?"

"He never speaks of the villain." Victor took a step toward her. "Do not think to distract me. Your disappearance devastated your father. It was fortunate that I managed to convince him to come after you."

His scolding made her want to weep. She had disappointed him, too. "I had no choice in leaving the mission. I *saw* Jo. I saw her running toward me in terror." Mary sank down on her chair again. "Or perhaps she was running from her kidnapper."

"The curse. I thought you'd renounced that wicked nonsense." Victor narrowed his eyes disapprovingly. "So. Have you seen anything of Miss Josephine since? Anything to tell you where she is?"

"I've heard her voice." Mary swallowed hard, remembering that haunting plea. "Just her voice, without an image."

"Did she say . . . who she'd gone off with?"

"No, only that she was frightened of him. Terribly, terribly frightened." Mary held her clasped fingers to her chin. "Oh, why does God not lead me to her? Why has He forsaken her?"

Victor paced slowly, his hands behind his back. "Perhaps God in His infinite wisdom does not wish you to know. And He would not wish you to foster this unnatural bond to your sister's mind. You must promise not to contact her again."

"But if it could help us find her—"

"Don't damn your own soul for her sake." His voice was deep and melodious, as compelling as a choir of angels. "Miss Josephine chose her own destiny. Never forget that she entered the fleshpots of London of her own accord."

If only he knew, Mary thought. If only she dared to confess the dark sin that lurked in her heart, that she had betrayed her sister for him. "Why did you never come after Jo?"

"I realized that she is weak in moral fiber, while you . . . you, Miss Mary, have a strength of character." He scrutinized her from head to toe. "Although I cannot pretend to be pleased that you would associate with the duke of St. Chaldon, no matter what the reason."

"Nothing happened between us. He was the perfect gentleman." It was only a small lie, she rationalized.

"Yet you permitted him to see you dressed so immod-
estly. Without any chaperon to protect your virtue."

His gaze lingered on the sheer gold gown, and Mary put
her hand to her throat, fancying that he could see through
the buttoned spencer. Was it possible . . . he was jealous?

The thought startled her. After Jo's departure, Mary had
felt so guilty that she had suppressed her dark longings,
never permitting Victor more than a quick kiss on the
cheek, not even when he had fulfilled her shameful dreams
with his proposal of marriage. Yet she had gone willingly
into Adam's arms, opening herself to the turmoil of emotion he stirred in her. Surely she could no longer shun
physical contact with her own fiancé.

On impulse she went to him and placed her hands on his
upper arms. He had the hard, muscled physique of the
laborers to whom her father preached. "You've spoken
nary a word of welcome. Are you not pleased to see me
again?"

Without awaiting an answer, she pressed upward on tiptoe and brushed her lips against his. They were dry and
cool, the lips of a statue. His widened eyes were not the
deep midnight hue of Adam's eyes, but the heavenly gray
of a cloud.

On a sharp intake of breath, Victor closed his arms
around her. He slanted his mouth against hers and kissed
her with stunning fervor. She stood frozen, shocked by his
unexpected display of passion. His musky odor tickled her
nose. His mouth tasted of the onions in the pasties he'd
eaten. His tight embrace seemed more like a prison than a
haven. The punishing force of his kiss plumbed the secret
darkness within her, and panic swamped her in a nightmar-
ish wave.

But he was not Peterbourne. Victor was her intended
husband. Many women would adore being in her place.

Yet no amount of reasoning could slow the frantic drumbeat of her heart. She jerked her mouth to the side and flailed her fists against his massive shoulders. "Let me go. Let me go!"

He lifted his head and stared at her through bright, glassy eyes. Breathing hard, he made no move to release her, and his arms felt rigid and powerful.

Suddenly a growl emanated from the stairway, and a small gray shape hurdled itself across the kitchen.

Prinny latched onto Victor's pant leg. The deacon let Mary go so abruptly she stumbled backward, her hands meeting the table. In the same move, he bent down and struck at the dog. The animal yelped and staggered away, shaking its matted head.

Mary dropped to her knees beside the dog, cuddling it against her. "Prinny, for mercy's sake! Are you hurt?"

"Better you should ask me that," Victor grumbled.

Mary scrutinized Prinny's scruffy body and decided he was only a bit stunned. As the dog licked her hands, she looked up to see Victor rubbing his calf. "Did he injure you?"

"The cur did no real damage, praise God."

"I'm sorry about his attack. He thought he was defending me."

At the sharpness of her voice, Victor straightened. For a long moment, their gazes held. The fire hissed and whispered like the lament of lost souls.

"Oh, Miss Mary. Can you ever forgive me?" Humble contrition in his tone, he knelt a short distance from her and bowed his head. "I've struggled against the temptations of the flesh. It was wrong of me to touch you without having our union sanctified by God. I can only think this is a sign."

"A sign?"

"Dearest, the Lord wants us to join in holy matrimony. Immediately. Please agree, else you'll break my heart."

Her stomach dropped. It was the closest he had ever come to a declaration of love. Yet something inside her balked. "Papa wishes us to wait a few months. To be certain of our feelings."

"He would be happy to have you back in his fold. So happy he won't object. Please, go with me tonight and we'll tell him."

At one time she would have been overjoyed to do so. But now she couldn't fathom the dark well of resistance in her. Nor could she understand why she'd felt such a strong aversion to his kiss. Was not a wife supposed to cleave to her husband? Was not Victor devout and humble, generous and kind, possessing all the virtues of a good man?

Life with Victor would lack the excitement she had known with Adam. But wasn't that for the better? Did she not wish to dedicate herself to her father's mission?

Weariness jumbled her thoughts, and she hugged Prinny against her. It must be the tussle with Peterbourne that disturbed her, made her unable to appreciate Victor's ardor. Why else would she be so startled to learn that behind his saintly facade dwelt a man like any other?

The truth rushed out at her. She didn't really know him. She had mistaken girlish worship for womanly affection. The promise she had made to him suddenly struck her as wrong, dreadfully wrong.

He knelt, regarding her with such honest adoration that she felt sickened at the thought of hurting him. Yet she must. "Oh, Victor, you ask the impossible. I cannot marry you. Not now . . . or ever."

A shadow crossed his face. He rose to his feet, the movement almost too elegant for a man of the cloth. "It is the duke, is it not? You are enamored of him."

"No!" She spoke quickly, sharply, needing to deny it. "Our betrothal should never have come about. I took you from Jo, and I cannot forgive myself for that."

"You took nothing. She left of her own willful accord. As soon as we're wed, you'll realize the rightness of our union."

"I cannot," she whispered. "Do try to understand why."

He compressed his lips and took a step toward her. Prinny growled, his small body stiffening against Mary.

Victor halted, frowning at the dog, then at Mary. "I must leave London for a few days with your father. But I'll return and speak to you again of this. When you've had time to reflect, you'll see that we belong together."

"I don't think—"

"Do think," he said gently, worry illuminating his handsome face. "Think about how you'll fare without me. How will you live? As a drudge in some lord's mansion? As the mistress of a nobleman who might cast you out onto the street at any moment? Or will you take the honored role of my wife?" With one last concerned look at her, he turned away and mounted the stairs.

Left in the kitchen, Mary slumped on the cold flagstones and gathered Prinny close. The dog wiggled happily and licked her face. Yet misery and pain and fear exerted a tight pressure inside her breast. What had she done?

In one fell swoop, she had cut herself off from both Victor and her father. Yet how could she ever return to the caravan and the mission that until a few days ago had been the focus of her life? How could she marry a man she did not love?

The future that had once seemed so safe and secure now loomed like a black cloud. Other than the ability to read and write, she had no skills. And she could not—she would not—throw herself on the mercy of St. Chaldon. With the masquerade over, he had no further use for her.

The ache in her heart intensified. If only she did not feel so alone. If only she could find Jo. If only Lord Cyril could regain his senses and reveal who had shot him.

The thought grabbed at Mary, and she straightened her spine. Now *there* was the key! Though Adam had expressly forbidden her to do so, tomorrow she would steal inside Brentwell House.

She would awaken Lord Cyril.

⊸ **Chapter 11** ⊱

Adam sat with his head tilted back, his eyes closed. A damp towel wrapped his face in soothing heat. He could hear Fenwick moving around the dressing room, preparing the shaving items on a silver tray.

The rare moment of peace lulled Adam. It had been the very devil of a disappointing day, and a command appearance at teatime still awaited him. Weariness weighed on every bone of his body. Only his brain seemed energized, moving with a will of its own to the one topic he should avoid.

Mary Sheppard.

She, her father, and her fiancé would have left the city by now. She would be arrayed as she had been when he had first met her, in that drab, shapeless gown, her tightly braided hair anchored atop her head. She would be riding inside the caravan, perhaps stitching a Bible verse on a sampler or practicing a hymn like a dutiful daughter.

Or perhaps she and Victor would be renewing their betrothal vows. Perhaps that bloody paragon already had sampled the sweetness of her lips. It was his right, after all.

Or worse, he might punish her for her imagined sins. He might humiliate her in front of an entire congregation of onlookers. Where would Mary go to heal her wounded heart?

The sense that he had failed her somehow had plagued

Adam through a restless night. He had tossed and turned in bed, sometimes drifting into an uneasy sleep in which he dreamed of pearly breasts and flowing red-gold hair, and eyes so green he could gaze into them forever.

Oh, Adam, I've never felt this way before.

A queer ache lodged in his chest. What nonsense. They had shared a few extraordinarily pleasant kisses, that was all. If Mary Sheppard hadn't gone away, they likely would have become intimate. She had a passionate spirit that no code of morals could repress. But their association would have ended in due course. No matter how refreshing he found their spirited debates, no matter how soft a woman lay beneath her thorny exterior, he would have tired of her eventually. After all, one did not keep a mistress forever.

Except for Cyril.

Adam clenched his teeth. His brother was an incurable romantic who had been duped into proposing marriage to a fickle conniver. Upon finding a new lover, she had shot Cyril in cold blood and left him for dead. The note she'd written proved it.

The towel grew unbearably heavy. Adam yanked it off, and cool air struck his face.

Fenwick stood at the dressing table, scowling down at a dish of foamy shaving soap. Odd that, for the valet seldom showed emotion. Even odder, he appeared to be muttering to himself.

Adam held out the towel. "Hadn't we best get on with it?"

Fenwick dropped the brush with a clatter. "Forgive me, Your Grace." He scurried forward and bore away the towel, then returned a moment later with the tray. "If you will lie back now."

Adam complied, tilting his head so that Fenwick could brush on the lather. The familiar aroma of sandalwood enveloped him, as did the faint rasp of the blade gliding across his cheek. Usually he enjoyed the small luxury of shaving twice a day. It was one of the few indulgences he allowed himself. But today he could only reflect that Mary would accuse him of overworking his servant.

Curse the little radical. Why could he not purge her from his mind?

"If you would be so kind as to cease frowning, Your Grace. I should not like you to entertain your lady guests with sticking plaster dotting your face."

The reminder of his impending visitors irritated Adam. But he forced his muscles to relax. "So you say. And while I am sitting very still, you may tell me what is troubling you."

Fenwick paused, the long razor gleaming in his hand. "Me, my lord duke?"

"Yes, you. Something has been occupying your mind. Perhaps I can help you resolve it."

Prepared to offer sage advice, Adam settled more comfortably in the chair and closed his eyes. He seldom probed into the personal lives of his servants. He paid them well and made certain of their creature comforts, and that was that. But ever since Mary's lecture, he had become uneasily aware of his ingrained aloofness to the people in his employ.

"It's that . . . that female," Fenwick said.

Adam cracked open one eye. "Who?"

"Mrs. Primrose. A trumped-up name if ever I heard one." The valet pinched his lips into a bloodless line. "Though, of course, Your Grace, I do not belittle your kindness in showing charity to her."

Adam was careful to remain still as Fenwick plied the razor. "She is shirking her duties?"

"Not precisely. She's fetched the coal and made up the fires and changed the linens. But not without rude complaint. She simply refuses to behave with decorum like any sober-minded domestic."

"Hmm."

"That is not the worst of it. Yesterday evening in the servants' hall, rather than taking her rightful place at the

lower table, she sat down to supper with the upper staff."
Leaning over Adam, the razor moving in expert strokes,
Fenwick fairly vibrated with indignation. "Imagine, a mere
housemaid sitting in the company of the butler, Her
Grace's abigail, and I. Next we shall have the scullery maid
demanding a place with us."

"No doubt."

"I suggested that she move, of course. And can you
imagine what that hussy said?"

"I shudder to think."

Fenwick planted his hands at the waist of his somber
black suit. "She said, 'Oo are ye ta be orderin' me about?
Ye ain't no duke. Ye're a servant no better'n me.' " The
valet resumed his shaving. "Needless to say, I was shocked,
utterly shocked to be spoken to thusly. I sent the ill-bred
female straight off to bed without any supper."

Adam raised an eyebrow. He had never known Fenwick
to be so long-winded. Or so indignant about the actions of
one particular female. "A harsh punishment."

"Standards, Your Grace. We servants must maintain our
standards. If I may be forgiven for saying so, the hierarchy
of the domestic staff is as exacting as that of our employ-
ers."

The servants had their pecking order, Adam had known
as much. Yet he had never thought of it as comparable to
that of the ton. It seemed the upper class had no exclusive
claim to prejudice. He wondered what Mary would think of
that.

"Of course," Fenwick went on, setting aside the razor
and picking up a clean linen towel, "one cannot help but
pity a woman with such bruises on her face. Put there by a
drunken sailor who wanted to . . ." A faint ruddiness
colored the valet's cheeks.

Interesting, this switch from indignation to sympathy.
Was there an attraction brewing? Adam decided to put the
theory to the test. "Ah, I see. Well, I cannot be employing
women of low moral character, can I?"

Fenwick blinked. "I did not mean to say she is wicked. She claims to have fought off her swain successfully."

"And what brought about her heartfelt confession?"

His flush deepened. "She, er, said she can get the better of any man, even me, Your Grace." He fussed over dabbing the last of the lather from Adam's face. "An idle threat, no doubt."

Rising, Adam removed the protective towel from his dressing gown. "Nevertheless, I will not abide strife among the staff. If Mrs. Primrose is disrupting the household, I shall dismiss her at once without reference."

"But Your Grace, I would not wish to put the poor woman out on the street. At least not without giving her a week's trial."

Adam suppressed a smile. "So be it, then. I hereby appoint you to oversee her training."

Fenwick's protests lasted for the next half an hour, while Adam finished dressing. Ordinarily, he would have no tolerance for chattering servants, especially not one whom he expected to perform his duties with grave decorum.

But Adam welcomed the distraction. It kept him from brooding about Mary, from reflecting on the dismal duty that awaited him. She was gone from his life, and the less he thought of her, the better.

"Turn left at the statue of Mercury," Mary muttered.

As she tiptoed around the corner and down another passageway, she glanced up at the work of art. The wing-footed god posed in naked glory, his bronzed chest gleaming, a strategically placed fig leaf his only covering. She found herself wondering if Adam would look so splendid without any clothing. Hastily she returned her attention to the paper in her hand.

"Go to the end of the passageway and turn right."

Lady Sophy had written out explicit directions. Although Mary had been here once before, she would have lost her way through the myriad corridors. Rounding yet another corner, she craned her neck to peer at the ornate moldings, the plaster decorations. The place should belong to a university or a church. How fantastical to think that one man could possess such a magnificent dwelling. And that she would have to skulk like a thief for fear of encountering the duke.

"May I ask your business, Miss?"

Mary whirled around to see a small man, meticulously dressed in black, glowering at her from a gilt-framed doorway. "Who are you?" she blurted.

"I am His Grace's valet. And more to the point, who are you?"

Looking beyond him, she glimpsed an enormous, sunny chamber dominated by a bed decked with azure and silver hangings. Her pulse danced in her throat. Adam's bedroom. Was he in there? Surely not. Surely he had already gone down to tea.

Seeing suspicion on the face of the stiffly formal valet, she bobbed a curtsy. "I'm Lady Sophy's modiste," Mary said, silently begging forgiveness for the lie. "She sent me to fetch a basket of thread from the sewing room."

"That would be on the upper floor. The servants' staircase is beyond that door." The valet pointed at the wall at the end of the corridor.

"Th-thank you."

Mary turned to go, but the man's voice stopped her. "Er, you would not have encountered a Mrs. Primrose just now, would you?"

The apple seller, Mary thought. "I've seen no one, sir."

His mouth formed a prim line. "Should you meet a rather stout maidservant with a bruised face, tell her I have another task for her. The woman has a habit of dawdling."

Sweet heaven, Mary thought as she walked slowly to the door cunningly hidden in the paneling. Had she made a mistake in persuading the duke to hire the woman? No, every person deserved a chance. Mrs. Primrose would learn to abide by the exacting standards of this household.

The valet stood watching, so Mary opened the door and
found herself standing in a dimly lit shaft with plain
wooden steps. She waited a few interminable moments,
then peeked out. The servant had vanished. Her heart
pounding, she stole back out and retraced her steps. To her
relief, the duke's door was closed.

Adam had called her brave, but she had always thought
herself a coward. Now she wished she had allowed Lady
Sophy to accompany her even though it was necessary for
the girl to keep Adam and the dowager occupied for an
hour. At this very moment, they were entertaining guests
at tea. One of the visitors, Sophy said with a wrinkle of her
pert nose, was the lady Adam wanted for his wife, though
he had yet to ask her.   ·

Mary's stomach twisted. What should it matter to her
that he had not yet betrothed himself? Sooner or later, he
would marry a gentlewoman who had been bred to the role
of duchess. These aristocrats were dedicated to preserving
their exclusive circle. Thank goodness she herself would
never be a lady.

Her footsteps whispered over the carpet runner. She
passed countless paintings of ducal ancestors, some scowling and others smiling. It was strange to think of Adam as
one of a long line of peers stretching back to Lord knew
when. It was even odder to know that she herself had a
trace of noble blood. If the past had been different, if her
grandfather had wed her hapless grandmother, would she
now live in such grand surroundings with scores of rooms
at her disposal and servants to do her bidding? And would
she be affianced to a man who viewed commoners with
benevolent hauteur? A man like Adam.

She huffed out a breath. It was pointless to entertain
flights of fancy, she admonished herself. The past could
not be changed. And she took pride in her lowly heritage.
Rather than frittering away the hours at balls and tea parties, she lived a useful life. Or at least she *had*.

The coldness of grief throbbed in her breast. Sometime

in the pre-dawn hours, her father and Victor had departed without saying goodbye. She missed them sorely. Half of her longed for the safety of the caravan; the other half recognized the painful impossibility of clinging to her childhood. She must take a different journey, make a niche for herself elsewhere. Surely she would not feel so lonely once she found Jo.

Mary turned another corner and stopped. She recognized this door with its gilded molding, the silver vase of flowers on a nearby table.

Aware that she had only a short time to accomplish her purpose, she glanced up and down the deserted corridor. Then she took a deep breath, turned the scrolled handle, and stepped into Cyril's bedchamber.

The medicinal aroma of the sickroom wafted to her. Despite the warmth of the afternoon, a fire snapped on the hearth. The glow of candles penetrated the gloom, illuminating the sturdy maidservant who sat dozing in the rocker near the four-poster bed. Recognizing her, Mary stopped short. That placid face had a healthy, attractive glow now that the bruises had begun to fade.

"Mrs. Primrose."

The woman jumped and opened her eyes. The creaking of the rocker ceased. "M'lady! Wot a start ye gave me."

"I've come to sit with his lordship," Mary said, walking briskly forward. "You're wanted by His Grace's valet."

"The rotter's workin' me ta the bone, 'e is," she grumbled.

"Are you unhappy here?" Mary asked anxiously.

Mrs. Primrose beamed a smile as she got up from the chair. "Oh, nay, m'lady! I bless ye fer gettin' me the post. As ta Mister Prig, why, I can 'andle the man. Might even get 'im ta likin' me." She winked, then sauntered out of the room.

Picturing the woman nose to nose with the supercilious valet, Mary felt the rise of a giggle. But the moment of mirth faded as she turned to the canopied bed. Against the white linens slept the man who loved her sister.

A thick bandage wrapped Lord Cyril's head, and a few strands of fair hair dipped rakishly across his brow. Wearing a plain nightshirt, he lay with his arms slack atop the coverlet. The stillness of his form wrenched Mary's heart. How could he recover in the stifling closeness of this room?

She marched to the bank of windows and drew back the ivory curtains. Late afternoon sunlight poured in to brighten the gloom. She opened the casement, and gusts of fresh air began to disperse the noxious ill humors.

Returning to the bed, Mary seated herself on the edge. She had only a vague idea of how to proceed. Hesitantly, she reached out and took hold of his hand.

His fingers were long and elegant and smooth. Though his hand lay limply in hers, his flesh was warm with life. With these fingers, he had touched her sister with tenderness. With his caresses, he had brought Jo happiness when she had found no joy in the bosom of her family.

Mary blinked hard, her grasp on his hand desperately tight. "Cyril. Cyril, you must awaken. Please, you're the only one who can help me." Could she make him believe she was Jo? Could she reach him with the voice of his beloved? "I need you here with me. Come back, my love. Come back and hold me in your arms again."

Opening her mind, Mary probed the vast darkness and caught the moonsilvered thread of connection. Then somehow, without losing her own identity, she became her sister, too, an amalgam of the both of them. She spoke in half-formed phrases of love and hope and despair, of the feelings that streamed through her with a clarity that lacked only imagery to make them complete. She gave voice to the echoing call of her twin, to the poignant pain of longing, to the terrible cry of fear that surged from the very center of her soul.

Save me, please save me, please, before it's too late.

The pounding of her pulse brought Mary back to herself. Her bosom rose and fell in quick agitation. Despite the warm breeze that undulated the draperies, she was chilled to the bone. As the tentacles of terror slowly released their grip on her, she found herself looking at Lord Cyril's face. The sunlight revealed faint lines bracketing the corners of his mouth as if he smiled often.

But not now.

She watched for a telltale fluttering of his eyes, any sign that she had reached him. He lay as insensible as ever, his tawny lashes unmoving against pale cheeks.

She had failed.

By degrees, she loosened her grip so that his hand slipped from hers. Palm up, it lay on the counterpane. Dear sweet heaven. Jo was in danger. Mortal danger. Yet Mary knew not how to save her.

"I know she's trying to contact me, to tell me where she is," she whispered to the unconscious man. "But I can't see her as clearly as before. I've lost the ability through my own stupid, selfish folly. Unless you awaken, she could die."

He gave no response, not even a twitch of his lips.

Bowing her head, Mary slumped on the bed. She should depart before someone discovered her here, and she faced another awkward scene. Yet instead she envisioned the last time she had been in this room, when Adam had touched his brother's cheek with unguarded tenderness. He had worn a look of fierce intensity, as if he could heal his brother by the sheer strength of his will.

How he wanted to see Lord Cyril restored to health. That had been her wish, too, the secret hope of giving his brother back to Adam, a bonus in addition to finding her sister.

The tightness in Mary's chest loosened, releasing a tide of tears that flowed down her cheeks. Seated sideways on the bed, she bent her forehead to her knees and wept. She wept for Adam's pain as well as her own, and for Jo, who faced an unknown peril all alone. She wept until her eyes burned and each breath seared a ragged path in her throat. And still the tears ran hot and wet from the depthless well of her misery.

Someone stroked her hair.

The touch penetrated the darkness in her heart and delivered her back to the sickroom. With a start of shock, she lowered her dampened hands to her lap and sat up straight.

Lord Cyril's eyes were open. He was gazing at her.

She sat very still, stunned by the joy that rushed through her, afraid that she was dreaming. Viewed through the lingering haze of her tears, Lord Cyril had beautiful eyes, a lighter version of Adam's mysterious blue.

Those eyes studied her, from the gown of lustrous cinnamon silk to the artful styling of her hair. A faint frown furrowed his brow, and then very slowly a smile of tender warmth softened his mouth.

Dear God, he must think she was Jo. He would assume his beloved was safe and sound.

For the first time, Mary wondered if she had done wrong to wear her sister's clothing. Perhaps she ought to have dressed in her customary drab hues. She had put off the return to her old self, and deep down she knew the reason was vanity. She had prettied herself on the chance that she might encounter Adam.

And she might now, after all. The wonder of it surged in her. He would be so pleased with her success. Unless the blow of her news about Jo plunged his brother back into unconsciousness.

Lord Cyril still stared at her in bemusement. She moistened her lips. She must reveal the truth about Jo very, very gently.

Before she could form the words, he lifted his head slightly. His voice rusty with astonishment, he said, "Good God . . . you're *Mary*."

* * *

Adam was bored.

He had never been fond of sipping a thimbleful of tea from a dainty china cup, of nibbling rich pastries while exchanging inane pleasantries. Today, the custom was all the more annoying. Especially when the conversation turned to gossip.

"I heard the most fascinating tidbit at the milliner's this morning," said his sister. "I could scarcely believe my ears."

Dressed in a pink gown decorated by ice-blue ribbons, Sophy looked rather like one of the confections on the tea cart. Not even Cyril's grave condition had dampened her spirits. Animation flushed her rounded cheeks. Like a queen holding court, she regarded her mother, Lord Harry Dashwood, Lady Camilla Crockford, and Lady Camilla's mother, the marchioness of Amberly.

"I am fairly trembling with curiosity," Harry drawled from the Sheridan chair beside hers. "If you keep us waiting any longer, I may expire from the suspense."

Sophy flashed him a withering look that had no effect on his insolent grin. Turning her wide-eyed innocence on the others, she said, "At the Stanhopes' ball last night, Mr. Jacob Pennington danced three times with Miss Layshire. People are whispering that he is about to make an offer for her. Is that not delicious?"

"Stuff and nonsense," Lady Amberly said, her thin nostrils flaring in a narrow, foxy face. "How could such a man aspire to the daughter of a viscount? He is a cit, a mere tradesman."

"Yet a very rich one," Lady Camilla added in a stately, modulated voice. "He made his fortune in coal, I believe."

"Humph." Her mother set her teacup into its saucer. "A merchant who feeds our fires attending the same parties as his customers. What is this world coming to?"

"We should wish Miss Layshire well, Mother. Not every lady is so fortunate in suitors as I am."

Lady Camilla lifted her Goddess of Winter gaze and

graced Adam with a cool smile. Sitting beside her on the gold chaise, he knew he should appreciate her sloe-eyed loveliness, the rich dark hair that set off her milky complexion, the dainty figure in a gown of pale green muslin. Less than a week ago, he would have welcomed her attentiveness. But that was before he had met an exasperating reformer who valued a man's character more than his class.

He could well imagine how Camilla would look down her noble nose at Mary. Thank God the two women would never have occasion to meet.

"It seems your beauty has St. Chaldon tongue-tied," Harry said, lifting his quizzing glass to peer at her. "No doubt he considers himself the fortunate one, for you are a camellia in a garden of weeds."

Camilla granted him a small smile.

Sophy shot him a black look.

His eyes gleamed. "Present company excepted, of course."

"You must forgive my son his preoccupation," the duchess told Camilla. "He has much on his mind these days."

"But not so much that I cannot enjoy the company of a lovely lady." Adam forced himself to smile at the woman beside him. "Mother is right. I most humbly beg your pardon."

Camilla touched his hand in an appropriately sympathetic gesture. "My dear duke. On the strength of our long acquaintance, allow me to express my distress at your brother's condition."

"Thank you. Your compassion is much appreciated."

Yet he couldn't help but note that Camilla had never offered to pray at Cyril's bedside. The very suggestion would scandalize a well-bred lady. Why did that observation irritate him today?

Beauty. Biddability. Breeding.

Camilla had every trait he wanted in a wife. Yet he felt as if he were tolerating her for his mother's sake alone.

And for a moment the melancholy lifted from the duchess's features as she gazed fondly at the pair of them. It was her dearest wish for he and Camilla to marry. The duchess and her childhood friend, Lady Amberly, had planned the betrothal for years. Over the past year, he had let himself drift closer to the alliance.

Now, to his consternation, he found Camilla's formal manners tedious. He felt restless with the need to escape.

The deepened age lines on his mother's face betrayed the exhaustion of unrelenting anxiety. Only concern for her kept Adam from walking out of the grand saloon. He had far better uses for his time than entertaining society guests. First and foremost, he wanted to renew his acquaintance with Lord Peterbourne.

Rayburn had reported seeing the earl return home shortly after the masquerade, and there had been no suspicious activity for the remainder of the night. Adam had had a man watching the house all day.

We're not who we seem to be, are we?

The earl's remark still nagged at Adam. As soon as this interminable tea ended, he intended to call on the rascally lord.

"Please don't worry, Mama," Sophy said, her voice strangely agitated. "Cyril will be fine. Trust me, I know."

"We continue to hope." The duchess twisted the napkin in her lap and gazed at their guests. "The doctors warned that Cyril could not . . . survive long without nourishment. But Adam has seen to his brother's continued health. Adam will take care of everything."

He didn't deserve the desperate faith shining in her blue eyes. He felt only the crushing weight of helplessness that he could not give his own life to save his younger brother.

Lady Camilla turned her refined face to him. "What miracle is this, may I ask?"

Her polite demeanor set his teeth on edge. "I've devised a tube-like affair that can be put down Cyril's throat. So he can be fed the liquids he needs to live."

As expected, the blunt explanation drew gasps from the two lady visitors. Silence settled over the stately room with its tall Corinthian columns and gilded furniture. Lord Harry stared down at the carpet. The duchess blinked her misty eyes. Even Sophy grew subdued, pushing the tines of her fork through the crumbs on her plate.

Lady Amberly fanned herself. "Oh, dear me. Is there no potion the doctor can administer? My abigail has a recipe for fainting spells. An infusion of hartshorn—"

"My brother has not swooned like some corseted maiden." Testy from the lack of sleep, Adam felt his control wear thin. "He was shot in the head. By his mistress."

Lady Amberly flushed so brightly she looked on the verge of swooning herself. The duchess said warningly, "Adam, do remember there are ladies present."

She was ghostly pale, and remorse flooded him. "Forgive me, Mother. I should not have spoken in so boorish a manner."

The duchess weakly waved her hand. "You only stated the unfortunate truth. Ah, if only men of rank would never mix with women of that class."

Adam's chest throbbed with tension as he thought of Mary with her charming naïveté, Mary with her refreshingly unladylike opinions. She would take issue with his mother's remark. And he would have enjoyed sparring with Mary. God help him, he missed her. The unsettling realization made his frame of mind all the darker.

"Perhaps it's time you rested upstairs," he said to his mother. "I'll escort you to your chambers—"

His sister set down her cup with a clatter. She sprang to her feet, her hands raised to forestall him. "No! I mean, not yet. Why, there are still cakes left on the tray. And we have not finished our hour of visiting."

"Sophronia!" the duchess said.

Sophy sat back down on the edge of her chair, regarding Adam closely, as though prepared to keep him from putting an end to her gossiping. "I only wished to be civil to our guests."

"Sophronia is right, and there is no need to coddle me," the duchess told him. "Indeed, I find the mere thought of more rest quite wearisome."

The gentle quip elicited smiles around the circle.

"And perhaps," the duchess went on, "a certain amount of frankness is permissible. So long as talk of this situation does not go beyond these walls."

"In light of that, I should mention a rather delicate matter," Camilla said in a subdued voice. "Yesterday I was forced to quash such a rumor on behalf of your family."

Sophy leaned forward, her eyes big. "Rumor? Do tell."

Camilla looked at Adam as if seeking his approval. He wanted to shout at her to speak her mind and be done with it. But he would not upset his mother anymore. He would not.

"You may go on," he said tersely.

She turned her gaze modestly downward, the picture of dull decorum. "It happened while Mother and I were taking the air in Hyde Park. I dare not name the guilty parties, but they were whispering . . . oh, I cannot say it."

"You can, indeed."

"Yes, my lord duke. It was horrid, scandalous. I knew it could never be true, but the gossips are murmuring that Lord Cyril had intended to marry that vulgar female."

Adam's temper snapped. He surged to his feet. "You were right to deny it. Josephine Sheppard is nothing but a schemer and a murderess. And should people have the temerity to ask, you may tell them that I intend to see her hang."

His words echoed in the vastness of the saloon. Into the ensuing quiet, a small sound came from the doorway. A strangled moan.

He pivoted sharply, wondering who dared to eavesdrop. His frustrated rage melted away when he found himself confronted by the one woman he had thought he would

never see again. The woman who had forced him to face
the dark side of his own superiority.

Mary, who now gazed at him with horror in her green
eyes.

⚙ Chapter 12 ⚙

"Curse the duke."

Mary jammed the tip of the trowel into the rain-softened dirt and uprooted another weed, adding it to the mound beside her. The scent of damp earth perfumed the air. Atop the brick wall, the one-eared tabby lazed in the sunshine, oblivious to the robin that pecked at the freshly turned loam. In the center of the X-shaped path slept Prinny, his fuzzy head resting on his paws.

The small garden behind Jo's town house had begun to lose its forlorn look of neglect. Pink blooms adorned the crab apple tree. Freed from a prison of weeds, rose bushes and daisies promised beauty for the summer. Now visible in a shaded corner was a patch of lily of the valley, the tiny white flower bells peeking out from thick, dark green leaves.

But today Mary took little pride in the fruits of her labor. Nor did she hum as she usually did while gardening.

Trowel in hand, she attacked a particularly stubborn weed. "Curse the duke of St. Chaldon," she muttered again, using the strongest oath she knew. "Curse all the nobility. Papa was right. They're corrupt, every last one of them. They're snobs and liars."

She gave the weed a vicious yank and flung it onto the pile. Breathing hard from anger and exertion, she sat back on her heels and turned her face to the afternoon sun. Its warm rays could not banish the core of ice inside her.

Adam Brentwell had used her most foully. Over the past week he had duped her into trusting him. He had made her believe he had her sister's best interests at heart. He had so cleverly gulled Mary that she had succumbed to his spell and kissed him.

Kissed the very man who wanted to see Jo dead.

Swallowing convulsively, Mary blinked back tears. She lowered her gaze to the clods of loam stuck to her gray skirt. Inside, she felt just as dirtied, stained by the darkness of his deceit. She had placed her faith in the duke. She had believed him when he'd called her brave and brilliant and beautiful. Worst of all, she had begun to think of him as her friend. Her friend!

How could she have been so terribly mistaken?

In her mind she relived that telling scene of the previous day, when she had raced downstairs, eager to impart the happy news of Lord Cyril's awakening. Adam's brusque tone had pricked the bubble of her excitement. He had stood before his guests in the grand saloon, tall and imposing in a dark blue suit with silver buttons, a snow-white cravat at his throat.

Josephine Sheppard is nothing but a schemer and a murderess . . . I intend to see her hang.

The marble floor had seemed to pitch and roll beneath Mary's feet. For as long as she lived, she would never forget those brutal words or the painful surge of her heartbeat or the voice inside her head crying, "No . . . no . . . no. . . ."

She must have made a small sound of distress, for he pivoted toward the entryway and saw her. The cruel twist of his mouth softened. His black brows lifted over the intense blue eyes that only the night before had regarded her with kindness and warmth.

He took a step toward her. "Mary?"

His voice vibrated with surprise and something else,

something akin to remorse. But he was incapable of so human an emotion. The truth stabbed Mary like a knife. The duke had never intended to help her. He was driven by his twisted hunger for vengeance.

Whispers like the rustling of leaves came from the rest of the small group. Sophy held a pink frosted teacake poised at her rosebud lips. Lord Harry abandoned his indolent pose and sat up straight. A woman with a fox-like face sourly turned down the corners of her mouth. The exquisite lady on the chaise wore a look of chilly disdain.

They all stared at Mary as if she were a ragpicker come to take tea with them. Her tongue felt frozen, her body a block of ice.

"You had express orders to stay away," the duchess said. Using the arms of her chair for support, Adam's mother rose to her feet. "Who admitted you into this house?"

She looked every inch a queen, from the sumptuous lavender gown to the imperious elevation of her chin. Yet her aging face bore the ravages of suffering.

In the raw wound of Mary's heart grew a tiny shoot of compassion. No matter how haughtily the duchess behaved, no matter how superior she believed herself, she was a mother who grieved for her injured son.

Mary found the strength to walk into the saloon. Deliberately she kept her gaze from Adam, though her skin prickled from the force of his stare. "Please, my lady duchess, I have good news for you. I've just come from Lord Cyril's bedchamber—"

"And you may now leave the premises." Adam strode to her side and took hold of her bare arm. "Before you distress my mother any further."

The pressure of his fingers startled her. Mary looked up at him, into the concentrated blue of his eyes. All the yearnings of the previous night—the desire to be clasped in his arms again, to know the tenderness of his touch and the ardor of his kiss—surged over her in a warm wave. She wanted to believe that the widening of his pupils meant he too was caught up in the rushing current of memory.

But his gentleness had been a lie. He had meant only to lull her suspicions so that he could send her away before she discovered his duplicity.

"Adam," the duchess said, "before Miss Sheppard leaves, I will hear her news."

"This is Miss Sheppard?" screeched the fox-faced older lady. "The hussy who shot Lord Cyril? Why was she allowed in his private chamber?"

"This is Miss *Mary* Sheppard," Adam said sharply. "Josephine's sister." Then his hand fell away from Mary, and she stepped around him. In a gesture of unquestioning respect, she dipped into a curtsy before the dowager.

"Your Grace, forgive me for intruding." Up close, Mary could see the fine lines of strain on the woman's proud face. "I must tell you that your son . . . Lord Cyril has awakened."

A stunned silence spread over the room. Then a babble of voices rose from the stillness.

"She is surely hoaxing us," said the younger lady in a silky smooth voice. "Women of her kind think nothing of vicious tale-telling."

"You did it," exclaimed Sophy, flinging her arms first around Mary, then around Lord Harry. "She truly did it."

His cheeks flushing, Lord Harry held Sophy by the waist. "Will wonders never cease?"

"I cannot believe . . ." The duchess held her trembling hands to her bosom. Painful hope glazed her eyes. "I must go to Cyril. I must see my son."

She brushed past as if Mary wasn't even there and walked swiftly toward the entrance hall. Lady Sophy grinned and squeezed Mary's hand, then hastened to assist her mother. Lord Harry took the duchess's other arm.

Mary slowly turned to Adam. She wouldn't think of how he had shattered her trust. Not just yet. First, she would relish his admiration, his thankfulness for resuscitating his brother.

But he wasn't even looking at her. He walked out of the saloon without a backward glance.

"How dare you burst into a private party and harangue the duke." The soft, cultured voice cut a swath through Mary's thoughts. "Leave this house at once."

The younger lady regarded her with cool contempt. This was the lady Adam would ask to be his wife. A strange sort of longing came over Mary. This was the woman he would smile at over the breakfast table, the woman who would bear his children, the woman with whom he would grow old. But she wasn't the duchess yet.

Mary lifted her chin. "You've no right to give orders here," she said, surprising herself with her imperiousness. "Unless you've done something highly improper with the duke."

Lady Camilla sucked in a breath. Her brown eyes filled with venom, and she fisted her fingers in her pale green skirt. "Why, you ill-bred bit of muslin. . . ."

Mary didn't linger. She marched away, her pride already deflating. Her chest felt as tight as an overwound clock. No matter how much she dreaded the prospect, she must join Adam at his brother's bedside.

As she hurried into the entrance hall, she barreled straight into him. For an instant, she was aware of his solid chest, his sandalwood scent, the supreme masculinity of him. In flustered confusion, she backed up a step and met the wall.

He pressed his hands to the wall to box her in. The lines of fatigue etching his brow and mouth enhanced his dangerous appeal. He looked every inch a gentleman . . . and a demon.

"Why did you not leave with your father?" he demanded in a harsh undertone.

"Because I had a feeling that I couldn't entrust my sister's welfare to you." Her voice sounded hoarse to her own ears, squeezed by the hurt in her throat. "And I was right."

The barest flicker of emotion crossed his hard features. "I suppose you would have found out sooner or later."

He gazed down at her with such icy hauteur that the taut ball of her pain burst, and she shoved at his chest. "Kindly move aside. I want to be present when your brother exonerates Jo."

"I will not have you badgering Cyril with your questions. He'll have a relapse if you remind him of Josephine's betrayal. You should never have come here in the first place."

The iron band of his arm encircled her waist. Mary found herself being marched through the domed hall, the scuffing of her slippers a faint echo of his determined strides.

A blank-faced footman opened the massive door, and before she could do more than sputter in protest, Adam deposited her outside on the portico, where the towering columns framed a view of the high iron fence that isolated the mansion from the common folk of London.

Even now, a day later, the metallic click of the closing door rang inside Mary's head.

She knelt in the garden and felt the bitter sting of humiliation all over again. Adam had dismissed her like an insubordinate servant. He had never even acknowledged her role in bringing his brother back to life. He had never apologized for using her. Instead, he had forbidden her access to the one man who could vindicate Jo.

She jammed the trowel into the dirt. She wanted to rage and rant. The need to do so lodged like an indigestible lump in her belly. Curse the duke. Curse him for treating her as if she were dirt beneath his expensive boots. . . .

A dark shadow blocked the sun. A man's shadow.

Mary gave a squeak of surprise. She turned on her knees and saw a pair of glossy black boots, two long, muscular legs encased in tan breeches, a broad chest in an indigo coat and elegantly tied cravat. And then the diabolically handsome face of her nemesis.

Sweet heaven. She had conjured up the duke of St. Chaldon.

He bowed. "Good afternoon, Miss Sheppard," he said in his deep baritone. "I beg your pardon for startling you."

Adam decided she looked more than stunned. She looked utterly adorable, from the smudge of soil on her cheek to the faintest scattering of freckles over the bridge of her nose. The breeze played with her hair, coaxing red-gold strands from the severely braided coronet. She wore a faded gray gown, but today he wasn't reminded of the timid mouse.

Hostility sparked in her green eyes. Her disapproval made his chest ache. He deserved no less for the pain he had caused her.

The mangy cur trotted forward, wagging its stub of a tail. Bending, Adam scratched the dog behind the ears and braced himself for Mary's blistering set-down.

It was not long in coming.

She resumed digging. "Obediah should have known better than to let the riffraff in," she said over her shoulder.

"I gave him no choice."

"You never do, not to anyone. You're accustomed to instant, unquestioning obedience."

Adam frowned down at her slender back. That shapeless gown might fool another man, but not him. Her feminine curves, the softness of her body, were indelibly etched on his memory. "Will you kindly stand up?" he said. "I prefer not to address your back."

"No. I've work to do."

He lowered his voice to a persuasive pitch. "I came to beg forgiveness for my boorish behavior yesterday. At the time, I was exceedingly worried about my brother."

"Apology acknowledged." Without looking up, she waved her trowel toward the rear door of the town house. "You may go now."

Adam tensed in spite of his resolve to remain calm. Who did she think she was to dismiss him?

Then again, perhaps he deserved a taste of his own medicine. "Not yet. There's a matter of importance I need to put before you."

"Unless you've come to admit that my sister isn't a murderess, we've nothing to discuss."

He chose his words with care. He couldn't afford to antagonize her further. "Of course. Josephine most certainly is not a murderess. My brother is very much alive, thanks to you." The high joy of his recovery warred with the low blow of Cyril's anger. But Mary needn't know about that. "I'm pleased to report that he's eating again, and the doctors say he should be out of bed within a fortnight."

Mary assaulted another patch of weeds. "Praise God for that."

Adam shifted his weight from one foot to the other. "I should also like to thank you."

"For letting you dupe me?" She jerked the clump out of the ground. "Why, it was my pleasure, Your Grace. I live to serve you and your kind."

He refused to rise to her bait. "Cyril said it was you he heard. It was your voice that brought him back from the dead."

She looked up at that, the weeds clutched in her grimy hand. With a swipe of her wrist, she brushed a strand of hair from her forehead and left another charming streak of dirt.

She sat back on her heels. The wary vulnerability in her eyes struck straight into his heart. "What else has he said?"

"Precious little. I've tried to protect him from undue strain."

"You must have asked him what happened the night he was shot."

"Indeed so." Adam gritted his teeth. This was the part that galled him, the part that had him pacing the floor deep into the night. "I'm afraid the sequence of events are rather cloudy in his mind. When I very gently suggested that Josephine might have run off with a new lover, he . . . said he will speak to no one but you."

The words Cyril had really uttered would scorch Mary's ears. He had exhibited such fierce anger that Adam still reeled from the blow of it. Cyril had always had a blithe smile, a quip to brighten the most solemn occasion, an irrepressible charm that brought warmth into the cold corridors of Brentwell House.

Of course, he also had a streak of adolescent daring, and ever since their father's untimely death, Adam had been forced to guide Cyril with a firm hand. He was accustomed to receiving respect and even a bit of hero worship from his much younger brother. But Adam's influence had ended with Josephine Sheppard. Cyril had stopped listening to reason. Caught up in romantic illusions, he had acceded to her every wish, even when she demanded the unthinkable, marriage to a nobleman far above her reach.

Guilt gnawed at Adam. God help him if Cyril ever learned of the means by which Adam had tried to stop the marriage. His brother wouldn't understand that he had acted solely out of the desire to save Cyril from making a terrible mistake.

Balanced on her heels, Mary glowered up at Adam, her face a haunting replica of her sister's. Uncomfortably, he felt his private thoughts pierced by that knowing stare.

"Ah, now I see why you deigned to come here." Mary aimed her trowel at him as if she were God pointing at a sinner on Judgment Day. "You want to use me again. Just as you did when you threw me to Peterbourne and all those other lechers."

The image of her with that aging rake still haunted Adam. "I should never have subjected you to such an ordeal. I most humbly beg your forgiveness again."

"How prettily you apologize. You, who led me to believe you had my sister's best interests at heart. And all the while you were plotting to hang her from the nearest gibbet."

He needn't feel ashamed, Adam told himself, for wanting to bring Cyril's assailant to justice. He clasped his hands behind his back. "The courts will determine her fate. If she's innocent, she has nothing to fear."

"Yet you've already condemned her."

He was tempted to deny it. He wanted to see warmth on Mary's face instead of accusation. But he would not hide behind another lie. "Yes, I have."

"You . . . you . . ."

Mary pinched her lips together like a maiden aunt, though her heaving bosom bore no resemblance to that of anyone so prim. From his superior vantage point, he couldn't help but notice her shadowy cleavage through the unbuttoned throat of her gown. He should avert his gaze. He should not think of how soft and sweet she had felt in his arms. . . .

"You *nobleman.*"

Scrambling to her feet, Mary hurled a handful of weeds at him. The suddenness of her attack caught Adam off guard. He stepped backward, half tripping over the dog that leaped up with a yelp. But Adam did not move fast enough. Dirt and leaves rained down on him, adhering to his clothing. Grit slid inside his cravat and clods of earth rolled down his boots.

"Good God!" He dashed the debris from his shoulders. With forefinger and thumb, he plucked off a bedraggled plant that had landed on his blue waistcoat, and the roots left a brown smear. "There is no need for such uncivilized behavior."

Mary dusted off her hands. She had the audacity to look pleased with herself. "Pardon me, Your Grace. We common girls don't know the polite ways of the ton."

"You should know better than to sling mud."

"Perhaps you would have preferred me to slap your

cheek and demand a meeting at dawn with pistols. Isn't that how you aristocrats settle your differences?"

He whipped out a crisply starched handkerchief and wiped the mess from his boots. "Dueling is not for females. Its purpose is to settle a point of honor between two gentlemen."

"Gracious. One might almost believe you rank yourself among men of integrity."

Adam paused in the act of scrubbing his boots. Every muscle in his body went rigid. No one had ever dared to dispute his honor. No one.

Straightening very slowly, he folded the soiled handkerchief with military precision and tucked it in an inside pocket. Then he graced her with his most frigid stare. "I will pretend I did not hear that."

"Then allow me to elaborate. You lied to me. You led me to believe you were my sister's savior when you're really her enemy." She ticked off each statement on her grimy fingers. "You have no decency, no principles, and certainly no morals."

That did it. Grasping her arms, he dragged her against him, then moved his hands to her slim waist to hold her in place. His blood surged with untimely heat. He detested men who used force on a woman, yet his sense of reason seemed to have evaporated. "Perhaps you'd care for a demonstration of precisely how low my morals have sunk."

Mary blinked. Her lips parted and she looked cautiously at him from beneath the fringe of her lashes. Then she lifted her chin and fixed him with a glare. "That reminds me. I've one more sin to lay at your feet. You nearly stole my innocence."

Her maidenly outrage pierced the black thundercloud of his wrath. Adam could only stare at her a moment; then a grin quirked his lips. In his silkiest tone, he said, "Oh, did I? Just when did this momentous event nearly happen?"

Pink tinted her cheeks. "You know perfectly well that

you kissed me. Three times. All to satisfy your wicked lust."

An unexpected tenderness crept past his defenses. He couldn't resist running the pad of his thumb over her lips. Her soft, moist lips. "A kiss wouldn't begin to satisfy a man. You've a lot to learn about bodily pleasure, Mistress Mary."

Her blush deepened to a furious rose. She slapped his hand away. "Stop addressing me so. I'm not your mistress."

"We can both be thankful for that."

But Adam suddenly ached to take her to bed. He wanted to see that glorious red-gold hair spread against the white linens. He wanted to feel her untried body awaken beneath his, to hear her voice cry out to him in ecstasy. He wanted to sate the burning obsession that kept him awake at night.

Just as much, he wanted to coax her to laugh. She was both irksome and invigorating, for he never knew what peculiar opinion she would toss at him. An undeniable fondness for her warmed the coldness inside him, the frigid core that he had not even been aware of before meeting her.

How ludicrous. Mary Sheppard was not the sort of woman who attracted him. He preferred a skilled seductress who knew precisely how to please a man. And he liked to take his pleasure with a minimum of fuss. Not while being harangued by a self-righteous virgin who reminded him of his shortcomings.

When he released her, his arms felt empty. "Enough of this bickering," he said crisply. "My brother wishes to speak with you. If you're truly determined to locate your sister, you'll come with me."

⁓ **Chapter 13** ⁓

An hour later, Mary found herself back in Lord Cyril's splendid bedchamber. The draperies were half drawn, and an opened window let in a waft of sunshiny air. She settled herself on a stool beside the four-poster bed that was hung with elaborate swags of cream silk tied back with gold cord.

She had washed in haste, scrubbing the dirt from beneath her fingernails and exchanging her old soiled gown for one of immaculate pale green. She left her hair in its coronet, loath to let the duke think she had primped for his benefit. He had said little to her on the journey to Brentwell House, beyond that he had persuaded his mother to take a refreshing drive in Hyde Park and packed Sophy off with her.

With restrained energy, he paced near the foot of the bed. He looked impeccable as always except for the dark smudge of dirt on his blue waistcoat. A belated bubble of humor rose in Mary as she remembered his undignified leap backward, his finely tailored coat decorated by debris from the garden.

Of course, it was God's right to mete out punishment. But oh, she did not regret her act of temper. She did not.

She primly adjusted her skirts and turned her attention to her sister's fiancé. Lord Cyril lay propped against a mountain of pillows. The pallor of illness bleached his skin.

She thought for a moment he was sleeping; then his fair lashes lifted.

His eyes were the clear blue of the summer sky. The bandage wrapping his head gave him a rakish air. His lips curved into a friendly smile, the antithesis of his older brother. "Miss Sheppard," he said in a raspy voice. "I'd hoped you would come back."

She almost hadn't. She had almost let the duke nettle her so much that anger had taken precedence over her sister. "My lord, I've been praying for your recovery. And please call me Mary."

"Mary it is." Cyril's amiable features hardened as he glanced at his brother. "I should like to speak with her alone."

Adam braced his hand on the bedpost. "I've a right to be here. To look out for your interests."

"*My* interests? Or yours?" Cyril dug his fingers into the embroidered counterpane. "You're concerned only for your own sacred reputation—"

"Please don't quarrel," Mary broke in. "Let him stay if he likes. There's been too much secretiveness already." She touched Lord Cyril's fisted hand. "It's high time he accepted the truth about Jo."

Slowly the look of animosity eased from Cyril's face. He appeared all the paler as if the moment of hostility had drained his meager resources.

He turned his hand over and held hers in a warm grip. His keen eyes studied her as if searching out the similarities and differences to his beloved. "Mary the peacemaker. You're just as Jo described you."

Wistful pain knotted her throat. So many times she had intervened when Jo and their father argued. "She spoke of me, then?"

"Often. She longed to see you again. To make amends and ask your forgiveness for leaving without saying farewell."

It is I who needs to beg forgiveness.

Mary hung her head in shame. She wanted to confess her sin, but the words would not leave her lips. She had coveted Victor. She had rejected her sister. She had let pride and self-righteousness stop her from going after her twin.

"Jo wondered . . ." Lord Cyril paused to clear his throat, his voice hoarse. ". . . why you never responded to her letters."

Mary's head shot up. Shock clenched deep inside her. "Letters? I received only one letter from her in three months."

"But she wrote many . . . unless with all your traveling . . . the mail didn't reach you." He succumbed to a fit of coughing.

Mary leaped up and poured water into a tumbler on the bedside table. When she turned to the bed, Adam was already there, his arm beneath his brother's head to lift him for a drink.

Lord Cyril sipped a moment, then lay back, taking several breaths. "Throat aches . . . that's better now."

Adam stepped back, his attention concentrated on his brother. "Try not to waste your strength on reminiscing. Just tell us what happened on the night you were shot."

Lord Cyril raised one eyebrow in the same imperious way that Mary had seen Adam do. "I've thought about little else since yesterday. It's come back to me in bits and pieces. . . ."

"Such as?" Mary sat down very quietly, breathless for his answer.

He stared into the distance. "Jo and I quarreled at dinner that night. You see, I wanted to post the banns for our marriage and give her a proper wedding at St. George's with all the ton present. But she . . . wanted to cry off the engagement."

Mary blinked in astonishment. "Why? Surely she loves you."

He smiled, his eyes bleak. "That's precisely the problem.

The disapproval of my family had shaken her. She couldn't bear the thought of causing me to be cut off from the people who are dear to me."

Of course. Jo would have been thinking of her own familial estrangement, Mary realized with a heavy heart. Her gaze went to Adam, who stood motionless at the foot of the bed, a closed expression on his face. She wanted to rant at him, to tell him precisely what she thought of him for denying his blessing to the love match.

Yet she could not lay all the blame on his broad shoulders. She herself had caused her sister much unhappiness.

"What happened then?" Mary whispered.

"Like a petulant child, I stormed out of her house." Lord Cyril's mouth twisted in self-reproach. "For hours, I walked the streets, angry and hurt that she would give me up so easily, that she would not use her beauty, her wit, her warmth to charm society. *I* could laugh off the malicious gossip, the snubs, the icy glares. Then slowly I realized that as the outsider, Jo would bear the brunt of the cruelty." He picked at a thread in the bedcovers. "And so I conceded we should marry quietly and live at my country estate. To see Jo happy was more important to me than pleasing my family and friends."

The breeze stirred the curtains. Mary felt a great welling within herself, the yearning to know such love herself. Did Victor feel so strongly for her? He had kissed her with an almost frightening fervor. If she'd told him of her secret dream to live in a house with a garden, would he have agreed? Would he have sacrificed for her his place in her father's mission?

She would never know the answer now, for she did not love him. How vastly different were her and Adam's views on marriage. No doubt he had selected Lady Camilla for her impeccable breeding.

He paced slowly, staring at the floor as if it held the secrets of the universe. *Love is of little consequence in choosing a wife,* he'd told her. *To a man of noble birth, marriage is a dynastic alliance, the union of two eminent families.*

Mary forced her gaze back to Lord Cyril. "And then you returned to tell Jo what you had decided."

He nodded grimly. "I let myself in with my key, not wanting to wake the servants. The house was silent except for Prinny whining and scratching at the garden door." His tawny brows drew together in a frown. "I remember thinking it odd because when I wasn't there, Jo let the dog sleep in her room."

"She hated being alone," Mary whispered. "It frightened her, she said."

"I know." Lord Cyril swallowed, his hand to his throat. "I went upstairs to her bedroom. From the doorway, I could see Jo lying in bed, the glow of the moon on her face. She was asleep." His expression went soft with memory, but only for a moment. Every bit of light left his face. "And then I saw him. The black shape of a man, leaning over her."

"The kidnapper," Mary breathed, sitting on the edge of her stool.

Adam stopped pacing. "Did you recognize him?"

Lord Cyril rubbed the bandage across his brow. "No. I think . . . he might have been wearing a hood over his face. And I was blinded by fury, a murderous fear that he would harm Jo. I rushed forward and he turned toward me. There was the explosion of a shot. . . ." His jaw tight, Lord Cyril slammed his fist into the bed. "Damn him to hell. Who is he? Where did he take Jo? Why haven't you found her?"

Tears filmed his eyes, and he turned his head away, pinching the bridge of his nose with his thumb and forefinger.

Mary perceived his wrenching pain as if it were her own. And it *was* hers. They shared a deep love for Jo and an even deeper sense of loss. She sat down on the bed, uncertain of how to comfort him . . . or herself.

The bedropes creaked as Adam sat down behind her, his knee pressing lightly into her bottom. He drew forth a handkerchief and held it out to his brother.

Blinking hard, Lord Cyril waved away the offering. "Now, Mary, I'll have you know I haven't acted like such a watering pot since I was seven."

"When I thrashed the tar out of you," Adam said. "Because you hid in a cupboard and watched the governess at her bath."

A phantom grin flitted across Lord Cyril's lips. "A harmless prank."

"Oh? She screeched to the high heavens and fled that very day, never to return."

"And good riddance to the shrew."

Listening to them, Mary felt like an outsider. They spoke so casually of a way of life that she had never known and would never know. But for an accident of birth, she might have been raised in a world where children were kept tucked away in a nursery, cared for by servants. Her own upbringing seemed warm and intimate by comparison, she and Jo and their father living together in close quarters, sharing meals around a campfire.

Lord Cyril frowned again at his brother. "Jo does not have another lover. If you so much as allude to one again, I shall thrash *you* within an inch of your life."

Angled on the bed, Mary glanced from one man to the other. The two brothers shared a hard stare for a moment. Adam was the first to look away.

A muscle worked in his jaw as if he wrestled with his disbelief. "I suppose," he said slowly, "if she had been intending to run away with the man, she would have been awake and dressed for travel. Therefore, she may well have been abducted."

The reluctance in his voice irked Mary. He ought to be groveling, apologizing. "On the contrary," she snapped, "I'm certain Jo planned the ruse. She cleverly donned her nightgown and pretended to be asleep in order to make it look like an abduction."

"Just in case I should happen by," Cyril added blandly.

Adam sat very still. Then his frosty expression thawed into a wry smile. "All right, I deserve your most scathing mockery. For assuming the worst of Josephine."

A mighty surge of relief rose in Mary. Purely on impulse, she threw her arms around his neck. "Oh, Adam. Do you really mean it? You finally believe what I've been telling you all along?"

His arms closed around her. "Between the two of you, I don't seem to have a choice," he said gruffly into her ear.

His warm breath tickled her skin. His nearness enveloped her in his unique spicy essence. Against her breasts, his heart thrummed with a steady beat. A sweet, heavy ache settled deep within her, that yearning for something just beyond her reach, something she felt only with him.

Lord Cyril cleared his throat. Mary and Adam sprang apart. Mortified, she glanced at Lord Cyril. He watched them, unsmiling, one eyebrow arched, though he said nothing.

Adam got to his feet. A ruddy flush colored his cheeks. "Yes, well, now that we've established what a fool I've been, let's solve the mystery. Do you remember anything else, Cyril? Was there perhaps a vehicle waiting on the street?"

Closing his eyes, Lord Cyril rubbed his brow again as if it pained him. "Do you know . . . there *was* something. . . ."

"What?" Mary prompted.

"I saw a hackney coach parked in front of the neighboring house. I remember thinking that the neighbors were entertaining rather late." He opened his eyes, his expression hard. "The kidnapper must have used it to take Jo away."

Adam prowled beside the bed, his hands clasped behind

his back. "Were there any distinguishing marks on this coach? Something that might help me identify it."

"I think . . . the name of a livery stable was painted on the door in white lettering. . . ." He pressed both hands to his bandaged head. "Devil take it. I can't remember anymore."

"You've exhausted yourself," Adam said. "Rest now, and we'll talk more in the morning."

Mary rose reluctantly. "May I return tomorrow?"

"Of course." Warmth shone through Lord Cyril's weariness, and he reached for her hand. "Wait. What of the special bond between your minds? Has Jo tried to contact you?"

Her mouth went dry. "You know . . . ?"

He nodded. "She feared you'd trained yourself to ignore her messages. Because your father called the ability to hear each other's thoughts an evil curse." His fingers tightened around Mary's. "But I think it's a fascinating gift."

Adam made an impatient gesture. "It's a delusion, that's what it is."

"You can't see it, therefore it doesn't exist?" Lord Cyril said. "It's a wonder you believe in God or the devil."

They glowered at each other, and Mary said, "Jo did try to contact me. A few days ago, I received a faint communication from her."

Lord Cyril turned his head toward Mary. "What did she say?"

"The message was garbled. I could distinguish only a few words." She subdued a shiver, determined to hide that impression of cold terror from him. "Jo conveyed nothing to indicate where she is or who's holding her."

"Ah, if only I could get out of this blasted bed and track her down." He struggled to sit, but fell back against the pillows and slapped his palm on the mattress. "Hellfire and damnation, lifting my head makes me dizzy."

"I'll find her for you. I promise I will."

"You must." Cyril reached out and squeezed her hand. "Just as Jo said, you're the best of sisters."

As Adam guided her out of the bedroom, despair dragged down Mary's heart. The best of sisters. If only Lord Cyril knew the truth. If only he knew there was another, darker reason why she had repressed the heart bond.

She had come here in the desperate hope that he would identify the kidnapper. But it was to no avail. And now she held the burden of her sister's fate in her own frail hands.

"Come now," the duke said in a deep timbre. "You needn't pull such a melancholy face. I'll track down Josephine. If I can determine which livery stable the hackney coach came from, I can obtain a description of the man who rented it."

They stood at the top of the curving staircase that led down to the domed entrance hall. Mary braced herself on the wrought-iron railing as lingering suspicion returned to haunt her. "Why would you help my sister? If Jo never returns, it neatly solves the problem of your brother's marriage plans."

"I've never denied that the alliance is ill-judged. As head of the family I cannot permit him to make a mistake he'll regret later." Adam placed his hands lightly on her shoulders as if to convince her of his sincerity. "Yet credit me with some honor at least. I would never stand by idly while an innocent woman is held against her will."

Mary wanted to believe him. She wanted to press her cheek against his chest and seek refuge in the warm embrace of another human being. *His* embrace. She wanted to think there was a worthy man inside the duke's haughtily handsome exterior. Could she really trust a man who had lied to her already?

Resisting temptation, Mary started down the stairs. Over her shoulder, she said, "You needn't bother yourself. I'll find my sister alone."

He kept pace with her, his footfalls grating on the marble steps. "You play a dangerous game, Mary Sheppard. This is an unprincipled villain you're facing."

"Oh, so you admit you lack principles."

"I was not referring to myself," he snapped. "The kidnapper could take you hostage, too."

"How convenient. You would be rid of me as well."

"This is no time for jests. You will tell me precisely how you intend to imperil yourself."

"Why, Your Grace, can't you guess?" Quelling the doubts about her ability to succeed, she stopped at the base of the stairs and gazed straight into his scowling face. "I mean to delude myself. To reach my sister through my thoughts."

"Practice your smoke-and-mirror nonsense if you must." His glower altered subtly into a frown of concern. He took her hand in his and lightly stroked the back. "Only promise me that you won't endanger yourself. Please. Any man who would abduct a woman at gunpoint is ruthless indeed."

His warning stirred a shudder in Mary. Or was it his warm touch that roused the shivery tension deep in her belly?

Her disappointment that Adam still scoffed at her unnatural gift was tempered by the secret thrill that he wanted to protect her. Standing before him in the great hall, feeling the caress of his blue eyes and hearing the faint sounds of traffic in the street outside, she knew an inexplicable sense of rightness.

And a bond as undeniable as the joining of their hands.

In another part of the city, the earl of Peterbourne lounged naked in bed.

The housemaid who serviced him in the dimness of his bedchamber was as ugly as a hound and as eager as a bitch in heat. The skirt and apron hiked to her waist, she squatted over him, displaying her broad thighs and wiry-haired privates. The sight, combined with her expert pawing of Tall Dick, would at one time have driven the earl into a frenzy of lust.

Instead, his member lay as limp as a cold white worm on his groin.

The humiliation of his impotence enraged him. Not even fantasizing about the fruitful exploits of his randy youth could stiffen him. He gave her a hard shove in the belly. "Get away, you slut."

With a canine yelp, she retreated to the edge of the bed and crouched there, panting. "Please, m'lord. Lemme 'ave another go at ye. If ye were t' suck me titties—"

A discreet knocking on the bedroom door interrupted her. The earl pushed himself into a sitting position against the pillows. His joints were sore, and the movement pained him. Testily, he squinted as a shaft of afternoon sunlight penetrated a crack in the draperies. "Answer the door, you witless whelp."

"Aye, m'lord." She scrambled to obey, and her feet thumped onto the fine carpet. A moment later, she returned to the bed and handed over an envelope. Against the pale cream vellum lay the red seal of the archbishop.

As Peterbourne opened the missive and examined the contents, his wrath disintegrated beneath a burst of triumph. He shook the paper in the air. "Ha—ha! The game has taken a new turn."

The servant gaped uncomprehendingly. "Wot game, m'lord?"

" 'Tis the amusement of a lifetime. And now all my pawns are in place."

The scent of victory roused a hunger in his loins. For the first time in months, Tall Dick rose to the occasion. The earl dropped the paper onto the bedside table. Then he yanked down her bodice and pinched her large teats.

The bitch loosed a growl of pleasure. On all fours, she crawled onto the bed. He turned her around and tossed up her skirts, thrusting his finger into her wetness. Her ample white tail wagged an invitation at him.

"Oh, m'lord. I die, m'lord!"

So would he soon, Peterbourne thought grimly. But now he could take a certain person to hell with him.

She wept in darkness.

The ceaseless song of the sea underscored her quiet sobbing. Today he had come to her again. He had placed a devil's bargain before her: wed him or he would sell her to an Eastern whoremaster.

She had not believed him at first. She had stared straight into those unearthly eyes and laughed.

He had slapped her into silence. So hard that she struck her head on the stone wall and fell to the floor. While she lay there stunned, he gave her until dawn to decide.

As he left her alone and she heard the key rattling in the lock, she already knew her answer. She could never marry such a man. Never. Enslavement could be no worse than suffering the terrible pain of losing Cyril.

The agonizing memory seized her again. The explosion of the shot. The jolt to awareness. The horror of finding her beloved sprawled at her bedside, blood flowing from his head.

She shuddered, wrapping her arms around herself. Her throat felt raw from weeping, and the damp chill of the night lived in her bones. Never had she felt so cold, so alone. She wanted to shriek out her despair like the gulls that swooped the sky at daybreak. She wanted to moan like the wind that blew through the window slits of her prison. But the well of her strength had run dry.

*She curled herself into a ball on the stone floor. Mary. Oh,
Mary, don't trust him . . . don't trust him. . . .*

Mary swam to the surface of the dream. Disoriented, she
blinked into the darkness. The sound of the sea echoed in
her ears. Sluggishly she lifted her hand to her cheek and
touched the dampness there. As she did so, something
white flashed in the shadows above her.

She gasped, her heart speeding in alarm. *Don't trust him
. . . don't trust him. . . .*

The nightmare receded like a dark tide, and she came
fully awake. How foolish of her. She had glimpsed her own
ghostly reflection in the large mirror that was tucked into
the canopy.

She pushed up onto one elbow. Gloom lurked thick as
thieves around the bed. Her gaze picked out the somber
shapes of chaise and wardrobe and chest. Across the room,
moonlight lacquered the dressing table, and the cosmetic
jars and perfume bottles shone with a celestial silver glow.

This was her sister's bedchamber. Mary had chosen to
sleep here tonight instead of occupying the guest room. By
surrounding herself with Jo's possessions, she had hoped
to strengthen the bond between their hearts. All around
her, she felt the presence of her twin wrapping her in
warmth and despair.

She fingered the wetness on her face again. She had
been weeping as her sister wept.

Mary sat up straight against the pillows as realization
struck her. Sweet heaven. Her plan had worked! She had
seen her sister imprisoned, dreading the return of her captor. There had been the rhythmic lapping of waves. . . .

Jo was not in London, then. Perhaps she hadn't been all
along. Her gaol lay somewhere along the coast. No wonder
they had been unable to find her!

Too agitated to remain in bed, Mary threw off the coverlet. She slid from the mattress, and the bare floorboards
chilled her feet. She thrust her arms into a dressing gown

that belonged to her sister. The silk caressed her skin as she paced from moonlight to shadow and back again.

Waves. Seagulls. Stone.

Jo's cell was made of stone with several narrow slits for windows. A stone structure by the sea. Mary's spirit soared with unbearable hope. Just as quickly, it sank into despondency again.

Perhaps Jo's abductor had already sold her to a foreign brothel. During her week here in London, Mary had glimpsed a few episodes from her sister's past. Was the dream just another memory? Was Jo already confined aboard a ship to an Eastern port? Or was she still waiting in her chilly stone prison?

Mary, don't trust him . . . don't trust him. . . .

Her kidnapper must be someone familiar to Mary. Or perhaps someone Jo would expect to seek out Mary in London. But who? Lord Peterbourne? Another unknown suitor?

A small, dark shape stirred on the hearth rug. Prinny stretched, paws extended and rump elevated. The dog trotted over to nudge her with his cold nose.

She knelt in a whisper of silk and hugged the animal, rubbing her cheek against the matted fur of his neck. "It can't be too late. I won't let myself believe that."

Prinny whined and licked her hand.

She rewarded him with a scratch behind the ears. "If only you could tell me who locked you outside that night. If only you could tell me who abducted Jo."

The dog's stubby tail thumped on the floor. His mournful brown eyes gleamed through the shadows.

Mary sighed. Her gaze stole unwillingly to the dark blemish on the floor where Lord Cyril had fallen. Jo thought him dead. Dead! If only she knew.

Mary closed her eyes and concentrated all her energy on her sister. *Jo, are you listening? Cyril is alive. He's recovering. You mustn't give up. Do you hear me? Please answer. . . .*

She sensed the black passage stretching out . . . out

. . . out. Yet no radiance shone at the end of it. Through
the long murky miles came a faint rippling like a voice
muffled behind a thick door. Surely Jo wouldn't close her
thoughts, not when she desperately needed aid. Mary
clenched her fingers into fists. Dear God, their estrangement was her fault. By shutting her sister out, she had lost
the ability to contact Jo.

Frustrated to the verge of tears, Mary sprang to her feet.
She couldn't just sit and wait for morning. Yet the vastness
of her quest daunted her. It would take weeks to search
out every stone edifice on the coast of England. By then, Jo
would have been spirited away.

Adam would know what to do. Yes. She must go to him
straightaway.

Mary hastened out of the bedroom and dashed toward
the darkened staircase. Halfway down, she stopped, her
hand on the wooden banister. How cockle-brained of her.
She could hardly brave the streets of London clad in
nightrail and robe. Nor could she bang on the duke's door
and awaken his household. If Adam refused to receive her
in daytime, it wasn't likely he would welcome her in the
dead of the night.

No matter how strong the impulse, she shouldn't confide
in him. Once already, he had played her for the gullible
country miss. Yet she could not forget the look of steadfast
remorse on his face, or the caring in his eyes when he
regarded his brother. Had Adam really meant it this time
when he promised to help her?

*I would never stand by idly while an innocent woman is
held against her will.*

She sank to the step and propped her chin in her palms.
The dog lay down on the riser behind her and wedged
himself against her back, a warm comforting presence in
the dark. When Adam had spoken those words, only hours
ago, she had resisted the pull of his magnetism. Once a
liar, always a liar.

No, she could not believe that. It went against her nature

to be so cynical. Hadn't she lectured her father on forgiveness? She would far rather choose to have faith in her fellow human beings than to assume the worst of them.

Even if this particular human being was an aristocrat.

Somehow, the darkness made her thoughts shine clearer. She had been too quick to accuse Adam of dishonor. She hadn't stopped to consider *why* he had deceived her, that he had acted out of the misguided wish to bring his brother's assailant to justice. She could not fault him for that. She herself would do anything, say anything, to protect her sister.

And when faced with Cyril's testimony, Adam had been honest enough to admit his error. Mary's doubts dissolved into a reluctant trust. She must depend on him. Else Jo might die.

Her sister's fate weighing on her mind, Mary cautiously felt her way downstairs, into the depthless gloom of the foyer. Obediah would be asleep in his cellar room, but she could light a candle with the tinderbox on the writing desk in the parlor. The dog loped ahead, his night vision keener than hers, his claws clacking on the marble floor of the entryway.

The faint ticking of the mantel clock sounded like the beating of a heart. Sorrow seemed to pulse through the darkness as if the house were a living entity that grieved for its absent mistress.

Loneliness caught Mary in a sudden, fierce grip. She had lost Jo and Victor and her father. She had no one left, no one to depend on but herself. She ached from the emptiness of solitude, from the awareness of a soul-deep yearning for . . . Adam. If only he was here with her. If only she could forget her troubles and burrow into his warm arms. If only she could experience the tenderness of his kiss again and know that she was not alone.

Nothing could ever come of their association, she reminded herself. They lived in worlds as far apart as the sun and the moon. Yet curiously, she had felt more separated

from Victor, as if she were the lesser being, a mere mortal
who knelt humbly at the feet of a saint. Adam, on the other
hand, was human.

In the space of a few short days, she had come to see
beyond his image of lofty nobleman. Like her, he was more
sinner than saint. How strange to realize they shared human foibles, that beneath the veneer of opinions and
creeds, she and Adam were flesh and blood, man and
woman. The notion was both unsettling and seductive.

Mary patted the surface of the writing desk, found the
small oval tinderbox, and opened it. She would pass the
solitary hours of night by writing a note to Adam that
Obediah could deliver in the morning. Then she would find
a map and determine the most likely places to begin the
search. And she would pack her valise in preparation to
depart for the coast.

Of course, Adam would scoff when she told him of the
message from her sister. He would order her to stay out of
danger. Not that she intended to heed his dictatorial command.

Striking steel to flint, she watched a tiny shower of
sparks fall to the tinder and wink out before she could
blow them into flame. Excitement curled inside her at the
prospect of seeing him again. She should not dwell upon
how impossibly handsome he looked when he smiled. She
should not remember the way his intense blue gaze could
make her melt. She should not dream of kissing him again
. . . and more.

And yet she did. Her immodest longings crowded past
her conscience. In the most secret place of her heart, she
ached to learn the mysteries of sexual passion. And God
forgive her, she wanted Adam as her teacher.

The clock struck the hour of half past midnight, the
doleful chimes scolding her for her wicked thoughts. She
must subdue her unchaste urges. She must not surrender
to this weakness of the flesh.

Yet a forbidden image stole into her mind, and her skin

flushed with warmth. Knees like jelly, she sat down in the darkness, the unlit candle forgotten in her lap. As if their souls were joined, she saw Adam lying in his grand ducal bed with the azure and silver hangings. His naked body would be dark against the white linens, his black hair boyishly tousled, and his eyes closed in slumber. . . .

Adam lay awake, the back of his head pillowed on his arms.

Instead of the darkened chamber, he pictured Mary curled up in her bed, asleep. Her red-gold hair would be wild and loose, her nightdress fashioned of a pale silk that showed a tantalizing hint of womanly curves. From beneath the hem, one bare leg stretched out to him like an offering. He would touch her there first, with infinitely more finesse than he had at their first meeting. He would caress her slender foot and move his hand up the shapely calf to the silky warm thigh and beyond. . . .

Devil take it. No matter how weary he was, he would sleep no more tonight.

He thrust himself from the bed and stalked across the fine Axminster carpet. In the shadows of the dressing room, he donned breeches and shirt and coat at random, tying his neckcloth with a carelessness that would send Fenwick into a swoon. But Adam had no intention of encountering the valet or anyone else.

He strode out into the gloomy corridor and made his way downstairs, his footsteps a sharp tapping in the quiet house. The clock in the library bonged the hour of half past midnight, echoing the casement clock in the grand saloon. All the servants lay abed and his mother and Sophy retired early. Cyril slept, too, exhausted from the strain of the day. There was only the watchman to avoid on the front portico.

As stealthy as an escaping prisoner, Adam let himself out a side door. Unerringly, he followed the stone path through the formal garden. When he reached the iron

fence, he used his key to unlock the gate. He waited in the
shadow of a plane tree as a carriage rattled past. Then he
stepped across the street at a brisk pace.

Free. He was free from the strictures of his rank. Out
here he was just another pedestrian hurrying to an unknown destination. The relief of it eddied through Adam
with startling intensity. Why had he never done this before? And why would he consider his exalted station a hin-
drance?

It was only that he needed time alone. Time to think.

He breathed deeply of the night air, relishing its sweetness despite the ever present odor of horse droppings and
rubbish. In the city, he strictly adhered to the Brentwell
custom of riding about in carriages or on horseback. It
wouldn't do, his mother always said, for the duke of St.
Chaldon to be seen striding afoot like a costermonger.

At the family seat in Derbyshire, however, Adam often
took long walks in the evening. He did his best thinking
that way, alone, without chattering guests or endless social
functions to distract him. Then he could concentrate on
the problems of running the huge estate, analyzing the
crop yield or weighing the advantages of purchasing additional dairy cows.

Tonight, his nocturnal wanderings served the need to
clear his head and cool his loins. He had brooded about
Mary far too much of late. Especially since she had ques-
tioned his honor.

*You lied to me. You led me to believe you were my sister's
savior when you're really her enemy. You have no decency, no
principles, and certainly no morals.*

Her low opinion shouldn't matter to him. Yet it had
shaken the foundation of his belief in himself. She made
him wonder uneasily if he was no true gentleman, after all.
He, who prided himself on his integrity.

"You there!" snapped out a harsh male voice. "Come
lend my men a hand."

Adam looked across the street and saw a coach stopped

in the shadows beyond the circle of light cast by a gas lamp. The vehicle was tilted drunkenly, one wheel lying on the cobblestones. While the coachman and postillion struggled to right the carriage, a portly man in top hat and evening dress paced nearby.

He gestured imperiously to Adam. "Don't dally, man. I'll pay you a shilling for a few minutes' labor."

Adam's spine stiffened. No one addressed him in that tyrannical tone. No one.

Then he realized how he must look, clad in nondescript garb, on foot like a servant or tradesman who could not afford the fare of a short-stage. Perhaps anonymity had a price.

He headed toward the coach and hunkered down to peer into the gloom beneath it. "Broken axle?" he asked the coachman.

"Nay. Blamed nut came loose. If ye and Roach 'ere could 'elp lift 'er up, I can slide on the wheel."

Adam nodded. He and the lanky postillion gripped the undercarriage and heaved upward. The weight of the coach strained Adam's muscles. Especially when the pair of matched blacks shied nervously, dragging the vehicle forward a few inches and setting the load off balance.

"You there, hold the horses," he ordered the gentleman.

"I beg your pardon?"

"Do not stand there like an ass. Make yourself useful. Now."

Apparently surprised by Adam's aristocratic speech, the well-heeled man gawked a moment at him, then hastened to grab hold of the traces. In short order, the wheel was remounted and the coachman tightened the axle nut. Adam took out a handkerchief and wiped a spot of grease from his fingers.

The gentleman trotted forward. "Forgive me, m'lord, for not recognizing you to be Quality." All fawning attention, he peered through the shadows. "If I might make your acquaintance—"

"You may not," Adam said.

Turning on his heel, he strode away into the night. Yet he was not so much disgusted with the gentleman as with himself. A week ago, he would have thought nothing of addressing a tradesman with the same negligent disdain. How mortifying to realize that Mary was right about him.

A duke is born to command. Never forget, you are superior to other men.

His father's deathbed proclamation had guided Adam into adulthood. He had taken great pride in making himself a model of gentlemanly behavior. But now he could see he had deluded himself. Deep within his soul resided a man who fancied himself on a pedestal above his fellow human beings, a man so arrogant he believed himself justified in lying to a commoner.

It was painful to be stripped of his pretenses. Painful to face the fact that he deserved every word of Mary's dressing down. He, of the venerable name of St. Chaldon, possessed the same frailties as any person, rich or poor. Perhaps he was no better than the lowliest mudlark who combed the banks of the Thames for useful castoffs.

A part of him resisted the disturbing thought. The common man of the streets lacked the wisdom to rule the country, while men of rank had been groomed to sit in Parliament and make the laws. Were the nobility stripped of power, anarchy would reign as it had in France during the bloody revolution.

As young as he had been at that time, Adam retained the vivid memory of hearing guests of his father exchange terrifying tales about peasant mobs sending entire families of aristocrats to the guillotine. Adam would never permit such violence to invade the shores of England. He would not be reduced to mere *Citoyen* Brentwell while hotheads like the Reverend Thomas Sheppard seized his lands and destroyed all that he and his predecessors had worked to amass.

He'd like to tell Mary so right now, to watch her face

light up with the fervor of the debate. Like a lodestone, she drew him and he found himself walking toward that quietly genteel neighborhood near the Strand.

But she would be asleep at this late hour. At this very moment, she would be lying in bed, her body soft and warm and womanly. Perhaps she would be hugging her pillow and dreaming in the moonlight, a secret smile bowing her lips. . . .

Heat seized him with a vengeance. How adolescent of him, to let fantasies rule him. Better he should pay a visit to Madame Antoinette's establishment. He could purchase the services of a discreet ladybird who would not irritate him with her contrary opinions. Yes. He would release his physical tension and be done with it. He would prove to himself that he had not lost his head over Mary Sheppard.

His steps sharp on the pavement, he headed toward his new destination. The elegant town houses of Mayfair gradually gave way to a less prestigious district, where the homes were smaller and the streets less traveled. Here, fog rolled in off the Thames, curling like sea foam around his ankles. The glow of an occasional gas lamp shone hazily through the mist. With the scarcity of watchmen on patrol, danger could be lurking in the shadows.

Adam relished the thought of encountering a footpad. A bout of fisticuffs would expend his pent-up energy, though he would much rather lay his hands on the man who had shot Cyril.

Adam clenched and unclenched his fingers. He had alerted the magistrate at Bow Street about the change in Josephine Sheppard's status from criminal to victim. They were to seek the mysterious intruder who had invaded her bedroom and presumably abducted her. The man had rented a hackney coach, and tomorrow the Runners would commence the gargantuan task of checking every livery stable in London. God! If only Cyril could remember the name painted on the door of the coach.

His long strides disturbed the cold gray fog. He dared

not press his brother for fear of causing a relapse in him.
The thought troubled Adam. He had failed too many people lately. His mother, while he delayed offering for Lady
Camilla. His brother, by not guiding him with a firmer
hand. Mary, by deceiving her without a care for her rights
or feelings.

His chest ached. He had believed the worst of her beloved sister, only to discover that Josephine Sheppard was
not a cold-blooded killer, after all. No wonder Mary had
spurned his offer of help. He had destroyed the precious
gift of her trust.

From the very start, he had been suspicious of Josephine's intentions. Women of her station milked their
wealthy patrons for jewels and money, but respected the
boundaries of class. Josephine had seemed all the more
devious for devoting herself to winning Cyril's heart. She
had beguiled him with her charming smiles, her quaint
manners, her wide-eyed love of life.

Adam had been certain that only the most cunning ad-
venturess would set her sights on marriage. Thusly, he had
made that foul offer to her in the hope of forcing Cyril to
realize the truth. But perhaps, Adam reflected, he had
seen only what he wanted to see. Perhaps she was sincere
in her affection for his brother. So sincere that she would
end the engagement rather than force Cyril to be cut off
from his family and friends.

It was the act of a selfless, loving woman, not a greedy
fortune hunter. And she *was* Mary's twin, after all. Mary
had vouched for her sister's character, and Mary knew her
better than anyone. Mary, who possessed honor and integrity to the core of her soul.

Unlike himself.

Adam swallowed the bitter pill of his pride. If he had
kept an open mind, he might have come to know Josephine's true character. But did virtue make her a suitable
bride for Cyril?

A week ago, Adam would have denied it. Now he hesitated. Marriage within one's own class was the way of the world; it ensured compatibility between husband and wife. Each followed the same customs, and there were no awkward moments when one partner encountered the other's circle of acquaintances. It was a sensible, rational system. So why, Adam wondered, did he balk at the prospect of wedding Camilla? And why was he gnashing his teeth at the mere thought of Mary in the arms of Victor Gabriel?

His footfalls rang hollow on the cobblestone street. The fog had thickened, rising to his waist. Moonlight glimmered on the ghostly pale mist. Then suddenly he was approaching a familiar door with a lion's head knocker glinting through the gloom.

Adam stopped short and frowned at the modest pillars that flanked the entry. The brothel was more than a mile away. How had he come to be at the town house where Mary lived?

She must have drawn him here by that strange connection he sensed between them.

Balderdash. He didn't believe in prescience or mystical bonds of the mind. Besides, Mary was asleep. Against his will, his fantasy took flight again, and he imagined himself trying the door and finding it unlocked, stealing upstairs to the velvet darkness of her bedroom. He would stand for a moment at her bedside and admire her slumbering form. Then he would kiss the downy softness of her cheek, and her eyelids would flutter open. She would smile and reach out her arms and draw him into her scented warmth, and he would no longer feel so cold and empty.

Good God. Now he was contemplating the criminal act of breaking into her house. What madness had invaded him?

Were he to surprise Mary in her bedroom, she would be far more likely to scream the place down. And his illicit action would hardly restore her faith in him. He would do better to put her from his mind once and for all.

Adam turned resolutely away, though the spectral fingers of the fog snatched at him as if to stop his departure. Then from the corner of his eye, he noticed the faint glow of a candle inside the front room. His pulse surged out of control. Perhaps . . .

Without giving himself time to reconsider, he mounted the steps and rapped on the front door.

♠ **Chapter 15** ♠

Mary dropped her quill.

She had just dipped the nib into the inkwell when the knocking startled her. Now, black specks ruined the neatly penned and sanded note lying on the desk. She had spent an hour composing and tossing out drafts until she achieved the proper tone of polite urgency. It had seemed imperative to impress Adam by perfecting her first letter to him.

She wanted him to think her his equal. She wanted him to rush to her aid not out of duty or a sense of justice, but because he couldn't bear to see her unhappy. Because, beneath all his lordly hauteur, he cared for her.

Foolish, foolish dreams. She might as well hope to pluck a star from the night sky.

The quiet rapping sounded again. Her heartbeat stumbled, and thoughts of footpads and robbers darted through her head. Then common sense prevailed. A criminal wouldn't announce his presence.

Perhaps it was something to do with Jo.

Snatching up the candle, Mary hastened into the foyer. Prinny whined and prowled, his dark eyes glowing in the feeble light. The dog sniffed the bottom of the door and his stub of a tail wagged frantically.

If the dog didn't regard the visitor as an enemy, then neither would she. Mary set the candle on a bench. She clutched the edges of her dressing gown together, turned the key, and opened the door a crack.

She opened it wider.

Against the moonlit mist, Adam Brentwell loomed like the devil himself. For once, he looked less than impeccable, and his black hair was tousled as if he had just risen from bed. Despite his plain suit and simple neckcloth, no one could mistake him for a commoner. The shadows heightened the masterful angles of his face, and the grim set of his mouth alarmed her.

Heedless of her thin nightclothes, she stepped out into the chilly air and touched his sleeve. Fear made her throat dry. "Have you . . . heard something of Jo?"

One dark eyebrow shot up. "No."

"Then is it Lord Cyril? Dear heaven, has he taken a turn for the worse?"

"Of course not. He was sleeping soundly when I left."

Mary looked past him. "Where is your coach?"

"I came on foot." The duke glanced over his shoulder at the street, where the low-hanging fog swirled and danced. Abruptly he slid his arm around her waist and propelled her inside. The door closed with a quiet click.

His furtive behavior disturbed her. "Something *is* wrong," she said. "Tell me."

"A carriage turned the corner, that's what." His gaze burned into her, scorching downward from her loose hair to her silk robe to her bare feet. "You would face a scandal if you were seen with me like this."

Her skin grew overly warm. Beset by the return of shyness, she lowered her chin and studied him from beneath her lashes. "I very much doubt that. Who would bother to gossip about a provincial nobody?"

"You might be surprised. I will not see your name bandied about in the drawing rooms of London."

His fearsome expression left her breathless. She marveled at the virility of his form, the broadness of his chest, the length and strength of his legs encased in shiny black knee boots. Although his manner was as courteous as ever, she should send him away at once. But she couldn't bear the thought.

"We can talk in the parlor." Mary picked up the candle and led the way. "It's uncanny that you would come to see me just now. Why did you?"

He strolled to the shadows near the fireplace and gave her a strange, piercing look. "I couldn't sleep. So I went for a walk."

The simple explanation didn't satisfy her. How amazing that he stood here, fantasy taken flesh. "You must have read my mind," she said.

"Pardon?"

"I'd just finished writing a note asking you to call on me. So that I could tell you what happened."

"Explain yourself."

The chilling reality of the dream came rushing back to her. Hand shaking, she set the candlestick on the mantel. "I received a message from my sister tonight. A terrible, frightening message that came in a dream."

He raised both eyebrows. "A dream."

"I know it's farfetched," she said, half irritated. "But you must believe me. My sister and I have always been able to share our thoughts. For as long as I can remember."

"So you've said." Sinking onto one knee, he rubbed Prinny's ears with a delicacy that had the dog squirming with pleasure.

"Tonight I saw Jo very clearly. She isn't being held here in London as we thought. She's locked in a stone building somewhere on the coast."

"Hmm. Quite gothic."

"It's true. I heard waves crashing onto the shore." Awash with lingering horror, Mary knelt beside him, the white silk nightdress pooling around her on the rug. "The kidnapper gave her an ultimatum. If she refuses to marry him, he's going to sell her to an Eastern whoremaster."

A half smile cracked the mask of his aloofness. "By

chance you weren't reading a lurid novel right before you went to sleep, were you?"

Her patience snapped. "This isn't some cheap trick at a country fair," she said, wishing she had a pile of weeds to hurl at him. "And I don't make a habit of telling fanciful tales when my sister's life hangs in the balance."

His smile faded. "I've done it again, I see."

"Done what?"

"Insulted you. Behaved with ungentlemanly disregard for your feelings, just as I did when I deceived you. Can you forgive me?"

His deep blue eyes mesmerized Mary. Without taking his gaze from her, he continued to massage the dog's head. She had the sudden, overwhelming desire to know the splendor of his touch.

She placed her hand on his and stilled its motion. Awareness of him prickled over her skin. How elegant his fingers were, how warm his flesh. That mysterious connection surged between them, the bond deeper, more intimate than the one she shared with her sister. With Adam, it was less a meeting of minds than a miraculous glimpse into his soul.

Did he feel the spiritual union, too? She wanted to believe it was so. Even though she feared he would break her heart.

"I cannot exonerate you," she whispered. "Not in regard to my sister."

Frowning, he turned his hand over so that their palms nestled together. "I've behaved like an arrogant ass. Just know that I meant only to act in my brother's best interests."

"I do understand that. But that doesn't excuse you."

"Let me finish. I condemned your sister as a fortune hunter without bothering to learn her true character. Yet if she was willing to give up Cyril rather than cost him his family, then I can only admire her unselfishness." He grimaced as if peering into dark memories. "I was wrong about her. Terribly wrong."

Mary laced her fingers through his. She could sense the turmoil in him, the difficulty of his admission. "Do you truly mean it, then? Would you give them your blessing?"

He hesitated, his expression moody. "I'll be honest, Mary. I cannot abide the notion of subjecting my mother and sister to the scandal of this alliance. However, Cyril is of an age to make his own choices. I promise you, I will stand in his way no longer."

She had thought Adam inflexible in his beliefs. Yet now he would permit the marriage of his younger brother to a commoner. In time he would come to love her twin as she did. How could he not? "Oh, Adam. I don't know what to say."

"It's a wonder you'll speak to me at all." His eyes caressed her, and he lowered his voice. "Especially alone here in the middle of the night. Without your fiancé to protect you."

Her heart beating faster, she sat back on her heels. Dear heaven, she hadn't told Adam her news. Would it matter to him? "We're no longer plighted. I ended my betrothal to Victor two days ago."

Adam's face darkened. "By God, if he raised his hand to you—"

"No! He did nothing to hurt me. He's not like that."

"Then why?"

Shame escaped the strongbox of her emotions, the sting of her secret so sharp that it corroded her heart. She ached to unburden herself and lowered her gaze to his cravat. "The fault is my own," she said in a halting whisper. "It was wrong of me to promise myself to him in the first place. You see . . ."

When she hesitated, tortured by the fear that Adam would think ill of her, he gently prompted, "Tell me."

"Victor . . . was once my sister's fiancé."

"I know."

Jolted, she looked at Adam again. "You do?"

"I told you I'd sent a man to investigate Josephine's background."

So he had. They had quarreled over it on the day she and Sophy had stolen into Brentwell House and encountered the duchess, Mary recalled. And in the carriage on the way home, Adam had kissed her for the second time.

Kneeling before him now, she felt like a penitent who deserved his reproach. But there was no censure in his midnight eyes, only an acute attentiveness.

"Don't you understand?" she asked. "I wanted what Jo had. I was so envious of her that I shut her out of my mind and heart. My coldness made her run away." Mary's throat constricted. "I'm afraid . . . that's why I've had trouble contacting her. It's my punishment to know that she desperately needs me, yet I cannot find her."

He tenderly rubbed the back of her hand. "Try not to be so hard on yourself. You made a mistake, that's all."

"It was more than a mistake, it was a sin." Torment tasted bitter in her mouth. "I coveted Victor. The man who belonged to my own sister."

The faint rasp of Adam's breathing disturbed the quiet night air. "Do you love him so much, then?"

His voice was low and vibrating as if the answer mattered to him. She shook her head, her eyes blurring. "I thought so at first. But now . . . now I can see that I only loved the *idea* of Victor. I admired his goodness and his faith and his perfection. I wanted to be like him. Yet more than that, I wanted . . ." Unable to admit the rest, she dipped her head.

With his forefinger, Adam nudged up her chin. "Wanted what?"

She would die before she would tell him. She would. But those compelling blue eyes coaxed the truth from her. "I wanted to know physical love," she whispered. "I wanted carnal passion."

Her body burned as it had when she had lain in the dark

of the caravan, hearing the hum of voices as Jo and Victor sat outside, and feeling a restless envy within herself, the anguish of wicked, wanton desires.

Tears spilled down her cheeks in a hot, scourging rush. Now Adam would realize she was not a devoted sister. Nor was she a virtuous angel of mercy. She was only a weak-willed woman.

He clasped her shoulders and drew her against him, so that her tears wet the smooth fabric of his coat. "Hush, Mary. Don't chastise yourself for perfectly natural desires. It's no sin to want happiness."

"But I wanted it at the expense of my own sister. My dearest friend. . . ."

"And so she came to London and met Cyril." Adam brushed away the strands of hair that clung to her damp cheeks. "Don't you think she's glad of that? I know my brother certainly is."

Mary took a shuddering breath. He was right. Perhaps things *had* worked out for the best. For so long, she had borne the crushing weight of guilt. Now, hope glimmered within her . . . a hope extinguished by fear. "But I sent her away. And because of that, she could die."

"Sssh." He captured a teardrop with his fingertip. "She isn't going to die. I'll do everything in my power to find her. You have my word on that."

His expression held a steadfast determination, a lordly self-assurance that only a day ago she might have labeled conceit. Slowly the ice of her apprehension melted away. Adam would use his vast resources in the search. A true gentleman, he would save even the woman who had caused disruption in his family. How could she have ever thought him unworthy of her trust?

A voluptuous warmth crept into the cold places inside Mary. She was aware of the clock ticking on the mantel, the sleeping dog curled on the hearth rug, the darkness veiling the world beyond the golden circle of candlelight in which she and Adam knelt.

Unable to resist, she caressed his stubbled jaw. "I never thought I'd be saying this, but you're a man of honor, Adam Brentwell."

His jaw tightened beneath her fingers. "Am I? I wonder."

His gaze dipped to her bosom, where the flimsy silk outlined her curves. A flush of awareness heated her skin. The smoldering fire in his eyes seemed less like a violation than a baptism. She felt pure again, cleansed of guilt, awash with a yearning that overflowed her modesty.

"I'm so pleased you came to visit," she admitted shyly. "I'm happy you thought of me when you couldn't sleep. I was thinking of you, too."

"God help me," he muttered, "I couldn't stay away from you."

His lips came down on hers with a rough urgency that answered her most secret romantic fantasies. Closing her eyes, she gave herself up to the temptation of his mouth. She linked her arms around his neck and twined her fingers in the rough silk of his hair. The solidness of his chest felt good against her breasts, and she absorbed every beat of his heart as if it were her own. Deep inside, she grew aware of a hollow ache, the desire to draw him into her body, to be possessed by him. He made her feel like a woman, warm and desirable.

His fingers slipped inside her dressing gown and cupped her breast over the thinness of her nightrail; then his thumb glided over the sensitive peak and made her shiver. How wickedly wonderful it felt to be caressed by him. How sinfully sweet his stroking of her flesh.

In the dark reaches of her mind, Mary knew she should not grant him such liberties, yet a marvelous madness swept away logic and conscience and wisdom. Her soul cried out with a need that overpowered her will . . . the need to feel his mouth in places no man had ever touched . . . the need to sweep away all barriers between them

. . . the need to know mysteries that were beyond the bounds of her imagination.

The firmness of muscled arms enclosed her in a loving embrace. His big hands smoothed a course down her silk-clad back, molded around her bottom, and lifted her to his loins. The heat of him flowed into her, and she obeyed the irresistible urge to press herself against him. Sweet heaven, even there he was hard.

A groan shuddered from him. Swiftly he brought his hands up to her face. "Mary. Mary, I must leave you now."

A cold wind blew through her heart. Opening her eyes, she looked at his thinned mouth and tight expression, and struggled to make sense of his abrupt withdrawal. "Why? Don't you like kissing me?"

Tender humor lit the brooding darkness of his gaze. "Too much, I fear. Far too much." He traced the bow shape of her lips. "But I cannot take advantage of you."

She kissed his fingers. "How is it taking when I choose to give freely to you?"

"You don't know what you're saying." Roughly, he grasped her shoulders and thrust her to arm's length. "Think, Mary. There is nothing honorable about what I want from you. I can no longer be content with just kissing."

"Nor can I."

"If I stay, I'll make love to you. So for God's sake and your own, send me away."

He was giving her the chance to preserve her virtue. Yet morals couldn't fill the emptiness inside her. Ethics could not keep her warm at night. She had lost everyone dear to her, yet she had found Adam.

Mary, don't trust him . . . don't trust him. . . .

A faint shiver brushed the fine hairs at the back of her neck. She eased out a breath. Her sister had been speaking of the kidnapper. Not Adam. Not the man who knelt before her with unguarded fervor shining in his eyes. His respect for her gave Mary a blessed sense of soul-soaring freedom. How bleak and bereft she would feel without him, how incomplete. In that moment she understood the connection between them. She was bound to him because he owned her heart.

"I want you to show me passion." Aware of a momentous relief, she reached for his hand and shaped it around her breast again. "Please, Adam, I know what I'm doing. Stay with me tonight. I need you."

He had dreamed of this. He had dreamed of seeing the softness of surrender in Mary's green eyes, of hearing her invite him into her bed. Yet Adam had never expected his fantasy to come true. The miracle of it tightened his throat and rendered him speechless.

Her hand felt small and warm as she held his fingers against the lushness of her breast. Her unbound hair cascaded around the white dressing gown, the red-gold strands as wild and free as her spirit. How had he ever mistaken her for a straitlaced shrew?

She knelt before him, her smile so sweet and young and hopeful that it disturbed his conscience. She could not have stopped to consider the consequences of her offering, Adam thought. And there was one aspect to his association with her sister that Mary did not know, an episode best left forgotten. It would only turn her against him to learn what he had done, and he could not tolerate the thought of losing her, of being alone. If he had any principles left at all, he should walk out the front door and never look back.

But she harbored secret longings. She yearned to know the mysteries of physical passion. And she wanted him to initiate her.

In one fluid motion he rose to his feet, swept her up into his arms, and bore her out of the parlor.

She clung to his neck, her eyes huge and dreamy. "Where are you taking me?"

"To bed."

A sigh quivered from her, and she tucked her cheek into the lee of his shoulder. Her feathery breaths stirred him more than the most intimate caress of a courtesan. He mounted the darkened stairs, her body warm and yielding against him, the folds of her skirt trailing over his arms.

Little did she know, he would gladly have made love to her right there on the floor. But he wanted to shield her from Obediah's spying. The crusty retainer would censure Mary, and she had suffered enough needless guilt in her life already.

Adam knew the layout of the upper floors from inspecting the house after the shooting. Ignoring the master bedroom, he strode down the gloomy corridor and found one of the smaller chambers reserved for guests. Misty moonlight lit a silvery path to the four-poster bed. He gently lowered Mary to the counterpane and his hand lingered on her, following the curve of waist and hip and thigh.

The dog padded to the bedside and whined, tail wagging. Adam retraced his steps to the door and snapped his fingers.

Head hung low, Prinny slunk back out into the passageway. Adam leaned down to give the animal's patchy fur a conciliatory rub. "Sorry, old boy. I'm afraid you'll be sleeping alone tonight. Unlike me."

Impelled by erotic tension, Adam closed the door and turned. Night enfolded the room, though the faint light from the casement window illuminated the bed. Mary lay on her side, watching him though he could not discern whether with anticipation or misgiving. As he approached, she leaned forward, her low-cut bodice revealing shadowy cleavage. The moonlight glimmered on her bare leg, just as he'd imagined it.

A deep river of yearning coursed through him. He still could not quite believe they were here together, with several long, private hours until dawn. He had the irrational fear that she might fade away like a spirit, leaving him cold and alone.

Settling on the edge of the mattress, he shaped his hand around her foot. Ah, she was real, all warm flesh and delicate bones. Her ankle was as exquisitely formed as the rest of her. She belonged to him tonight. The thought blazed through him, and he disciplined the urge to raise her skirts and consummate their union in one swift thrust. He would not let his own burning need spoil the pleasure that awaited her.

He slipped his hand beneath her hem and slowly moved it up her leg. As he lingered over the trim muscles of her calf, she shivered again.

He bent down to brush his lips across hers. "You needn't be afraid," he murmured. "If ever you want me to stop, you need only say so."

"Never mind stopping. I want you to *start*."

Her impatience surprised a chuckle from him. "All in good time," he murmured. "Like fine wine, lovemaking is meant to be savored."

She touched his cheek consideringly. "Oh, Adam, I just want to *know* . . . to *feel*. . . ."

He smiled through the darkness. "As my lady wishes."

He shucked his stock, his coat, his boots, dropping them in a haphazard heap on the floor. His unbuttoned shirt and breeches he left on for the moment. He doubted she had ever seen a man unclothed, let alone in full arousal.

Lowering himself to her side, he gathered her close and blended their mouths in another deep, searching kiss. Mary tasted of enticing mysteries and artless desire. Unlike the cloyingly perfumed women of his acquaintance, she exuded the chaste fragrance of soap. There was a purity to the way she touched him, her hands gliding over his shoulders and back and waist as if she marveled at his male form.

She certainly gave him cause to marvel. She was both bashful and bold, winsome and passionate. She made no protest as he removed her outer dressing gown, but when he loosened the tiny pearl buttons of her nightrail, she put her hands on his.

"What are you doing?"

"I want to see you," he whispered. "Trust me, love."

Her eyes shone luminous in the moonlight. "I do."

This time she helped him, lifting her hips and sliding out of the sleeves as he drew the gown over her head. Like a virgin offering, she lay naked upon the altar of the bed, her only covering the loose strands of her hair. And the lady-like hands she clasped over her breasts.

Her natural modesty only enhanced his need for her. Over the years he had learned to use skill and finesse to gratify himself and his partner. Yet this untried girl roused him to the brink of madness. And with her he must leash his lust.

"How beautiful you are, Mary Sheppard," he said, his voice husky with a strange, aching tenderness. "How I've longed to be with you like this."

Setting himself to the torturous delight of seducing her, he kissed the fluttery pulsebeat in her throat, then drew his fingertips downward over silken skin, tracing a path over her spread-out hands to her abdomen and back up again, reserving the ultimate delight until she was ready. He caressed her shoulders and throat and arms until her hands unlocked and they came to rest inside his opened shirt. "I feel so . . . alive," she whispered against his mouth. "Is it always this way?"

"Only when the man and woman care for each other."

It was true. He hadn't known that before now. He had spoken without thinking, without his usual cynicism. But of course, this richness of affection he felt for her could only be a fleeting aberration. Thrown together by circumstance, he and Mary had been caught up in a storm of emotion.

She was anything but prickly now. She snuggled closer, brushing kisses along the underside of his jaw. Each tiny movement she made bedeviled him with the skin to skin contact of their upper bodies. It was hell . . . and it was heaven.

With agonizing patience, he explored the lush valley between her breasts before permitting himself to cradle her

in his palm. He stroked the budded peak before allowing
himself to taste her.

His heart melted at her small sounds of yearning. Her
hands slipped down to his waist, and her hips lifted to his
as if she were inquisitive, searching. She could not know
what she wanted . . . but he did. Ah God, he did.

Sending his hand on a downward quest, he sought her
most private place. Her gasp of surprise preceded a whimper of unguarded euphoria. She arched to him and her
hand alighted on his wrist. For a moment he feared she
might stop him; then her fingers shamelessly encouraged
his caresses.

"Sweet heaven," she said, turning her head from side to
side on the pillow. "Oh, dear sweet heaven."

Her untutored movements excited him beyond belief.
This was the moment when he should seek his satisfaction.
Yet more than his own, he wanted hers. And now he
wanted it quickly.

Parting her delicate folds, he gave her the most intimate
kiss of all. She gasped, and her fingers dug reflexively into
his shoulders. "Adam?" she said on a rising pitch. And
then it happened . . . the small jerk of tension, the
quivering of release, the keening sigh of wonder.

Exultation seized him by the throat, the joy of giving joy
to her, of introducing her to ecstasy. Shedding starched
shirt and breeches, he brought himself down on her. Down
on the woman who set fire to his soul.

She lay replete and glowing in the moonlight, her legs
parted in the instinctive pose of submission. Yet he had the
oddly compelling sense that he was the one yielding to her.

He took her face into his palms. "A woman feels pain
her first time with a man. I fear I may hurt you. . . ."

She pressed her fingers to his lips. "More than anything
in the world, I want us to be one. In every way."

A fierce hot pressure expanded his chest. She was his.
His alone. Easing himself into her chaste passage, he met
resistance and breached it. She whimpered and clutched at

his back, and he went instantly still. Crooning soft words into her hair, he trembled with the effort to hold himself back, to give her a moment to adjust to his penetration.

How good she felt. How tight and warm and pure.

"Mary," he whispered. "Ah, Mary."

He could not say more, though his heart swelled to bursting, and he sensed they were joined irrevocably by more than their bodies. The curious feeling slipped away when the force of her grip on him gentled and she moved sinuously beneath him.

Bracing himself on his forearms, he pushed more deeply into the wellspring of her, and she responded with all the sensuality of a pagan goddess. She closed her eyes and tilted back her head, her bare breasts inviting the adoration of his mouth.

His body rejoiced in its perfect mate. Splendor shimmered just beyond his reach, and his breath came hard and fast with the enticement of it. Yet still he held back until he sensed the same need mounting in her, carrying her up and up and up until she shuddered and moaned his name on her plunge into primal rapture. The brilliance of it lit his soul and with a hoarse cry, he succumbed to the madness and let his own ecstasy pulse into her.

In the drowsy aftermath, he luxuriated in a strange, new feeling of peace. He could not remember the last time he had felt so relaxed, so contented. He drifted in a dark, warm cocoon shared by the precious woman he cradled in his arms. Mary . . . Mary . . . not contrary. . . .

Their closeness made him unbelievably happy. Their bodies were still linked and for once he felt no compulsion to draw away from his bed partner. He wanted to stay here forever.

A sigh eddied from her, and she nestled her cheek against his shoulder. Her fingertips trailed over his chest and she made a low sound of sleepy pleasure. "That was like flying."

A chuckle rumbled from his throat. "Though I'm thankful you don't have feathers and a sharp beak."

Adam felt her smile against his chest, felt the fluttery wings of her heartbeat. Then she spoke again, musingly, "I only just remembered . . . there were seagulls."

"Seagulls?"

"Outside my sister's cell."

He sensed as much as heard the troubled thought that invaded her tranquillity. His mind lifted another degree toward wakefulness. Yet he resisted the pull of reality, wanting to bask in the bliss of holding her.

"Adam? I do wish I could convince you."

Her voice was husky, its sadness tugging at him, prodding him into opening his eyes. She lay in a cloud of hair, her face touched by moonlight. The sweet echo of passion lingered in his loins, and he cupped her face in one hand. "Mary. About this power you and your sister share. If it were anyone but you, I wouldn't even consider it."

Kitten-like, she rubbed her cheek against his hand. "If only I could tell you exactly where Jo is, you'd believe me. You would. . . ."

Her anguish flooded him, and absently he stroked her ear, tracing the delicate whorls. He could feel her pain like a sharp ache inside him. It was almost miraculous, his attunement to her emotions. They were one heart, one soul, one mind. If he could sense such a bond to a woman he had only known for a week, then why could not Mary feel an even stronger connection to her twin, the sister who had shared their mother's womb?

Yes. He wanted to take the leap of faith.

"Ssshh, now," he whispered into the fragrance of her hair. "I believe you. *I believe you.*"

"Truly?"

"Truly. Come morning, I'll organize a search, just as I promised." He drew the coverlet over them and brought her close again, shaping her softness to the length of him. "Sleep now, my love. Sleep."

He kissed the top of her head, and she slipped her arm around his waist, cuddling her face into the crook of his shoulder. He felt a clenching of heat in his groin, the desire to make love to her again, although the intensity of their coupling should have sated him. A curious tenderness stopped Adam. She lay against him, the rise and fall of her breasts coming slow and easy. He thought she had drifted into slumber when she stirred once more.

"Adam," she murmured in a drowsy tone, "I love you, too."

She touched her lips ever so lightly to his earlobe. Then she relaxed completely and the evenness of her breathing told him she was asleep.

He lay unmoving in the darkness. *Too?*

Of course. He had called her *my love.* She lacked the experience to know that men spoke endearments in bed, though he himself seldom—never—used that particular one. It was just that her guileless nature inspired a sense of protectiveness in him.

Adam, I love you. . . .

His eyes and his throat burned. In all his twenty-nine years, he could not recall anyone ever saying those words to him. Civilized people did not voice powerful sentiment. He knew without hearing the declarations that his mother cared deeply for him, as did Cyril and Sophy.

And yet no one had ever spoken those words to him. No one but Mary.

She lay sleeping in his arms, all warm, trusting woman. Only a deep-rooted sense of morality made her believe she loved him, he told himself. Otherwise, she could not in good conscience have given herself to him.

What had he done, seducing an innocent like her?

He should go now so that he would not be tempted to take her again. He should go before she realized her mistake, before he caused her more hurt. He never lingered after bedding a woman; he had never seen the point. Yet he could not bring himself to part from Mary. Not just yet.

Weariness rolled through him like a warm sea. He hovered on the edge of sleep, basking in the gently lapping waves of that rare serenity, the peacefulness he had not known in a long, long time. He would allow himself a few more moments of holding Mary.

Just a few moments. . . .

✎ **Chapter 16** ✎

M ary awoke to the patter of raindrops on the casement window.

She stretched luxuriously, her sleep-warmed skin tingling at the slide of the linens. Lifting her head, she blinked at the rosewood furniture, the plump chair by the fireplace, the pale green silk of the bedhangings. For the briefest of moments, she could not recall why she occupied the larger of the two guest chambers; then the events of the previous night tumbled over her in a gentle cascade of memory.

Adam had made love to her. Right here in this bed, he had shown her an intimacy so incredible it was like a dream of heaven. And in the quiet aftermath, just before sleep overtook her, he had called her his love. The marvel of it overflowed her heart.

Yet he was gone now. He had left without saying good-bye.

Her blissful contentment ebbed into emptiness. In the same moment, she turned her head and noticed the greenery lying on the pillow beside her. Wonderingly, she gathered up the bouquet with its stalks of tiny, white bells peeking from the broad leaves. Lily of the valley. Adam had left a gift.

Happiness flowed back into her as she closed her eyes

and inhaled the delicate fragrance. How beautiful an expression of his feelings for her.

Sleep, my love. . . .

Raindrops still dampened the leaves. He must have stolen out into the garden and plucked the nosegay, then tiptoed back and placed it on her pillow.

Mary glowed at the thought. Holding the cluster of flowers, she rolled over and pressed her cheek to the pillow, where his scent lingered. The movement brought a hedonistic awareness of her nudity. Never in her life had she slept without a stitch of clothing. She blushed to remember all the ways Adam had caressed her, ways she had not imagined in her most daring fantasies.

A pulse of heat stirred deep in her loins. Sweet heaven, he had even kissed her . . . *there.* The shocking glory of it had delivered her into spasms of rapture. And then the miracle had happened again after he had joined their bodies in the most amazing, wondrous manner.

She had a hazy memory of snuggling against his muscled length afterward, his skin warming her, his steady breathing lulling her to slumber. For a man so strong, he had held her so gently, as if she were the most important person in the world to him.

Turning onto her back, she smiled at the gilded canopy. At last she understood why Jo had given herself to Lord Cyril. She must have felt this sense of oneness, this bond as strong and indivisible as twinship. Jo's love for Cyril was a blessing that soon, God willing, would be sanctified by the Church.

All because in the space of a few short days, Adam had modified his views on marriage between the classes. A sudden thought awed Mary. Was the transformation of his character rooted in his love for her? Would he follow in his brother's footsteps and take a commoner as wife?

She drew a shaky breath. She must not think such impossible thoughts. And she mustn't be weak again. She had turned to Adam in a vulnerable moment, and the episode must not be repeated. But oh, the exhilarating experience had been worth the risk to her soul. That one treasured memory meant more to her than a thousand nights of loneliness.

A sharp knocking shattered her reverie. Mary sat up, clutching the flowers to her bare breasts. "Who is it?"

" 'Tis me," came a gruff, muffled voice.

Obediah. Her gaze widened on the door. Did he know what she had been doing? Had he seen Adam depart?

Her languor slipped away, and she dropped the stalks of flowers in her haste to find her clothing in the tangle of sheets. "I can't come to the door," she called out. "If you'll wait downstairs, I'll meet you there in a few minutes."

"Nay, miss. 'Tis a matter of import."

Oh, dear. Why had he chosen this moment to be obstinate? And what could be so important at such an early hour?

Merciful heaven. He *must* know.

Mary scooted off the bed. Her valise was in the smaller guest room, and she had no choice but to don the crumpled nightrail and dressing gown. Her fingers fumbled over the buttons, and the garments now seemed scandalously revealing.

As she walked to the door, her breasts felt heavy, sensitive to the brush of the silk. She caught a glimpse of herself in the pier glass and paused, startled by her reflection. Wild waves of hair flowed around her shoulders. Her lips were reddened, her cheeks glowing. Instead of girlish naïveté, her eyes shone with the sultry wisdom of a woman. A wanton.

Abstain from fleshly lusts, which war against the soul.

Resolutely she turned away. She would not let herself feel shame for expressing her love for Adam. She would not.

Clutching the robe together at her throat, she opened the bedroom door and peered out.

In the dimness of the corridor stood the servant, wearing

his usual pea green livery. A scowl made his squatty face all the gloomier. "I brung yer mornin' tea." He held up the silver tray with its china cup and pot, the charred toast slathered with orange marmalade.

He knew she detested orange marmalade. Was he angry at her, or just feeling grumpy?

"Thank you." She reached for the tray, wondering if there might be a note tucked beneath the plate. A love letter from Adam. "Is there a message for me?"

Obediah stubbornly clung to the silver handles. "No message."

She held onto the tray, too. "But . . . you said something about an urgent matter."

" 'Tis yer breakfast that's urgent when the clock shows ha' past ten."

"Ten!" Mary only just kept herself from blurting that she never slept so late. "Goodness, I must have been weary. I appreciate your bringing this to me."

They had a brief tug-of-war with the tray; then Obediah shouldered the door open. "I'll carry it fer ye," he growled.

Before she could protest, he stumped to the bed and set the tray down at the foot, the china clinking. Planting his hairy fists at his hips, he glowered at the rumpled sheets, then back to her.

"Seems ye've some explainin' t' do, young miss."

Her courage faltered in the face of his fatherly outrage. "Explaining?"

"I ain't no green recruit," Obediah thundered, stabbing his finger at her. "Ye were up to mischief last night. An' I know who led ye t' it."

"Y-you do?"

"Aye. 'Twas the almighty duke o' St. Chaldon. Caught the cocky rogue sneakin' out the door at nine. Nine! When all o' London could've seen him, God rot his black soul."

Guilt hovered at the edge of Mary's mind, but she resisted its dark pull. "Kindly refrain from speaking of Adam that way."

"Adam," the servant repeated in disgust. "Ye fell like a guinea in the gutter fer his seducin' ways." Obediah limped around to the side of the bed and yanked back the covers. "An' there's yer virgin's blood t' prove it."

The rain murmured into the silence. Mortified, Mary blinked at the small rusty smear on the linens and lifted her hands to her hot cheeks. She hadn't even known to look for the mark, although Adam had warned her that a woman felt pain her first time. Memory flared golden in her, the stunning intimacy of his caresses, the burning ache of his entry, then the irresistible feel of him, thick and strong, forging a miraculous bond between them.

"I thought ye had higher morals than that flighty sister o' yers," the servant said darkly. "What would yer Papa say t' know ye chose a Brentwell, too? What?"

Her father would be horrified that she had succumbed to mortal temptation. He would denounce that beautiful union as wicked fornication. The sharp pain of loss pierced Mary's throat. Adam might forsake her tomorrow, but her father would always be her father. Yet by giving herself to a nobleman, she had ended any possible hope of reconciling with him.

Her anguished gaze stole to the lily of the valley scattered forlornly over the pillow, and she swallowed hard, unwilling to let fears and regrets spoil the magic of the night. How could such a meaningful closeness be cause for shame?

Folding her arms over her bosom, she met Obediah's glower straight on. "Papa's fire and brimstone views don't hold true for me anymore. Perhaps they never did."

His keen blue eyes softened against his bulldog features. "Ah, girl, ye need a father's guidance. Men like His Grace only want one thing from a female o' yer station. An' ye gave it t' him, all wrapped in silk an' lace."

"Adam isn't like that. Not anymore. Why, he even gave permission to Lord Cyril to marry Jo. He told me so himself."

"Humph. An' now ye're thinkin' the duke'll wed ye, eh?"

The very thought shone like a ray of sunshine through the rain. Adam . . . her husband? She sank onto the bed and leaned against the post. She could share her life with him, bear his children, sleep beside him every night.

Victor had never roused such sweet yearning in her. With him, the murky shadow of her own wrongdoing had tainted her emotions. With Adam, however, it was not the darkness of lust she felt but the radiance of love.

And yet . . . marriage? Would he . . . could he . . . allow himself the same freedom to choose as he had afforded his brother? Could she herself disregard the teachings of a lifetime?

If she married Adam, she would be a duchess. The thought was too fantastical to imagine. She could never be haughty like his mother or Lady Camilla. How much better it would be if Adam was a commoner. If they could live in a vine-covered cottage with a garden. . . .

"There ye go, lookin' all dreamy-eyed again," Obediah said.

She sat up straight. "I was merely thinking."

"Aye, I can see that," he said, gruffly disapproving. "Ye force me t' be the one t' take the wind out o' yer sails, then. Just have a look at this an' tell me the duke's a fine and honorable man."

Obediah fumbled in a pocket of his coat, limped to her, and stuffed a book into her hand.

Mary glided her fingertips down the spine of the slim, leather-bound volume. "What is it?"

"Yer own sister's journal. I found it t'other day, stuck behind the bedside table in her chamber."

With trembling hands, Mary clutched the unexpected treasure. "I never thought to look for a diary. Jo has never been fond of writing."

"Then yer in fer a surprise. Read what she wrote there on May the fourteenth."

Mary stiffened. "You read my sister's diary?"

A ruddy flush suffused his face. "Aye, 'twas fer yer own good. Someone around here needs t' have his wits about him."

His evasive manner puzzled Mary. Before she could wonder at it, Obediah hobbled away, his wooden leg thumping on the rug.

At the door, he paused to regard her gravely. "Since yer papa's not here t' advise ye, I'll give ye a word o' warnin' meself. Once the duke plants a barstard in yer belly, ye'll never see him again."

The door clicked shut. Against the windowpanes, the rain tap-tapped like skeletal fingers. Mary pressed her hands to her stomach in awe. Dear heaven. Adam might have started a baby in her. *A baby.*

A bastard.

Her grandmother had been seduced by an earl and then abandoned. She had raised Mary's father in poverty, dying from a lung ailment when she was not much older than Mary was now.

No. She wouldn't compare Adam to her cruel, faceless grandfather. Adam had too much integrity to renounce his own child. Nor would he forsake her. Now that he had stepped down from his pedestal, now that they had shared the ultimate closeness, he had come to realize how much she meant to him.

Sleep, my love. . . .

A smile gentled her mouth. She picked up a sprig of lily of the valley and tucked it behind her ear. Obediah was wrong. Nothing could change her mind about Adam. Nothing at all.

Lowering the diary to her lap, she began to read.

His mood as low and dark as the clouds, Adam strode across the stable yard. Muddy water splashed his boots. Rain wet his face and trickled inside his starched collar. On any other occasion, he would have dispatched a servant with the message while he himself stayed within the fire-lit comfort of Brentwell House. But today a restless energy drove him.

The door of the coach house stood open, propped by a wooden bucket. The interior was dim, and the familiar aromas of leather and hay and manure brought a flash of memory from his boyhood, when he had been forbidden to play here. He had longed to do so, to escape the tedium of the schoolroom and the stultifying study of Greek and mathematics and geography. One spring day, Cyril had talked him into disobeying their father's edict, and they had spent a gleeful hour climbing over coaches and swinging by rope from the rafters. Until John Coachman caught them and sent the both of them to the duke. Although Cyril stoutly took the blame, Adam earned the whipping. He was the elder, the heir, the one whose behavior must be exemplary. That ingrained lesson had guided his life.

Until recently.

A horse stamped its hoof in the stable, followed by the soothing voice of a groom. Just ahead in the shadows, the state coach reposed like a mighty Zeus flanked by the lesser deities of phaeton, landau, and post-chaise.

He stepped deeper into the building. His hollow footfalls harmonized with the plopping of the rain. "Coachman."

A massive man stepped out of the harness room. Polishing rag in hand, he stopped and gawked. Then he tossed the rag aside and came hastily forward, snatching off his cap and holding it to his barrel chest. "Yer Grace," he said in a rumbling voice. "No one told me t' bring up yer carriage."

"I haven't come to chastise you. I need your advice, that's all."

"Mine?"

Adam nodded. "At dawn tomorrow, I'll require three traveling carriages, one for myself, one for Fenwick, and another for Dewey. There's you and the second coachman for two of them, but you'll need to secure a third driver.

Do you know of someone for hire, someone trustworthy and discreet?"

The servant turned the cap round and round in his meaty paws. "No need to hire out. There's young Whitby, if ye won't be needin' a postillion. He could handle a team. Where shalt ye be journeyin'?"

Adam grimly wished he knew. "To various destinations along the coast. I'll be able to tell you more come morning."

The man bobbed his head. "Ye can count on John Coachman, Yer Grace."

"Very good." Adam retraced his steps. At the doorway, he stopped, turning back to the man who had served the Brentwells for some twenty years. There had been his father before him, by custom also called John Coachman. "May I ask your Christian name?"

The coachman had crouched to retrieve his polishing rag. He straightened, his bushy brows lifting. " 'Tis George Crookes."

"Have you family, Crookes?"

"A wife and six youngsters back in Derbyshire." His broad face took on a glow of pride. "A right handful they be. Ever time I see 'em, they be growin' faster'n weeds."

Adam had never considered that while the Brentwells spent several months each Season in London, Crookes was forced to live apart from his family. Also the times when Adam or his mother went on week-long visits to friends, jaunts to Bath, or the annual tour of his other estates. Servants were supposed to be unobtrusive, devoted, uncomplaining of long hours, of toiling seven days a week. Those who behaved otherwise were replaced. It was the practice in any genteel household.

Going back out into the rain, he crossed the short stretch to the house. He would break tradition. He would hire additional staff so that every servant could take an occasional holiday. No doubt the nobility would be aghast at his reform, but Mary would applaud the endeavor.

Mary. His fingers clenched around the brass knob of the back door. Cold droplets pelted his hair, his face, his suit. Memory burned inside him: the softness of her skin, her feminine cries of pleasure, the incredible moment when he had buried himself inside her and they had been joined in soul as well as body.

In the sober light of day, his actions of the previous night struck him as astonishingly rash. He had taken a virgin to bed. A *virgin*. He had ruined a respectable girl. And if that deed were not black enough, he had trampled on her tender heart.

Adam, I love you, too. . . .

Louder than the voice of wisdom or reason, her voice sang in his memory. To his chagrin, he wanted to hear her whisper those words to him again. He wanted it with a fierceness that clouded rational thinking. Seized by warmth, he remembered awakening to the sweetness of Mary snuggled against him. It was the first night in weeks that he had slept so soundly, the first morning he had felt refreshed and invigorated. He had wanted to lie there forever, to kiss and caress her, to enter her again even before she came fully awake.

A belated sense of reason had stopped him. Never before had he made the mistake of staying with a woman until the light of day. The longer he tarried, the more likely that someone of consequence would spot his departure from the house. He did not fear so much for himself, but for Mary. The gossips would lash her raw.

And so with great reluctance he had dressed, crept downstairs, and gone out the back door. He intended to exit by way of the mews, yet as he walked through the small garden behind the house, a reckless sentimentality caught at him. Mary would wake up alone. She would be hurt, disillusioned, perhaps even bitter. Without further thought, he had picked a cluster of lily of the valley and had borne it upstairs to her pillow.

He deplored the impulse now. It was a wildly romantic

gesture, more the token of a moonstruck swain than a gift befitting a man of dignity and rank. And Mary, in her inexperience, would view the offering as a sign of his undying devotion.

No, he should not have left the flowers. They had brought trouble down on him already.

Heat crawled up his neck. If only he had left that first time, he would not have encountered Obediah coming out the cellar door. A succession of emotions had crossed that spider-veined face: surprise, comprehension, fury. He had blasted Adam with a barrage of insults: *Ye scurvy, black-hearted wretch! Ye spoiled an innocent angel, ye who ain't fit t' wipe her shoes. Go on out o' here, afore I'm tempted t' send ye t' hell. Damn ye, get out!*

Never before had Adam met with disrespect from a servant. And what was all the more humiliating, he could not take the man to task over it. Because Adam knew he deserved every harsh word of condemnation.

He opened the glass door and wove a path through the maze of yellow and blue chaises and chairs in the morning room. His footsteps rang hollow on the marble tiles of the outer passage, as hollow as the beating of his heart.

He could never give Mary the honorable life she deserved. He certainly could never take her as a wife. The very notion was unthinkable. The liberty he granted his brother was not one he could bestow on himself, for his position required him to adhere to a more rigid code of behavior.

Yet he could offer Mary his lifelong protection. She would protest at first. But he would vow to be as faithful to her as a husband. He would purchase a house for her, a home with a fine garden in Derbyshire, near his ducal seat so that he could ride over to visit her from time to time. Once she became his sister-in-law, their relationship might pose awkward moments. But if they were very discreet, she could find contentment as his mistress.

Already his seed might have met fertile ground in her.

The thought of Mary rounded with his child, Mary nursing his infant at her breast, ignited the fire of fierce longing in him. He doused the feeling with icy rationality. Better he should instruct her in methods of preventing pregnancy than saddle her with his bastards. It was the honorable thing to do. So why did he feel so bleak?

His revised plan for his life meant postponing his own nuptials for a few more years at least. His mother would be displeased, but she would survive her pique. If Lady Camilla chose not to wait, she could find another husband. Eventually, he would have to take a blue-blooded wife and sire an heir. That duty struck him as oppressive now. Worse, it seemed unthinkable.

"Adam, I need a word with you."

His mother sailed like a sleek brigantine down the corridor, her shoulders squared, her blue silk tea gown rustling. Now that Cyril was on the mend, she was the picture of health and vigor, her silver hair upswept and affixed with a pearl comb.

Without realizing it, he had arrived at the library. Organized chaos reigned within the stately, book-lined walls. Fenwick stood in the middle of the long chamber, directing a queue of footmen, who were depositing crates along one wall. An army of clerks sat at tables and poured over piles of documents.

And there was another matter to look into, Adam recalled. This morning, his man had brought word that the earl of Peterbourne had departed London for his estate in eastern Sussex. Adam meant to find out if the aging lord owned land on the coast.

The duchess reached Adam's side. "What in heaven's name is going on here?"

Adam smoothed back his damp hair and wondered if she knew he had stayed out all night. Surely it had been the talk of the servants' hall at luncheon that the master had returned home at mid-morning, wet, rumpled, and unshaven. Her maid might well have carried the news to the duchess.

"These men," he said carefully, "are examining records I obtained from the government."

"But why? And why here?"

Anticipating her fury, he said, "Let's speak in private."

He escorted his mother down the corridor and into his study. It was a comfortable room decorated in deep shades of green and brown, a masculine retreat from the ornate embellishments of the rest of the house. A tidy arrangement of quills and inkwells lay upon the mahogany desk, alongside a locked document case. Behind the desk, a globe rested in a wooden stand beside a tall window.

"I would have come to your apartments had you but asked," he said.

"I shan't be coddled." She waved him away when he would have settled her into a leather wing chair by the hearth. "So tell me this business of yours that has men tramping in and out, and the maids cleaning mud from the floors."

Not for the first time, Adam wondered if he were financing a wild goose chase. Was Mary's dream of her sister mere fancy? To think otherwise defied logic, and logic had always ruled his life.

Yet he trusted her. And he could not sit idle.

"I have reason to believe that Josephine Sheppard has been imprisoned somewhere along the coast."

His mother drew a sharp breath. "At last. So tell me, who caught her? We must provide a handsome reward to the magistrate responsible."

"She isn't being held by lawful means." He watched the duchess closely. "She was abducted. On the night Cyril was shot."

His mother slowly shook her head. "You can't believe that Banbury tale, too. Why, the Runners concluded she did the deed and then ran off with her new lover. You yourself said she deserves to hang for her crime."

Vengeance had burned inside him. For as long as he lived, he would never forget the sight of Mary standing in the doorway of the grand saloon, her beautiful green eyes rounded by horror.

Finding Josephine was the least he could do to atone for that sin and others.

"I've since ascertained that an intruder shot Cyril and kidnapped Miss Sheppard. Cyril himself says that she had ended the engagement rather than see him lose his family." Hands clasped behind his back, Adam paced a path from his desk to the map of England on the wall. He couldn't forget the guilt that still shadowed him. "She would accept no money from us. That alone proves her love for Cyril is true."

His mother stood perfectly still. "My dear son, a clever female can make a man believe he is God Almighty. It is how some women procure what they want."

Her wise blue eyes seemed to pierce his very soul. Yet surely she could not know with whom he had spent the dark hours of the night. Surely he had not betrayed his fascination for Mary Sheppard.

Even so, he felt the perplexing urge to shout to the world that Mary loved him. Hiding the truth was more painful than he ever could have imagined.

Discomfitted, he turned to the map and pointed along the vast expanse of southeastern coastline. "I've discovered that Miss Sheppard is being held in a stone building somewhere along here. Fenwick is compiling a list of possible sites from official records. Tomorrow morning, I'll be leaving to begin the preliminary search along this section." Adam touched the easternmost shore, then moved his forefinger to the west. "Fenwick and Dewey will assist here. I've also engaged the services of Harry Dashwood."

The duchess glided forward in a whisper of silk until she stood at his side. He was surprised as always at the smallness of her. The top of her head barely cleared his shoulders. He thought of her as strong, invincible, larger than life.

"A stone building," she scoffed. "Where did you come by this information?"

If only she knew. "Suffice to say, the news came through unusual channels. But I intend to scour every inch of the coast until I find her."

"You truly believe that woman to be innocent."

"I do."

Frown lines appeared in her forehead. "It is commendable that you would aid a woman in distress. You were ever the honorable one, a joy to my heart. But have you considered that people will question your taking such extraordinary measures? Miss Sheppard's fate is best left in the hands of the law."

"And left to inept, provincial magistrates, she would likely never be found." He lowered his voice. "Surely that is not what you wish."

She met his gaze unflinchingly. "Of course I would not wish her ill. I simply do not care to see my sons involve themselves with unsuitable females."

Adam braced himself for another storm. "Mother, there is something else you should know. I've granted Cyril permission to marry Miss Sheppard."

She stiffened, her knuckles white against the antique lace of her bodice. "Have you gone mad? You know as well as I the scandal that would ensue. Such an alliance is inconceivable."

"Difficult, but not inconceivable. If you set your mind to the task, you could convince the ton to accept her. You and I and Cyril and Sophy. And no doubt Harry as well as others of my friends and yours." Convincing her suddenly seemed the most vital task in the world. He clasped her shoulders and gazed down into her patrician face. "You could manage it, Mother. You're one of society's leading hostesses. If you were to accept Josephine, no one would dare do otherwise. No one would flout the duchess of St. Chaldon."

She shook her head slowly, staring at him as if he'd sprouted horns and cloven hooves. "Why would you make such a drastic alteration in your opinion? This isn't like you, Adam."

"We almost lost Cyril. We owe him a second chance now, the happiness of securing his heart's desire."

"Happiness is of little consideration in making a suitable match. I myself married as my parents bade me. Cyril needs guidance, not the ruination of his life."

"Yet it is his life. And his decision."

The duchess paced to and fro like a diminutive general. "You baffle me, Adam. You know as well as I that her father is a traveling preacher of unknown stock. And her sister is cut from the same cloth, both of them ill-bred hussies."

His muscles tensed. He gritted his teeth so hard it set his jaw to aching. "That is no way to speak of your future daughter-in-law." Or Mary, he wanted to add.

Her face paled. "I might have expected Cyril to behave rashly, without judgment or thought. But you! You are St. Chaldon."

"And as such, I will use my authority to do what is best for my brother."

"Rescue her if you must. But I cannot permit this marriage, Adam. I will not."

The duchess fixed him with a freezing glare, one that would have sent a shiver through him as a youth. But he was no longer a malleable boy. Very softly, he said, "Then perhaps you would be more comfortably situated in the dower house at Derbyshire."

Her blue eyes rounded, and hurt flared behind her regal veneer. She took a step backward. They stood staring at each other, the only sound the rain sighing against the windowpanes.

It was galling to recognize himself in her, the arrogant

conviction of one's own superiority. But no more. She would obey him in this.

The sound of footsteps shattered the highly charged moment. With a cheerful disregard for manners, Sophy burst into the study. Oblivious to the undercurrents in the air, she called, "Adam!"

"What now?" he snapped.

"Look who I found waiting on our doorstep."

She stepped back with a flourish. And then Adam's heart plummeted in his chest as he beheld a wet and woebegone Mary Sheppard.

❧ Chapter 17 ❧

In the throes of a righteous rage, Mary had stormed out of her sister's house. Lacking any means of conveyance other than her own two feet, she marched through the rain-swept streets of London like a soggy St. George on his way to slay the dragon. Passing vehicles splashed water on her. Numerous puddles soaked her shoes. The damp chill invaded her bones. Yet she hardly noticed the physical discomfort. Clasping the small, leather-bound diary within the protection of her hooded cloak, she was caught up in composing the scathing rebukes that she would hurl at Adam.

Now, faced by him and his mother, Mary thought her mouth must be the only dry place about her. The courage dribbled out of her like the water that dripped from her sodden hem. The duchess looked every inch the stately lady in a blue silk gown trimmed with scallops of lace. Her elegantly arched eyebrow conveyed her annoyance at the intrusion.

Standing at his mother's side, Adam had the same refined bearing, even the identical raised brow. Dressed impeccably in dark blue, he looked remote and untouchable, unlike the tender man who had shared her bed. No smile of welcome graced his mouth; he might have been regarding a disobedient servant.

Sweet heaven. She had lain with him. She had given

herself to a peer of the realm, a man as far from her reach as a rainbow.

His lord of the manor magnificence jolted her to the truth. She had been impetuous to come here. She didn't belong amid the extravagant trappings of his house. Now, in the cold light of day, she knew that intimacy had deepened the chasm between them, rather than bridging it.

"Adam, how uncivil of you," scolded Lady Sophy. "The least you can do is to greet our visitor."

"It's all right," Mary murmured. Her anger deflated into awkward humiliation. Lowering her gaze to the leaf pattern in the rug, she took a step backward and her shoes gave off a wet, squelching sound. "I can wait outside. Please excuse me for interrupting."

She dipped into a deep curtsy as Adam had taught her, wobbling a bit from the weakness in her knees. As she rose again, he appeared at her side, his fingers warm and firm on her arm.

"Miss Sheppard," he said in that smooth, skin-tingling tone. "Come sit by the fire and dry yourself. My mother was just now leaving."

Mary found herself walking beside him, too discomfited to voice a protest. The perfect, condescending gentleman, he brought her to a leather chair near the snapping coal blaze. She sank down, fighting an innate sense of insignificance. Surely he thought she should be stoking the fire rather than benefitting from its comfort.

"I'm so glad you came to call," Sophy said, her blue eyes dancing with something like glee. "It was such a dull, rainy afternoon."

"And it shall continue to be dull," Adam told her. "For you, at least, since you're on your way out."

"You will require a chaperon," the duchess said. "Allow me—"

"I require privacy." Adam spoke with quiet authority. His gaze locked with his mother's, the tension between them so vibrant, Mary fancied she could see it shimmering in the air.

Had they been quarreling . . . about her? Merciful God. Did the duchess know where her son had spent the night?

"As you wish, then." Though her posture remained erect, his mother spoke in a subdued tone. She flicked a guarded glance at Mary. "No doubt Miss Sheppard has taken a chill. I shall have tea sent here."

She glided away amid a rich rustling of her skirts. As she passed Sophy, she said, "Come along."

"But Mama—"

"Sophronia."

Lady Sophy flashed a pouting look at Adam and Mary; then she trudged from the room. The door swung shut . . . almost. It was clear the duchess wished to retain that small semblance of propriety.

The masculine domain seemed unbearably intimate to Mary. As Adam walked toward her, she noticed the streaks of mud that marred the polished black leather of his boots. His long legs drew her gaze upward over his loins, and her heart throbbed with a desire she should not feel.

Clutching the slim, leather-bound book in her lap, she reminded herself that she was angry at him. Furious. After reading in the diary what he'd done to her sister, Mary had come to confront him. Now was her chance to voice all the brilliantly blistering insults she had formulated on her walk here.

Before she could unlock her tongue, he sank down on one knee and took hold of her ankle. He slipped off her shoe and then did the same to the other. He propped both sodden bits of leather on the fender, where they hung like forlorn discards from a cobbler's shop.

His warm fingers curled around her right foot and rubbed briskly over the damp cotton stocking. "Your skin is like ice. You must have walked miles."

Resisting the pleasure of his massage, she glowered at

his face. His handsome, square-jawed, lying face. "Few of us have a dozen carriages at our command, Your Grace."

"I fear I must disappoint you, then." His eyes twinkled; his expression lost the unrelenting severity so that he looked human again. "I have a mere four vehicles at my disposal. One belongs to my brother. Another is used by my mother and sister. So you see, I am not quite so decadent as you would believe."

He moved his hands to her other foot, and his blissful stroking sent a river of heat over her skin. Her tight muscles relaxed involuntarily, the chill leaving her limbs. She couldn't help remembering how he had touched her in the dark, his big hand sliding up and up and up her leg . . .

She jerked her foot from his grasp. "On the contrary, you are the very devil of decadence."

The caprice vanished from his face. He crouched before her, one arm resting on his bended knee. "Ah. You're displeased with me. You've every right to be angry after what happened between us last night."

Unsure of how she fit into his life, she sought refuge in sarcasm. "I'm displeased with your lack of welcome. Though I should have expected as much of you."

His mouth twisted contritely. "I'm afraid you walked straight into a fracas. My mother—"

"Disapproves of me. And you would prefer that I remove myself from your home, where my presence causes you embarrassment."

"You misunderstand me. Mother and I had just exchanged words. Not about you, but about Cyril and Josephine."

Mary regarded him suspiciously. "Did you tell Her Grace what you've decided about their marriage?"

He nodded. "It will take time for Mother to accept my verdict. But she'll come around eventually, just as I did." His voice lowered, caressing her. "I owe that to you, Mary. You made me see the error of standing in the way of their happiness."

A ray of light penetrated the darkness in her heart. She tightened her fingers around the diary. When he gazed at her with warmth in his eyes, it was difficult to believe he was the same haughty aristocrat who had made a despicable offer to Jo just hours before she had been kidnapped.

The shameful need for him burned like a flame inside Mary, and she decried the weakness that made her want to trust in him, to acknowledge that he had changed. For her.

He rubbed her foot again, his firm touch reassuring somehow. "I'll deal with my mother later," he added. "At present it's more vital that I find your sister. As swiftly as possible."

Mary bit her lip. "There must be a thousand places where someone could have imprisoned Jo."

"Ah, don't despair. At this very moment, my men are combing over deeds of property, making a list of possible sites based on what you saw in your dream. I am determined to depart at dawn."

"So that's why you were gone when I awakened," she said. "You came home to organize the search."

"Yes."

His hair was damp and gleaming, and she wanted to smooth back the single black strand that dipped onto his forehead. Feeling unexpectedly shy, she gazed at him from beneath the screen of her lashes. "I haven't yet thanked you for the lily of the valley. It was lovely of you."

He compressed his lips as if her words somehow displeased him. Then he leaned forward and cradled her cheek in his palm. "Mary, you're a fine woman, a woman I respect with all my heart. It was wrong of me to make love to you last night. Though I cannot in all honesty say that I regret it. I could never regret experiencing the joy we shared."

It was the most romantic soliloquy Mary had ever heard in her sheltered life. "Nor could I," she whispered.

The connection between their souls seemed to draw taut, quivering with energy. Against her cheek, his palm felt warm and protective, utterly reliable. He knelt so close that she could see the tiny silver stars in the deep blue dusk of his eyes.

Heeding the behest of her heart, she bent toward him, craving his kiss . . . and more. His tender expression altered to something deeper and darker, something that made her remember the feel of his mouth on her bare skin.

His breath warmed her lips. "Let me take care of you," he said, brushing a kiss over her mouth. "Let me provide for you and grant you my protection. God knows I never meant to bring you dishonor, but there's no going back now. And there's no denying that once could never be enough for me."

Mary's pulse pounded in her ears. He was proposing . . . what? "I don't understand."

"I want you to share my bed. I want to give you as much happiness as you've given to me." His fingertips skimmed over her face. "So long as I remain unwed, I'll be faithful to you. I give you my word on that. And you'll never want for anything."

A tapping on the door interrupted him. Frozen in her chair, Mary saw a footman enter the study, carrying a huge silver tray in his white-gloved hands. He must have seen her and his master posed intimately by the fire, their lips almost touching. Yet her stunned mind couldn't give her body the command to draw back.

Adam rose to his feet, his movements unhurried. "Thank you, Marples. That will be all."

The footman bowed and departed. The fire gossiped on the hearth. Out of the corner of her eye, Mary registered Adam's fawn breeches and the midnight blue of his coat as he went to the tray and lifted the silver pot.

Dear God. He didn't love her. He never had. All he wanted was a mistress. A female body to warm his bed.

She should have known. She should have *known*.

He walked toward her, bearing a cup of tea. His big

hand dwarfed the rose-patterned set. "I added a spoonful of sugar. I hope that suits you."

On a blinding rise of anger, she surged up and struck both cup and saucer from his hand. The porcelain shattered into shards on the hearth. Dark liquid seeped like a bloodstain over the pale marble.

"I did not come here for tea, Your Grace. Nor did I come to be insulted by your repulsive offer."

A troubled look lowered his eyebrows. His chest rose and fell beneath the snowy white shirt and pale blue waistcoat. "Mary, I meant no insult, truly I did not. But have you given a thought to your future? Where will you go? What will you do?"

"I'll manage somehow. Without becoming your whore."

His face hardened. "Don't cheapen what we have. Marriage is impossible, but I'm offering you a long-standing liaison. The chance to live comfortably for the rest of your life."

"Money." Hurt crowded Mary's chest, and she folded her arms to hold back the pain. "Jo was right. You believe you can buy whatever you like."

"I beg your pardon?"

"Indeed you should. This morning, Obediah came to the bedroom. He wasn't pleased to learn—"

"That you'd made a gift of your innocence." His voice grew husky. "To a man who did not have the right to accept it."

There it was again, that thread of regret. She refused to acknowledge it.

She turned to the chair and picked up the slim book that she had dropped, holding it like a talisman to her breast. "Obediah gave me this. He found it wedged behind the night table. It's my sister's diary."

"The wily rascal. He ought to have given it to a magistrate at Bow Street." Adam came forward. "Have you read it, then? Does she say anything to indicate who might have kidnapped her?"

Nonplussed by his nearness, Mary could only shake her head.

"Are you certain? There must be some clue, perhaps the mention of a suitor who paid her an excessive amount of attention."

He reached for the volume, but Mary backed a few steps away from him, holding it protectively to her bosom. His black eyebrows drew together. He stood with his arm stretched out, comprehension dawning on his proud features.

He lowered his hand to his side. "She wrote about me."

"Yes." The fact that he didn't offer a denial shuttered all light from Mary's heart. "The day after Cyril brought her here to meet you and your family, you paid a visit to her. You offered her ten thousand pounds if she would renounce Cyril and become *your* mistress."

He bowed his head in acknowledgment. "I believed I was acting in my brother's best interests. I wanted to prove to him that she was fickle."

"And that gave you the right to humiliate the woman he loves?"

"You don't know my brother. He's reckless, easily led astray. He'd had his heart broken before. I thought your sister had deluded him."

"And you didn't bother to learn her true character. You judged her to be a cunning commoner who snatched at the chance to invade your exalted circle."

He combed his fingers through his hair, ruffling the dark strands. "Yes. I can only offer my deepest apologies."

He conveyed a sincerity that endangered the shield of Mary's anger. He must never know how anguished she felt to learn that he, too, had chosen her sister first. "Why did you never tell me of this sordid offer?" she demanded. "Better yet, why did you never tell the magistrate? Unless you were afraid that we might think you guilty of the crime."

He flinched as if she'd struck him. Unguarded shock

widened his eyes. "Mary, you have every reason to believe my honor is tarnished. But surely you can't think I would shoot my own brother. Or attempt to stop his marriage in so foul a manner as kidnapping his bride."

She blinked down at the diary in her hands. "No, I don't think even you would stoop so low. Yet if you had wanted to cause Jo pain, you could not have chosen a more vicious mode of attack." Opening the book, she turned to the middle and found the passage, thrusting it at him. "Here, Your Grace. Read for yourself exactly how you ruined my sister's life."

He took the volume from her. Overcome by the turmoil inside her, Mary walked to the casement and pressed her forehead to the cool glass. Raindrops wept against the window as if to mimic the tears that she refused to let fall.

She wanted to make him suffer. She wanted to punish him for the sins of the past. Yet she was as guilty as he.

In her mind she saw Jo's childish, blotted handwriting, the poor penmanship due to their father's insistence that she use her right hand even though her left was more adept. Each painstaking entry began the same way: *Dear Mary . . .*

Denied the link between their hearts, her sister had poured her hopes and fears into the diary. She had filled a daily journal with the sort of confidences they used to share, cheery anecdotes about her life, joyful observations on falling in love, humorous descriptions of people she had met, both common and noble. Yet through it all ran a thread of discontent, the yearning for her twin.

Mary did not have to read the words as Adam did, for she had experienced Jo's torment as she wrote the final entry.

> *Dear Mary,*
> *A terrible thing happened today; St. Chaldon came to call on me. He is a frightening man, cold and distant, rather like Papa when he's in a fury. But*

unlike our Papa, St. Chaldon never smiles. He looks at me as though I were a worm he would dearly love to squash, if only it didn't require dirtying his polished boots. He offered me ten thousand pounds to become his mistress and forsake my Beloved.

Can you imagine how shamed I felt, how sick at heart? For I knew then that His Grace would never, ever accept me into his family. I bade him leave at once, with as much dignity as I could muster, though I was weeping inside.

And in the end, the duke accomplished his purpose without expending a single penny of his blood money. For as soon as I closed the door, I knew that I could never ask Cyril to choose between me and his brother. At supper, I told my Beloved that our betrothal is ended. He stormed out in a rage, and I have not seen him since.

The pain on his face yet haunts me. It shall be my private purgatory in the years to come, my punishment for the vanity of seeking love at any cost. Tomorrow, lest my resolve weaken, I shall depart London, return to Papa, and beg his forgiveness. I pray that you, too, Mary, can forgive me, perhaps when you read these letters.

And praise God you will never have occasion to meet St. Chaldon. You alone will understand why I am determined to keep Cyril from learning of the despicable act of his brother. If only you would listen when my heart speaks, Dearest Sister, you will know why I could never again destroy the bond of family. . . .

"Mary. Mary, are you listening?"

Adam's voice pulled her from the mire of misery. Realizing that her hand was fisted around the casement latch, Mary loosened her rigid fingers and slowly turned around.

He stood directly behind her. God—or perhaps the

devil—had lavished him with stark male beauty, from his
blue eyes to his high cheekbones and thick black hair. He
had a habit of cocking his head to the side, of gazing intently at her in a shivery, heart-melting way. She searched
for the callous aristocrat who had propositioned her sister,
but saw only the brother who would go to any lengths to
guard his family, the lover who had swept her up to the
pinnacle of glory.

And the nobleman who had asked her to be his mistress.

Just as he had done her sister. It shouldn't hurt. But it
did. Dear God, it did.

"Didn't you hear me?" He held forth the opened diary,
pointing to the inner spine, where a thin, ragged edge jut-
ted. "Look at this. Someone has torn a page out."

Adam disciplined the urge to tap his fingers on the leather
seat of the coach as the conveyance lumbered with unbearable slowness through the crowded streets of London. He
would have preferred to drive himself in the phaeton, but
that would have meant exposing Mary to the miserable
weather. He could not bear to think of her taking another
chill.

She sat across from him, her hands folded in her lap as
she gazed out at the rain-soaked city. The hood of her
cloak framed a face of quiet beauty and pensive grace. She
had spoken scarcely a word since insisting on accompanying him to confront Obediah. Coldly, she had pointed out
that her reputation was in tatters, anyway, so what did it
matter if anyone saw her alone with him in the St. Chaldon
carriage?

His throat closed around the knot of his own treachery.
She would not permit him to protect her, not even now,
when he had made her his own.

No. She wasn't his. And her refusal to become his mistress shouldn't surprise him. He told himself it didn't matter, that she had done him a favor. A long-lasting
relationship would only keep him from his duty to marry.

Yet he could not help wondering that if only she had not found the diary, if only she had not discovered his perfidy, she might have answered him differently.

At least there was time to make amends. They were bound together by their search for her sister. For now, he did not have to say goodbye to her.

The coach slowed. Mary leaned forward and pressed her nose to the window. "There's Obediah now," she said, pointing her gloved finger down the street. "I wonder where he's going."

Crouching to avoid striking his head on the roof, Adam sprang to her side, aware of the scents of damp wool and sweet woman. He peered out into the gray afternoon as they drove past the row of quaint town houses. By pressing close to her, he spied Obediah's husky form, swathed in a greatcoat and hat, limping toward the cross street.

The coach eased to a stop before the columned edifice where Mary resided. "Wait here," Adam commanded. "Please."

He unlatched the door and emerged into the drizzling rain. Mary clambered down after him, and he turned just in time to lend her a hand. Her hood tumbled off, and beads of rain glistened on her red-gold hair.

"I don't suppose you've decided to wait in the house," he said resignedly.

She pressed her lips together in that prim, woman-on-a-mission manner. "If Obediah is hiding something, I intend to discover what it is."

Adjusting her hood, she marched down the street. Adam signaled Crookes to stay with the coach, then strode to her side and took her arm. She cast him a sidelong glance as they hurried to the corner. Only a few pedestrians braved the weather, a housewife with her shawl drawn over her head, a boy balancing a bundle of rags atop his head, a coster and his cart sheltering beneath the awning of a haberdashery shop.

Even if the byway had been crowded, Adam was sure he

would have spotted Obediah. The footman had a distinctive gait, the memento of his service in the King's army. "He's heading toward the Strand. There's something furtive about the way he's looking around. As if he fears to be followed."

"Nonsense," Mary said. "He's probably on his way to market."

"The stalls would be closed by now."

"Then he has another household errand. Perhaps he's going to the chandler or the stationer or the apothecary."

"Perhaps." Adam spoke absently, keeping his attention on the hurrying man and also the task of negotiating Mary around the puddles and potholes.

She squeezed his hand suddenly, luring his gaze to her. Puzzlement clouded the misty green of her eyes. "Jo probably tore out that page herself. It's too ridiculous to think Obediah had anything to do with her disappearance."

"He has no alibi. The other servants who were in the house that night have yet to be located."

"He said he dismissed them because they were lazy and taking advantage of Jo."

"And he told the magistrate they'd run off rather than risk being blamed for the crime."

That silenced Mary, but only for a moment. "You're resentful of him because he dared to stand up to you this morning."

Her accusation should not have hurt. She had commented often enough on his arrogance. He kept his expression closed, his eyes watchful on the foot traffic ahead. Then a strange happening distracted him.

"Now there's a curious sight." He drew Mary into the doorway of a tobacconist's shop. Pungent aromas saturated the damp air, along with the stink of the Thames. "Look. In the churchyard."

They both peered through the misting rain at St. Clement Danes with its tall spire piercing the sullen sky. The pale stone structure dwarfed the man who stood amid the trees behind the church, his shoulders hunched and his balding head hatless despite the rain. He walked forward to greet Obediah with a handshake. The scene struck Adam like a fist in his gut.

"Papa?" Mary whispered, her voice reedy with astonishment.

When she took a step forward, Adam touched her arm. "Not yet. Let's see what they're about first."

He might have known she would not obey him. She shook off his hand and dashed headlong down the street, dodging a clerk carrying a satchel and a housewife with a half-wrapped fish tucked beneath her doughy arm. Muttering a curse, Adam sped after Mary, going as fast as he dared, his polished Hessians unsuited for mad races over wet paving stones. She clutched the sides of her skirt, and the hood fell back again, exposing the richness of her hair.

He caught up to her just as she reached the churchyard. There was no need for subterfuge now; the two men had spotted them. Obediah passed a white paper to Thomas Sheppard, who tucked it inside his black coat.

As they drew nigh, Mary hung back. The mouse again, Adam thought, his heart lurching with tenderness. Her father had trained her well.

He took her arm again and conveyed her around the few gravestones, the sodden earth giving with each step. She lowered her chin, staring from her father to Obediah and back again.

Adam took a protective stance in front of her. "Reverend Sheppard. What an unexpected pleasure."

Thomas gave a curt nod. "Mr. Brentwell."

"But where is your minion?" Adam asked. "The virtuous Deacon Gabriel."

"I bade him wait at the caravan," Thomas Sheppard said, his face stony. " 'Tis parked down the lane."

"Ye followed me," Obediah accused Adam. "Ye with yer devious ways."

"He has found me out, and there is naught to hide now,"

Thomas said. " 'The wicked flee when no man pursueth; but the righteous are bold as a lion.' "

Adam raised an eyebrow. " 'He that diggeth a pit shall fall into it.' "

A droplet of rain rolled down Sheppard's high forehead and into his thick graying eyebrow. He glowered at Adam, then at Mary, and the stern lines of age seemed to cut deeper into his face. Abruptly, he said, "Obediah is in my employ."

That was the last answer Adam had expected. Yet perhaps it fit. Yes, it did.

Mary caught her breath, the tiny sound almost lost to the hissing of the rain. "I don't understand, Papa. Jo hired him, not you."

"I sent him to her." Thomas Sheppard rubbed his jaw, his gray-green gaze veering to the church. "Without her knowledge."

"Because you knew that if a half-crippled soldier came begging at her doorstep, she would take him in," Mary whispered. "You knew she would give him work in her house."

"And then he could spy on Josephine and send back reports to you," Adam surmised. "A clever arrangement."

"It weren't spying." The servant smacked his broad chest with his fist. "I did me chores, an' did 'em good. The reverend only wanted a letter now and again t' know that Miss Josephine were safe." He glowered at Adam. "An' Miss Mary, too."

She walked slowly to her father. The voluminous dark cloak made her look fragile. Too fragile. "Then you lied to me. You said you'd cut Jo out of your life, and you insisted I do the same. But you didn't, not really. *You didn't.*"

His troubled gaze met hers. "I committed a sin of weakness, daughter. And I've begged God's forgiveness for it."

"Weakness?" Mary flew to embrace him, pressing her cheek to his coat. "Oh, Papa. How can love be a weakness?"

Thomas hesitated, then brought his arms up to clasp her close. He bent his head, displaying the diadem of graying hair that encircled his bald pate. Just then, the bells in St. Clement's tower began to peal.

"There now," Obediah said with satisfaction. "Four o'clock and all's well."

Moodily, Adam regarded him. "So tell me," he said over the music of the bells, "what part did you play in Josephine's abduction?"

The older man bristled. "I was asleep in me cellar room that night."

"Then tell us the true reason you sacked Josephine's servants."

Obediah adjusted his squat hat. "Miss Josephine found me out, is all. That evenin' she saw me writin' the envelope t' her papa and wanted t' know why. Whilst we was havin' words, Cook walked in. I feared she'd blab it t' the magistrate, an' I'd take the blame fer shootin' his lordship."

"I knew there was a reasonable explanation," Mary said.

"And what of the page you tore from Josephine's diary?" Adam asked the servant. "The one you handed to Reverend Sheppard. I should like to know what it says."

The two older men exchanged a furtive glance. "It is a family matter, one that has nothing whatever to do with you," Thomas said coldly. He turned to Obediah. "You may go now. I've no further need of you."

"There's one more thing first." The footman jabbed his stubby forefinger at Adam. "Tell the reverend what ye did. Git on yer fancy knees an' beg his pardon fer seducin' Miss Mary." Muttering to himself, the servant limped out of the churchyard.

Thomas Sheppard stiffened. His hands fell away from his daughter, and his face darkened. The church bells ceased their music. Into the sudden quiet, the plop-plop of the rain blended with the noise of traffic from the Strand.

"Is this true, Mary Elizabeth?" he asked hoarsely. "Have you fallen as low as your sister?"

She dipped her chin. "I thought it was an act of love—"

"Love. It is lechery! Men of his kind will say anything to lure a godly woman into sin. Just look at him, standing there so proud of his vile deed."

Mary's gaze focused on Adam, and a deep, knowing pain shone in her eyes. His chest seized up with the urge to tell her what she wanted to hear. But how could he lie to her again? He didn't love her; he couldn't love her. Love was a gentle warmth, not this burning obsession, this fierce possessiveness.

"There, you see?" Thomas Sheppard thundered. "He feels no remorse for turning you into a whore. You are no more to him than a nameless doxy who plies her trade on the street corner."

Coldness ran through Adam's veins. Was this a taste of how others would treat her? He would not tolerate it.

In one swift move, he grabbed the preacher by his black lapels. "Do not ever again speak to Mary in such a manner," he snapped. "The situation is entirely my fault. And I intend to put matters to right—"

"Indeed you shall, Mr. Brentwell."

With lightning swiftness, Thomas brought up his fist and smashed it into Adam's jaw. The blow sent him staggering backward, jolting into the solid trunk of an oak. A shower of droplets cascaded on him. He tasted blood in his mouth. Pain radiated outward from his jaw and into his skull. Half dazed, he clenched his fists, his muscles tensed to return the attack.

Yet he could not—would not—strike Mary's father.

She stood as if paralyzed, her hands over her mouth and her eyes wide with shock. Moist curls framed the delicacy of her face, and he could only think that he had brought her to this. To shameful disgrace in front of her own father.

Unexpectedly, she spun toward Sheppard. "How dare you interfere, Papa? I don't need you to fight my battles. I'm not a child any longer."

She ran toward Adam, slipping and sliding on the wet

grass, until she reached his side. The scent of woman filled him as she arched against him, reaching up to cradle his jaw in her cold palm. Her show of spirit both warmed him and deepened his guilt.

Thomas Sheppard watched them, his shoulders slumped and his gaze fathomless. "Go to your lover," he said in a quiet voice. "As to you, Mr. Brentwell, I would advise that you keep her within the safety of your house. God forbid I should be tempted to turn my righteous wrath on her."

Wheeling around, he strode off into the rain, a black-garbed figure against the stark monolith of the church.

Sheppard's threat held Adam paralyzed. He was keenly aware of Mary shivering within the protection of his arms, and how vulnerable and afraid she must be. Damn her father to hell!

Yet Adam's anger at Sheppard was overshadowed by anger at himself. By his own arrogance, he had put her in this untenable predicament. By his lack of restraint, he had doomed her to a life of dishonor. There was but one way to atone for ruining her. With fatalistic acceptance, he knew it was the only way.

He must make Mary his wife.

❧ Chapter 18 ❧

"Gather your things," Adam said. "You'll be staying with me tonight."

Mary blinked at the St. Chaldon coach, parked in front of the town house. During their walk back here, she had been reliving that dismal scene at the churchyard, and misery held such a grip on her heart that for a moment his words failed to register. Then the reminder of his sordid proposal made her freeze.

"I shan't be your mistress. I told you so already."

"I meant that you'll be my guest at Brentwell House. It isn't safe for you here with only a crippled footman to protect you."

God forbid I should be tempted to turn my righteous wrath on her.

A chill prickled over her skin, and she rubbed her arms beneath the cloak. "For heaven's sake, you can't suspect my father. Certainly he's punished my sister and me from time to time, but only when we richly deserved it. Besides, he was with me on the night Jo was abducted."

"And what of his deacon, Victor Gabriel?"

"He'd gone to Dover to fetch a bundle of tracts." When Adam frowned, she quickly added, "He was only to stay overnight. That would hardly be sufficient time to abduct a woman in London, convey her to a prison on the coast, and return to the caravan. Besides, Victor is . . . good."

"Unlike me."

"I didn't say that."

"You didn't need to."

Adam regarded her broodingly. Ever since they'd left the churchyard, he seemed to have drawn into himself, the remote and unapproachable duke. Yet the attraction of him pulled her like a moth to the flame of a candle. The rain had dampened his hair again, and a strand lay like a black half moon on his forehead. A bruise already darkened his jaw. It lent him the dashing look of a pirate.

"Please stay at my house," he said. "I would feel more at ease knowing you are protected under my roof."

No smile softened his formal invitation. He must be furious that her father had dared to strike him. Somehow she felt guilty as if she herself had hurled the blow. That, more than her own security, decided her. "All right."

She entered the dim, silent house, her footsteps echoing in the small foyer. Prinny padded out to greet her, then went to Adam, who crouched down to pet the dog. Mary mounted the stairs and packed her few possessions in the valise. She changed out of her bedraggled gown and donned a lovely amber silk with short, puffed sleeves and a daring bodice. What she had once thought scandalous, she knew now to be the fashion for all ladies.

Going to her sister's dressing table, she picked up the silver hairbrush. She was no longer afraid to gaze into the oval mirror and see her reflection. With her damp hair hanging loose and her bosom milky pale in the shadows, she looked utterly different from the meek, frightened girl who had come in quest of her sister only a week ago. Now she looked like a woman in love.

Men of his kind will say anything to lure a godly woman into sin.

Her father was right. She had known that for certain in the terrible moment when she had looked into Adam's face to see the truth written starkly on his features. Yet she had gone to him anyway. In spite of pride and self-protection, she wanted to feel his heart beating against her cheek and his arms holding her close. She wanted to give herself into his keeping, to accept whatever crumbs he might toss to her. She wanted to trust a nobleman. What had she become?

She had become her twin, her lost half.

A dizzying vulnerability swept over Mary. Brush in hand, she sank to the floor and rested her cheek on the flounced stool. "Jo," she whispered into the stillness. "I feel so alone without you. There's no one to advise me, no one who loves me as you do. Please listen, please. My heart is speaking to you."

The silence mocked her. Despair washed through Mary, the feeling expanding until it flooded her chest and inundated her spirit. She squeezed her eyes shut against the threat of tears. Then into the darkness of her heart appeared a star of light.

Mary? Is it you? Listen . . . I'm so afraid . . . Papa is . . . you will never guess . . . Peter . . .

The garbled words disintegrated into a sibilant noise like the sound of the sea hissing onto the shore. Then the urgent voice faded away altogether.

Mary sprang to her feet. The hairbrush dropped from her shaking hand and clattered to the floor. Jo had heard her. She had been trying to tell Mary something vital.

God have mercy. Had Jo implicated their father?

"We shall have to be married," Adam said.

The well-sprung coach swayed slightly as the horses drew away from the curbstone. Keeping his emotions under strict control, he gauged Mary's reaction, anticipating her disbelief, then her cautious acceptance. But she gazed blankly at him as if her mind were a hundred miles away. No doubt she thought he was jesting.

"As soon as we locate your sister," he went on, "I shall see to obtaining a special license. It should present no problem. The archbishop will balk, of course, but in the end he will acquiesce. We can be married quietly in the church of your choosing—"

"No."

Her rejection caught him off guard. "If you prefer, we can speak our vows at my home. Then afterward, a small reception with the closest friends of the family in attendance—"

"I said, *no.*" She clenched her gloved fingers in her lap. Her eyes were deep green pools of anguish against the pale oval of her face. "No license, no archbishop, no church, and certainly no reception. I am not marrying you."

He frowned. "But you must."

He sent the force of his willpower to bear on her. He had to do right by her. Didn't she comprehend how agonizing this decision had been for him, how he was sacrificing his ordained duty for her? And didn't she understand the enormity of what he was offering? The honor of his ancient name. The promise of riches. The chance to take her place as his duchess, a position scores of ladies would clamor to fill.

But of course this was Mary. He should have expected as much. "You surely cannot allow any misguided nonsense about the aristocracy stop you from accepting."

She shook her head. "It isn't so much that."

"Then what?" Anger built in him, an anger sparked by frustration. He felt as if he were trying to speak with her across an abyss, but the wind kept whipping away their words. "If you are pained by my actions toward your sister, I can only humbly beg your forgiveness. I promise to make amends somehow."

"It isn't that, either." Mary pleated the edge of her cloak between her fingers. "You don't wish to wed me of your own accord. You feel coerced into making this offer. My father shamed you into it."

So that was it. Remorse gnawed at him, the feeling stronger than the ache in his jaw. "I will not permit others to revile you as he did. When you are my duchess, no one will dare to insult you."

She studied him with those direct eyes. "Had we not spent the night together . . . had you not been caught at it . . . you would be asking Lady Camilla for her hand instead."

He sat silent, unable to deny it.

"I am not your love, not really," Mary added, a husky quality entering her voice. "I should have known those words meant nothing to a nobleman."

Adam, I love you, too.

A fist of longing gripped his throat. What *did* he feel for her? Lust, certainly. He wanted to take her to bed and stay there for the next ten years. Admiration, too. He appreciated the quickness of her mind, and he could take lessons from her on frankness. But love? How could love cause this agitation inside him, this undignified turmoil of emotion?

A strange, exhilarating panic swept him. It was shattering even to wonder if this unconventional miss might already hold his heart in her soft little hands.

"I care for you," he said. "In time, that affection will grow."

"Resentment is more likely to grow. How can it be otherwise when you view me as something less than yourself? When you feel forced to take a wife who is only suited to be your mistress?"

The dreary light illuminated her delicate features, the chin she held so proudly. Yet there was a wounded quality to her eyes and mouth. He had hurt her. Badly. Because she saw the reluctance behind his offer.

The thought of being refused suddenly terrified him. He leaned forward, clasping his hands before him and resisting the powerful urge to kiss her for fear she might think he was using her again. "Mary, please try to understand. I meant you no insult when I asked you to be my mistress. I only wished to offer my protection as amends for ruining your reputation. But now I can see that I owe you more than that temporary arrangement. Honor demands it of me."

The moment she pursed her lips, he knew he'd spoken wrongly. "Damn your honor," she said in a sharp voice. "I could never accept a man who thinks he is lowering himself to marry me. You may take both your offers, my lord duke, and go to perdition."

Mary pretended to eat her creamy turtle soup unobtrusively. The few sips she managed stirred a protest in her stomach. Her nerves were so overwrought that she could taste little.

It had been a mistake to accept Adam's invitation to dine with his family. His cool formality made her want to run and hide in her sumptuous bedchamber. But she was no longer a mouse, she reminded herself. No man could make her cower ever again. As a guest here at Bridewell House, she had every right to sup at Adam's table. She was the equal of any nobleman or lady.

Besides, being alone meant agonizing over that distorted message from her sister. Jo could not have meant their father was involved in her disappearance. Mary had misunderstood. And who was Peter? Her head ached from the effort to make sense of it all. After dinner, she would write a note to Obediah and ask him if he knew.

She dipped her spoon into her bowl again, but could not bring herself to swallow any more soup. Never before had she attended such a fancy gathering. Across from her sat Lady Sophy and Lord Harry, with Adam and his mother presiding at either end of the long table. Lady Sophy was describing a merry escapade involving one of her friends, while her mother and Lord Harry offered a comment every now and then.

As they chatted, Mary tried not to gawk like a bumpkin at her surroundings. The walls were hung with blue silk damask that matched the gold-trimmed draperies on the tall windows. Ornate plasterwork decorated every inch of the ceiling. A chandelier cast sparkling prisms of light across the bone china and heavy sterling silver.

This could have been hers, all of it. She might have taken her place as mistress of this grand household with its endless corridors and dizzyingly high ceilings and elegantly appointed rooms. How very strange to consider that.

A keen yearning rose within her. Was she so shallow that she craved wealth and luxury?

No, it was the master of the house she desired. In spite of all that had transpired between them, in spite of wisdom or judgment, she longed to be his wife.

His magnetic presence drew her gaze, and as always, the sight of him made her heart constrict. Darkly handsome, he sat at the head of the table, listening to his sister's chatter. A bemused smile eased the arrogant set of his face. The bruise across his lower left jaw lent a dash of danger to his attractiveness. From the perfection of his cravat to the richness of his brocaded waistcoat, he was the epitome of rank and privilege.

And he wanted to marry her.

She carefully set down her spoon lest her trembling fingers spill soup onto the pristine white tablecloth. Not *wanted*. He had felt obliged to offer for her. No doubt he was relieved that she had refused him. She fit his exalted life as well as a snake in the Garden of Eden.

How foolish she was to love him. Still.

He turned then and looked at her. His smile faded and his eyes gazed piercingly into hers. Breathlessness seized her lungs. If only she had accepted him, he would come to her bed again. They would share that miraculous bond of body and mind. Was he thinking of their lovemaking, too?

"Did you not care for the soup, Miss Sheppard?" he asked.

Mary's mouth went dry. Every coherent remark flew from her mind. "It's good, but rather . . . green."

He quirked an eyebrow. Lady Sophy giggled. Lord Harry grinned.

The duchess said, "I am sorry the dish displeases you. I shall inform Monsieur Bernard not to serve you any more green soup."

Mary's cheeks grew hot. "Please don't trouble yourself. I'm really just not very hungry."

"It's no wonder you've lost your appetite," Lord Harry drawled, his eyes twinkling. Tonight he wore a turquoise coat over a pale salmon waistcoat. "St. Chaldon was glaring at you. 'Tis a habit of his, intimidating his guests. You'll grow accustomed to it as the rest of us have done."

"Here now," Adam chided. "Don't reveal all my secrets."

"Speaking of secrets." Lady Sophy leaned forward, the pink ruffles on her bodice in danger of taking a dip in her soup bowl. "I should like to know about that bruise on your face. Why won't you tell us how you came by it?"

"As I said, I ran into a door. Quite clumsy of me."

"Hah." She turned to Mary. "Do *you* know? He did not have the bruise earlier today, I'll vow."

Adam's cool gaze dared Mary to reveal the truth. Gooseflesh prickled her skin. Did he expect her to be so gauche?

Lord Harry saved her from blurting out an unladylike set-down. "I do fear, Miss Sheppard, there's another eccentricity to which you must accustom yourself. And that is Lady Sophy making a nuisance of herself."

"I beg your pardon, Lord Toad," huffed Sophy. "She shall have a harder time getting used to *you.*"

They squabbled good-naturedly as if Mary were a member of their closed circle. A wistful smile touched her lips; then a grievous thought shook the remnants of her composure. If . . . *when* Jo married Cyril, Mary would be his sister-in-law. She would be invited to this house on many occasions. From time to time, she would see Adam with his blue-blooded wife, Adam with his blue-blooded children.

A liveried footman cleared away the bowls while another served a course of fish in cream sauce. Mary watched to see which fork Lady Sophy picked up, and did the same herself. If nothing else, she would be a credit to her sister. Adam could go to the devil.

She managed to finish the meal without committing another faux pas. Afterwards, Lady Sophy took Mary by the arm and drew her from the dining room.

"Now we ladies must go sit in the grand saloon for another half an hour of polite conversation while the men smoke their cigars and drink their brandy." She wrinkled her nose. "I should like to stay with them for once, wouldn't you?"

"Sophronia," the duchess chided. "Mind your behavior."

"But Mary agrees with me. Don't you, Mary?"

Their footsteps echoed through the entrance hall with its paintings of Julius Caesar on the vaulted ceiling. Mary balked at being the pawn in a mother-daughter quarrel. "I'm afraid I would make dull company tonight with either group." She smiled to soften her words. "I'm most weary. May I be excused?"

"You will stay a moment at least," the duchess said. She wore a look of grave concentration. "Sophronia, wait in the saloon."

"But Mama—"

"Kindly do as I say."

The girl heaved a sigh and flounced through the gilded doorway, a pleasingly plump figure in pink sprigged muslin.

Mary's heart beat with apprehension. Why did the duchess desire a private moment with her? Dear heaven. She must have discovered that Mary had lain with Adam in blatant disregard for the laws of society and the Church.

Mary reluctantly followed the duchess into a small alcove off the grand staircase. There, the duchess folded her hands at her waist. For all her imperious bearing, she stood no taller than Mary. "I have never thanked you for what you did for my son."

"Did?" Mary squeaked. What had she done for Adam that would make his mother express appreciation?

"There is no need to be modest, Miss Sheppard," she said in a kindly voice. "You awakened Cyril, perhaps saved his life. I shall always be grateful to you for that." She smiled, lending warmth to her queenly features.

Mary felt a rush of intense relief, along with a surprising flash of affinity. Adam's mother did have a human side. "How is Lord Cyril?"

"He is recovering rapidly, much to the amazement of his doctors. And he has become quite the ill-tempered patient. Although sitting up makes him dizzy, he is determined to be on his feet again."

"Because he wants to find Jo," Mary said.

The gentleness vanished from the duchess's countenance, and a rigidity seemed to grip her. "Naturally he would wish to aid a woman in distress. He is a gentleman, albeit rash at times."

Mary gritted her teeth. "Jo is more than a woman in distress. She is Lord Cyril's intended wife."

A furrow appeared in the duchess's smooth brow. As if in reassessment, she looked Mary up and down. "I am perfectly aware of that."

"Then of course you also know that the duke has granted his approval of their wedding."

The keen blue eyes wavered, but only for a moment. "I admire you for defending your sister. Yet you seem a sensible girl, Miss Sheppard. I am sure you'll understand that I want only the best for my son. For both of my sons."

Mary bristled at the slight to her and her twin. How shocked the duchess would be to learn that Adam had made his offer of marriage already, and that Mary had refused him. She wanted to hurl that fact at the duchess, but it would mean exposing her own private pain.

Then the duchess did something unexpected. She

reached out and wrapped her cool, dry fingers around Mary's hand. "I do not mean to distress you," she said. "But perhaps frankness is in order. Of late, the duke has been restless, weighed by the duties of his high station. He needs a generous woman who will give him ease."

Mary's mouth went dry. "Ease—?"

The duchess inclined her head. "My son cares for you, I can see that in the way he looks at you. If you truly return his regard, Miss Sheppard, do not burden him with unreasonable demands. He must marry within his own world. For the duke, it is not a choice, but a sacred trust."

Mary felt hot and cold all over. The duchess was urging her to become Adam's mistress. Because if he married her, he would be shirking his responsibilities. He would be failing to fulfill the duty that had been drummed into him since boyhood.

A footman approached and bowed to the duchess. "There is a man at the door, Your Grace. He is asking to see Miss Sheppard."

"Where is his card?"

"He presented none." The footman curled his lip as if offended by the breach of etiquette. "He gave his name as Mr. Gabriel. I bade him wait at the tradesman's entrance."

"Victor?" Mary blurted. "I should like to see him, please. Bring him to me. In the library."

Without awaiting the duchess's permission, Mary hurried out of the alcove and down the immense marble corridor. She could think only of seeing a friendly face, a person from the comforting familiarity of the life she had left behind.

The tapping of her slippers echoed through the vast residence. After a few wrong turns, she found the library at last. Adam's men had been working here. Crates were placed against the shelves of books, and long worktables held piles of documents. Quills and inkwells lay beside several flickering lamps as if someone had stepped away for a few moments, perhaps to dine.

Too agitated to sit, she paced until Victor came striding through the doorway, clutching a black, curly-brimmed hat in his hands.

"There you are at last," he said with uncharacteristic terseness. "I was beginning to think I might never be allowed inside these hallowed halls. First the porter at the front gate insulted me, then that footman sent me around back. As if *I* were a rag peddler."

His angry tone surprised her. Unlike her father, whose temper snapped easily, Victor was always as serene as a saint. "I'm sure they meant only to be cautious. You're a stranger to the staff, and there are many valuables in the house."

"You speak as if you belong here now."

Feeling torn between two worlds, Mary sheltered herself with anger. "And you speak as if you were my master."

His silvery eyes widened. Then he inhaled deeply, the frown lines vanishing from the classical perfection of his features. "Forgive me, Miss Mary. I was worried about you, that's all. Praise God you're safe."

"Of course, I'm safe. Why would I not be?" A thought struck the breath from her, the dreadful memory of that broken message from Jo. "Is it Papa? Is he . . . coming to see me, too?"

Victor shook his head. "I'm here on my own to rescue you from the duke."

"I don't need rescuing. His Grace has treated me with all the respect due a guest in his house."

"Respect! St. Chaldon tempted you into sin. He stole your virtue."

Victor loomed over her like a golden archangel barring her way into heaven. She almost hung her head in shame for disappointing so many people: Obediah, her father, the duchess, and now Victor. Yet she could not regret that extraordinary union with Adam. Oh, she could not.

And she was done listening to everyone scold her about morality. "Adam couldn't steal what I chose to give. And if you're so keen on punishing me, then feel free to announce my fall from grace on the front page of the newspaper."

"This is no time for jests. Consider what happened to your father's mother when she fornicated with a nobleman. She suffered for her sin, and I fear you will do the same."

"My actions are not for you to judge. Not any longer."

Victor's eyes narrowed. He stood as still as the statue of a martyr who devoutly bore the ravages of suffering. Mary felt a stirring of dark chaos inside her. What was wrong with her, that she could still feel drawn to a man so holy? The man she had once coveted enough to shut out her own sister.

. He fell to his knees then. Grasping her hands, he bent his golden head. "Renounce the duke, Miss Mary. Come away with me. Right now. I can give you a life of honor and goodness. My love for you remains as strong and firm as a rock. Please say you'll marry me. Please."

His impassioned speech shook her. Sweet heaven. She had not imagined him so tormented by the loss of her. Yet even in the midst of her compassion, she could not stop an agonizing thought. Why did the wrong man love her?

"A touching scene," spoke a harsh voice. "You must forgive me for interrupting."

Mary whirled around to see Adam walking toward them. The autocratic set of his mouth, the deliberation of his strides, radiated fury. Yet her heart took a joyful leap. "I thought you were with Lord Harry."

"I came to fetch some papers prepared by my steward." He fixed a hard stare on Victor. "We are mapping out our route to find Josephine. My men and I depart for the coast at first light."

Victor rose to his feet. "Your Grace," he said, inclining his head submissively. "Am I to hope you've discovered where she's hiding?"

"Perhaps so. Or perhaps not."

"Has Lord Cyril awakened, then? Has he identified the villain who seized her?"

"The answer to that is not for your ears."

Victor's face paled. "You surely don't think *I* would wish her harm."

"You, the jilted fiancé? I surely do."

The two men eyed each other with unguarded hostility. Dear God. Adam didn't know of the garbled message from Jo that pointed to her father. And Mary dreaded to have him find out.

She stepped between them. "What is the harm in telling him?" she chided Adam. Turning to Victor, she explained, "Lord Cyril could give us no clue. But I had a dream, a vision that might help us locate Jo."

" 'Tis the work of the devil," Victor grumbled. "But tell me, where is she? I'll join the search party."

"No," Adam said crisply. "And there's a door right there, if you would care to remove yourself from the premises." He indicated the same glass door where Mary and Lady Sophy had once entered on their secret visit to Lord Cyril.

"Your Grace, I will pray for the success of your mission." Victor bowed, then turned to Mary, his eyes soft with yearning. "Miss Mary, please consider what I said. It is the best solution for all who love you, including your poor father. I'll return for my answer soon." He walked away, setting his hat over his fair hair before stepping out into the night.

The latch clicked shut, and silence settled over the library. Mary rounded on Adam. "Was it necessary to be so antagonistic? Accusing Victor without any evidence."

"You're a veritable angel of mercy. Tell me, do you plan to accept *his* offer of marriage?"

He made no attempt to hide the fact that he'd listened in on their conversation. Anger blazed in her, an anger beyond the situation. "Lurking in the corridors, Your

Grace? You have no right to invade my privacy, not even in your own house. I would have your apology."

"When hell freezes over." Adam stepped to the desk and impatiently rifled through a pile of papers. "Thank God my mother told me of your impropriety, skulking off alone to meet that man. I never realized you were so lacking in common sense."

"And *I* never realized you would stoop to the ungentle-manly practice of eavesdropping." Hardly aware of what she was doing, she seized a crystal paperweight. "The only time I lacked common sense was when I let you seduce me."

He reached across the desk and removed the paperweight from her hand. "Mind your temper, Miss Sheppard."

"I never knew I *had* a temper until I met you." Mary flattened her palms on the desk. "And if we're naming suspects, what of your mother? Maybe she sent a hired minion to dispose of a threat to her exalted family. He might have shot Cyril in a panic."

Adam glowered at her. "Don't be absurd. My mother has an unshakable core of decency."

"So does Victor. He's a hardworking man, devoted to the cause of bringing equality to this nation. What better way than to see one of us commoners marry into your exclusive society?"

Adam threw down a sheaf of papers. "You're behaving like a besotted fool. Gabriel could have hurt you. He could have carried you off into the night and locked you up like your sister."

Had Adam spoken with any warmth, she might have hoped his mother was right, that he cared for her. But he stood regarding her in his cold and unforgiving manner, the man who had asked her to marry him purely out of obligation. Adam didn't love her. To him, she was another duty to discharge, of no more significance than keeping his horses fed and stabled.

To her chagrin, his image went misty and tears spilled hotly down her cheeks. Not trusting herself to speak, she picked up her skirts and hastened toward the door before he could notice her lapse into weakness.

She heard his footsteps behind her. His fingers closed on her arm before she could escape, and he brought her around to face him. "I'm not through with you—"

The imperiousness of his expression faded away. He blinked, his eyes a startled blue against features that had become more dear to her than anyone else in the world.

"Mary," he said softly, contritely. He pulled her against him, holding her close while stroking her hair. "Ah, Mary, why must we hurt each other? Why can we not find joy instead?"

Too distraught to answer, she hid her face against the smooth fabric of his coat. Her senses expanded with the scent of him, the beating of his heart against her cheek, the strength of his muscled body. More than anything, she craved the comfort of his embrace, yet not even that could stop her tears. The past twenty-four hours had been too much for her, the tumultuous night of discovery, the revelations in the diary, his offer first of dishonor, then of marriage. She wept for the upheaval in her life, and most of all, the terrible connotation in her sister's message.

Adam drew back slightly, his hands rubbing up and down her bare arms. "I never meant to snap at you," he murmured. "But when I saw that holy paragon touching you, holding your hands. . . ."

It dawned in her that he was jealous. But how could that be when he didn't love her? The answer was simple. "I'm not one of your possessions."

"Of course not." As if to deny his own words, he flexed his fingers around her shoulders, keeping her near him. "But surely you see the need for caution. You shouldn't be alone with him, Mary. He might very well be the man who abducted Josephine."

Her head ached. She had to unburden herself, to reveal

the truth. Jo's life depended on it. "Victor isn't the one," Mary said haltingly. "I was afraid to tell you . . . while I was packing my valise earlier, I heard my sister."

Adam's gaze penetrated her. Taking her by the arm, he guided her to a sofa and sat her down beside him. He held both her hands in his. "Tell me exactly what you heard."

He believed her. And ironically, for once Mary had hoped he would not. "The message was . . . broken. Only snatches of phrases. She said she was afraid. And right after that, she mentioned a name. . . ."

"Who?"

His large hands warmed her cold skin, giving her the strength to speak. "Papa."

The confession hung in the hushed air of the library. Yet still she could not believe their father would hurt Jo. Granted, he'd been furious when she'd run off, but deep down, he loved her. He'd even dispatched Obediah to act as her guardian angel.

Yet he had threatened Mary.

God forbid I should turn my righteous wrath on her.

Her lower lip quivered, but she held her head high, willing herself not to flinch from Adam's certain exultation.

He merely said, "Is that all? She didn't give more details about her prison? Or a reference to anyone else?"

"She said . . . the name Peter." Mary grasped at the straw of hope. "But does she know a man named Peter? She said nothing of him in her diary, and she wrote about all her suitors."

"You said the message was indistinct."

"Yes. Her voice kept fading in and out."

Adam compressed his mouth into a grim line. "Then it's clear enough to me. She was referring to the earl of Peterbourne."

∽ Chapter 19 ∞

Astride his favorite black mare, Adam rode south along the Brighton turnpike. The horse's hooves splashed through puddles left by the previous day's rain. The road was muddy and his traveling coach lagged far behind, but the afternoon sky shone a brilliant blue and a refreshing breeze blew across lush green pastures, where sheep and dairy cows grazed in the sunshine.

Ordinarily, the rustic scene would have roused in Adam a deep longing for his lands in Derbyshire. But not today. Gripped by tension, he concentrated on the interview that awaited him.

Why would Peterbourne kidnap another man's fiancée? Cyril had no more than a nodding acquaintance with the man, and that ruled out vengeance over some slight.

Perhaps Josephine's rejection had insulted Peterbourne's manliness. Had she so angered him that he'd felt compelled to enter her house at night and shoot Cyril?

Ridiculous. Peterbourne was a lecher who went after anything in skirts. If one female refused him, another would take her place. There were scores of women who would gladly accommodate an earl, no matter how far past his prime.

Unless the rake had developed an unnatural fascination for Josephine. Perhaps his hunger to possess her had consumed him until it overwhelmed his sanity.

Obsession. Now *there* was an explanation Adam could begin to fathom.

He guided the mare past a treacherous quagmire in the rutted road. The mud sucked at her hooves, and the elegant animal pranced sideways, the silky black mane lifting in the breeze. The horse's every step carried him farther away from Mary.

The thought of her made his heart clench like a hot fist. He had not seen her this morning. Only a few yawning servants had been awake when he and Crookes had departed at dawn.

As he had done half the night, Adam brooded on that highly charged meeting in the library the previous evening, when he had driven Mary to tears with his unreasoning jealousy. He ought to have been more cognizant of her delicate emotions. She had endured a trying day, from his rash seduction of her in the early hours of the morning to the distressing encounter with her father in the afternoon. If that were not enough, Adam reflected grimly, he had insulted her twice, first with his ignominious proposal of a liaison, then with his coldly reluctant offer of marriage.

His arrogance had been inexcusable. He didn't own her. He had behaved like a beast, and his lack of self-control appalled him.

Yet he couldn't regret seizing the chance to comfort her. She fit his arms to perfection as if her slim body were made for him alone. Holding Mary had calmed the storm of his temper if not his irrational possessiveness.

She had wanted to accompany him today, of course. But when he pointed out the dangers of confronting Peterbourne and bade her stay at Brentwell House, she'd put up only a token resistance. And no wonder. Her shoulders had drooped from exhaustion as she'd gone upstairs to her bed.

It had taken every shred of Adam's willpower to keep himself from following her. Though his loins ached for her still, he vowed to cage his uncivilized passion. He was done offending Mary with his unwanted attentions. Henceforth, he would keep himself at a prudent distance from her. In truth, this journey was a godsend. A few days' separation from her would surely cool his hot blood.

A distant *halloo* caught his attention. He reined the mare to a halt and turned in the saddle, shading his eyes to look behind him. Some four hundred yards back, the St. Chaldon coach lumbered along the dirt road, and Crookes waved his black top hat. It was their cue to stop at the next inn.

Adam swore under his breath. Little more than an hour had passed since they'd changed the team of horses during a brief pause for luncheon. Crookes knew they needed to press on if they were to reach their destination by nightfall. That he would signal now meant trouble, either with the coach or the horses.

Irked and impatient, Adam rode toward a shabby posting inn in the distance. Not for the first time, he regretted the need to bring the coach. He could have made better time riding alone. But when—if—he found Josephine, he would require a closed carriage in which to return her to London. A soon-to-be member of his family did not travel by public mail coach.

A gaggle of geese ran squawking across the muddy yard of the inn. A mastiff trotted forward, its tail wagging. Several ostlers hastened out of the stables, one to take Adam's reins, two others to hold the team of matched grays.

He dismounted, heedless of the mud that squelched beneath his boots. Striding to the coach, he scrutinized the four horses, then the outside of the vehicle, but could spy no visible problem.

Hands on his hips, he frowned up at the coachman and the footman who peered almost fearfully past his bulky companion. Both servants wore the St. Chaldon livery, dark blue trimmed in silver. "Well, Crookes? What is the difficulty here?"

George Crookes shifted on the wide seat, the ribbons

loose in his great paws. He cleared his throat. "Er . . . need t' make a convenience stop, Yer Grace."

The man must have taken leave of his senses. "There is no shortage of trees along the roadside."

" 'T'ain't so simple as that."

"Are you ill, then?" Adam gestured to him. "Don't dally there. Climb down, we're in a hurry."

But Crookes made no move to obey. A ruddy hue stained his cheeks. "Er . . . 'tisn't me. Nor Drabble here," he added with a nod at the footman.

"Then who?"

The coachman pointed the handle of his whip toward the coach. " 'Tis the lady."

Hearing their voices, Mary took a deep breath and braced herself for Adam's wrath. She pushed open the door and poked her head out. The bright sunshine dazzled her for a moment. Then she found herself gazing straight into his thunderstruck face.

She forced her lips into a brilliant smile. "Good day, Your Grace. Lovely weather for a journey, isn't it? I've been enjoying the scenery. Your coach is ever so much more comfortable than riding in Papa's caravan—"

"Never mind that."

The sprightly commentary dried in her throat. But Adam wasn't addressing her; he imperiously waved away the footman who had clambered down from the driver's seat to lower the step for her. The hapless servant retreated hastily, standing at rigid attention by the door.

She had expected Adam to be angry. But not at his servants.

"If you must rant, do so at me. It isn't the fault of your men. They didn't see me creep into the coach this morning. They only found out when I . . ." She bit her lip, aware of her blush. An increasing discomfort had forced her to address the coachman through the brass speaking tube.

Adam stalked toward her. She was determined not to flinch from this cold stranger. She would stand her ground and make him listen to reason—

"Oh!" .

Her exclamation slipped out as he swung her up against him. Automatically, she clung to his neck as he carried her toward the inn. Each hard stride jostled her against his muscled chest. His spicy masculine scent made her giddy, and the sudden need for him spread a seductive heat through her.

"Put me down," she said, glaring up at his jaw, where the sunshine illuminated the faint yellow bruise placed there by her father. "I can walk."

"Mind your tone. Lest I be tempted to drop you in the mud."

She gritted her teeth against a retort. He was furious enough already. And she didn't want to quarrel anyway, not when she was tense already from the nervous strain of this journey. Not when she could tuck her cheek into the hard pillow of his shoulder, close her eyes, and pretend for one sweet moment that he loved her.

The innkeeper greeted them at the door, fawning and rubbing his pudgy palms together. At Adam's terse command, the portly man showed her to a small, private room with a chamberpot tucked discreetly behind a partition. Ladies, apparently, did not use the outdoor privy.

In short order, Mary accomplished her purpose, did a quick washing up, and tidied her hair. Adam's displeasure troubled her far less than the apprehension that had gnawed at her since the previous day. Was Peterbourne the kidnapper, or was it her own Papa? Would she find Jo, or would the trip end in disappointment?

A sense of desperation prodded Mary. She found Adam waiting for her in the common room. Pacing near the long tables, he cut a splendid figure from top hat and chocolate brown riding coat down to buckskin breeches and muddy

black boots. The tightness of his expression made him look
more forbidding than forgiving.

But she had no patience for sweetening his temper.

She hastened to the door, where he tossed a coin to the
obsequious innkeeper. Without a word, Adam picked her
up again and conveyed her to the coach. He set her down
on the step with all the care of a farmer ridding himself of
a sack of grain.

As he strode toward his black horse, a thought struck
into her preoccupation. He could bid the coachman return
to London. In a panic she held onto the door and called
out, "Adam! You aren't going to send me back, are you?"

He turned, his look grimly inscrutable. "No."

She scooted thankfully into the plush confines of the
coach with its velvet cushions. Adam would ride ahead,
and she could be alone with her anxious thoughts. She had
scarcely slept a wink last night, alternating between worry
about her family and concern over missing his early departure.

Tapping her toes on the floor, she waited for the coach
to start off again. They should reach Peterbourne's estate
by dusk. But the interminable hours of the afternoon
stretched out before her, another half a day of wondering
about her sister, of sensing the foreboding that loomed like
a black cloud on the horizon—

The door opened. The springs jolted as Adam stepped
inside, filling the coach with his domineering male presence. A moment later, the vehicle resumed its journey
down the rutted road.

Mary stiffened as he seated himself opposite her and
tossed his hat into the corner. The air felt thick with the
dark force of his fury. Rather than alarm her, his hostility
delivered a stab of bitter frustration to her breast. Couldn't
he see that she needed comfort and closeness and understanding?

As he peeled off his riding gloves, he focused his gaze on

her. "So," he said in a clipped tone. "Would you care to explain your presence?"

The cold burn of those blue eyes incensed her. So did her own untimely rush of desire. "Surely you didn't expect me to sit and embroider handkerchiefs while my sister is in mortal danger."

"So instead, you'll place yourself in mortal danger, too."

"I'll do whatever is necessary. If Peterbourne is holding Jo hostage, I intend to be there when she is freed."

"You shall not be. If Peterbourne is guilty that also means he shot my brother. Are you so wooden-brained as to think I'll permit you to meet with the unscrupulous blackguard?"

"Are you so pig-headed as to think I *require* your permission?"

He leaned forward, looking more dangerous than any blackguard. "I'll brook no interference from you, Mary. If I must tie you to the bedpost, you're to stay at the lodging house while I call on Peterbourne. Is that clear?"

She was an annoyance to him, a common thorn in his noble side. The reminder cut deeply into her heart. And how, in the face of his coldness, in the face of her own desperate fears, could she still feel a foolish yearning for him?

"On the contrary, Your Grace, I shall do as I see fit. In case you've forgotten, you don't own me. You haven't any hold over me. None whatsoever."

Watching her, he drew his gloves across his palm once, then again. Very quietly, he said, "Oh, haven't I?"

Dropping the gloves, he lunged across the coach and hauled her against him. His mouth crushed hers in a plundering kiss that brought her wildest dreams to vivid life. All her dread and anxiety vanished beneath a tidal wave of passion. Trembling from the violence of it, she stroked his face, his hair, his shoulders, yet none of that satisfied her craving for human closeness, for this man above all others.

His hands delved beneath her skirts, and at the burning

movement of his palms over her stockings and garters, she uttered a whimper of surrender and parted her thighs to him. Instead of touching her there, he caught her waist in both hands and lifted her to face him, her legs straddling his lap.

For all her inexperience, she knew his intention. Knew, and wanted it with such sweet ferocity that she hiked up her skirts and adjusted her underclothes while he wrestled open his breeches. Then in one blessed slide she came down on him, and the keen pleasure of it shattered at once, drowning her in endless ripples of rapture. At the same moment Adam spoke her name in a low, savage cry, and shuddered with the force of his own release.

She melted against him, her arms inside his coat and her cheek pressed to his starched shirt. His chest rose and fell with the slowing of his breath, and his hands cupped her bottom with thrilling possessiveness. She was conscious of the gentle jouncing of the coach, the joining of their bodies. And a wondrous sense of well-being that she had known only once before, on the night he had made her a woman. His woman.

He slid his fingers into her hair, tilted up her face, and brushed a kiss over her lips. Then he pressed his forehead to hers. "Ah Mary, I vowed not to dishonor you again," he whispered. "What am I to do with you?"

"Make me your mistress."

He jerked up his head and stared at her. "You cannot mean that."

But she did. She had surprised herself as much as him, yet how else would she have a chance at happiness? She was alone now, and not bound by convention as he was. And she could not imagine ever loving any other man.

Lightly touching the bruise on his jaw, she struggled to put the rightness of her decision into words. "With you, I feel . . . complete. In a way I never felt before, not even with Jo." She gazed earnestly into his blue, blue eyes.

"Adam, don't you see? You're my lost half. The part of me that was missing."

His chest expanded with a deep breath. His dark eyebrows drew into a frown, and he turned his gaze downward, watching his fingers stroke her bosom. Then he kissed her again, gently, deeply, thoroughly. The pressure of his renewed arousal stirred her. He wanted her again, so soon. As she wanted him.

Yet he made no move to repeat their ecstasy. He gripped her by the shoulders and looked into her eyes. "I'll make you happy," he said quietly. "You'll never want for anything. No matter what happens, I'll take care of you always."

Marriage would happen. *His* marriage, not hers. Never hers.

It is not a choice, his mother had said, *but a sacred trust.*

Hiding her pain behind pride, Mary curved the corners of her mouth upward. "If you insist upon adhering to duty, then being your mistress is the only way I can have you."

"I wish that circumstances could be different, Mary. God knows this can't be the life you planned for yourself. But I shan't forsake you, not ever. I swear it."

He still looked too serious, and she needed his smile. Craved it with all her heart. Moving her hips sinuously, she murmured, "I'm sure we'll find a way to settle our differences."

The sound he made was half groan and half laugh. "Minx," he said, his features relaxing into a grin. "I can see that I'd best be careful, or you'll be leading me around by a tether."

"Don't you mean . . . by *this?*" Swept by a sense of daring liberation, she shifted on him again.

He sucked in a breath, his head briefly tilting back against the cushion. "Where the deuce did you learn that move?"

"You inspire me, my lord duke."

"And you, me." He nuzzled her ear, his breath moist

and tantalizing. "I'll have you know, I've never before made love in a carriage."

"It's terribly undignified for a man of your rank."

"Mmm." His mouth descended to the tender hollow of her throat. "Nor have I ever taken a woman with my boots on."

"Muddy ones at that."

He kissed her bosom, raising gooseflesh over her skin. "I've never before committed myself to one woman, either. Granted, there have been women in my life, but no one who mattered to me."

The affection in his voice called to her aching heart. If only he could love her. If only . . .

He drew the velvet curtains across both windows, shutting out the world. Then he unbuttoned the back of her dress, pausing from time to time to explore the flesh he exposed. She lost herself to the beauty of the feelings he aroused in her and readily complied when he took her from his lap and pressed her down onto the seat. There, in the cramped quarters of his coach, he made love to her again, lingeringly this time, worshipping her body with his own.

Afterward, they straightened their clothing and then sat side by side. His arm was a pleasantly heavy weight on her shoulders, and she leaned against him, resting her own arm across his waist. The troublesome thoughts crept back to haunt her. "It seems a sacrilege to feel so happy when my sister is in grave danger."

Adam tilted her face up. "Tell me about her . . . and you. I know little about your upbringing."

"What do you wish to know?"

"Anything. Everything. Having a twin. Traveling all over the country. Growing up with a caravan for a home."

And so Mary began to talk, describing chilly nights around a campfire, the tiny gardens she planted and left behind, the mystical bond she and her sister shared.

In turn, Adam related stories of his own childhood.

Then he described his estate in Derbyshire, painting so vivid a picture that she could almost see the rolling pastures and the rocky streams, the stately manor house where Brentwells had resided for hundreds of years.

Mary sensed his pride as he spoke of his lands and the work he had done to modernize the cottages of his tenants. In defiance of common sense, she yearned to share every part of his life. But she would never live in his elegant mansion. She would never receive his friends and family for long, comfortable visits. She would never raise his heir to be as fine and honorable a duke as his father.

She could only hope to settle nearby and to see Adam whenever he could spare a few moments from his busy schedule. Eventually, another woman would take his name and bear him children.

Would *she* bear him children, too? She might already have conceived. The possibility roused a wistful ache inside her, a feeling of both joy and sadness. Her baby would be a bastard.

Mary knew it could be no other way. And yet her heart whispered, *if only* . . .

If only . . .

If only he could linger with her.

With great reluctance, Adam eased himself from the warm, slumbering woman in the bed. Mary stirred and sighed, snuggling her cheek against the pillow. She lay curled on her side, the coverlet drawn up to her breasts. The dawn light washed a pale radiance over her skin and lit the golden tones in her coppery hair. She looked sweet, adorable, and he wanted her again with aching fervor, although they had spent half the night making love.

As he got up, the bedropes creaked under his weight and the planked floor chilled his bare feet. This small, drafty chamber with its sloping ceiling was the best the Five Bells Inn had to offer. The mattress was lumpy, the food mediocre. But the room was quiet and clean, and he'd had Mary to himself.

His mistress. That was exactly what he'd wanted. Wasn't it?

Adam frowned as he donned a fresh pair of riding breeches. Thinking of her as his ladybird made him uncomfortable, dissatisfied somehow. Upon their arrival at the inn, he had found himself maintaining the polite fiction that Mary was his cousin. He had procured the adjoining room for her and stopped the proprietor's leer with a freezing glare.

Adam had wanted to tear the man limb from limb.

He couldn't bear for anyone to think ill of her for being under his protection. Mary wasn't a professional courtesan who had schemed to catch herself a rich duke. She was a vulnerable girl who longed for love.

Did he love her? He must. Never in his experience had he known this fierce tenderness mixed with insatiable passion, the need to find oneness with a woman again and again and again. Unlike the civilized warmth between husband and wife, however, his fiery infatuation might well burn itself down to ashes.

Whatever happened, he promised himself, he would give Mary a good life. He would devote himself to pleasing her. They would reap whatever happiness they could from a world that would never countenance their marriage.

But would that be enough?

Shirtless, he mixed the shaving soap with a few drops of water from the basin. It was the first time he had traveled without a valet. He had bade Fenwick to stay in London and wait for word from him. That way, if the meeting with Peterbourne failed to yield results, Adam could send a swift message by mail coach.

He picked up the razor and removed a day's growth of whiskers. When he was done, he leaned closer to the cracked mirror to examine his jaw for any missed spots. And he saw Mary sitting up in bed, watching him.

Seized by pleasure, he turned and smiled, walking across the room to kiss her. She smelled of womanly secrets and the faint musk of their lovemaking, an erotic blend that sent the blood rushing to his loins. "Forgive me for awakening you," he said. "I did try to be quiet."

"I don't mind." She sat cross-legged with the sheets drawn modestly to her breasts. Wistfulness curved her lips. "When I was a girl, I loved to watch my father shave. He let Jo or me apply the lather to his face. We had to take care not to squabble, else we'd miss our turn."

Adam selected a folded shirt from his trunk. "I can't recall ever seeing my own father in an unshaven state. He was so stiff and formal a man that I used to wonder how he had ever managed to sire three children."

Mary giggled; then a soft somberness shadowed her face. She scooted off the bed, picked up his discarded shirt from the previous day, and slid it over her nakedness.

"That isn't amusing, not really," she murmured, coming forward to help him with his buttons. "Think of all he missed by not showing love to you. Think of what *you* missed." With wifely attentiveness, she straightened his starched collar. "Never fear, though. I plan to love you enough for ten people."

His throat thickened, choked by the turbulence of emotion she stirred in him. What could he give her in return? Money? Material comforts? She was no whore.

Not trusting himself to speak, he donned a gray waistcoat and stepped into his boots. Mary assisted him in drawing on a charcoal riding coat. Then he went to the trunk and lifted out a rectangular case of dark leather, which he opened to reveal a pistol nested in maroon velvet.

Somewhat smaller than one used for duels, the weapon had a spring-loaded trigger and a curved mahogany stock trimmed in silver. He carefully loaded the gun, first the black powder, then the ball in its linen patch.

Mary leaned against the bedpost and watched him. She looked extraordinarily fetching in his white shirt, the collar opened to reveal an enticing glimpse of cleavage. The bottom hem brushed her slim, bare thighs. His blood heated as he noticed her staring with intense concentration at his groin.

"Do you truly think you'll need that?" she asked.

"I beg your pardon?"

"The gun. Surely you won't use it."

"Ah." Feeling foolish at the turn of his thoughts, he glanced at the weapon in his lap. "It's only a precaution."

"Adam. What if Peterbourne isn't the one?"

Anguish lurked in her green eyes. Understanding its source, he lay down the pistol and walked to her, pulling her into his embrace. Gently he stroked her tumbled hair. "You're worried about your father."

Nodding, she clasped her arms tighter around his waist. His lust somehow transformed into an aching warmth, and he sensed her pain as if it were his own. He wanted to assure her that the culprit wasn't Thomas Sheppard. Yet he could not lie to her.

"We'll know soon enough. Now mind, you're to stay here while I'm gone."

She studied him from beneath the veil of her lashes. "If I refuse, would you really tie me to this bedpost?"

"No." Smiling only briefly, he took her face in his hands and gazed into her eyes. "But I'm asking you, Mary. Please. Let me deal with Peterbourne in my own way."

"What of Jo? She'll need me."

"If your dream proves true, she won't be at the earl's house since it's a good five miles from the coast. I shall have to persuade him to tell me where he's keeping her."

Her gaze flitted to the gun, and she shivered. "All right, then, I'll stay."

"Promise?"

"Promise."

"No purloining the coach and following me?"

"No."

"Excellent." He kissed the tip of her nose. "I'll return as quickly as I can."

"Take care, my love."

Like butterflies, her hands alighted on his shoulders, and she raised her sweet mouth to his. Adam allowed himself a taste of her tempting softness, indulged just for a moment his need for her. His hands flowed downward over the curve of her back and lower, where only the linen shirt covered her bare bottom. More than satisfying his physical desire, he wanted to stake his claim on her. Yet Mary would never truly be his. She might very well leave him someday if she met a man who would give her the honor of his name. The thought depressed him mightily.

It was torture to end the kiss, torture to release her warmth and step back. But he did. As he picked up the pistol and took his leave of her, he faced the troublesome truth.

They had settled nothing. Certainly, Mary had agreed to be his mistress. She had given him the precious gift of her love. Yet Adam felt no peace. And he knew not what else he wanted of her . . . or himself.

"His lordship cannot be disturbed," the footman said. His coarsely handsome features drew into a sneer as he glanced at the sway-backed nag cropping the lawn. "If you insist upon waiting, you may go to the tradesmen's entrance."

Thomas Sheppard saw the studded oak door start to swing shut. With a rage born of fear, he thrust his shoulder into the opening and knocked the servant out of the way.

He strode into the gloomy entrance hall, his hobnailed boots ringing on the marble floor. Rooms opened to either side of the paneled walls. He hastened first to a palatial saloon hung with tapestries, then to a library that housed as much naked statuary as books.

No one occupied either chamber.

"See here!" snapped the footman. "His lordship don't allow riffraff in his house."

When the servant stepped in front of him, Thomas gave that fancy, gold-liveried chest another shove. The footman landed on his bottom and skidded backward, crashing into a chair.

"Help!" he shouted. "Somebody, help!"

Knowing he had little time, Thomas half ran down a wide corridor and ducked his head into a music room, then a dining chamber, startling a housemaid who polished the baseboards. Muttering an apology, he backed out and looked wildly around the passageway, which split off in three directions.

Where was that spawn of Satan?

Crimson hangings. Carved headboard. Tangled sheets.

The images clawed into Thomas's mind. He had suppressed the inherited taint for so long that its reappearance startled him. Then he realized what the vision meant.

The curst sinner lay abed.

A pair of footmen came running down the corridor. Thomas dashed back to the hall and made for the broad staircase. The clatter of the men's shoes echoed like gunshots.

"Ho there! Stop, you!"

Thomas ignored the order. As he passed the newel post, one of the men grabbed at his arm. He chopped the edge of his palm onto the servant's lace-cuffed wrist. Spitting an oath, the man fell back.

Thomas stormed up the marble steps. He had advanced no more than halfway when both footmen caught him from behind. He fought viciously, but the younger men prevailed, locking his arms behind his back.

Panic filled him. He could not be thrown out. He had to thwart whatever malicious game the earl played. Josephine's life depended upon it.

"Peterbourne!" Thomas roared. "Show yourself, you hellhound!"

He dug in his heels, but the men dragged him slowly down the stairs. Pain throbbed in his arms. Regardless, he continued to struggle.

"Let the preacher go."

The command floated down from on high. Thomas looked up to see the earl standing at the stone rail that ran the length of the upper floor. He wore a dark green dressing robe and his bald head was bare. He peered downward through a quizzing glass.

Thomas felt the surge of a hatred so painful that he scarcely noticed when the footmen released him. The black emotion crawled through him like a disease, and he had the shameful urge to run like a child from the demons of the night. With a silent prayer, he overcame his weakness and stalked up the staircase.

Peterbourne strutted down the corridor and vanished into an opened doorway. Thomas followed, passing through a sumptuous antechamber and entering the semi-darkness of a bedroom. Several lighted candles on the bedside table illuminated the satyr's lair. Dominating the chamber was an enormous, canopied bed hung with crimson curtains. The headboard displayed carvings of bare-breasted mermaids. Though it was mid-morning, the sheets were rumpled as if the earl had only just arisen.

Thomas strode to the window and threw open the heavy draperies. Sunshine flooded the room, highlighting its erotic decadence.

Peterbourne threw his arm over his face. "What the devil—? Close that!"

Thomas ignored the order. "Where is my daughter?"

"Which one?" Lowering his arm slightly, the earl blinked his pale green, bloodshot eyes.

"You know which one."

"So Josephine is still missing, eh? We don't hear much juicy gossip out in the provinces."

That gleeful smirk enraged Thomas. "You were in Lon-

don only two days ago. Then you left suddenly." He took a
menacing step forward. "Tell me where you're hiding her."

The earl groped for the bed and sat down, rubbing his
scrawny legs as if they pained him. "Last I saw of your
daughters, Mary was masquerading as Josephine. And a
pretty filly she is."

Thomas flew across the room and caught a fistful of
green satin dressing gown. A putrid odor came to him, the
stench of a rotting soul. "You filthy old goat. If you so
much as touched my Mary—"

"How could I, with St. Chaldon standing guard over
her? Now release me, else I'll call my men."

"Josephine wrote in her diary that you tried to seduce
her."

" 'Twere only a jest. A chance to take a close look at
her."

"Soulless vermin. Thank the Almighty she didn't know
who you are. A lecher so depraved you'd go after your
own . . ."

Breathing hard, Thomas stopped. He could not say the
word aloud. He could not acknowledge the truth, not even
now.

"Granddaughter," Peterbourne said, his lips curling into
a sly grin. "They are my twin granddaughters."

Thomas stared at the monster who had sired him. The
monster who had seduced a serving girl, then cast her and
her whelp out to starve.

Only once before had Thomas come face to face with his
father. As a lad of fourteen, he had received a summons to
attend the earl at his London residence. Though he'd
blamed Peterbourne for his mother's early death, secretly
Thomas longed for his father to acknowledge him. He had
been thrilled to learn that Peterbourne had kept track of
him over the years. And so Thomas took his foolish hopes
to the interview, and the earl lured him upstairs to a bedroom where three courtesans waited to initiate him. His
young body responded shockingly, shamefully, to their ca-

resses. Even so, he might have won the battle against temptation had it not been for his father's presence. With uncanny accuracy, the earl had voiced every lustful thought that consumed Thomas, had sent his own darkness into his son's mind . . .

Now, Thomas hungered to commit murder. He tightened his fist around Peterbourne's dressing gown and yanked him off the mattress. "Where is my daughter?"

Those pale eyes bulged. "I don't . . . have her . . . I swear."

"But you know something. Tell me!"

"First . . . let . . . me . . . go. . . ."

When Thomas relaxed his fingers, Peterbourne fell back against the pillows and rubbed his throat. "Honor thy father," he croaked. " 'Tis written in your Bible."

"It is also said that the wicked shall burn. As you shall do this very day if you don't reveal where Josephine is."

"Go on, kill me," Peterbourne taunted. "I'm dying already from the French pox, and I'll gladly bring you down to hell with me."

Thomas's heart slammed against his ribcage. So that was why the chamber stank of decay. His father's imminent mortality dulled the edge of his fury, and for all that he told himself to rejoice, he felt hollow inside.

"The will remains in your name," the earl said with a crafty look. "Everything I own except for this entailed pile and my title, which reverts to the crown. It can all be yours."

"I wrote to your solicitor last year, renouncing the money."

"Bah. There's wealth enough to tempt the most pious of men. Seventy thousand acres of prime English land, a coal mine in Wales, cloth mills in Lancashire."

"Wealth you've stolen from the blood of the poor."

The earl slapped his palm onto the bedlinens. "Ungrateful wretch. I'll have you know, I've sired other bastards. But I've favored you, the eldest."

Favored. Thomas looked into the earl's once-handsome face and saw a pitiful, selfish man who had wasted his life. Who lacked what Thomas had in abundance, the love of his children.

The realization penetrated the darkness that had ruled his soul. For a lifetime, he had lived with his hatred for this man, attributing Peterbourne's degeneracy to all the nobility. But how blessed he was not to have grown up under this man's tutelage.

And how blessed he was to have two daughters who loved him.

A great cleansing river washed through Thomas. He glowed with the riches of love and ached with the anguish of knowing he had spurned both his children. If not for his blind pride, he would have gone after Josephine months ago. She would be safe. . . .

"She isn't safe," the earl said. "Nor is Mary."

His bald head was cocked in a listening pose, and his fiendish eyes glittered with triumph. The dark, misty cloak of corruption snaked around him.

Thomas stiffened with fear. "What have you done to them?"

"I? You sealed their fate when you scorned my generosity. You see, I intend to rewrite my will in favor of my youngest bastard. On condition that he marry one of your daughters."

Thomas braced his hand on the bedpost as a dizzying sense of unreality swept through him. "Who—?"

"Can't you guess? You've known your half-brother for quite some months. He's your very own disciple."

With a sickening jolt in his gut, Thomas knew. "Victor."

❧ Chapter 20 ❧

By mid-morning, Mary could bear the suspense no longer. Darkness still hovered at the edge of her consciousness. It was like the approach of a violent storm, and she struggled against the fear that crowded her heart. Each time she tried to contact Jo, she met a blank wall of silence.

Dear God. Was her sister dead?

Hands shaking, Mary donned her pelisse and hurried downstairs in the hopes that a brisk walk in the sunshine would clear her mind. As she passed through the common room, she saw two men drinking ale at a table. Both sprang to their feet.

The burly coachman snatched the clay pipe from his mouth. "M'lady."

"Good morning, Mr. Crookes. And Mr. Drabble."

The gangly footman blushed, gazing curiously at her. Mary felt awkward knowing that they must have guessed her intimate relationship with their master. This was how it would always be, she told herself. She had to learn to cope with the disapproval. The pity. The disdain. "If you'll excuse me, I'm going outside."

Crookes followed. "I'll attend ye. By orders of His Grace."

Of course, Adam would wish to protect her. The notion warmed Mary, yet the prospect of making conversation seemed a burden. She wanted only her own company, the chance to calm the turmoil of her thoughts.

"Please, I'd rather be alone."

"Go on ahead now," the coachman said in a kindly but firm voice. "I'll keep an eye on ye, is all."

In front of the gabled inn stretched a narrow cobbled road lined with houses and shops. A tradesman lifted his cap to her, then continued whistling on his way. The rhythmic clanging of iron came from the blacksmith's beyond the inn yard.

Mary felt rather foolish to have a guard pacing behind her as if she were royalty on parade. But restlessness drove her, and she strolled along, peering into shop windows. Drawn by the heavenly scent from the baker's, she went inside and bought a gooseberry tart. She took a bite and the sweet jam oozed over her tongue. Finishing the pastry with delicate greed and licking the crumbs from her fingers, she headed toward a medieval gate that arched over the street.

Several yards thick, the interior formed a cave of sorts. Mary leaned against the sun-warmed stones of the outer wall. Crookes took up a post outside a nearby public house and set to cleaning his pipe.

Idly, Mary traced the uneven outline of a stone, marveling at how old it must be. Long ago, the gate must have been part of a wall around the town, perhaps a fortification like a castle. An odd sense of familiarity trembled inside her. She explored the feeling, but met the ominous haze instead.

In that moment the darkness receded. There came a rushing inside her like a deep, endless river of love. Mary closed her eyes and savored the richness of emotion that flowed into her. Yet its source was not her sister. She could not say how she knew so, but the river had existed all her life.

Papa? But she had never been able to sense his thoughts.

Confusion from afar swirled into the serenity of her heart. Confusion and a sound like the hush of waves upon the shore.

Mary, it's you . . . please say it's you.

Yes! With unexpected clarity, the tunnel of light opened, and Mary rejoiced. *Jo, I'm in Sussex. Where are you?*

That beastly blackness . . . must have been a nightmare. I thought you closed your heart . . . but 'twas the distance, then. The distance kept us from hearing each other.

The realization coursed through Mary in a warm wave. The trouble she'd had contacting her sister wasn't her fault. Then the woozy quality to Jo's words disturbed her.

Are you ill?

Laudanum . . . in the tea last night . . . should have known better.

Concentrate, dear sister. Show me where you are.

Again, Mary had the impression of clouded thoughts. Then slowly a picture took shape in her mind of gulls wheeling over the dense blue of the sea, over the ruined remains of a castle on a cliff. A single tower stood intact in the curtain wall. She felt herself moving through the gatehouse and into a vast yard littered with rubble. A tall, square keep loomed ahead, but she veered away from it, going instead to the tower.

The shadows grew thick and cool as she mounted the spiraling stairs to a sturdy wooden door. Then suddenly she found herself in a round room where her sister sat huddled on a cot, her face buried in her hands.

Jo, don't despair. I have happy news. Cyril is alive.

Her sister lifted her head, the long braid of coppery hair draped over the shoulder of her pale gown. Tears coursed down her cheeks, and Mary felt the rise of exquisite gladness as if it were her own. *My beloved . . . lives?*

He's recovering at home. And Adam will rescue you. He may already be on his way.

A fuzzy astonishment came from Jo. *Adam . . . the duke?*

Yes, I'll explain later. Now tell me quickly. Is Peterbourne your kidnapper?

An earthquake of fear shook Mary. *No! Don't ask me! He said he'd kill you if I told . . . I can't . . . I can't. . . .*

The light at the end of the long passage dimmed like the shutting of a door. And her sister's voice faded into darkness.

"Mary? Mary Sheppard! Answer me."

Someone was shaking her by the shoulders. With a gasp, Mary opened her eyes and blinked from the bright sunshine. Before her stood a tall man clad in sober black with a cleric's collar. His fair hair haloed the unearthly perfection of a painted archangel.

"Victor? What are you doing here?"

"I accompanied the Reverend Sheppard to the village. He had an errand to attend to this morning."

"An errand . . . here?" Mary glanced in bewilderment at the cobbled street with its shops and houses, the villagers strolling here and there. "But he was in London when last I saw him."

"He came to fetch you." Those cloud-gray eyes studied her reprovingly. "You see, he learned that you were traveling with His Grace, and he couldn't bear for all the world to see you become a nobleman's harlot."

A lump formed in Mary's throat. Pain pulsed through her body as if a hole had opened in her heart. She hadn't wanted to think about how much she had hurt her father by becoming Adam's mistress.

Papa. Oh, Papa, I'm sorry. . . .

She pressed her palms to the stones behind her. "Papa will have to accept my choice. I love the duke, and I shan't feel shame for that."

"Only a week ago, you loved me. Until a man of wealth and rank came along."

"I regret the pain I've caused you," she said softly. "And I know how my association with Adam must appear to you

. . . and to the rest of the world. But truly, his position in society doesn't matter to me."

"And what of him? Will he give you the honor of his name?"

Looking away, Mary bit down hard on her lower lip.

He must marry within his own world. It is not a choice, but a sacred trust.

"I thought not," Victor said with a trace of contempt. "But that is neither here nor there. I believe I may have found Miss Josephine. Yesterday, a woman fitting her description was seen standing on the battlements of a castle near here."

Mary's heartache vanished beneath a crushing fear. She clasped her hands so tightly her bones hurt. "Yes, it's a ruined castle by the sea!" Several passersby glanced curiously at her, and she lowered her voice. "Do you know where it is?"

"Yes. I grew up in this district." He gazed at her without expression. "I'd hoped you would come with me, and I took the liberty of procuring a cart and pony. Though we'll have to evade the duke's man."

For the first time, she noticed the small vehicle waiting in the cool shadows beneath the arched gate. And Crookes strolled toward them, his ruddy features alert and the stem of his pipe clenched between his teeth.

"I'll return to the inn," she whispered. "I'll pretend to go to my chamber and then slip out the back door. Where shall I meet you?"

"There's a copse of beeches south of the village, just around a bend in the road." Victor smiled. "Godspeed."

He walked toward the ponycart, and Mary started toward the inn. Her heart beat faster when Crookes fell into step beside her.

"Was that man botherin' ye, m'lady?"

"Oh no, he's a friend of my father's. Fancy meeting a familiar face in a strange town."

The concern in Crookes's expression eased. " 'Tis a small world, they say."

The rest of her escape proved ridiculously easy. She entered the common room of the inn, smiled at Drabble and caused him another blush, then went up the stairs. At the landing, instead of proceeding to her chamber, she veered down the narrow steps to the kitchen. The cook had her back turned and was singing so lustily that Mary had no trouble stealing out into the alley and thence between two cottages to the woods beyond. She felt a twinge of guilt, for when Adam returned, his servants would suffer the brunt of his temper. But she didn't dare wait for him. He might be hours, and anyway, Victor would protect her.

And there was another reason she didn't want Adam with her.

The thought pricked at Mary, needling her until she opened herself to the pain of it. Her father had gone off on an errand this morning. Had he come not in pursuit of her, but to visit his other daughter? Had he paid someone to kidnap Jo, just as he had paid Obediah to watch her?

Fiercely praying that it wasn't true, she hastened out of the village. With all the emotion in her heart she called to her sister. But like an eclipse of the sun, darkness blocked the light.

He said he'd kill me if I told.

Papa wouldn't threaten his own daughter. He was a peace-loving man who would sooner carry a spider out of the caravan than squash it.

But he'd been in a fury when last she'd seen him in the churchyard. He had lashed out with his fist at Adam. And with his words at her.

God forbid I should be tempted to turn my righteous wrath on her.

Knees as weak as water, she hurried around the bend in the road. Victor sat in the ponycart beneath the shade of a beech tree. He gave her a hand up, and she settled beside him on the narrow seat.

Snapping the reins, he guided the pony off the main road and onto a rutted track that wended past orchards and fields. Along a ditch, clumps of violet mixed with wild garlic and buttercups. The cultivated land soon gave way to the windswept hills of the Downs, treeless and desolate except for gorsebushes and a few grazing sheep. In the distance, a windmill stood alone like a man with his arms raised.

"When I came upon you in the village," Victor said over the clopping of the pony's hooves, "you were communing with Miss Josephine, were you not?"

Mary was so wrapped in misery that she had almost forgotten his presence. "Yes."

"What else did she tell you, other than where she's hidden?"·

"Very little. She'd been drugged."

"And did she name her abductor?"

He said he'd kill me if I told. . . . "No."

As the cart jolted up a hill, Mary held onto the railed seat. A dirge of dread played over and over in her mind. Could her father hate Josephine so much? Over her involvement with an aristocrat? Would he now turn on Mary?

Then something in what Victor had said struck a discordant note. She turned and stared at him. The breeze blew his fair hair, and the sunshine lent a harshness to his celestial face.

Slowly, she asked, "When did you change your mind?"

"I beg your pardon?"

"Just now you referred to Jo's abductor. I thought you still believed that she'd run off with a new lover."

He slid a glance at her. His tense mouth relaxed into an engaging smile. "Reverend Sheppard convinced me she was kidnapped. We had much time to talk, for we traveled all day and through the night in an effort to catch up to you."

A reasonable explanation. And yet . . .

Victor lifted his arm and pointed. "Now there's the place we're seeking."

The ponycart rattled over the top of a hill. In the distance, a tumbledown castle sprawled across a cliff overlooking the endless blue of the sea. Mary's stomach clenched into a tight knot of dread. Was Papa here? Was he even now with her sister?

Victor patted her hand. "There now, Miss Mary. You needn't look so fearful. I have the strength to overcome any villain. Soon we shall make our way to the tower and free your sister."

The tower. A chill skittered down Mary's spine and stabbed into her belly. She was sure she hadn't specified in which part of the ruins Jo was imprisoned.

Yet Victor knew. He *knew*.

And that tale about Jo being seen on the battlements? How could she walk about at will, when she was imprisoned?

Don't trust him . . . don't trust him. . . .

Her sister had meant Victor.

Mary resisted believing it. He was utterly pure in his devotion to God. She had known him for months, worshipped him. . . .

Yet certainty drenched her in horror. As if seeing him for the first time, she gazed at his gloriously sculpted profile, the high cheekbones and smooth skin, the sensual lips and finely molded chin. And she sensed a dark agitation emanating from him, swirling around her like the spell cast by a sorcerer.

She had believed him to be a saint. She had blamed her own weak will for the turmoil he stirred in her, the passion that had tempted her into betraying her own sister.

But perhaps the darkness wasn't desire at all. Perhaps it was the call of evil.

God in heaven. *God in heaven.*

Her heart thudded in rhythm with the pony's hooves. As the cart drew closer and closer to the castle, a single thought galvanized her. She had to divert Victor. She had to keep him from her sister.

She forced herself to touch his sleeve. When he glanced at her inquiringly, she assumed a meek and remorseful expression. "Dear me, I don't remember that gatehouse. This must not be the right castle, after all. We'll have to turn back and ask in the village. I'm ever so sorry."

"Nonsense. This is the only castle for many miles. Since we've come this far, surely we can spare the time to look around."

She moistened her dry lips. "I'd truly rather go back. My father can help us search—"

"No." Victor's hand covered hers, cold and heavy as a manacle. "My dear, we must go on. Your sister's life could hang in the balance."

He smiled as he spoke, though his deep, resonant voice held an undertone of menace. Why would he kidnap Jo? Could he resent her so much for breaking their betrothal?

As the castle loomed larger, Mary's panic increased. She wanted to flee from his darkness, but she could not desert her sister. Somehow, she must keep Victor off guard and watch for a chance to rescue Jo.

"You're right," she said, summoning a smile. "I'm only being silly. It's very courageous of you to help Jo."

"I'm doing it for you, Mary. It is you I love. You, I want."

Though he spoke seductively, her skin crawled. He was lying to her. How had she failed to see his hypocrisy before?

Because loving Adam had taught her that true passion was clean and good. Not a dark presence, foul and sinful.

She swallowed hard. "You've never spoken much of your past, beyond that you were orphaned and grew up in a workhouse. Did you really live in this district?"

"Yes. And I shall tell you everything about my past . . . soon."

His silvery eyes were like mirrors, reflecting the sun and

barring her from his thoughts. Mary shivered as the pony cart came up the final grade and approached the gatehouse.

"What a forbidding place," she said. "I don't believe I would have liked to live here."

" 'Tis the former stronghold of the Goacher family. Perhaps you're more familiar with the noble title associated with the place. This is Peterbourne Castle."

Mary's heart jolted. His gaze seemed to delve into her soul as if seeking a reaction from her. Did he know where Adam had gone? But she had been tragically mistaken about that garbled message from Jo. Her sister had been naming the castle.

"Peterbourne." Mary tried not to let her revulsion for the man color her voice. "I believe I've heard of an earl by that name."

"The builder of this fortress was a mere baron. A descendant of his was elevated to the earldom for his loyalty to the crown during the Dissolution. In the reign of Queen Bess, the family moved inland to its present manor."

"You know much of their history."

"It was a hobby of mine when I was a youth, to study the great local dynasty." His mouth formed a small, secretive smirk. "Did you know the present earl has no legitimate heir?"

She shook her head slowly, wondering at the light of fervor on his face.

"He's an old, sick man," Victor continued. "When he dies, his title shall revert to the crown, along with his entailed estate. However, there are many additional holdings, rich holdings that he may dispose of as he pleases."

Mary hardly heard him. As the cart rattled through the arched entrance of the gatehouse and into the rubble-strewn bailey, her stomach tightened until she felt ill. To the left stood the tower with its tiny slits for windows. Jo's prison.

And beside Mary sat her sister's gaoler.

* * *

The mid-morning sun did little to dispel Adam's dark thoughts. As his horse cantered down the long drive, he gazed upon the gloomy Elizabethan mansion with its mullioned windows and numerous chimneypots, a monument to grandeur in the midst of rolling green pastures dotted by the crofts of poor tenants. It was a bloody waste that Peterbourne didn't improve his lands. He had never even bothered to marry and sire an heir. Not that Adam would wish any boy to have the dissipated knave for a father. A man who would abduct a woman and shoot her fiancé.

A pair of sphinxes flanked the terraced garden outside the east wing. Adam felt the rise of grim anticipation. The roué likely presumed he had covered his trail well. And indeed he had. He had nearly gotten away with his crime.

Suddenly a man emerged from the house and hastened down the stone steps. Adam shielded his eyes from the sun. There was something curiously familiar about that husky build, that balding pate. . . .

The Reverend Thomas Sheppard.

Shock reverberated through Adam. Only Mary knew that Peterbourne was their culprit. Unless Josephine had written something damning about Peterbourne on the diary page that Obediah had handed to Sheppard. Unless Sheppard himself was the culprit.

Mary's father hurried toward a sway-backed horse whose reins were tied to a rhododendron bush. Adam drew up, the mare dancing a sidestep. Controlling the animal with a squeeze of his legs, he watched the preacher swing into the saddle. "What the deuce are you doing here?"

"St. Chaldon, thank the Almighty! Come, there's no time to waste. My daughters are in grave danger." Sheppard slapped the reins and the nag lurched into a walk, then a trot, its ragged mane flying.

Daughters?

Seized by foreboding, Adam touched his bootheels to

the mare and caught up to Sheppard. "Mary isn't in any danger. My men are watching her at the inn."

"I cannot hold that hope." Deep lines of distress cut into the old man's face. "She trusts the demon. He's surely found a means to lure her away."

"Demon? Peterbourne?"

"Nay. Granted, he's the devil who masterminded this game. But 'tis his minion we seek now." Sheppard pinched his lips shut in an expression reminiscent of Mary.

"For God's sake, man, tell me who we're after."

Staring straight ahead, the preacher heaved a breath like an agonized groan. "Victor Gabriel."

Adam bit out a curse. "You're saying he's in league with that ancient rake?"

"Aye." Sheppard cast a glance at Adam. "Victor is Peterbourne's bastard son. As am I."

Adam gazed into Sheppard's haunted, gray-green eyes. Peterbourne's eyes.

The truth of it staggered Adam, and he struggled to sort out the tangled relationships. Hell. Bloody *hell*.

Provoked to fury, he brought the mare around to cut off Sheppard's nag. "You pious impostor. How do I know I can trust you? You, who let Mary betroth herself to her own uncle."

"I swear before God I didn't know it. I only learned today that Victor and I are half brothers, both the spawn of that devil." Sheppard's voice cracked. "I cannot blame you for being angry, Your Grace. But if you care anything for my Mary, you'll come with me now."

Suspicion died hard in Adam. He urged his mare to a canter, easily keeping pace with Sheppard's straining mount. "Explain this wretched business."

"A year ago, the earl discovered he was afflicted with the pox. He wrote a will leaving his worldly possessions to me. When I renounced claim to the money, he was enraged. He summoned Victor and proposed to rewrite the will on one condition." Sheppard paused. "That Victor wed one of my daughters."

"He'll go to prison instead. I'll see to that."

"You haven't heard the rest." A tear leaked down Sheppard's grizzled cheek. "The earl has procured a special license for Victor. Victor plans to use it today. By threatening my Josephine, he'll force my Mary to wed him."

Fear spilled through Adam in an icy torrent, plunging him into a cold pool. He had failed to protect her. Had he not destroyed her faith in him by proposing a love affair, had he not offered marriage with such reluctance, she might have heeded him when he bade her to remain in London. Now, because he had withheld his love, because he had embraced duty instead of her heart, he might lose Mary.

He gripped the smooth hilt of his pistol. "Tell me where to find the devil."

The salt smell of the sea tainted the air. Built of stone like the rest of the castle, the chapel held the remnants of fine carvings on the walls. To one side of the altar, Christ labored under the weight of the cross. On the other side, the angel Gabriel visited the Virgin Mary.

Mary shivered at the ironic symbolism of that particular engraving. A breeze blew through the open slits of the windows, as cold as the dread that blew through her soul.

Victor paced before the doorway of the vaulted chamber, blocking her escape. From the quickness of his steps to the smile on his face, he exuded a peculiar excitement. His exultant mood fed the panic that had paralyzed her as he'd hauled her into the keep and up the stairs to this chapel, where a pudding-faced cleric had awaited them. Before Mary could appeal to the man for help, Victor had sent him away with a sharp command to fetch Jo.

She must keep her wits, she reminded herself. She must not let fright immobilize her ability to think. Her only hope was to act the mouse. To make him believe her harmless while she searched for a weapon.

Keeping a wary gaze on him, she strolled to the window as if to look out at the sea. Her fingertips brushed a chunk of masonry that lay upon the ledge.

"Come away from that rubble," Victor said. "You'll dirty your gown."

Her heart thudded wildly against her breastbone. She curled her fingers around the stone and then turned, secreting the weapon in the folds of her skirt. "I'm sorry," she said plaintively. "I'm worried about my sister. Why is she here? And when can I take her home?"

"Very soon." Victor grinned, a profane darkness shadowing his male beauty. "As soon as you and I are married."

For a moment she thought she had not heard him right. She stood paralyzed, the concealed rock heavy in her hand. Her mind could make no sense of his purpose. "Why? Why would you force me to marry you?"

"Force? I'm saving you from a life of dishonor." A strange satisfaction underscored his words. "You can thank me by saying 'I do' at the appropriate moment."

"And if I don't?"

"You will. Believe me, you will."

The sudden menace in his voice jarred her. "You surely see the wrong of this. It's a sin to make a false vow before God."

"To hell with your religious claptrap. I'm done pretending to be holy." Victor reached up and ripped the cleric's collar from his throat. He threw the white scrap to the floor and ground it beneath his heel. "Reverend Fabor should return with your sister shortly. Then we can start the ceremony."

A sense of unreality spun through Mary. She hardly recognized this conniving stranger with his too-perfect features. Why would he join her father's mission and play the devout deacon for months? And why was he so bent on marrying her? Was he mad?

Adam. Oh, Adam, my love.

But he could not hear her. He had not the gift. And he was miles away at Peterbourne's estate. It might be hours before he returned to the inn and discovered her gone. And then how could he find her? She had only herself to depend on.

The rock rested solid and deadly in her sweaty palm. She wondered fleetingly if she could kill another human being.

She must. Now. Before Victor's crony returned with Jo, and she had two to contend with.

The stone hidden, she walked toward Victor. "A marriage can't be sanctified without a license. Nor without calling the banns for three Sundays."

"That is true only for those poor souls without a special license. Those who lack money and influence."

This time, her puzzlement was genuine. "But you have neither."

He strolled across the chapel and met her halfway. "The Lord works in mysterious ways, as you believe. Soon I shall have more wealth and influence than you can imagine." Victor stroked his thumb across her lips. "And you will be my wife, Mary Sheppard. I ought to have seduced you long ago and forced your father's hand."

He bent closer as if to kiss her. At the heat of his breath, the gorge rose in her throat. His touch was an abomination.

With a savage cry, she brought up the stone and aimed for his face. His eyes widened in a flash of silver. He shied back, but not before the rock met flesh and bone.

Victor loosed an unearthly howl. Both hands catching at his bloodied nose, he stumbled backward against the wall and slid to the floor. Mary's pulse beat with fierce exultation. Then she picked up her skirts and ran out the door.

The breath sobbing in her chest, she raced full tilt down the narrow stone steps. There was a hall down there, a vast

echoing space strewn with rubbish. She paused to peer out
the slit of a window. A rook pecked at the dusty soil of the
bailey below. There was no sign of Jo or the cleric.

How many minutes had passed since he'd left to fetch
her? Mary didn't know.

Jo! Jo, where are you? Speak to me!

No answer. Dear God, no answer.

Intending to steal down the outside stairs, Mary hastened toward the adjoining guard room. The noise of footsteps from outside startled her. Hand shaking, she
snatched up another stone and hid behind a column by the
door.

The pudding-faced priest entered the keep. Jo sagged
against him as if unable to walk alone. She wore a wrinkled
white gown that made her look impossibly fragile, and a
single thick braid hung down her back. Mary's heart sang
out with bittersweet joy, and she held back the urge to
embrace her twin.

She waited as they shuffled past, tensing herself to take
Pudding Face by surprise.

Jo brought her head up then. Those dazed green eyes
focused on Mary even as Mary launched herself from behind the column.

No! There's two of them!

Jo gave the cleric a push. Mary whirled to look behind
her and saw a giant barreling at her.

With a cry of panic, she drew her arm back to hurl the
stone. But he caught her wrist and squeezed. Her fingers
went numb and the makeshift weapon clunked to the floor
and rolled away.

The goliath wrenched her arm behind her back. Her
wriggling and kicking only made him tighten his grip. Jo
fared no better, for Pudding Face had managed to hook his
arm around her throat.

Mary looked at her sister in despair. *I'm sorry I'm sorry
I'm sorry. . . .*

"I see you've met my men," Victor said.

Walking unsteadily, he came into view. He held a red-stained handkerchief to his face, and his nose looked crooked. Yet this time Mary felt no glee. A dismal sense of failure settled like a stone in her stomach.

Refusing to cower, she stared Victor full in the face. "They are not nearly as vile as you."

Victor regarded her a moment, his face sulky like that of a fallen angel. Then he raised his hand.

Though Mary saw the blow coming, she could not escape it, for Goliath held her firmly. The slap caught the side of her head. Stars burst in a blinding flash across her vision. The pain brought tears to her eyes.

"Now," Victor said, "you'll marry me. Else I'll kill your sister and the noble brat she carries in her belly."

Adam crouched in the shadows of the gatehouse. Pressed to the gritty stone wall, he watched the fat cleric shove Josephine up the outer stairs of the keep. A giant of a man tramped after them, his shaggy head swaying from side to side.

Mary must be inside already. With Victor Gabriel.

Fear left a dusty taste in Adam's throat. Victor was greedy, ruthless, desperate to secure the inheritance from his father. If Mary defied him, he might well hurt her.

Or even kill her and marry Josephine instead.

The thought shuddered through Adam, leaving his skin clammy. With effort, he mastered his emotions and took stock of the situation. Josephine and the two men had vanished inside the keep. He couldn't count on help from Thomas Sheppard, who lagged ten minutes behind on a horse fit for the knacker's yard.

There were three men, and the pistol fired a single shot. Adam grimaced to imagine the odds he'd get in the betting book at White's.

Alert for guards, he crossed the bailey and made his way up the stairs and into the keep. Nothing but rubble on this floor. Pistol in hand, he quietly mounted the narrow stairs to a large, sunny room that must have been the solar centuries ago.

And then he heard the voices.

Hoping the crash of the sea would mask his progress, Adam moved along the wall until he came to the door. He eased a look inside and saw a chapel. At the far end, the giant stood sentinel near the stone wall, his arms crossed over his tree trunk chest. Clearly bored, he stared out the open window. In front of him, her head bowed, Josephine wavered like a wilting lily.

Adam inched closer. His line of vision expanded to include the altar and the couple standing side by side, their backs to him. The tall man clad in black was Victor Gabriel. Beside him, the bride wore topaz silk, her hair a fiery tumble down her slender back. Mary.

His Mary.

Adam felt his heart plunge into hellish torment. God! It should be him who stood at her side. Him who had his arm around her slender waist as they faced the marriage altar.

A fury of possessiveness exploded in him. Focusing his attention on the fair-haired man, Adam caressed the curve of the trigger. But he forced himself to think. If he shot Victor, the giant would seize Josephine. If he shot the giant, Victor would grab Mary and use her as a shield.

The agonizing choice tore at him. Swaying on the verge of a swoon, Josephine was clearly the weaker. Yet how could he deliver Mary into the clutches of that scoundrel?

Then he noticed Josephine staring with rounded eyes at him. Quickly she shifted her gaze back to the altar.

The piggish cleric squinted down at the Book of Common Prayer, and the pounding of the surf nearly drowned his voice. "Mary Sheppard, do you take this man, Victor Gabriel, to be your lawfully wedded husband?"

"I . . . I . . ." Mary turned her head toward her sister, and their gazes held for a brief moment as if they were communing. Abruptly she spun back toward Victor. "I do *not.*"

She drove her fist into his crotch. With a yelp of agony, he doubled over, clutching himself.

With simultaneous swiftness, Josephine struck at the giant. But he barely winced from her blow. Loosing a mighty roar, he snatched her up as if she were a rag doll.

Mary wheeled to run, but Victor caught a handful of her skirt. The material ripped and she stumbled to the floor. Even as the bastard reached down to grab her, Adam took aim and fired.

The report echoed deafeningly against the walls of the chapel. A small hole appeared in Victor's coat, and he looked down at the blood staining his shirt. He staggered drunkenly against the fat cleric, who squealed and retreated to the corner, leaving Victor to collapse beneath the stone altar.

Mary sat up on the floor. Even as Adam rejoiced in her safety, Josephine whimpered in fear. He turned the pistol over, holding it like a club as he advanced on the giant. Somehow, he had to induce the titan to release his captive.

Out of the blue, a missile whizzed from behind Adam. The rock struck the giant square in the forehead. His arms loosened and Josephine lurched to safety just before he crumpled into a heap like Goliath of old.

Thomas Sheppard hastened into the chapel. He ran straight for his daughters, gathering the both of them against him. Sunlight streamed through the windows and haloed the tender reunion in radiance. The two sisters looked remarkably alike, two halves of a whole as they embraced one another, laughing and weeping and chattering with their father.

Adam ached to join them, to share their love. But he held himself back, keenly aware that when he had taken Mary as his mistress he had forfeited the right to be a part of her family. An unbearable pressure gripped his chest.

The tightness rose to thicken his throat and sting his eyes. And in that moment he knew the truth.

Duty be damned. Life was too short for him to deny the need burning in his heart. He wanted only to be a father who loves his children. And a husband who loves his wife.

∾ Chapter 21 ∾

Awash in the joy of reuniting with her sister, Mary looked around for Adam. He stood conversing with her father by the door of the chapel.

The happiness in her heart spilled over as she gazed at Adam's noble profile, the broad shoulders clad in charcoal gray, the windblown hair, the long legs in black riding boots. With all the strength of her love, she willed him to turn to her. But he merely nodded to her father and, without a backward glance, strode from the chapel.

Jo stared from the empty doorway to Mary. "I don't believe it. You . . . and the duke?"

The wave of appalled astonishment radiating from her sister didn't surprise Mary. Seeing their father walk toward them, she whispered, "I'll tell you about it later."

"His Grace has gone for the magistrate," Thomas Sheppard said, his expression sober. "And Peterbourne will have to be told that Victor is dead, may God rest his avaricious soul."

"The earl? What has he to do with Victor?" Shuddering, Mary glanced at the sprawled form by the altar. "And why did Victor try to force me into marriage? I haven't any money."

He placed an arm around the waist of each daughter. "Come out of this darkness and into the sunshine. I've some explaining to do, and pray you'll find room in your heart to forgive me."

And so with Mary and Jo in the ponycart, and their father riding George the Third, they returned to the outskirts of the village and found the caravan parked in a thicket of oak. Like times of old, they sat down together, Jo and Mary next to each other on a fallen tree trunk, their father on his favorite stool.

Though Jo had already heard some of the story, he told them of the man who had sired him and the spiteful game the earl had played. In shock, Mary learned that Victor was her half uncle, that his religious devotion had been nothing but an act calculated to win one of his nieces and to satisfy his greed for the earl's wealth.

Jo added that Victor had intercepted the letters she'd sent, including the one that contained the news of her betrothal. Enraged that she had chosen a legitimate lord over him, Victor kidnapped her and hid her with Peterbourne's aid. She told Victor of her pregnancy in the desperate hope of convincing him to release her. But to her horror, he'd gone after Mary instead.

Seeing tears well in her sister's eyes, Mary grasped Jo's hands in an effort to cheer her. "Is it true? About the baby?"

A tremulous smile bloomed on Jo's face. "I'm not completely certain, but I hope . . . oh, I do hope."

Thomas sprang up, his hands on his hips. "I won't have my grandchild born out of wedlock. That man of yours had best honor his promise of marriage."

Jo set her chin at a familiar, mutinous angle. "Don't growl at me, Papa. Cyril and I love each other, and you'll come to love him, too. Not even the duke can stop our marriage now."

"You *will* wed Cyril," Mary said. "Adam has given his blessing to the match."

Jo's mouth dropped open. "Well, mercy. Mercy me."

The sisters fell to making plans for the wedding as their

father prepared a belated luncheon of bread and cheese. There was much news for the three of them to catch up on, including their father's surprising admission that he, too, had the ability to sense thoughts and feelings, though not with the clarity that the twins possessed.

"The bond between your hearts is good," he said heavily, "not evil. I forbade it because I feared to see Peterbourne's taint in either of you. Had not hatred for him ruled my life for so long, I might have kept my daughters from harm."

Jo threw her arms around him. "I'm not sorry," she declared. "If I hadn't run away, I would never have met Cyril."

Watching her sister's face glow as she spoke of her beloved, Mary realized with a bittersweet pang that she and her twin had grown beyond the insular bond of their childhood. She was aware of an aching need in herself, the need of a woman for a man.

The need for Adam.

Yet she saw him only briefly that evening, when he stopped by to report that the giant had suffered a concussion and now rested in gaol along with the cleric, who had been found at a public house, drowning his terror in ale. Victor's body had been delivered to Peterbourne's house.

Then Adam's gaze bored into Mary. "I'll return to the inn now." He walked toward her, and the intensity of those blue eyes brought a powerful rush of emotion to Mary. She wanted him to hold her again and to love her with his body if not his heart.

But Thomas Sheppard stepped into the duke's path. "Both my daughters shall be spending the night in the caravan."

"Of course." Bowing, Adam took his leave.

Disappointment nagged at Mary as she watched him mount his·horse and ride away into the purple shadows of dusk. Sweet heaven, she wanted to run after him, to beg him for a kiss. But they must not flaunt their illicit relationship. She could not bear to cause her father more distress.

Lying in the dark with Jo that night, Mary poured out the story of falling in love with Adam, whispering of her hopes and her misgivings, her dreams and her reality. Of course, her sister understood. "You'll always have Cyril and I," Jo vowed. "Even if the duke forsakes you."

Through the shadows of the caravan, Mary found her sister's hand. "Can you forgive me for shutting you out of my heart?"

" 'Tis your forgiveness I should beg. I sensed the sinful darkness in Victor, too, and I ran off to London. I never, ever dreamed that he would turn to you."

The heavy burden of guilt lifted from Mary, and for the first time in months, she felt at peace. Yet long after her sister fell asleep, Mary lay awake, thinking of Adam. She was aware of an emptiness as if a part of herself were missing. It pained her to know that his feelings for her lacked the depth of commitment. Would he tire of her without love to bind them together? Could she live with the constant dread that he might leave her?

As dawn gilded the countryside, the St. Chaldon coach rumbled into the clearing. There was no opportunity for private conversation, and Mary stepped into the plush vehicle with her sister. As the coach started off, turning a bend in the road, she pressed her nose to the window and looked back.

Adam rode his horse alongside the caravan. Incredibly, the two men appeared to be deep in conversation. Or rather, Thomas Sheppard was speaking and Adam was listening gravely.

"I hope Papa is blistering the duke's ears," Jo declared, peering out the window, too. "The rogue ought to be shamed into marrying you."

Mary's throat constricted. Jo simply didn't understand how the conventions of his world bound Adam. Though he had proposed to Mary once, he had done so with great reluctance, and she very much doubted he would ask her again.

Nor would she accept him if he did. She could not bear to think of him resenting her for the rest of their lives.

Yet, with a shiver of longing, she remembered their tryst at the inn, the tender way he had held her and teased her and brought her to a glorious completion. His rescue of her in the chapel had only strengthened the love that burned in her heart.

But she mustn't expect him to change his mind. Duty was too deeply ingrained in his character. He wanted Mary as his mistress, not his wife. It was foolish to dream of more.

The thought echoed in her mind like the rhythmic rattling of the coach wheels.

Foolish. Foolish. Foolish.

"I have just the thing, Your Grace." Fenwick brought a cobalt blue coat from the clothes press. "The tailor delivered it during your absence."

The valet held the coat while Adam donned it. Adjusting the fit, he studied himself critically in the pier glass. Cravat tied to perfection, silver buttons shining, tan breeches snugly molded to his thighs. Even his shoes gleamed with the high gloss of polish. Would Mary approve?

It was a new sensation, the anxiety, the uncertainty. The journey back to London had taken the better part of two days. Because of the caravan, they had traveled slowly. He had restrained his impatience and given Mary time with her sister, time to renew their bond without him making selfish demands on her.

And of course Thomas Sheppard had acted the vigilant chaperon. Though the restriction chafed at Adam, he could not fault the man for protecting his daughters. And for unbending—just enough—his views on the aristocracy.

The memory of their discussion brought a twisting anticipation to Adam's gut. "That's sufficient," he growled at the valet, who plied a brush at invisible lint on Adam's coat.

"Yes, Your Grace. Only allow me to add the sapphire pin."

Fenwick scurried away and brought back the oval-cut jewel. The far-off clang of the dinner gong sounded. The valet promptly dropped the sapphire and it rolled beneath the dressing table, requiring him to get down on hands and knees to fetch it.

"So sorry," he mumbled, his fingers trembling as he affixed the large, silver-mounted gem to Adam's cravat.

For the first time, Adam noticed the man's nervousness. "Is something weighing on your mind, Fenwick?"

"No . . . er . . . yes. May I ask Your Grace's permission on a matter of . . . er . . ."

"Speak up, man."

Fenwick stood rigidly at attention. "I should like permission to marry."

Adam lifted an eyebrow. "Who is the lucky bride?"

"Mrs. Primrose."

"Ah. The new maidservant. That was swift work."

Fenwick's cheeks reddened. "She . . . ah . . . suffice to say I've compromised her. She is a decent woman and I must do right by her."

A sense of camaraderie rose in Adam. Gazing keenly at the servant, he saw beyond the plain brown suit and sober mien to a man with the same hopes and fears as any prospective bridegroom.

"Fenwick, I believe we've far more in common than I once thought."

"Do I have your permission, then?"

Grinning, Adam clapped the valet on the back. "You've never needed it. You're your own man, as much as I am."

Entering the grand saloon to the sound of the dinner gong, Mary found herself caught between serenity and strife.

The serenity emanated from Jo, who occupied a gold-striped settee with Lord Cyril. They made a perfect match, she in deep green silk and he in fine dinner attire, his bandaged head lending him a rakish air. They were both smiling, holding hands, whispering to each other. Mary could have sworn that stars shone in their eyes.

The strife came from the opposite side of the fireplace, where the duchess of St. Chaldon sat rigidly on a gilt chair beside Mary's father. Thomas Sheppard looked distinctly uncomfortable on his own ornate chair, his black suit in stark contrast to his hostess's bejeweled elegance, the rose silk gown and upswept silver hair.

With a sharp, stabbing sensation in her breast, Mary knew that she didn't belong in this house as Jo did. And in the years to come, how would she fit into this family? As sister-in-law, she would be welcome. As the duke's mistress, she would be a pariah.

Heartsore, she seated herself on a chaise in the corner and picked up a book of poetry from a nearby table. The duchess afforded her a distracted nod before returning her ice blue gaze to Thomas Sheppard. Mary paged through the volume and strove not to eavesdrop. But temptation proved more than she could bear.

The duchess said, "I understand that you claim a connection to the Goacher family of Sussex. The earls of Peterbourne."

" 'Tis on the wrong side of the blanket," he said bluntly. "But never mind our connections. My daughters and I are people, not pedigrees."

"I appreciate your candor, Reverend Sheppard. Yet I merely wished to know—"

"If my daughters are worthy of your sons." The chair creaked as if he shifted position. "You might be surprised to hear, duchess, that I asked a similar question about *your* children."

Her back stiffened. "I beg your pardon."

"I beg yours, too. But since we're soon to be related by

marriage, I'll pass along a bit of advice, something I've learned quite recently."

"I will not be spoken to thusly."

"You will, indeed," he said, his low tone vibrating with righteous indignation. "At first I, too, despised the notion of our families uniting. I assumed your sons to be worthless nobles who lacked all human decency. Just like you, I committed the sin of judging a person not by his actions but by his birth."

Mary stared in blind anguish at the book in her lap. Did he not realize she would never be more than Adam's mistress?

"Mr. Sheppard," the duchess murmured, "I don't scorn your daughters. They are bright, lovely young women. However—"

"However, bah. Give your approval to them. If you don't bend, you'll lose your children. You'll lose the joy of knowing your grandchildren, too. You'll live as a bitter, lonely woman with only your pride for company."

The duchess was silent, and Mary ventured a glance at her. A flush colored those high cheekbones, and she gazed across the room at Cyril and Jo, who sat talking quietly, absorbed in their happiness. The queenly disapproval on the duchess's face altered subtly. She looked pensive, the corners of her mouth softened by wistfulness.

Her gaze flitted to Mary and an enigmatic assessment entered those blue eyes. Caught staring, Mary felt her cheeks grow hot. Surely the duchess could not approve of *her*. Yet Mary suddenly longed for that approval. She ached to have respect from the mother of the man she loved.

Foolish. Foolish. Foolish.

The duchess lifted her gaze to the doorway beyond. "Ah, here's Adam now."

Mary's heart beat in slow, painful strokes as he strolled into the saloon. Magnificent in a finely tailored coat of the same cobalt blue as his eyes, he looked every inch the duke. Yet unlike the arrogant aristocrat he had once been, today he was smiling as he went to greet his brother and Jo.

Were she his wife, she needn't sit hidden in the corner. She might go to him, speak to him, touch him. But she was merely his mistress.

Misery overwhelmed Mary. She could not spend her life as someone less than the man she loved. She could not live with herself if she allowed him to treat her as a woman unworthy of his name. The realization thrust her toward an anguished decision. As soon as she could find a moment alone with Adam, she would tell him so. She would end their association.

Aware of a trembling in her fingers, she closed the unread book. She watched as Adam crossed the room to his mother, bending to kiss her on the cheek.

The duchess looked rather startled at his show of affection. "What a delight it is to have all my children safely together again," she said. "And there's Sophronia now, returned from her stroll."

Resplendent in tangerine silk adorned by flounces of lace, Lady Sophy entered on the arm of Lord Harry Dashwood, who almost outshone her in his lime green coat and gold pantaloons. From the redness of her mouth to the hectic flush on his cheeks, they looked as if they'd been up to mischief.

"The garden is perfectly beautiful at dusk," declared Sophy.

Cyril drawled, "Since when have you developed an interest in flowers, little sister?"

Sophy flashed Lord Harry a secret smile. "Since they make a lovely setting for Lord Toad to turn into a prince."

The duchess cleared her throat reprovingly. "It is nearly time for all of us to sit down to dinner."

"Not quite yet," Adam said. He turned to Mary's father and bowed. "If I might beg your indulgence, sir, I should like to have a word with your daughter."

The two men exchanged a long look. Then Thomas Sheppard smiled and waved him away. "Take all the time you need, St. Chaldon."

Mary's heart commenced a wild dance as Adam walked toward her. He wished to speak to her. In private. With her father's approval. There could be only one reason why. And those deep blue eyes held a warmth that beckoned to her dreams.

Foolish. Foolish. Foolish.

She shot to her feet. "I'd like a word with you, too, Your Grace."

"I'm glad we're in agreement for once," he murmured.

As if in a wine-induced haze, she felt his warm fingers close around hers, felt herself rise from the chaise and accept the support of his muscled arm. Only with effort did she hold onto her resolve to break off their relationship. To do otherwise meant sacrificing her newfound pride, her very self-respect.

Dying inside, she walked beside him down a passageway and around a corner and into his study, where a cozy fire burned on the hearth and a ledger lay open on the desk. He shut the door and guided her toward the very chair that she had occupied on the cold, rainy day he had asked her to be his mistress. That sobering memory only reaffirmed her resolution.

Marriage is impossible, he had said. *Impossible.*

Nothing had changed since then. Nothing.

She stopped abruptly. "I have something to tell you—"

"I have something to ask you—"

They both paused and stared at each other.

"You first," Adam said.

"No, you."

"You're the lady."

The tender intensity on his face nearly unraveled her willpower. But she couldn't bear for him to be forced into a union that he did not want with all his heart. "The answer is no."

Smiling, he cocked his head to one side. "But I haven't asked you any question."

Sweet heaven. Was she mistaken? She flushed from her scalp down to her toes. "All right, then. I'll tell you what I've decided about us."

"Decided?" He came closer and lightly rubbed his thumb over her mouth. "Strange, I've decided something about us, too."

Her liquefied legs gave way, and she sank into the chair. He knelt before her, and the sudden seriousness of his expression left her breathless. In spite of her resolve, she couldn't help asking, "What did you decide?"

He brought her hand to his lips. "That I can't live without you, Mary. That you've come to mean more to me than duty or convention." His voice lowered to a husky murmur. "That I love you with all my heart."

The brightness of the dream enveloped her again. Except this time it felt real, the solidness of the chair, the warm pressure of his hand on hers, the utter need on his beloved face.

"Mary Sheppard, will you do me the great honor of becoming my wife?"

The very thought roused a reckless yearning in her. "But I don't fit into your world," she whispered.

"I wouldn't want you to change. Let the rest of society learn from your sweetness and your fire."

"Oh, Adam. I don't know how to be a duchess."

"You know how to be *you*. That's more important. And think of all the good you can do. Building orphanages and hospitals and schools. Giving away all our riches to the needy." He smiled as if pleased by the prospect, and tiny diamond stars sparkled in the sapphire depths of his eyes.

Her resolve threatening to melt, she forced herself not to move toward him. "You'll grow to resent me. I'll never be a lady."

"Thank God for that. You must promise you'll never become conventional. Else I might turn back into the priggish duke I was before we met." He tightly gripped her hands. "I cannot bear the thought of losing you. You own my heart, Mary. You always will."

A wealth of emotion shone on his face. Not prideful hauteur, but the quiet desperation of a man. A man who needed her. And in that moment she believed. Adam truly did love her. Forever.

With a cry of gladness, she went into his arms. "I love you, too, my lord duke. So very much."

Their lips met in a kiss of passion and wonder, a kiss that expressed the full commitment of their love. She clung to the solidity of his body and knew on a rush of bliss that he was no dream. Adam was her reality, her future, her life. The man who would be her husband.

When at last he lifted his head, he held her close so that she could feel their hearts beating in tandem. His hands stroked up and down her back. "Now what," he murmured into her hair, "did you mean to tell me in private?"

"Never mind." The lightness of joy drew a bubble of laughter from Mary. "It was just foolish. Foolish. Foolish."

Don't miss Barbara Dawson Smith's next fabulous historical romance: ONCE UPON A SCANDAL— coming from St. Martin's Paperbacks in September 1997:

London, 1818

It was the perfect night for thievery.

As she climbed out the attic window and onto the third story ledge, Lady Emma Coulter felt blessed by luck. The fog hid her presence high atop the row of elegant town houses. The dense mist also kept her from seeing how far she could fall.

Hugging the brick wall, she inched her way toward the home of her quarry. Only the faintest glow from the lower windows penetrated the darkness. The soup-thick moisture in the air gave the illusion of solidity, as if she could step off her perch and sink into a black feathered bed . . .

Emma shuddered. One false step, and she would break her neck. This narrow shelf was intended as decoration, not as a walkway for the Bond Street Burglar.

She slid one slipper along the ledge, then the other. Right foot, then left. Right foot, then left. These supple soles had once graced ballroom floors in the finest mansions of London. She smiled, thinking of how horrified the *ton* would be to learn the use to which the marchioness of Wortham now put her dancing slippers.

Not, of course, that she intended to get caught.

A series of robberies had plagued Mayfair over the past few years, the most spectacular of which had been a daring daytime theft on Bond Street, when the earl of Farleigh had had his jewelry case nipped from his carriage while he visited his tailor. Residents of the exclusive area had raised a hue and cry to apprehend the criminal, but to no avail. They never dreamed the culprit was one of their own. A woman.

Born to privilege and wed to wealth, Emma knew she was above suspicion, in spite of her ruined reputation.

Most men had no inkling that she even possessed a brain. After all, her dainty figure made her appear childlike, helpless. And at one time, she *had* been helpless. But never again.

Never again.

Though the damp chill bit through her snug black coat and pantaloons, the heat of determination warmed her. She crept past the connecting wall to the neighboring town house. At last the shadowy square of a window loomed through the fog. Deftly, she inserted a wire into the frame, wriggled the latch, and eased open the casement.

The hinges squawked. Emma froze, listening for sounds of alarm, but she heard only the clopping of horse hooves and the rattle of carriage wheels from the street below.

She hoisted herself over the sill and into a small, gloomy chamber. An odor of neglect hung in the air. Apparently, Lord Jasper Putney's taste for luxury did not extend to the attic rooms occupied by his servants.

Emma felt her way through the darkness toward the faint outline of a door in the far wall. She paused to check her mask and the hood that hid her blonde hair. Then she twisted the doorknob and cautiously poked her head out. A guttering candle in a wall sconce illuminated an empty corridor. Silent as a wraith, she stole down a small staircase and slipped through a door cleverly concealed in the paneling.

In contrast to the barren passage allotted to the servants, this corridor was decorated with sumptuous abandon. Watered green silk adorned the walls, and Greek statuary cluttered the side tables. Gilt moldings edged the ceiling and framed the doorways. Through the eye slits of her black domino, Emma appraised the richness of the decor. Yes, the master of this house could afford to relinquish his ill-gotten gains. The conniving blackguard.

Voices rose from the dining chamber on the floor below. According to Emma's informant, Lord Jasper was entertaining a large party of friends, and his valet was assisting the footmen in serving the guests. The upstairs should remain deserted for at least another hour.

Her heart pounding with anticipation, Emma found the

master bedchamber and entered the adjoining dressing room. The heavy scent of pomade mingled with the smoky odor from the fire that burned low on the hearth. A branch of candles flickered on the dressing table, casting light on a large coffer of studded Morocco leather.

It was unlocked, of course. Despite the previous burglaries, these aristocratic gentlemen seldom considered themselves potential victims. Only their lust for gambling surpassed their arrogance. They thought little of bleeding the pockets of a too-trusting old man.

But tonight, Emma would rectify that wrong.

She lifted the domed lid of the coffer and assessed the contents. On the white velvet lining lay an array of stickpins, jeweled sleeve links, and silver waistcoat buttons. She picked up a ring and examined it in the candlelight. The cabochon ruby glowed a deep, rich red against a figured gold setting. Sold at a certain shop where no questions were asked, the precious stone would yield a tidy sum.

Emma tucked the ring into a special pocket inside her coat, then selected several other items until her booty approximated the amount her grandfather had lost to Lord Jasper a fortnight ago. She never took more than was strictly necessary. She was, after all, a seeker of justice, not a common thief.

Yet this once, she found herself caressing a diamond-encrusted pocketwatch. With the money it would bring, she could restock the larder and pay the account at the butcher. She could properly refurbish Jenny's wardrobe, rather than letting down the hems of her gowns again.

Emma held the watch to her breast and squeezed her eyes shut. How she ached to see her daughter arrayed in the finest silks and laces, with an ermine muff to keep her small fingers warm in winter and a frivolous bonnet to shade her blue-green eyes in summer. Jenny deserved so much more than Emma could afford to give her. Jenny, who was too sweet and innocent to comprehend the sins of her mother. Jenny, who needed the love of a father. From the prison of Emma's heart, a rush of bitter despair escaped. Jenny, who would never, ever be accepted by Lucas . . . .

"I say, who the devil—?"

The raspy voice pierced her anguish. Emma dropped the watch with a clatter and spun around.

A stout gentleman blocked the doorway of the dressing room. He looked like an overstuffed sausage in his broad, brocaded waistcoat and tight gray pantaloons. His pale eyes bugged out in a face crisscrossed by broken red veins.

Lord Jasper Putney.

Emma's heart slammed into her throat. Then the shock of discovery was eclipsed by a new terror as her gaze fixed on his hands. His fingers clutched the half-unbuttoned placket of his trousers.

Dear God. *Dear God.* Memory drenched her in a sickening wave. He meant to force himself on her . . . .

A whimper squeezed past her dry lips. Her limbs felt leaden, weighted by horror. Time stretched into an eternity.

"Help!" Putney bellowed. " 'Tis the burglar. The Bond Street Burglar!" He wheeled around and staggered drunkenly away.

Emma snapped to her senses. She had mistaken his intent. Trembling with relief, she sprinted toward the outer door of the bedchamber. From the corner of her eye, she spied Putney by the bedside table, fumbling in a drawer. He turned, his shaky hands raising an object that glinted in the firelight.

A pistol.

Panic iced her lungs. She was almost to the door when an explosion split the air. A numbing impact struck her left side, and she stumbled.

Lucas. Lucas!

Clutching at the door, she righted herself. She could not think why her mind cried out to the husband who had abandoned her.

The gabble of voices and the clatter of feet sounded from the main staircase. Spurred by hot pain, she lurched in the opposite direction.

Down the deserted corridor. Up the servants' steps. Into the dark attic room and out the window where the black mist waited.